"What exactly are you proposing?" Charlotte asked, her words cool.

"I'll make it very clear. I don't care what you've been doing for the past five years. I don't care what you do tomorrow, for that matter. I care about tonight. Tonight I want to make sure we finish what is between us. Tonight I want you in my bed."

Rafe jerked back when trembling fingers touched his lower lip. The shock of it immobilized him. It had been so long since he had been touched. So he stood absolutely still as she traced his lower lip, his upper lip, mimicking what he had just done to her. She traced his jaw and then moved her fingers, featherlight, down the side of his neck, where they came to rest on his pulse.

"Unless you're afraid of me," she said, "then it appears I still have the same effect on you that I once did."

He held her chin, keeping her still. "That may be. But one thing has changed. I do not love you, Charlotte. Quite the opposite. If I take you to my bed you will be giving yourself to a man who hates you. Though I wonder if that matters? Because it certainly doesn't matter to me. I find that I want you regardless."

"One night?" And this time a slight tremble worked its way into her words.

"Just one," he respon

She let out a long, slc
corridor around them

D0652981

THE ITALIAN'S PREGNANT PRISONER

BY
MAISEY YATES

MILLS & BOON

This is a work of fiction. Names, characters, places, locations and
incidents are purely fictional and bear no relationship to any real
life individuals, living or dead, or to any actual places, business
establishments, locations, events or incidents. Any resemblance is
entirely coincidental.

First Published in Great Britain 2017
By Mills & Boon, an imprint of HarperCollins*Publishers*
1 London Bridge Street, London, SE1 9GF

© 2017 Maisey Yates

ISBN: 978-0-263-92540-1

Our policy is to use papers that are natural, renewable and recyclable
products and made from wood grown in sustainable forests. The logging
and manufacturing processes conform to the legal environmental
regulations of the country of origin.

Printed and bound in Spain
by CPI, Barcelona

Maisey Yates is a *New York Times* bestselling author of more than fifty romance novels. She has a coffee habit she has no interest in kicking, and a slight Pinterest addiction. She lives with her husband and children in the Pacific Northwest. When Maisey isn't writing, she can be found singing in the grocery store, shopping for shoes online and probably not doing dishes. Check out her website: maiseyyates.com.

Books by Maisey Yates

Mills & Boon Modern Romance

Carides's Forgotten Wife
Bound to the Warrior King
His Diamond of Convenience
To Defy a Sheikh
One Night to Risk It All

Once Upon a Seduction…

The Prince's Captive Virgin
The Prince's Stolen Virgin

The Billionaire's Legacy

The Last Di Sione Claims His Prize

Heirs Before Vows

The Spaniard's Pregnant Bride
The Prince's Pregnant Mistress
The Italian's Pregnant Virgin

One Night With Consequences

The Greek's Nine-Month Redemption
Married for Amari's Heir

Princes of Petras

A Christmas Vow of Seduction
The Queen's New Year Secret

Visit the Author Profile page
at millsandboon.co.uk for more titles.

To the Presents team.

You believed in me first.

I didn't know when I sent in my chapters
eight years ago that this was where it would lead.

I'm so glad it did.

CHAPTER ONE

Once upon a time...

LET DOWN YOUR HAIR...

Charlotte Adair's heart was pounding so hard she was sure the person next to her could hear it. And she was shaking. Shaking and fighting against the rising tide of emotions and memories that were threatening to compromise her ability to think straight.

Although, it could easily be argued that her being here at all was proving she lacked any ability to think with clarity.

She had escaped. For five years she had been free.

But there was unfinished business. *Rafe.*

He would always be unfinished business. There would be no fixing that. But she could *see* him. She could see him one more time.

And, at least, he wouldn't be able to see her.

Pain burst in her chest, hot and acidic, her stomach tightening. Yes, his abandonment had hurt her. Immeasurably. But that didn't mean the thought of such a powerful man being injured in the way he had been wasn't painful.

Of course, any thoughts of Rafe were painful.

And as she stood in the darkened corner of the antechamber that led into the ballroom, her palms beginning to sweat, the red gown she was wearing started to feel so tight she could scarcely breathe.

She couldn't hold off the memories any longer…

"Let down your hair."

"You know I'm not allowed to," Charlotte said, moving away from Rafe, every nerve ending in her body tingling. Every part of her demanding that she follow his simply issued command, regardless of the consequences.

Which was basically the same demand she'd been issuing to herself from the moment she'd first seen him.

She wanted him. Whatever that had meant at first, she hadn't fully known. Only that she wanted to be near him. Always.

"I see. And what exactly are the rules concerning men in your bedroom?"

She blushed, her skin heating all over. "Well, I would assume that it's frowned upon. Of course, it is nothing my father ever thought to forbid me expressly from. I suppose I'm meant to take it as read."

Rafe smiled, and she felt the impact of it all the way down to her toes. He was the most beautiful man she had ever seen. That had been her very first thought about seeing him when he'd come to work for her father two years earlier.

She wasn't entirely sure of the circumstances, only that he was an apprentice of sorts, which made her stomach tremble in a not-too-pleasant way. Because while the circumstances of her father's business were kept largely secret to her, she wasn't stupid. Yes, she lived a secluded life at his villa in Italy, transplanted from their native United States when Charlotte had been just a child, but in that seclusion she had taken the opportunity to learn how to gain information by quiet observation.

Charlotte had become part of the wallpaper in the villa many years ago, and as a result she was often underestimated. She liked it that way.

Being invisible.

But then Rafe had appeared, and he had not allowed her to remain invisible. He had *seen* her. From the first. She had been sixteen the first time she'd laid eyes on him, when she had been certain that her heart was going to claw its way up her throat and out of her mouth. Not just because he was beautiful—though, he was certainly beautiful. In his early twenties at the time, with broad shoulders, a jaw so square she thought she might cut her finger on it, and dark, fathomless eyes that she wanted desperately to get lost in.

He was a tall man, well over six feet, and she had the feeling that if she were to walk up to him and stand just in front of him that she would only come up to the middle of his chest. Which, she could not help but think, would be solid, strong, perfect to rest against.

Yes, her obsession had begun that first moment, and it had not abated. Apparently, it had been the same for him. He had tried to warn her away from him. But she'd persisted. She'd made a fool of herself, following him around. But it had worked. Eventually, he had stopped telling her to go away. Eventually, they had begun to form a friendship.

Except, she supposed friends didn't have to sneak around. Friends did not have to wait until the house was dark, and everyone was safely asleep to meet out in the stables, or to catch a moment with one another in the brilliant light of day out in one of the fields well away from the house.

It was chaste. Always.

Until one afternoon when they'd been in the corner of the barn, and he had told her it was time for him to go back to his post—whatever that meant—and she'd been filled with a strange kind of desperation that she could not fathom or fight.

She had reached up, touched his face with her fingertips. And then she'd had his iron grip wrapped around her wrist, his dark eyes burning hotter than she had ever seen them before.

Before she could protest—before she could question anything—his mouth had been on hers. Claiming. Marking her as his own.

She had never been kissed before that moment. Hadn't even thought much about it. But kissing Rafe was like touching the surface of the sun. She could hardly bear it.

It was too hot. Too bright. Too much.

And far too brief.

But that night, he had climbed the trellis and come into her room. Her tower bedroom, high above the rest of the house, separated from everyone, as she always was. No one came into her bedroom.

But he had. And he had treated her to another kiss. Then another.

He had come to her room every night for the past two weeks. Their kisses had gotten longer, deeper. They'd begun shedding clothes. Lying on the bed together. Trading intimacies she would have found shocking before him. Would have found shocking if it were with anyone *but* him.

With Rafe, all these things felt right. She'd been asking him for more. Asking him to take her virginity. But so far he'd kept it to pleasuring her, and never taking things to their ultimate conclusion.

She had been okay to wait. But tonight she felt urgency. Tonight, there was a rock in her stomach, and she knew that she had to tell him about the conversation she'd had with her stepmother earlier that day.

Her father didn't often speak to her, if he did at all. Most of the relevant information was conveyed through Josefina, her stepmother, who was the most hardened, suspicious person Charlotte had ever known.

And given Charlotte lived in a compound with criminals, that was quite a feat.

Earlier today she had informed Charlotte that her father's ultimate purpose for her was about to be fulfilled. He had found another kingpin in a corner of Italy Charlotte had never been to who was looking for a wife. And it was an alliance her father wanted to cement with his own bloodline. A dynastic union. The one use he could think of for a daughter he had never wanted.

Josefina seemed nothing but happy to be rid of the stepdaughter she had always seemed jealous of. A jealousy Charlotte could not understand, given she was a glorified prisoner in her father's home. But Josefina had once been a poor girl from the village her father's estate was built near, and she had clawed her way from poverty to being Michael Adair's mistress, then ultimately his wife. She wasn't quiet about that achievement, and it was Charlotte's belief that her stepmother was secretly afraid she might someday lose her elevated position, which made her a bit vicious.

She had certainly seemed vicious when telling Charlotte of her upcoming marital fate.

Dimly, Charlotte had always thought that her life might come to this. Because her father was nothing if not a medieval lord, the master of his keep and all who depended on him for anything. And of course it was not outside the realm of imagination that he would try to cement his power in the criminal world through marriages. Like a dark king, trading family members to prevent wars. Or to start them. Depending on the present circumstance.

But even though part of her had always known it was a possibility, she had done her very best not to think of it. And now, there was Rafe.

Rafe, who made love and sex something that wasn't theoretical. Rather, something that she wanted. Something that she craved. Not in a general sense. She wanted it with him.

The idea of sharing her body with someone else… It could not be endured. Her need for Rafe, for his touch, his kiss, for everything… It was so intimate. It went deeper than the electric need that sparked over her skin.

It was heart. *He* was her heart.

"Yes," he said, "I suppose that is the letter of the law, if not the spirit of it." His dark eyes turned intense, a black flame that burned through her. "I would like you to break some rules for me. I know your hair is considered quite the asset. You're not allowed to cut it—is that true?"

Charlotte touched her heavy bun. "Not entirely. I get the ends trimmed. But yes. My father considers my hair to be part of my beauty." And the importance of her beauty had become shockingly clear with her marriage deal being brokered.

"Creepy."

She forced out a laugh. "You work for him. And here you are."

"I only work for him until my debt is repaid. I have no loyalty to your father. On that you can trust me."

It was the first time Rafe had said anything like this to her. "I didn't… I didn't realize."

"I am forbidden from speaking of it. But then, I am certain that I am also forbidden from being in here. And I'm also forbidden from touching you like this." He put his hand on her cheek, and then he kissed her. "Let down your hair," he whispered against her lips.

This time, she obeyed. For him. Only for him…

Charlotte was dragged back to the present, and her heart was beating out of control, as it had been in the memory. It had only been a couple of weeks after that when everything had fallen apart. When she had been left devastated, wounded beyond the healing of that devastation.

When Josefina had told her that Rafe had gone, that he didn't want her. And that she had no choice but to go and marry Stefan. Charlotte had protested. So much so, that she had found herself locked up. So much so that she had seen the true nature of her father. He did not love her. Not at all. He would kill her if she didn't marry the man of his choosing; that was what he'd told her. And Charlotte had been ready to believe it.

She had also not been ready to accept her fate. Because if there was one thing that being with Rafe had taught her, it was that there was more to life than the villa. More to life than her tower bedroom. More to intimacy with a man than a simple transaction.

And she had wanted those things. All of them.

So when her father had paid his men to transport her across the country and they had stopped at a petrol station in the middle of nowhere she had taken her chance.

She'd slipped from her restraints and fled, running deep into the woods, certain they wouldn't follow her there. Somehow, she was right. They had searched for her along the highways, perhaps checking in with passing motorists and various business owners.

They certainly hadn't expected *her*—cosseted princess of the Adair family empire—to take her chances with the wolves and foxes out in the thick forest.

But she had.

Ultimately, had found a certain measure of safety living in rural Germany, moving from cottage to cottage, never settling in one place too long, taking simple positions at shops and farms over the years.

It had been a lonely existence, but in many ways freeing.

It wasn't until years later that she had seen anything of Rafe again. But then, there he was, splashed across the cover of a newspaper. The story of a man who had worked his way up from nothing, from the Italian slums, to become one of the wealthiest men on earth.

A blind man. Wounded in an accident that he refused to speak of.

After that, she saw him on the covers of papers quite a lot. It never got easier. It never got less painful. She ached for him. For what they might have had, had he truly loved her as she had believed he had. For the accident that had taken his sight.

She thought very little about his billions. If only because she had never truly doubted that Rafe would overcome his circumstances in a spectacular way. He was a singular man. He always had been. No one compared to him. And no one ever would.

It was why, when she had gotten the news of her father's death, when she had found out about the invitation under his name to this event, and the fact that Rafe would also be in attendance, that she had decided to take her chances.

With her father out of the picture, no one was coming for her. And she very much doubted any of his men would recognize her now. She was no longer an eighteen-year-old girl.

And as for Rafe... Well, he would never see her. Just as he would never see anything ever again.

But she could see him. She needed to do that. Needed to put that part of her life behind her completely so she could move on. Her time of seclusion was at an end. And he was wrapped all up in it.

She was done hiding. But she had some ghosts to vanquish.

She took a fortifying breath and moved out of the shadows and into the light. She could honestly say it was the first time in five years she had done this. For the first time in five years, she wasn't hiding.

She sensed that heads were turning, following her progress as she made her way through the ballroom. But she didn't care. She wasn't here for generic admiration. Or curiosity. She was here for him.

She had dressed up for him. Even if it was foolish.

For one thing, he wouldn't be able to see her. For another, she didn't want him to.

It didn't take her long to see him, though. Her eyes were drawn to him, like a magnet. He was near the center of the ballroom, standing and making conversation with a group of men in suits. He was the tallest. The handsomest. He had always been the singularly most beautiful man she had ever seen. And he still was. Except at thirty he was much more mature than he'd been at twenty-five. He had filled out, his chest thicker, his face more chiseled. Dark stubble sat heavy on his jaw, and she wondered…she wondered what it would be like to touch his face with it there.

She hadn't touched a man since Rafe. She'd had no interest.

She needed to find some interest. Because she was going to have a normal life. After she claimed the inheritance she knew that she still had—untouched—in a trust at the bank in London, she was going to start her life in earnest.

Maybe go to school. Maybe start a shop of her own, since she had always enjoyed working in them over the past few years. Had enjoyed not being lonely.

Whatever she did, it would be her choice. And that was the point.

She didn't know what answers she had expected to find here. Right now, the only clear answer seemed to be that her body, her heart, was still affected by him.

He excused himself from the group, and suddenly, he was walking her way. And she froze. Like a deer caught in the headlights. Or rather, like a woman staring at Rafe Costa.

She certainly wasn't the only woman staring. He

moved with fluid grace, and if she didn't know better, she would never have known his sight was impaired at all.

He was coming closer, and as he did her heart tripped over itself, her hands beginning to shake. She wished she could touch him.

Oh, she wanted it more than anything. In that moment, she wanted it more than her next breath. To put her hands on Rafe Costa's face one more time. To kiss those lips again. To place her hand over his chest and see if she could still make his heart race.

It was easy to forget that her stepmother had told her how Rafe had left, taking an incentive offered by her father to end his tenure there earlier. How he had thought nothing of Charlotte when he left. Nothing of all the promises he had made to her.

Yes, it was so easy to forget all of that. It was easy to forget that and remember instead the way it had felt when he had kissed her. Touched her. The way that she had begged him to use more than his hands between her thighs, more than his mouth. The way she had pleaded with him to take her virginity, to make her his in every way.

But he hadn't.

For honor, he had said. And for her protection.

Except, really, he had never wanted her. At least, not enough to risk anything. So he had simply been toying with her.

She should remember that. Her treacherous, traitorous body should remember that well. But it didn't. Instead, it was fluttering. As if a host of butterflies had been set loose inside her.

He came closer, closer still, passing through the

crowd of people, everyone moving out of the way for him, as though he was Moses parting the sea.

Time seemed to slow. Everything around her. Her heartbeat. Her breathing.

Suddenly, he was there. So close that if she wanted to she could reach out and touch the edge of his sleeve with her fingertips.

Could bump into him accidentally, just to make contact. He wouldn't know it was her. He couldn't.

Suddenly, he turned. He was looking past her, his dark eyes unseeing, unfocused. But then, he reached out and unerringly grabbed hold of her wrist, dragging her toward his muscular body.

"Charlotte."

CHAPTER TWO

IT WAS IMPOSSIBLE.

Charlotte—for all intents and purposes—had disappeared five years ago. She hadn't simply disappeared; she had gone off to marry another man.

The triumphant smile on her stepmother's face was the last thing he had seen. The last thing he had ever seen. Beyond gray, amorphous shapes.

He mostly hung close to the walls in situations like this. He had a cane to help him navigate, but in a crowd this thick it was still difficult. Though, in a crowd this thick it was also normal to run into people. So there was that.

He could see sharp contrasts between light and darkness, but he couldn't make out features or colors. Nothing subtle.

But when he had walked by her, he had caught her scent. And in that moment, he had seen so many things. Color and light bursting through his mind, vivid and sharp. Sun-drenched days in Tuscany, that had been hell on earth except for her. Soft, pearlescent skin that was too fine, too exquisite for him to touch. And yet he had. And that beautiful blond hair that her father had had a strange obsession with.

Glossy, impossibly long and always kept wound up in a bun so that no one could truly see it or appreciate it. Memory gripped him tight…

"Let down your hair," he rasped against her throat as he kissed her, lying down on her large four-poster bed.

He begged her for that privilege, every night. The privilege of running his hands through her hair. Touching the silken strands, seeing her naked, her hair cascading over her pale body like a waterfall, light pink nipples just barely visible through the golden curtain.

She reached up, taking the pins out, obeying his command. In the past weeks since he had begun coming into her room he had asked her to do this for him every night, and every night she had complied. The fact that she never took it down before he appeared led him to believe that she enjoyed this game. Of his commands, and her acquiescence.

It was fine with him. He liked it too.

It was dangerous. This game. Easy to pretend that it was some sort of harmless assignation. That they might get caught, and might suffer a severe scolding. But Rafe was under no illusions. If he were caught with Charlotte, her father would have him killed. If Charlotte were found not a virgin, after her father had taken great pains to seclude her away from the rest of the world, Rafe would be killed. And possibly Charlotte, as well.

And so, he didn't take her virginity. Rather, he pushed the boundaries every night. And every night she begged him for more. Every night, he declined. But he was becoming weak. He would not be able to hold out for much longer. And in truth, he didn't intend to.

He simply needed to get to a place where he had shored up the assets he needed to be free of her father. He could hardly plunge Charlotte into a life of poverty after she had lived the cosseted existence of a gentleman gangster's daughter. Michael Adair's empire had the semblance of legitimacy, but it was anything but.

To most of the world he appeared to be a businessman. But that was only because the world didn't look too closely. Not at fabulously wealthy, powerful men who could offer a great many favors, and do untold amounts of damage if they were crossed. It benefited no one to examine those things too deeply. And so nobody did.

Rafe knew all too well about the power men like Michael wielded. He knew too what it was to go from a spoiled, cushioned life to one of abject poverty. His father was not unlike Michael Adair. Oh, he might not be a criminal, but he thought nothing of using the people in his life until they were spent.

Until he had no more use for them but to grind them under his boot for fun. That was what Rafe remembered most about the father he hadn't seen since he was five years old. How much he seemed to relish causing pain.

When he had kicked Rafe and his mother out onto the streets, the man had seemed to enjoy their distress. Or, if not that, then the fact he had the power to do so.

Power. Yes, men like that loved power.

And Rafe had spent many years with no power at all. Begging. Stealing. Doing whatever he could to help his mother survive.

He had begun doing odd petty crimes with a group

of boys. Delivering packages that he never asked about the contents of. Things like that.

He'd ended up getting caught by the police and charged with running drugs, in spite of the fact that he was only a boy. And a boy who'd had no idea what he was handling at that.

It was through that arrest that he'd met Michael Adair.

It was only much later that Rafe had realized the man must have had a connection to the drugs. To the particular ring of petty criminals Rafe had been working with.

Michael Adair had not only given Rafe his freedom; he had also provided Rafe with an education, paying for him to attend one of the finest private schools in Europe. Rafe had accepted greedily. Uncaring of what it might mean in the future.

Michael had promised him someday he would collect the favor. And indeed, he had made good on that threat.

For years, he had done various errands for Michael in Rome. Until finally, he had been brought to the estate to apprentice under the man himself.

That was when he'd really gotten to know the man he'd aligned himself with. Had seen how hard he was. How entirely without morals.

Rafe had asked him once why he had shown such an interest in a young boy from the streets. Why he'd helped him at all, much less sent him to school and provided for him.

He'd said it was because he didn't have a son. And he had thought perhaps Rafe was the protégé he needed.

Rafe might have been shocked or upset if he weren't

already the son of an amoral bastard. As it was, he just figured he might as well take advantage. At least this particular amoral bastard wanted to give him a hand up, unlike his actual father.

But after school he had started getting a deeper look at Michael Adair's twisted empire. By then he was living at the estate and there was no leaving. Not without being killed.

The entire business made Rafe ill. Michael was ruthless. He didn't care who was hurt by his business practices. And he was not above intimidation, or even murder to get what he wanted. He had a host of enforcers who meted out punishments on those who did not comply with his wishes. And Rafe could only count himself fortunate that he had not been forced to be part of that side of the business.

No, he was being taught the business. Because Michael had no son. And he wanted Rafe to be able to take control of the business portion, the front of house part of the empire.

But that did not mean that he found Rafe to be good enough for his daughter, and Rafe was under no illusions that it would be the case. Rafe had also decided that while he was content to get any education he could get from Michael, he was certainly never going to overtake the man's evil empire.

No. He was going to escape at his first opportunity. And he was going to do it with Charlotte.

Then. Then he would make her his.

She shook her head, her hair falling around her in a silken wave. His stomach tightened. And he couldn't breathe. He'd had more women than he could count. A side effect of being a young boy unsupervised far too early. One who looked much older than he was the moment adolescence had hit.

But none had ever affected him like this. None had ever made him feel as though his heart were being pulled out of his chest through his mouth. Had ever made him feel like he might die if he didn't touch her. But also made him feel so protective that...he would rather cut off his own hands than do her harm. And it was that need, that need that overrode all else, that gave him the strength to resist her, night after night.

He leaned in, sliding his fingers through her hair, lifting the silken strands to his face, and inhaling deeply.

Roses. Lavender. And something he couldn't name. Something that belonged only to her...

Rafe dragged himself back to the present. And to the feel of the woman he was currently holding on to. Soft. She was so soft. It had to be Charlotte. It could only be her.

Of course, it had been five years since he had touched a woman, so perhaps, his memory was faulty. Perhaps, they were all this soft. But he didn't think so.

Michael Adair was dead. And he had been on Rafe's mind this morning. Perhaps, that was why his body was playing tricks on him now.

Or perhaps, it was why Charlotte had resurfaced.

"Come with me," he said, his voice hard.

He held on to her with one arm, casually sweeping the ground in front of them with his cane in his other hand.

She said nothing. Didn't protest. Didn't speak at all. Frustration bubbled up inside him. And he wished...

oh, how he wished he could see her face. Yes, his other senses had been honed quite a bit since the accident. But in this moment, though, senses could not replace his sight. Not by a long shot.

He took them out of the ballroom, into some kind of alcove. Perhaps no one was around, it didn't seem as though anyone was. But if they were, he doubted they would have the balls to interrupt them. Something else Rafe had honed over the past five years was a fearsome reputation. He was a man who took no prisoners. He acted ethically. He was bound and determined that he would. That he would never bear any resemblance to Michael Adair, or to any man like him. But he was also determined that he would never go back to the streets he had come from.

It was power that insulated a man. He knew that well. The only reason he had been at Michael's mercy in the first place was because he had been vulnerable. Because he lacked resources. Because he lacked power.

He had made a vow that he would never return to that place. Never. There was no longer any vulnerability inside of him. And truly, his blindness—nature's last gasp at ensuring he wasn't all powerful—had only spurred him on to work harder.

It was an accident he wished hadn't happened. He didn't want to give it too much credit in his life. However, he was also certain enough that it had made him work harder. That it made him yet more determined to appear capable, infallible.

He was also certain that early on it had caused a great many to underestimate him. So when his corporation gobbled up theirs, when his success put them out of business—his electronics manufacturing conglomerate slowly and steadily taking over the world—they simply hadn't seen it coming.

Something he found deliciously ironic.

"What the hell are you doing here?" he asked. "Has your husband set you free? Or has he simply let you out for the night?"

"I…I…"

Was it her? Was that her voice? It had been so long. And memory was not infallible. If this was simply something conjured up out of his darkest desires, out of need he should no longer feel, his rage with himself would know no bounds.

"Charlotte Adair." He said her name like a curse. "Is that your last name anymore? After marrying Stefan did you take his last name?"

"I think you must be mistaken," she said, her voice a low whisper.

He slid his hand up her arm, following the line to her collarbone, up the side of her neck and to her chin, where he gripped her between his thumb and forefinger. "I am never mistaken. You would do well to remember that." He leaned in, and he could smell her again. Lavender. Roses. *Charlotte.*

His heart beat her name over and over again.

It had to be her. No woman had affected him like this in the past five years. No woman had affected him at all.

And then he'd walked through that ballroom and caught her scent, touched her skin. It was like being born again.

"If you lie to me, I will make you pay. There will be no end to what it will cost you."

She began to tremble beneath his touch, and he slid

his thumb upward, along her lower lip, heat and arousal tightening his gut.

"You cannot lie to me," he whispered, his mouth now so close to hers he could feel her breath. "You might have a husband, but believe me, there is no man on earth who knows you as well as I do."

She was burned into his memory in a way no one else could be. Because losing his head over Charlotte had nearly cost him everything. Had been a turning point in his life. He could not walk away from it, not really. He bore the mark of it.

Not just his vision, but the ugly scars on his body from where he had fallen off the balcony.

From where he had been pushed.

"My…my father is dead," she said, the words rushed. "I've come to London to sort out some of his business."

He laughed, the sound cold and hard even to his own ears. "Silly girl. Did you think for one moment that I would be unaware of your father's death? I nearly gave my staff a holiday. In celebration."

He slid his hand down her throat, holding it gently, feeling the flutter of her pulse beneath his thumb.

"I was under no illusion you would have given them a holiday so that you could wallow in your grief," she said, her breathing quick and shallow, betraying her fear when her tone of voice did not.

"I opened my best bottle of champagne that night."

She shifted, and he had a feeling she was looking directly at him now. Looking him full in the face, when before she had not been. "So did I. Do not think you have a monopoly on despising that man."

"Probably the last remaining thing we have in common, *cara mia*." She stiffened beneath his touch.

"It would not surprise me."

Her pulse was racing beneath his thumb, and he knew that his own heart was pounding just as hard. He was angry with her. So angry. He wanted to destroy her. Destroy her in the way he had been destroyed by the loss of her. By her betrayal.

But he also wanted her. That protection he had extended to her, the virginity he had preserved, simply so that she could throw it away to another man, so that she could marry another, galled him.

It had been his by rights. And out of some misguided sense of chivalry that he no longer possessed he had not laid claim to it.

"Is your husband here?" he asked.

She hesitated. "No."

"I believe you and I have unfinished business." He changed the way he held her, yet again moving his thumb up to her mouth, to trace her plush lips. "Do you not agree?"

He heard a faint sniff, and he imagined her tossing her head back, her expression haughty. He had seen her do it many times before. Years ago. "I don't know what you're talking about."

"Charming. But I think you do." He moved his fingertips to the edge of her mouth, then back down the side of her neck, coming to rest on her pulse. "This feels just as I remember it. I make your blood run faster. This makes me wonder if I still make you wet."

She gasped, and he waited for a slap across the face that didn't come.

"I'm frightened," she said, her voice breathy.

"I don't believe that. A woman who would dare set foot in London, into a place where you had to know I would be, so soon after her father's death… Well, I don't believe she's afraid of anything. No. I do not believe this is fear, Charlotte."

"What you believe or don't believe doesn't automatically become truth."

He chuckled. "See, that simply isn't true. I'm richer than your father ever was. People do my bidding, not because they fear me but because of what I can do for them. What I wish often becomes truth easily enough."

Five years. Five years since he had touched a woman. Longer since he'd had sex with one. There had been no one else from the moment he'd met her. And he'd held back out of deference to her innocence.

Now it had been five years since he had touched her.

"I can make you want me," he said.

And he hated that, for the first time in years, he doubted himself. Because as certain as he was of a great many things, he could not be certain that she would want a scarred, blind man in her bed.

"What exactly are you proposing?" she asked, her words cool.

"I'll make it very clear. I don't care what you've been doing for the past five years. I don't care that you married Stefan. I don't care what you do tomorrow, for that matter. I care about tonight. Tonight, I want to make sure we finish what is between us. Tonight. I want you in my bed."

He jerked back when trembling fingers touched his lower lip. The shock of it immobilized him. It had been so long since he had been touched. So he stood, absolutely still as she traced his lower lip, his upper lip, mimicking what he had just done for her. She traced his jaw, and then moved her fingers featherlight down the side of his neck, where they came to rest on his pulse.

"Unless you're afraid of me," she said, "then it appears I still have the same effect on you that I once did."

He held her chin, keeping her still. "That may be. But one thing has changed. I do not love you, Charlotte. Quite the opposite. If I take you to my bed, you will be giving yourself to a man who hates you. Though, I wonder if that matters? Because it certainly doesn't matter to me. I find that I want you regardless."

"One night?" And this time, a slight tremble worked its way into her words.

"Just one," he responded.

She let out a long, slow breath that echoed in the corridor around them. "Okay. One night."

CHAPTER THREE

CHARLOTTE WAS CRAZY. She supposed that was what years in isolation would do to a person. Not that she had ever been isolated truly. She had made friends wherever she had gone, but it was always on the internal understanding that she wouldn't be in one place for long. And, of course, she had been unable to share the truth behind her circumstances, no matter how wonderful her new friends had seemed.

It was too dangerous for them. Too dangerous for her.

That always put distance between herself and her friends, no matter how much she wished it wasn't there.

But her old life—no matter how far she ran from it—always had claws in her. She had spent five years looking over her shoulder. Five years fearing that one day her father's men, or Stefan's, would show up at the door of her home, or one of the shops that she worked in. Five years living abroad, traveling from place to place. Hiding.

But now her father was dead. And the last remaining claw stuck deep into her flesh was Rafe. Yes, she had come to London tonight to catch one last glimpse of him before moving on. But perhaps, this was better. Perhaps, this was what she needed.

She had been prepared to give him her virginity five years ago. He was the man she had meant for it. Perhaps, it was fate. No matter what the ensuing years had brought.

Yes, Rafe had hurt her. His abandonment had wounded her deeply. But, in the end, there would have been nothing he could have done for her. And she could not have gone back to him while her father lived.

If her father had known where she was, he would have come for her. And he certainly would have killed Rafe.

Her fantasies of him had been wound around anger, grief and sadness for the past five years. And, yes, she had blamed him for some things. In the dark of the night, when she lay there, feeling like there was a heavy weight resting on her chest, she had internally raged at him for not saving her. For not climbing the tower and carrying her away with him. Off to live in a forest somewhere. Where mice and birds would build them…a house or something.

Not a care. No contact with the outside.

But this was the real world. It wasn't a fairy tale, and she knew that none of that was actually possible.

It made for a lovely fantasy. But in the end, she'd had to escape the tower on her own. In the end, it had been up to her to save herself. Bringing anyone with her would have only put them in danger.

So, it didn't matter that Rafe had left. It was better. Better for him.

And she still hurt when she thought of him.

So maybe this was what she needed to do. Maybe

this was the grand letting go that she required. Maybe. Just maybe.

Whether this was the road to salvation or perdition, she imagined it remained to be seen. Either way, she was on it.

In his limousine.

It had been a great many years since she had traveled this way. Even tonight, dressed in a gown that had cost her entire savings, she had taken a cab.

She hadn't worried much about her savings, because she would come into her money in the next week or so. And tonight was supposed to be a strange fantasy. Or really, the last chapter on a life she had never chosen to live in the first place. That she wanted.

She tightened her hold on her clutch purse, staring straight ahead, the city lights flashing in her face as they drove.

Rafe pressed a hand to her shoulder. "Just checking to make sure you were still there."

"I don't believe for a moment that you thought I had gone." As if she was going to silently fling herself out onto the London streets and tuck and roll in her beautiful red gown.

"No," he said. "I can hear you breathing. I can almost hear your heart beating. Tell me, Charlotte. Are you nervous?"

"I told you I was," she said. "I told you I was frightened."

"You are not frightened. You know I won't harm you. I had a great many chances to do that. A great many times when I was alone with you, and I still possessed my sight. When I could have done anything to you, and by the time you had screamed it would've been too late for your father's guards to rescue you. I would say that with your father gone you have absolutely nothing to fear from me. Any leverage that you might have been has long since ceased to be."

What a strange thing. The introduction of the thought that he might have harmed her back then to escape working for her father. Or that he might have threatened to harm her. It had never occurred to her then. Never occurred to her that he might be using her. Because she had been so young. Because she had trusted him implicitly.

But he hadn't harmed her or held her hostage then.

And, in order for him to wish her harm now, it would have to be personal. He would have to want some kind of revenge against her. And for what? He was the one who had left her. And, if it had demonstrated anything it was that his feelings for her had never been all that strong.

His refusal to take her virginity had been all about him hedging his bets and saving his own skin. It had nothing to do with *honoring* her. With *protecting* her, as he had pretended it did all those years ago.

"I don't think you're going to hurt me," she said, her throat tight, speaking nearly impossible. "What would the headline say, after all? It isn't as though people didn't see us leave together. Nobody knows who I am, but if they found my body in a hotel room, they would connect me to you soon enough."

She looked over at him, saw his lip curl upward. He was still touching her. Still maintaining contact. "Please. I'm not going to kill you. That is more your father's style than mine. Such displays hold no interest for me. I have built my empire on the rock. Not the sand."

"Excellent. So when the rains come down your house will stand firm."

"That is the hope," he said, his tone caustic.

It all seemed so absurd suddenly. That she was in this dress, in this limo, with Rafe. She could hardly figure out how she'd gotten there. Just a few hours ago she'd slipped the dress on, ready so sneak quietly into the ball, see him just for a moment and then leave. But he'd…sensed her.

She hadn't counted on that.

She should know that anticipating Rafe was impossible.

"What is it you want with me?" she asked.

"I should think it is quite obvious. I want no more than to claim what I want. What I have always wanted. I want your body, Charlotte. I want all that was kept from me five years ago. Weeks of foreplay only to have my prize stolen from me. I did not take kindly to it then. I don't like it now."

She frowned. "How was I *stolen* from you? You left."

"I left? Is that the story then?" He chuckled, hard and dark. "I was certainly shown the way out."

"I was told one morning that you had gone, and that I would be sent to marry Stefan. That my father knew about our relationship and that he had offered you a bargain to leave. And that you chose the money he gave you over me. That you chose your freedom. I was hurt, Rafe, but I could understand. I know how my father is. I know what a wonderful thing it would be to be free of him. If I could've been free of him so easily, I would have done so. I'm not going to say I wasn't angry. But I accepted it."

She looked over at him, his face illuminated as they passed a lit-up storefront. His expression was blank.

"I did not leave you," he said finally.

"You didn't?"

"No. I was…told that you left. I was told you had gone to marry the man of your father's choosing. The path of least resistance."

She laughed. But there was no humor in it. "I suppose the fact that either of us believed anything relayed to us by Josefina or my father makes us fools. They were master manipulators, always. And that wasn't even a very master manipulation. It was just two vulnerable people ready to believe the worst, I suppose. Ready to believe the worst of the world and all of the people in it."

"Why would you ever believe anything else?"

Silence stretched between them.

"I do want this," she said, curling her hands into fists. "Do you?"

The streetlight caught his exquisite face, highlighting his razor-sharp cheekbones, the curve of his lips. Her heart stuttered.

"I have wanted little else for the past five years. I have amassed a great fortune, Charlotte, and there are two things that I have never been able to obtain in spite of my newfound wealth and power. My sight, and you. You, I can have. You, I will have. Seeing as I cannot have the other."

The car pulled up to a beautiful building, all ornate stonework, well lit, exquisitely visible even in the dark.

"We have arrived," he said. He removed his hand from her shoulder, and the two of them sat in the car and waited. The driver opened the door, and Rafe got out, his hand resting on the car as he walked around to the curbside, his cane sweeping the ground.

Her heart folded up like it was made of paper. Fragile and easily torn. Of all the misunderstandings between them, this was not one of them. Rafe had lost his sight, and though she had known it for a while now, it still hurt her. It wounded her that he was hurt. That he had lost something of himself.

And the fact that her father and stepmother had lied to them both…

Yes, she and Rafe did deserve this night. Whatever else lay ahead, they deserved this.

Her door opened, and she looked out to see Rafe, extending his hand to her. She hesitated, but only for a moment. And then she curled her fingers around his, and he lifted her from the limousine. She landed against his chest, her palm spread over his muscles, her hand over his beating heart.

It was raging. Just as hard as her own.

"Rafe…"

"We must go inside," he said. "Now. Otherwise, I'm likely to take you up against the side of the building."

For a moment, Charlotte couldn't quite work out why that would be a bad thing. "Okay," she said, her voice thick.

With a firm hand, Rafe led her into the building, and the two of them walked across the small gilded space to an elevator with golden doors. They swung open, and she followed him in, having to take two steps to his one.

Clearly, this was his domain. There was no hesi-

tation in any of his movements. The only indication
that he wasn't able to visualize his surroundings in the
quick sweep of his cane across the floor.

Suddenly, her breath was coming harder, faster.
She hadn't seen this man in five years. It had taken
two weeks of physical intimacy to build up five years'
worth of fantasies. And now she was here. Now she
was here, but he wasn't *her* Rafe anymore. Wasn't a
man in indentured servitude to her father, but one of
the most powerful businessmen in the world. A man
with billions of dollars. A man newspapers wrote of
in hyperbolic phrasing. A man that women spoke of
with awed reverence.

That thought sent a kick straight to her gut. She
wondered how many women he'd been with since their
time in her tower. How many women he'd touched.
Kissed. Been inside.

Of course, she had never truly had him. So it seemed
silly to worry about who else might have.

*Well, you'll have him tonight. And those other
women won't matter. This isn't about them. This is
about you. It's for you. It's not for anyone else.*

Yes, she had been stagnant for so long, and she was
done with it.

Tonight, she would have Rafe, and she wouldn't concern herself with the consequences.

Before she was prepared, the lift reached its desti-
nation and the doors slid open. They were here.

They hadn't even kissed. In five years, they hadn't
kissed. She had said yes to this because of a mere
touch. Because of his firm, warm hold on her throat.

She couldn't go back now. She wasn't even certain
that she wanted to.

He took her hand and led her inside, and she followed.

The loft was Spartan. Wide swaths of floor left blank, furniture pushed more or less against the walls.

He took his jacket off and hung it on a peg, and then placed his cane in a holder by the door. He straightened, his focus on the black space before them.

"My circumstances have changed quite a bit," he remarked, gesturing to the space around them.

"Your circumstances never mattered to me." She examined him, the hard set of his jaw, that cold, closed-off expression on his face. Tension radiated from that big, strong body in waves. She wanted to touch him. Wanted to move away from him, as well. He was frightening. Compelling and magnetic. All at the same time.

Finally, he spoke. "My circumstances mattered a great deal to me."

"Of course they did," she whispered. "I didn't mean…"

"I do not want your apologies, Charlotte. This is not an evening for recrimination. Not now. You and I should've both forgotten about a youthful dalliance a long time ago. Clearly, we did not. So, there is business yet to be finished between us. And I, for one, need to see it done."

After that, there was no waiting. He reached out, and she went to him. Then, he wrapped his arm around her waist and drew her up against his hard, muscular body.

He took hold of her chin, as he had done back at the party. Only this time, he didn't stop. This time, there was no slow, careful examination. There was no hesitation at all.

His lips crashed down on hers, unerring, his tongue parting her, delving deep into her mouth, slick and hot, and somehow even more than she had remembered.

He had been her first kiss. Her only kiss.

She had never let a man get so close to her since then. She had known that that way contained only heartbreak, and she had no desire to experience heartbreak again. Not when everything in her life was still in such peril. When it was still dangerous to breathe in too deeply, much less forge any kind of true emotional bond with somebody.

And it had never seemed…it had never seemed right to pursue a purely physical relationship. Perhaps because of the intensity of what she had felt for Rafe. She wasn't sure. Either way, the idea had never really appealed to her.

Except, that was what she was doing now. With him. There had been no promises made, and she wouldn't ask him for any.

This was about creating a new life. The life that she wanted, on her own terms, and free of her father's influence. She supposed that meant being free of Rafe's influence, as well.

And after tonight, she would be. At least, that was the hope.

But this kiss didn't taste like freedom. It tasted like deep, crushing need. Like willing bondage. Like she was committing herself to him again with each pass of her tongue against his.

But she couldn't do that. She couldn't. If she was going to take this night, then she had to be committed to her plan. To her freedom.

Freedom was the one thing she'd never had. Her

life on her own terms. She couldn't steal it from herself. Not before she had ever had a chance to hold it in her hands.

But she had never had a chance to hold him either. And now it seemed imperative. Necessary. Like the thing she needed more than air…

He bit her bottom lip and desire arrowed down straight to her stomach, down farther between her legs. She remembered this. It had rested in the back of her mind, a half-faded memory for five years. But now it was back. Bright, sharp and clear.

This thing that she had felt only ever with him. This thing that was like a wild, untamed beast inside of her. The only thing that ever was. The only thing that ever had been.

She had been hidden away, kept apart from the world on the estate, locked away from the world in a tower. And the only wild, untamed thing in her had always been for him.

It was astonishing how true that was now. How quickly she was transported back to that time. To her bedroom. When the only good and wonderful thing in her life had been Rafe. He had been worth everything. Worth risks she knew both of them took great pains not to dwell on.

They had of course spoken of the need for them not to get caught. But it had been like children sneaking around. Rather than two people who were in very real danger should they ever be discovered.

But there was no one to discover them now. There was no danger. Those things that had made it feel all the more special, forbidden, were gone now. There were no walls. No one was in chains, so to speak. They were here of their own free will. Making this choice.

She was not the only available body that he might find pleasure in. She was not a trapped girl who had met no other men that appealed to her.

No, she hadn't dated anyone but they just hadn't called to her. Not in the way that Rafe did.

No one ever had. No one.

She reached up, ready to unpin her hair, which he had always liked. Something he had always asked of her.

He gripped her wrist. "No."

"But—"

"There will be none of that. Leave it up."

Those words scraped her raw. Left her wounded. She couldn't quite fathom why. Except that maybe, no matter what he had said, he didn't want to be so conscious that it was her. He couldn't see her, after all. And asking her to keep her hair up was truly like asking her to stay shrouded in darkness.

She would have to decide, she supposed, if that wounded her enough to make her walk out.

No. It didn't. Because this wasn't about her. It wasn't about her feelings. It certainly wasn't about trying to recapture something that had happened between them long ago. This was a step forward. The closing of the door. She had to allow it to be that.

She had to allow it to be unique. Its own experience. And if he wanted to keep her hair up, then that was fine by her.

Her hair was another thing that had had far too much importance attached to it for far too long.

Maybe that would be another change she would make when all this was done.

She had left it unchanged for all these years, after all. And she knew why. It had nothing to do with her father. As Rafe had said long ago, her father's obsession with it had been nothing short of creepy.

This was for Rafe. Her hair was for Rafe. He had loved uncoiling it from its bun, loved wrapping it around his hand. Loved running his fingers through the silken strands. She had left it for him. For five years, she had left it.

Perhaps when this was over, she would not feel that compulsion.

Clearly, he didn't require it of her anyway.

"Take your clothes off," he said, his words cutting through the silence like a knife, slicing straight down into her soul.

She hesitated. Only for a breath.

"All right." She reached around behind her back, and gripped hold of the zipper tab.

"I want you to tell me what you were wearing," he said, speaking slowly. With supreme authority.

"To…to tell you?" she asked, the words choked.

"Yes. Tell me in great detail exactly what you were wearing tonight. A gown, I assume, and with an interesting material. Not silken. A thin layer over something heavier. Yes?"

"Yes," she confirmed.

"Describe it to me as you remove it."

He was standing in the center of the room, his expression impassive, his dark eyes resting behind her. Even if he had been looking directly at her, she knew that he wouldn't be able to see.

"It's…it's red," she began haltingly. She started to try to jerk the zipper down, but it was as halting as her words. "It has a V-neck, thin straps. It conforms to my figure. Hugs my hips. And follows my body closely all the way down past my knees. It flares out there. Like a mermaid's tail."

"Very interesting. And what is underneath this gown?"

She let the straps fall around her waist, a whispering noise as it fell away from her curves and pooled at her feet.

"Underneath…" She swallowed hard. "My bra is red. It matches the gown. It's made of lace."

"I see. And would I be able to see those beautiful nipples through it? They were very pale. I recall that clearly. All of you is very pale. Your nipples…they are a particular shade of pink that I find extremely arousing. Like candy. It makes my mouth water just thinking about it."

She swallowed hard, trembling now. "Yes. You would be able to see them."

"If I could see," he said, his tone dark.

"Yes," she said softly. "If you could see."

"Please tell me that your underwear matches. That they are red and lacy, and that I would be able to see your beautiful golden curls through the fabric."

She could hardly breathe. She felt dizzy.

"Yes." She swallowed hard again. "The fabric is transparent."

She had never played the part of seductress. Those weeks in her room *he* had been seducing *her*. And while she had certainly begged him to take things further— to take them all the way—he had still been the one in control of the situation. It felt different now. The air between them an electric shock. And his expression… Growing tighter, growing more tense as the moments wore on. His hands were curled into fists at his side, and he might have been made of stone.

Beautiful stone that looked as though it would be hot to the touch. There was a strange power in this moment. In him demanding that she paint a picture in his mind. She could have told him anything, but she found that she wanted nothing more than to give him honesty. Because here, in this strong man, was some sense of vulnerability. He was stronger than her. More experienced than her. As he had always been.

But she had some power. She did.

Because he had given it to her.

Even now, with things as they were between them, he had handed her this.

"I want you to remove the bra," he commanded.

Without thought, she obeyed.

"Now tell me," he said, his voice rough now. "Are your nipples tight? From the cold air? From my voice? From your arousal? Knowing exactly what I will do next. Because you know me, and you know I am insatiable when it comes to those breasts of yours. I'm going to suck one of those sweet buds into my mouth, lick you, taste you."

She shivered. "Yes."

"Yes, you want me to taste you? Or yes, they are tight?"

"Both," she whispered, the word husky, her voice unrecognizable as her own.

A smile curved his mouth, and she would be tempted to describe it as cruel.

"The panties next. Push them down your hips slowly." He smiled wider. "You did not tell me about your shoes."

"Stilettos. Red. Like the dress."

"And are you still wearing them?"

"You didn't tell me to take them off yet."

His mouth twitched. "Good. Leave them on."

She complied with his wishes, pushing the thin scrap of fabric down her legs slowly, then kicking them off to the side. And she prepared for more commands.

"Now tell me," he said, his voice like gravel. "Are you wet for me? There between your thighs, are you wet and aching for my touch? You have been touched by me there before. Remember. How I would put my hand between your legs and stroke you, draw the moisture out from inside of you and rub my thumb over your clit? Do you remember that?"

"Yes," she answered in a rush.

"And is that what you want from me now? My tongue sliding through those slick folds? My fingers deep inside you?"

She had tried. On more than one occasion to replicate the kind of pleasure he had given her with his hands with her own. It was never the same. It didn't work like that. She hadn't felt that kind of pleasure in five long years. And what he was saying now went beyond this kind of elevated need for closure. All of these excuses she had been giving herself. Yes, this went far beyond that.

This was just about want. Pure, undiluted sexual need. Something she thought she had lost touch with.

But apparently, Rafe had simply been holding on to it for safekeeping.

"I want that."

"Good." He turned away from her. "You can leave the shoes on. And I want you to walk with me to my bedroom."

CHAPTER FOUR

HE BLAZED THE trail to the room, and she followed, her high heels clicking on the glossy marble floor.

He pushed the door open, revealing a large, pristinely made bed that took her breath away. Because they would be in that bed together. And there would be nothing stopping them this time. Nothing stopping them from consummating this need that had blazed between them for so long.

Before there had always been something else. Always something stopping them. Some kind of obstacle. But that was gone now. There was no need to stop. No pretense available.

She sucked in a sharp breath and walked toward the bed, standing at the foot of it.

"Where are you?" he asked.

"Just in front of the bed. At the foot of it."

He oriented himself, then walked toward her. Following her voice and her instructions unerringly.

"What color is your lipstick? I hope it's red. Red like everything else."

Her heart slammed against her breastbone. "It is."

"I want it all over my body," he rasped. "I want you

to be able to see exactly what has happened between us. Come here."

She complied, taking two steps to close the distance between them.

"Kiss me," he demanded. "Right here." He lifted his hand and pointed to his neck. Just at his throat. She leaned forward, pressed a slow, firm kiss to his skin there.

She moved away, looking up at him.

"Have you left a mark?"

She surveyed her work, the red smudge left behind on his skin. "Yes."

"Good." A muscle in his jaw ticked. "Now. You will undress me next. Start with my jacket. Then my tie. Then my shirt."

Charlotte felt dizzy and breathless, but desperate to obey. She pushed his jacket from his shoulders, not caring where it landed. Then she undid his tie, the black silk sliding easily to the floor.

With unsteady hands, she undid the top button on his shirt, then pressed her fingertips tentatively to his chest, and then leaned in, kissing him there, just above his heart. "I've marked you there too," she said softly.

She undid the next button, then moved lower. The next button. And she followed the path, moving lower still, inhaling the scent of his skin. And then, she was lost in memory. Because this was still Rafe as she remembered him. She had unbuttoned his shirt many times.

Had seen him naked.

Yes, he was more heavily muscled now, with more hair on his chest. But he was still Rafe. And she *remembered* this. Remembered him.

The way his skin tasted. How starving she was for him all the time. How she couldn't get enough.

She untucked his shirt from his pants, spreading it wide, then kissed him, just above his belt before taking hold of it with trembling fingers and working it through the buckle. She had done this before. For him. She had forced him to accept it, actually. Because while he was playing the part of chivalrous knight, pleasuring her in various ways without technically taking her virginity, he had taken nothing for himself.

And so she had insisted. And once she had started, he had not been able to stop her. More accurately, she didn't believe he had wanted to.

He had played at honor back then, or at least at control, but he had certainly enjoyed surrendering it to her when she had gotten down on her knees. She hoped it would be the same now.

She pushed his pants and underwear down his hips, revealing that hard pillar of masculinity. Her heart thundered, her entire body seizing up tight. She remembered this too. Remembered him. The shape of him. The way he had felt in her hand. Hard, hot and endlessly enticing.

She reached up, curving her fingers around his hardened length and letting out a long, slow sigh of satisfaction. He jerked beneath her touch, and she smiled. And suddenly, the years melted away. As she leaned forward, sliding her tongue over him before taking him deep into her mouth, it was easy to imagine that she was back in her tower room during one of their hot, illicit nights.

He reached down, gripping her hair, which was still firmly coiled in the heavy bun at the back of her head.

And that reminded her. The sharp tug bringing her back to reality, the realization that her hair was bound. That reminded her that this was not five years ago. And they were not the Rafe and Charlotte that they had once been.

That filled her with an unaccountable sadness. But on the heels of it came a strong sense of empowerment. Because she had as much power here as he did. Because there was nothing looming over them. They had this night. All night.

For anything—everything—that they wanted.

After so long, she was essentially made of want. She would take every last one of the hours before them to satisfy it. She gripped the base of his shaft and took him deeper, and he tugged harder on her hair, pulling her mouth away from him.

"Enough of that," he said. "This, I have had from you."

"And somehow...you're tired of it?"

He pressed his thumb to the center of her bottom lip. "I will have your mouth on me later. Believe me. But for now, I wish to be inside you." He paused for a moment, tilting his head to the side. "Have you left lipstick there, as well?"

Her cheeks heated, and she examined him. "Yes."

He growled, a feral, untamed sound, and bent down, wrapping his arm around her waist and hauling her up against him. Then, he walked them both backward, tumbling with her onto the bed.

The rest of his clothes, and both of their shoes, were discarded onto the floor, and he kissed her like he was a lost soul on his way to hell and she might provide the necessary ingredient to his salvation.

"You're so soft," he said, abandoning her lips to press a kiss to the tender skin on the side of her neck. "So warm. I imagine you are flushed from arousal. I remember how you used to do that. Your pale skin turning pink, starting at your cheeks and moving down your neck." He pressed his thumb against her pulse again. "Yes. And your heart would beat fast, just like this. And then…" He moved his hand down to cup her bare breast, that deft thumb of his sliding over her nipple. "Yes. Your nipples were always so responsive. So tight. Just for me."

She gasped as he pinched her lightly, then replaced his hand with his mouth, flicking the tightened bud with his tongue before sucking her in deep.

It was a sensory overload. After so many years without physical contact, it was almost too much. But he was merciless, and when she let out a sob that was wrenched from deep within her body, one she could not have controlled if she had wanted to, rather than easing off, he pressed his fingers between her legs, pushing through her slick folds.

His thumb moved in a circular motion over her clit as he pushed his middle finger inside her and she saw stars. Then, he added a second finger, the fullness unfamiliar. He had never done this before. Part of sparing her innocence and all of that. But there was none of that happening tonight.

Thankfully.

She closed her eyes, letting her head fall back. And she ignored the uncomfortable lump created by her restrained mass of hair. Ignored the pins digging into her scalp. She didn't care about any of that. Didn't care about anything but the intensity of the pleasure burning through her like a wildfire.

Orgasm was closing in on her; she knew it. But she wanted to hold it off for as long as possible. Wanted to exist on this knife's edge until she couldn't possibly stand it any longer. That was what she had wanted back then too. To extend her time with him. Because once she was satisfied, he would leave. Lingering too long a risk that neither of them could take. And so she had learned to hold back. To find pleasure in the exquisite torture that came with denying herself release.

In the interest of having Rafe's hands on her for longer. In the interest of staying lost. Of no longer existing as Charlotte Adair, daughter of a notorious crime lord, but as a creature made entirely of pleasure. Of need.

But it had been so long. And it was too much. She couldn't bear to hold it off, not for one more moment. And so she gave in. Diving deep into that pool of pleasure, into that release that only Rafe had ever given her. She was breathless. Weightless. Thoughtless for an extended space of time. Made of nothing but deep, pulsing satisfaction that pounded through her like waves on the rocks.

When her release ended she looked up at Rafe. His eyes were closed.

Then he lifted his hand to his lips, and sucked the two fingers that had just been inside her into his mouth. Fire, white hot and savage, burned through her. She wasn't sure if it was shame or if it was need on a level she had never known before. Certainly, there was embarrassment, because that had been such a base and carnal act.

And yet, she understood it. Because hadn't she been

compelled to taste him? As she had once done. She
wanted more than a few quick strokes of her tongue.
She wanted all of him. But he was right. There would
be time for that later.

He grabbed hold of her legs and parted them, kneel-
ing before her, that most masculine part of him standing out from his body, thick and proud, and for the very
first time—intimidating.

Every other time she had been with him there had
been no expectation that he would be inside her the
way he was about to be.

She had always enjoyed the shape of him. The way
he had felt in her hand.

And somewhat foolishly she had imagined there
would be no virginal nerves tonight. Because wasn't
she familiar with his body? Hadn't they been naked together many times before? She'd had him in her mouth,
had brought him pleasure with her hand. It had given
her a false sense of experience.

One she certainly did not feel now.

He reached down, cupping her cheek, his fingers
curving around the back of her head as he lifted her
from the mattress, claiming her mouth with his own.
He brought her up against his body, wrapping her legs
around his waist, bringing his hardness right up against
the place where she ached for him the most.

He wrapped his other arm around her waist, his hold
like iron. Her breasts were crushed against his chest,
and she could feel his heart raging. And somehow, that
calmed her nerves. The realization that he felt all of
this too. He might look hard, unaffected and utterly
composed, but his body told another story entirely.

There was no more talking. There were no more

commands. There was just raw, unleashed desire, poured out onto her body like an anointing.

He slid his hand down to her lower back, then lower still, grabbing hold of her rear and squeezing her tight as he lifted her against him, the head of his shaft finding the entrance to her body.

She couldn't breathe. She began to protest. To say something about how she wasn't ready. How she didn't think she could take all of him, at least not without taking it slowly. But before she could, he tilted his hips forward, then pushed hard into her body, filling her in one breathtaking thrust.

It hurt. Her eyes watered, and she bit her lip hard and waited for the stinging sensation to subside. It didn't take long. Because she was so slick, and because there was something delicious about the way that he filled her, even if it was unfamiliar and painful.

A great many things in life were painful, and they weren't anywhere near this beautiful. She would take this pain gladly. Because finally she was joined to Rafe. The way that she had always dreamed of.

He was frozen. His face like granite, his unseeing eyes like ice. But he said nothing. Then, finally he closed his eyes, letting his head fall back. Slowly, without withdrawing from her, he laid her down onto the mattress, rolling his hips forward and going deeper—impossibly so—as he lowered his head and kissed her lips gently.

But the only gentleness came in that moment. And in the space of a breath, it was gone.

He reached down, gripping her hips and holding her steady as he thrust hard against her. She closed her eyes, and she saw stars. She was glad. She didn't want this to be a slow, easy coupling. Because they had never been slow or easy. The last five years seemed to shrink, and they disappeared altogether as his body met hers, fast, furious and deep.

She gripped his shoulders, her fingernails digging into his back, while his blunt fingertips were certainly making bruises in her pale skin. It was what she wanted. To be marked by this. Changed in a way that was visible.

So that tomorrow when she went back to the apartment she had just signed the papers for, the place that would be hers, and she looked in the mirror she would be able to see the changes in her body with just a glance.

She wanted to be sore between her thighs. Wanted to see the impression of his hands, where he had held on to her. She wanted to be wrecked by this. Ruined. So that she could rise from those ashes, instead of simply appearing quietly, meekly, from hiding.

He whispered things in her ear, dark and rough, in his native Italian. Words she didn't know. Words she had never heard. Which certainly ensured that they were dirty.

That sent a thrill through her body. Twisted that coil of arousal that was starting low in her stomach again, heightening it all. She moved her hands from his shoulders, sliding them up his neck, gripping his face firmly, and holding it steady, bringing his head down so that his forehead was pressed hard against hers.

She kept her eyes open, forced herself to bear witness to this. Because he couldn't.

Even so, those dark eyes bore through her. And she could almost swear that though he couldn't see the features on her face, he might be able to see into her soul.

The rhythm between them was frantic, desperate. And she clung to him as she lost herself in it. In him.

She pressed her lips to his, and then began to say things. Things she didn't understand any more than the Italian he had just spoken to her. Desperate demands, promises. Supplication. She spoke words to him she had never said out loud in her life, begging for more. Begging for him.

It wasn't just the way it felt physically. Being connected to him... It was more than that. It didn't satisfy a need; it simply unveiled how deep her need was. To be connected to someone else. To be needed. To need in return.

Pleasure stretched inside her like a wire, drawing tight from her lungs, down to her toes. She had the sense that it was holding her together. That when it snapped, she would fly apart, never to be put back together again.

Just like before, she fought against it. Fought against the end. But she could feel her hold on her control slipping. Could feel her mind starting to get hazy, her thoughts going fuzzy. It was hard to remember why she wanted to hold off her pleasure in the first place. Difficult to grasp on to where she was, and why she was afraid for the end to come.

But she never forgot who she was with.

It was Rafe. It could only ever have been Rafe.

And then he growled, his teeth digging into the cords on her neck as he began to slam into her, no consideration, no gentleness remaining at all. And she rejoiced. Letting go. Just as he had done.

She turned her face, curving it into his shoulder as she rode out the impossible release that flooded through her. There had never been anything like this. Like losing control with him.

They had traded pleasure in her room. Her hand, then his. His mouth, then hers. But they had never gone over together like this. She had never felt him pulsing inside her as he spilled himself.

It was everything. It was perfect.

It was finished. At least, that was the idea.

This was supposed to be the ultimate fulfillment. The satisfaction that she had been waiting for for the past five years. And yet, as soon as the storm passed, she wanted more. She wanted him.

He moved away from her, rolling onto his back, breathing hard. "Would you care to explain that?"

"I wouldn't have thought you would need the facts of life explained to you at this point, Rafe," she commented, feeling the need to put up some kind of shield between them. Because she felt so vulnerable. So exposed. Naked. When before it had all felt easy.

"That," he bit out, "is not what I meant. And you know it."

"We have amazing chemistry," she responded. "But we've always known that. We risked our health and safety to explore it, if you recall."

"I take it you are unmarried."

She frowned. And then she remembered that he had mentioned her husband back at the ball. It had all grown hazy in the interim. By the revelation that they'd been lied to by her father and stepmother. And then it had been lost in the pleasure.

It was incredibly distracting pleasure.

"I'm not. You assumed that I was. I never said either way. And frankly, with everything else going on I didn't really…think of it."

"And you were a virgin."

"The last five years haven't exactly been an ascent to success for *me*."

He chuckled, the sound hard and dark. "In contrast, they have been a walk in the park for me."

"I'm sorry," she said. "That was thoughtless of me. I escaped."

She looked over at him, and he was frowning. "You escaped?"

"My father kidnapped me and attempted to sell me into marriage, Rafe. When I refused to go willingly even after I was told that you had left me. I suppose they thought without you there I would have no reason to resist. Shockingly, I took exception to being married off to a crime lord. Fancy that."

Rafe pushed himself into a sitting position, his muscles rippling. "Your father tried to sell you into marriage?"

"You look surprised, Rafe. We are talking about a man that we hid our romance from so that he would not kill us both."

"And yet, in the end they clearly knew. And opted not to kill either of us."

She nodded. "I never quite figured that out."

"In my case I know that it was due in part to the fact that eventually I became too high profile." There was something strange and opaque in those words. But right now, her brain was scrambled, and she couldn't quite parse it.

"And you left."

"When I was told you had opted to marry another man I did not see why I should stay," he said, clipped.

"But I didn't. I was carted off. And I escaped. I have spent the past five years hiding. So, the opposite tactic to you. You became more visible. While I faded into invisibility. An easy thing to do, all things considered. You know, since I had spent all of my previous years hidden away at the villa."

His expression was utterly black. Terrifying. "If your father were not dead, I would kill him myself. And that is one of the very few sins I have never committed."

"He wouldn't have been worth it. It wouldn't have been worth destroying yourself for." She blinked, her eyes filling with tears. "It doesn't matter. We're free of him now."

"Yes. And we still have the rest of the night."

Her heart squeezed tight, need filling her. "Yes." She leaned in, kissing him on the mouth. "We do."

And after this, she would find herself. After this, she would find her freedom.

Finally. This was the end.

The end they both needed. So they could finally have a beginning that they chose for themselves.

CHAPTER FIVE

"DID YOU GET the report I asked for?"

It had been weeks since Charlotte had walked out of his penthouse and out of his life, yet again. It had been part of their agreement this time. Still, Rafe felt unsettled. He told himself it was because he was concerned for her safety. After all, she had been living in cottages in the woods and small villages for the past five years. She had not been trying to navigate London.

Why he should care, he didn't know. Except, he felt differently about her now, knowing that she had not abandoned him. Though, guilt was a new companion. He had taken her stepmother at her word.

Yet pursuing her would have been difficult. It had taken him months to heal from his injuries. And then, there were those that had never fully healed. By then, he had been certain that she was settled into her new life.

And he could think of nothing sadder than playing the part of injured, rejected boyfriend crawling after the woman who had willingly left him.

But he should have known. He should have.

"Yes, Mr. Costa. I got the files that you asked for,

though it seems to me that a great deal of this is a violation of privacy laws."

Rafe sighed heavily as he shifted the phone from one ear to the other. "Undoubtedly. But that is not my concern. And anyway, that is why I paid for a third party to acquire the information and not you, Alyssa."

"Well, it is all here. Shall I put together an email for you?"

"If you please."

Rafe ended the call with his assistant and turned toward the office window, which he had been told offered an expansive view of London. The Thames. The London Eye. Big Ben and the Abbey. A view such as this spoke of status. Of security. It was only the mortals that had to stand below and view bits and pieces of these icons rather than taking in the full reality of the city.

He couldn't see it; that was true. But it was there. He took a perverse amount of pride in that. In the fact he owned this view and had never even seen it.

It spoke of excess in a way that appeased him. Spoke of his power. As did his ability to keep tabs on Charlotte. Now that she was not in hiding, she was doing a very poor job of not leaving a paper trail.

He had obtained her address easily enough, and he had asked for his contact to keep him apprised of any other information about her that might be relevant. Anything that went into an online system that he could find a back door into.

Rafe loved technology. He had built his fortune on it. But more than that, he adored how it had such fatally flawed weak points. When everything was in hard copy it was much easier to keep secure. But the moment something was put out on a network…it had the potential to be exposed. To be obtained by those who were never supposed to see it.

His mobile phone buzzed, and he gritted his teeth in annoyance when the ringtone kicked in—the specific tone he had set for his friend, Prince Felipe. His Royal Highness and general pain in Rafe's ass.

He sighed, and then answered. "To what do I owe the pleasure?" Rafe asked, not meaning it at all.

"Hang on for just a second," Felipe said.

"*You* called *me*," Rafe said, his patience feeling stretched. But then, it had been feeling severely compromised from the moment Charlotte had walked out of his penthouse.

"I did. But I'm also calling Adam."

Prince Adam Katsaros had been his other friend at the private school he had been sent to by Michael Adair. It had been his happiest time. A time when he had been on his own, but had also possessed the resources that he needed to survive.

Of course, it had come with a price. The price of his indentured servitude. At the time, it had seemed reasonable.

"Hello?" Adam came on the line.

"Excellent," Felipe said. "I wanted to ask Rafe if he would fill us in on who the woman was that he was spotted leaving a party with some weeks ago."

Rafe gritted his teeth. "That's what you want to know? Why are you calling me now? Why didn't you call me weeks ago?"

"Because I *want* something from you now," Felipe said. "And I'm not one to waste a phone call."

"That isn't true," Adam said. "You are one to waste several phone calls. And a great many words."

"Your opinion is fascinating," Felipe said. "My wife finds me delightful."

"Then it's a good thing she married you instead of one of us," Rafe said drily. "Now, get to the point."

"Briar is spearheading an art exhibition in a couple of months. And I wanted to make sure that it was appropriately populated with my very influential friends. It is a showcase of my country's work. And also of her first original works. Now. All of you must come or the next time you do come to visit me I will throw you in the dungeon."

"I see no problem with it. Though, I find my enjoyment of art is somewhat truncated these days," Rafe said.

"Yes, but your enjoyment of beautiful women is suddenly not. A notable change from the past few years, is it not?" Felipe pressed.

"All signs point to it," Adam supplied.

"Perhaps you should both be concerned more with your marriages than with my sex life?"

"We worry about you," Felipe said, "because we are true friends."

Rafe mumbled something about friends being overrated. Then a tone went off on his computer, and he made his way back to his desk. He muted the microphone on his call, then gave his computer voice instructions to read his email to him.

The file was lengthy. His Charlotte had been busy.

He continued to half listen to Adam and Felipe talk logistics in terms of the exhibit in Felipe's country.

But his attention fell away from that as he continued to listen to the contents of his file regarding Charlotte. She had gone to the bank. She had secured a large sum of money. He had access to everything. Her balance, the account it had been transferred from. It surprised him to know that her father had left some money in a trust for her.

He wondered if the old man had forgotten about it. If it had actually been a way for him to hide some of his money. Money he had intended to move before he died. If he knew one thing about Charlotte's father, it was that he had certainly fancied himself immortal in many respects. He most definitely wouldn't have thought his death would come so soon.

There were mundane things in there too. Receipts for online shopping. Uninteresting. She had bought a table lamp. And oven mitts.

Then there was the last bit of information. She had made a doctor's appointment. At a private women's health clinic.

It was entirely possible that it was for a regular checkup. Entirely possible.

But it had been weeks since they were together. And the first time they had not used a condom. He hadn't been thinking straight, and neither had she. She had also been a virgin—something he hadn't counted on. But that led him to assume that she had not been on any kind of birth control.

A women's health clinic. The implications of that pounded their way through him like a battering ram. Felipe was still talking, but Rafe was past the point of listening.

The appointment was this afternoon. And the address was on the paperwork. He had just over an hour to get across the city, and he would be damned if he was going to miss it.

"I have to go. I will be at your party—don't worry."
He hung up the phone, and he quickly buzzed for his
secretary. "Get my helicopter ready."

Charlotte walked into the clinic with clammy hands.
Her heart was pounding hard, and she could scarcely
breathe. She had taken about ten home pregnancy tests,
so it wasn't as if she expected to get any other news
here at the appointment. But of course, this would be
real confirmation.

It was hugely expensive to book an early scan at a
place like this, but she didn't have a GP, and there was
a long waiting list to get in at the hospital, so she'd just
done a quick online search and decided to throw some
of her father's money at a private women's clinic.

If she really was pregnant with Rafe's baby, spending her father's money to confirm it was amusing in
some ways. Even if nothing else about the situation
was.

She could tell herself whatever she wanted about
being under stress, about life changes affecting her
cycle. But the fact of the matter was she had gone on
the lam for five years, constantly afraid that somebody
might find her, and had never once missed a period.
Most likely, it had more to do with the fact that she had
had sex for the first time in her life, and it had been
unprotected. Something she had blocked out of her
mind the moment she had walked away from Rafe's
penthouse.

She checked in at the front desk and then walked
into the plush waiting room. And her heart nearly ex-
ploded.

Because there he was. In the clinic. It wasn't possible. It didn't seem like it could be. She had spent five years running from one of the criminal world's most notorious bosses, and no one had found her.

But Rafe was here. He was here, and he had to know.

"What are you doing here?" she asked.

He turned toward the sound of her voice. "I would ask you the same question, but I have a strong suspicion that I already know."

"I'm here for a Pap smear," she said, staring him down.

"I doubt that."

"Ms. Adair." She turned to see a nurse standing in the doorway. "Dr. Schultz is ready to see you now."

"I will be accompanying her," Rafe said, standing up from his chair. He grabbed hold of his cane, black with a silver tip, and began to walk toward where the nurse was.

"You will certainly not accompany me," Charlotte said, keeping her voice low.

He moved toward her then, much more quickly than she expected him to. "Do not make a scene, *cara mia*," he said. "You will not like the way it ends."

She was too numb to protest further. She should have. She should have screamed and tipped over the ficus by the door. Then, maybe someone would have stopped him. But who would have? Who was going to physically accost Rafe Costa, known billionaire and powerful businessman? And even if they didn't know who he was, he was well over six feet tall and made almost entirely of muscle.

Charlotte imagined that she wouldn't find an ally here.

Her temples were pounding as they walked down

the hallway that Charlotte assumed would lead to the exam room. She felt like the walls were closing in on her. Like the sky might be crushing down on her.

And she had to ask herself why she had been so desperate to keep this from Rafe in the first place. It was his baby. There was no one else. There never had been.

That initial response, the one that had demanded that she keep all of this to herself, had been based in panic. He was here now. Didn't he deserve to know?

Her own father had played the part of villain in her life; that much was true. But Rafe wasn't a villain. She knew that.

Maybe there would be no baby. That would be a good thing. She was only just beginning to figure out what she wanted after a lifetime of being hidden away.

She was only just beginning to figure out who Charlotte Adair was. On her own. Without a group of men searching for her. She had no idea what she would do if she was supposed to try to figure that out while trying to figure out how to be a mother.

She had never even held a baby. There had never been any children at her father's compound except for her.

Yes, she had watched women push strollers around when she'd worked at the shops. She had watched them kiss away fat, angry tears from chubby cheeks. And of course, she had wondered what it must be like. To have someone to love. Someone who would love you so very much in return.

The thought made her chest ache. But her head hurt too. From the impossibility of all of this.

And then there was Rafe. Who loomed large behind her.

She was handed a small plastic cup and directed toward a bathroom. Her cheeks flamed as she went inside. And then she tried not to think about the fact that Rafe knew exactly what the cup was for as she completed the task.

She exited the restroom and went into the exam room. And the nurse left Rafe and Charlotte alone.

"When exactly were you going to tell me?" he asked as soon as the door had closed behind the retreating nurse.

"I was definitely going to wait until I had something confirmed by a professional. When you think about it, it's a little bit ridiculous that we're supposed to buy something from a grocery store that tells us something so essential, and just trust that it's correct."

"I see. And how many of those did you take?"

She waved a hand. "I don't know. Maybe ten?"

"I see." His jaw was hard, his face set into a grim expression. "And what did those ten tests tell you, Charlotte?"

"That I'm pregnant," she answered, feeling subdued.

There was a knock on the door, and Dr. Schultz swept into the room. After some risk preparation, Charlotte found herself staring at an ultrasound screen as the Doppler swept over her stomach.

"There isn't much to see at this stage," Dr. Schultz said, her eyes on the screen. "But we do want to confirm viability."

"What do you see?" Rafe asked, from his position in the corner.

"Nothing yet," the doctor said.

"Just black lines," Charlotte said softly.

Then the image on the screen changed. And she could see it. Just ever so faintly. A little bit of motion.

Charlotte couldn't help it. She giggled. The strangest response she could have imagined having to such a thing.

"What?" Rafe asked.

"Something moved," Charlotte said, looking up at the doctor.

"Yes," Dr. Schultz responded, changing something on the ultrasound machine, turning up the sound so that a watery noise filled the room. And beneath the kind of indistinct blur was a rhythmic whispering. "That's a heartbeat."

Charlotte looked over at Rafe, who had gone pale. And then a second, very similar sound filled the room.

Charlotte's head whipped back toward the screen. She looked up at the doctor. "Is that…?"

"That is a second heartbeat," the doctor responded. "Congratulations. Twins."

The words were ringing in Rafe's ears after the doctor left, and Charlotte was dressing. He could hear her rustling in the corner. She was otherwise silent.

The black hell that he lived in seemed to close in around him. His sense of the slight distinction between light and dark felt erased in that moment.

Twins. Charlotte was having twins.

And he—a man who had never had a father, a man who had no sense of how to be a father—was supposed to know what to do.

He couldn't see. He would never see his children. How would he care for them?

With nannies. Of course. That's the purpose of money.

He heard a sharp movement from Charlotte's direction. And that was when he realized he had spoken those dour words out loud.

"I doubt I'll need nannies," she said, her voice stiff.

"Did you not care for yours?" He had rather liked his. What he could remember of her.

He had spent only five years in that life. The life where there had been shining marble halls and nannies and all the food he could want. But he'd been happy then. As far as he recalled.

She huffed out a laugh. "On the contrary, they were an improvement to my father and stepmother. I imagine that perhaps my mother was fine enough. But I know nothing about her since she died in childbirth, and my father never spoke of her. I always got the impression that Josefina was his mistress before my mother's passing. All she did was change rooms. And gain an official title."

"So, then nannies are not so bad."

"But I won't need them. I will need to work at some point because the money that my father left me—whether he left it intentionally or not—won't last forever, but it will be sufficient for a time."

"You seem resolved."

"I am," she responded, taking a couple of steps toward him, wearing hard-soled shoes that made a distinct sound as she moved.

He cursed his lack of sight yet again. Because he would like very much to be able to see how she was reacting, truthfully. Not just with her brave, carefully chosen words. He wanted to see her face. If she was pale. If she looked as frightened as he suspected she probably was.

His whole life was structured to serve him, and he rarely thought much about his lost vision. But Charlotte—this piece of his past that she represented—brought out memories. Memories of what it had been like to hold her in his arms, to look at her pale body, to brush his fingers through her golden hair.

Visions of how she had looked standing in an open field with the overwhelming light of the sun pouring over her beauty, illuminating her.

And that brought out the contrast of what it was like to be with her now and to be robbed of that vision. To have this future—children—looming before him and yet to see nothing more than darkness.

"I am resolved, as well." He stood, walking across the space between them and holding out his hand. He could sense her hesitation. "Please take my hand," he said. "I am in unfamiliar surroundings, and it would be helpful."

While that was not strictly untrue, it wasn't really true either.

She took his hand, and he allowed her to lead him toward the door, which he could have found on his own.

"Did you take a cab to get here?"

"Yes," she responded. "I don't feel all that well and I didn't want the hassle of the Tube."

"I never do. But then, I rarely bother with traffic. Where do you need to go?"

"Home," she said simply.

She was not going home. He was resolved about that. And he was done at the office for the day. But he wasn't going to tell her that.

"I have a helicopter. Do you suppose it's possible to land on your building?"

He could tell by the resounding silence beside him that he had succeeded in shocking her. He was gratified by that. "You know, I didn't ask about helicopter parking when I moved in."

"An oversight."

"You don't need to give me a…flight back."

"Allow me to. My pilot will know exactly where he can land that's in proximity to your building." It didn't actually matter.

"Rafe…"

"I am told the view of London is quite spectacular. Of course, I am not able to see it. It would be nice if one of us could enjoy it."

Had he a conscience remaining inside him that was something other than a theoretical understanding of right and wrong, he might have felt guilty about that. But he didn't. So he didn't.

She sighed heavily. "All right. I'll let you give me a ride back. I've never been in a helicopter before. I've never flown before."

"Are you nervous?"

"No." She sounded somewhat astonished by that. "I'm not."

They went up to the top of the building, where the helicopter was waiting for them, and he allowed her to brace herself on his hand as she got into the vehicle. He followed suit, putting on his headset and holding hers back as the rotor started turning, creating a deafening sound around them.

He knew that she wouldn't be able to hear the instructions he was giving to his pilot.

"To the castle," he said.

Then he handed Charlotte her own headset. She

would figure it all out soon enough. When the flight took them over the ocean, and took more than an hour. But unless she was going to fling herself from the helicopter—and he doubted it—by then it would be too late.

It took a while. He wasn't quite certain what the view below looked like, but he had made the educated assumption that they were leaving London behind when Charlotte spoke.

"My flat is the other direction," she said.

"I like your English," he said. "An interesting mixture. American in some ways. Vaguely British in others. If I recall correctly, your Italian is quite good too."

"Wonderful. But that has nothing to do with what I just said."

"Because I'm not concerned about what you just said."

"You're not concerned about the fact that your pilot might be lost?"

"My pilot is not lost. He's going exactly where I told him to go."

"Where…where did you tell him to go?"

"Why, we're going to my castle in Germany, *cara mia*."

"I just escaped Germany," she said sharply. "Why would I want to go back?"

"You seemed to have fond memories of it. It is incredible to me that we spent some time in the same country and never knew it." He settled back in his seat, feeling more and more relaxed as the journey wore on. Because he had already won. "I heard about a castle for sale and simply couldn't resist it. After all, my two closest friends are royalty, and I didn't want to be left out."

"What difference does it make? You can't even see it."

She spat the words, and they hit him like a slap. He quite liked it. Enjoyed the fact that she was strong even though she had been raised by a madman who would as soon have used her as a pawn to shore up his empire as given her a hug.

"Yes, but it pleases me to know what surrounds me. Anyway, you must know a castle possesses a certain atmosphere. It cannot be replicated by a modern building. In fact, I would suggest to you that such atmosphere is more important to someone such as myself than it would be to someone like you. I can feel the history when I walk through the doors. I can smell the age of the rooms. The books. Everything in modern construction is so smooth. It lacks texture. In the castle… It is everywhere. I can feel how the walls look."

"Why are you taking me there?"

"Because," he said. "I find I have lost quite enough in my life to risk losing my children, as well. You weren't going to tell me. I think we both know that. Why, I cannot fathom. I thought we had come to some sort of agreement, some sort of understanding. I didn't abandon you, any more than you abandoned me. And yet, you're still treating me like a man you have reason to distrust."

"He says as he kidnaps me *in a helicopter.*"

Rafe chuckled and leaned back in his seat. "But I hadn't kidnapped you before."

"You worked for my father. You know what that says about you."

"You didn't mind when you were eighteen and letting me put my hands between your legs. And you certainly didn't mind a few weeks ago when you begged for my—"

"Stop it," she hissed.

"You and I will have plenty of time to talk over the next few months. So for now, I will stop. Because later…later you and I will reckon with each other. That is a promise."

CHAPTER SIX

CHARLOTTE WAS STILL numb sitting in an ornate bedroom in what looked like a fairy-tale castle hours later. The helicopter had landed in a clearing in a beautiful, orange-tinged forest, and left them there.

Then, as if summoned by the sheer force of Rafe's magnetism, a car had pulled up to the edge of the trees and driven them up the side of a mountain, up a winding dirt road that seemed chiseled into the side of it.

The castle was glorious, wreathed in gold, with dramatic turrets rising up and spiraling toward the sky. It seemed to be built straight from a rock face, or placed directly on top of the mountain.

At least there was a road. Otherwise, she would imagine it was impossible to escape this place. Like it, and its inhabitants, had been trapped here by some kind of enchantment.

Of course, there seemed to be no town for miles. At least none she had seen when they had flown in, or when they had driven to the castle.

It was…it was profound isolation. And she had none of her own things with her. Only her purse, which at least contained her ID and her credit cards.

But, seeing as she felt as though she had been transported back in time, it didn't feel like any of those things would be useful to her.

She stood up, moving to an ornate vanity made from beautiful inlaid stones—jade, jasper and obsidian—and lined with gold. She looked at herself, stunned by the ridiculous contrast created by her reflection.

Her hair was escaping its confines, her face drawn and pale. Her black turtleneck sweater and blue jeans looked outrageously casual in her exceedingly formal surroundings.

Actually, she looked a little bit too casual for a kidnap victim, truth be told. She frowned. This was not the first time in her life she had been kidnapped. Charlotte had accepted a long time ago that her life wasn't normal. But this…well, this was just pushing the boundaries.

There was a knock on her door, and she made her way across the room, pulling it open just a crack and looking to see who was there. "Yes?" There was a woman there, one she had never seen before.

"Mr. Costa has requested that you come down to the study."

"I would like to request that Mr. Costa jump in a lake. Though, I imagine he wouldn't take terribly kindly to that."

The woman only looked at her blankly. Charlotte sighed heavily.

"I don't have a choice, do I?"

The woman shrugged. "I have a feeling that were you to refuse him, Mr. Costa would come up here and carry you down himself."

"That does sound like him." At least it sounded like the man he had become. A little bit too close to her father for Charlotte's liking. A man who was not opposed to keeping her locked away if he thought it would serve him. That made her chest feel like it was caving in on itself. It was even more painful than seeing him without his vision.

That change, the change that had clearly occurred in his soul, was much more disturbing than any physical change. A much greater loss, in her opinion.

Instead of arguing, she simply complied, leaving her bedroom and following the woman down the labyrinthine hallways. She reached up, brushing her fingertips against the wall, against the golden fleurs-de-lis that were stamped into the plaster.

This was what he had meant when he had talked about feeling the texture on the walls. About having a greater sense of the space than he did in a room composed of modern architecture. His home in London had more space, and she imagined that made things easier in some regards.

Nothing for him to trip over, everything set out just so. But there was a richness here, a sense of place that she could not deny.

She would rather deny it. Because she would rather go ahead and just think he was crazy. That he was lost to her completely, and there was nothing of the man she cared for remaining.

Sadly, she didn't think that was the case. This was Rafe. The man, rather than the near boy she had known. He was successful. He was wealthy. She had read all about how power corrupted, and she had seen it firsthand over the course of her childhood.

She was only sorry to know that Rafe had not been immune.

She shook her head. She should have left him in the realm of fantasy. It would've been so much kinder to her poor heart. A heart that already felt so tender due to years of abuse and neglect.

She could have imagined Rafe forever as she wanted to think of him. But no. She had gone to find him. To have one blistering night with him, which had resulted in permanent consequences.

And him proving to be a controlling kidnapper.

The woman paused, then stepped to the side, opening up one of the ornate blue double doors, revealing a study, and Rafe, who was sitting in a wingback chair in front of the fireplace.

"Thank you," Charlotte said, turning to the woman, who had already vanished back into the gloom.

Charlotte sighed, then stepped into the study.

"Nice of you to join me," Rafe said.

Her heart began to speed up, then, as he looked in her direction, she felt it stall out completely. The way the flames highlighted his face was…intoxicating. Arresting.

His eyes looked black, fathomless. The stubble on his square jaw would be rough to the touch, as she already knew. And then there were his lips… Lips that she knew from experience would soften beneath her own, and then would get firm again as he assumed control. As he parted her lips and slipped his tongue into her mouth…

She felt her face heat, and she bit her cheek, doing her best to keep from making an idiot out of herself by betraying the fact that even now, when he had proven himself to be an undesirable louse, she still desired him.

"Well, much like my joining you here in this castle, I was left with very little choice."

"Still. It is very nice to put the veneer of civility over all of it, isn't it?"

"I'm not sure why you would care. It certainly isn't for my benefit. I don't have very much experience with civilized men. And you…you're no different. You're cut from the same cloth as my father, who thought nothing of physically moving me from one place to the other to do his bidding. Congratulations."

His face went hard as granite. "I am not like your father."

"Well, you could have fooled me. Dragging me off to a castle…intending to force me into marriage."

Rafe chuckled, pushing himself up from the armrests so that he was standing. He stepped to the side of the chair, held out his hand in front of the fire, then took a step closer, keeping his hand extended.

"I said nothing about marriage, *cara mia*."

She blinked, feeling incredibly stupid. Because he hadn't. "Well. As you're currently carrying me off like a marauder because I'm carrying your child—*children*—I assumed that you had designs on making them legitimate or something."

He shrugged, a casual and careless gesture. "I'm not legitimate. Why should I care if my children are?"

She didn't know what to say to that. Obviously, she had assumed that since he had kidnapped her, he wanted to keep her.

"This doesn't have anything to do with me, does it?"

She felt stupid. So stupid asking that question. And so very uncovered. Like he could see into her soul. See everything that she hoped way down at the bottom of her crushed heart. Because there were things she knew logically. Things she knew about him, about their situation, and about why it wasn't healthy in any way.

"This has everything to do with power," he said, his voice hard. It echoed what she had been thinking in the hallway. What she feared more than anything else.

That he wanted control. Whatever that might mean.

"And somehow, you had to take me back to a castle in order to feel like you had any? Honestly, Rafe, if I had not seen the contents of your underwear I would have thought that this had to do with some kind of inferiority complex."

He laughed at that, which surprised her. "You weren't going to tell me, were you?"

"I don't know," she answered honestly. "I really hadn't dealt with any of it mentally or emotionally. I still haven't."

"We do not know each other very well," he said, his dark brows locking together, lines appearing between them.

"I know you better than I know anyone else." She felt her face getting hot. "You have seen me naked, after all."

"You can see a great many women naked and never know them—on that you can trust me. You were certainly not the first woman I saw naked." His lips tipped up, his smile rueful. "You were the last woman I saw naked, though."

Charlotte didn't know what to make of that statement. She wasn't clear on when his accident had happened in relation to their parting. But it must've been soon after. Because she couldn't imagine him pining for her after he had believed that she had…

"Rafe," she said. "Did you really think that I went off and married somebody else without giving you a thought? Did you really think that I was just amusing myself with you?"

"That's what rich people do," he said, his voice hard. "They use those without power as pawns in games that only they know the rules to."

"And you thought that I…you thought that I was doing that with you. That's really what you believed?"

"I didn't believe it. I didn't until I went to your room and was met by your stepmother. Clearly, she knew about us. Which meant your father did too."

"And she told you that I…that I betrayed you."

Pain gripped Charlotte by the throat, squeezing it tight. Of all the things she had imagined as she had spent those years away from him. When she had begun to see articles about his success, it had never occurred to her that he had been led to believe she had not only abandoned him but had told her father about them.

She frowned, icy cold gripping her. "Rafe, how did you escape? My father's not a forgiving man. And we both knew…being together was risky. I can't imagine that he would have let you…"

"He did not let me escape," Rafe said, his tone dark. He turned away from the fire and began to walk toward her. "The only reason I got away from your father's estate alive is that he thought he had killed me, and by the time he discovered the truth…it was too late for him to do anything about it. It was his intention that I leave in a body bag. And in truth, I essentially did."

Rafe hadn't intended to tell Charlotte the story so quickly. But then, there was no reason not to. Here they were, holed up in this castle for the foreseeable future. He intended to keep them both here until she was ready to give birth. He already had a doctor lined up, and he had paid her a very decent sum to attend to Charlotte and to look the other way if Charlotte were to mention that she was being held captive.

Oh, the power that came with money.

But power aside, they had time. And there was no reason to keep the story secret from her. It was true; the world did not know. But Charlotte might as well. She might as well understand exactly what had happened to him as a result of their assignation.

Yes, she had been in hiding for five years. Yes, it had certainly been difficult for her. But he had suffered greatly. He had lost greatly.

And then, she had been considering keeping his children from him. Another thing that would be stolen from him by the Adair family. He could not reconcile that. He could not endure it.

"When I climbed up to your room your stepmother was there on the balcony, waiting for me."

"Josefina is a serpent. She always has been."

"A bit of a cliché," he said drily. "The wicked stepmother."

"One I feel she took to heart."

"She told me you had gone. That you had confessed that I had been coming to your room at night, that you had elected to marry Stefan, who you felt was much more fitting of a woman in your position."

"How could you have believed her?" Charlotte asked, her voice torn with pain. "I told you that I would have given you everything. You wouldn't let me give it. I was not unwilling."

"Because I understood what you did not. That while you might have been willing at the time, you would come to resent me later. For all that you had left behind. For all that you had lost. I was never going to move you straight into similar circumstances, Charlotte, but you were too cosseted to think of such a thing. Because you could not imagine life without a tower."

"All I wanted was life outside the tower," she said. "You do me a disservice thinking otherwise."

"Then I did you a disservice. But it is in the past. And this conversation does not lead up to what you wanted to know. How did I escape?"

He heard her swallow, heard the rustle of fabric, and he wondered if that indicated she was fidgeting. He wasn't sure what she was wearing today, so he couldn't be certain of the way the fabric would sound when it moved.

"Tell me," she said. "I promise I won't interrupt again."

"I arrived, and there she was, standing on the balcony. She told me I was too late, and that you had gone. She also told me that your father was going to send guards, and that I would be dealt with. She said I would surely leave the property in a body bag. Her words. She was not wrong. She was smiling… It was very grotesque. She enjoyed my pain. Enjoyed threatening me. Somehow, I think your father had cast some blame on her for our tryst. Because she was the lady of the manor, I suppose, and hadn't realized I was sneaking into your room. She told me she wasn't going to allow me to destroy all she had built. Would not allow us to be her downfall. I took a step away from her, and then I looked down over the balcony, and considered that I needed to climb back as quickly as possible and try to escape if I could. Because I knew she was correct. If your father's men found me, the only way I would leave was as a dead man. But while my focus was turned away... Josefina pushed me over the edge of the balcony. I was not paying attention, or there would have been no way she could have overpowered me. I was about to turn and climb down on my own, and she used that momentum against me."

He heard an indrawn gasp from Charlotte, a choked, distressed sound. "How did you survive that?"

"A true miracle and mystery," he said drily. "Though, the fact that I had my momentum broken by a couple of rocky ledges, and then again by the hedge that grows around the perimeter of the villa did help. Still, I sustained a severe head injury. And that swelling damaged my ability to see. For a while, they hoped that the swelling would go down, and that my vision would right itself. They say now that it is incredibly unlikely."

"But not impossible," Charlotte said.

"It does not benefit me to think of it as anything but impossible, Charlotte. I have never been one to hope for miracles. Everything I've ever gotten has come with bloodied knuckles and no small amount of struggle. My current status being no exception."

"Who helped you escape?" she asked.

"One of your father's men found me. Pietro. He was an older man who seemed...weary of the business. I had spoken with him a few times over the years. He used to talk about a woman he left behind when Michael called him in. He also owed your father a favor. He went to the estate, and he never returned home. He never saw the woman he loved again."

"That's sad."

"Life with your father was sad, as you well know. I think…I think he wished he could find his way back to something real again. To life. Love. He was sent down to the bottom of the tower to collect my body, and to have me removed. But when he got down there he discovered that I was still breathing. Though most of my bones were broken, and I was unconscious. He took his life into his hands rescuing me. Covered me with a sheet and told your father that he was off to dispose of me. Instead, he took me to a local doctor that he said we could trust. That man cared for me until I was stable. And then he paid to have me moved to a hospital far away. I was utterly dependent on strangers. My life was in their hands. I despise being helpless. But a broken blind man who would be as good as dead if his employer found out about his existence is as helpless as it gets. I don't know what became of Pietro when it was discovered that I was not in fact dead. I imagine it didn't end well for him." Rafe sighed heavily, thinking of that man and his heavily lined face. One that relaxed only when he spoke of his love. A love Rafe was certain the man had never seen again. "I hope… I only hope that he felt… He missed his humanity. He told me that. I hope that whatever price he paid in the end, he felt that what he did healed him in some way."

He heard her sit down, the heavy weight of her body as she plopped indelicately onto the settee he knew was positioned at about three o'clock.

"Rafe," she said softly. "I wish I would have known."

"Why?" He was truly curious about her rationale.

"Because I would have come to you. I would've come to find you. As it was I was off hiding. Hiding, and thinking only of myself. I had no reason to believe that you were in any trouble. I was told that you were fine. But you were off somewhere. And I didn't doubt it."

"So you would have come to find me, and then what? We would have been much easier to locate if both of us were in one place. And there would have been no way that I could have ever gone into the public eye if you and I were attached."

He wouldn't have cared. That much he knew. All those years ago, he would have taken the risk on her still.

But that would have been a mistake. Because his salvation had not come through Charlotte. It had come through money. It had come through power. Perhaps, the love of wealth truly was the root of all evil, but he would much rather that root be in his possession, something that he could grow and tend at will. Something that he could manipulate for his own ends.

He had been born powerless. And he had remained so until he had come into the position he was in now. It was irrefutable, undeniable.

"I just wish I would have known," she said. Silence hung between them, and he could hear her labored breathing. "I was very sorry. When I heard. And of course I did. When you became prominent, when you began to make the news, they said you were blind. And I knew it was because of some accident, which the media alluded to. But of course there were no details."

"There would be no details. Nobody knew what had befallen me. When I went to a hospital, I did not give them the real story. And so there was no way anyone could know. And unless your father purposefully chose to out himself and connect himself to me, there would be no way anyone could know."

"It was clever of you. Escaping him in that way. Because of that thin facade of respectability that he had. He would have known that he could not touch you. Not out in the open."

"He found it best to let it be. As it became clear that it was best if the both of us mutually did not acknowledge one another."

There was no sound then, nothing but the pop and hiss of the fire in the hearth. Then he heard her move, the faint slide of her fingers against skin, then through her hair.

It made him think of how that hair looked unbound. It made him ache. It made him want to shut out the outside world and take her in his arms again.

To erase the past.

But he couldn't go back. The sun was there. And he was here. Plunged into darkness.

"Money is the only real way to control your future, Charlotte," he said, his tone hard. "It is the leverage that is required to deal with difficult situations in life."

"True. Why would you talk to somebody when you can stick them in a helicopter and fly them up to a castle and detain them until you decide what to do with them?"

"You were not going to tell me about my child. I had no other choice. You don't understand. I have been manipulated too many times in my life, and I will not stand for it. Not again."

He heard her agitation. Her feet shuffling on the

marble. Her abrupt shift in position. "How? How have you been manipulated?"

"I believe story time is over," he said, his voice hard.

"Fine." He heard the slap of her hands against fabric. "I can't understand you if you won't let me. I can't actually know you if you won't share with me what there is to know. You were just saying that we didn't know each other, but you're not allowing me to."

"It is unnecessary for the situation that we find ourselves in. We are not children playing at games of love anymore. We are having children that are going to come into a world where their father cannot see. I can leave nothing to chance. Not even you."

"So you're not going to trust me. You're not going to trust that I won't keep your children from you?"

"No," he said without hesitation.

"There is nothing I can do to change that?"

He gritted his teeth, so hard that they began to ache. "Charlotte, I trust no one but myself. That which I can manipulate with my own two hands. It has been proven to me that unless I seize control of something it will not be as I wish. It has been proven to me time and time again."

And with that, he walked out of the room. He knew the layout of this castle better than just about anything on earth. The map of the place inscribed upon his soul. It had been his mission upon purchasing it. To create a sizable domain that he could maneuver about with ease. And so, there were very specific instructions given to every member of staff. Everything was positioned just so. To the centimeter, exactly like the Braille map he had memorized when he had first purchased it.

Nothing was to be moved. Ever. And so it had been

from the first. He spent a great amount of time here, and was more than able to conduct business from this location. Which was what he would continue to do until he came to a conclusion about exactly what he was to do with Charlotte. She had expected that he was going to force her into marriage of some kind, but he could see no benefit in that.

Marriage was simply a piece of paper. Easily walked away from. Easily destroyed. And Charlotte knew how to disappear. He needed something much more assuring.

Likely you could have gone with seduction if you had not kidnapped her.

He smiled ruefully at nothing and no one in particular. Yes, perhaps seduction would have been the better option. It said nothing good about him that he had gone to kidnapping first, he supposed. But it was too late.

That gave him pause.

Perhaps seduction was still the answer. Charlotte wanted trust. She wanted to feel as though she had some say in the situation. Wanted to feel as though she had some control. Charlotte wanted security and certainty. She wanted something of what they had once had.

He had lost that part of himself along with his sight, and it had never been an overly prominent part of him to begin with. She was the only person on the whole earth that he'd cared for in the way that he had. So, even then his faith in love had been somewhat tenuous.

It was gone altogether now, but that did not mean she had to believe so.

Control. That was the name of the game.

And what he had always found terribly inconvenient was that other people were so damned difficult to control. It was why he preferred his life stripped down to a series of transactions. Where there was him, and there was staff.

His dealings with Charlotte would require a different tactic.

But he was prepared for that. He had her exactly where he wanted. All he would have to do was maintain control of his own actions, and he would be able to obtain exactly what he wanted.

There were a great many things he found difficult these days. But control was not one of them.

CHAPTER SEVEN

CHARLOTTE WAS FEELING ANTSY. After her conversation with Rafe the night before she had gone to bed and slept fitfully. Then she had woken with her mouth tasting like the inside of an old fast-food wrapper, and her body feeling like it had been run over by a car. Her head hurt, and her entire being just felt stale. It was difficult to know what to do now. Difficult to know what the best course of action was.

It was terribly isolating, being in this castle. Not that she wasn't used to isolation. It was just that this was outside her control. And for the past five years her isolation had been self-imposed.

She had decided when she would move; she had decided where she would live and where she would work. All her interactions with her friends had been carefully planned, of course.

But she was supposed to be done with that, and Rafe had come in and uprooted her. Plus, she was having his babies.

All of that had been lost somehow. Probably in the kidnapping. It was very difficult to maintain one's wits when one was whisked to a castle in a helicopter against one's will.

She was having twins.

Her heart clenched tight, and so did her stomach.

She made a dash to the restroom, just in time to lose what little she had eaten the night before. She emerged again feeling clammy and unsteady.

She dressed slowly in the clothes she had been wearing the day before. Last night before bed a member of staff had provided her with a pair of pajamas, but there was still nothing else. She had been informed that a new wardrobe would be coming soon. But as concerns went, it was on the bottom of the list. She sighed heavily, looking at her reflection in the mirror again, which was yet more waxen and disheveled than it had been yesterday.

She opened up the door to her bedroom and saw a tray laden with breakfast sitting outside. She wrinkled her nose, then stepped over it. She wanted nothing to do with food. Not at the moment.

She walked down the circular staircase, and found herself standing in a large antechamber. She thought it was perhaps at the front of the castle. But she found the whole thing mazelike and disorienting. She couldn't fathom how Rafe navigated it. She had a hard enough time using all of her senses, and he was deprived of one of his and seemed to have no trouble getting around.

But then, as with all things, Rafe liked to maintain control. Which meant getting around the palace wasn't difficult. That much she could surmise from just knowing him.

Her heart twisted. The way he had talked about being dependent on other people after his accident…

What a horrible thing. For a man like him, feeling powerless, feeling helpless. It truly was one of the worst imaginable fates. Aside from death. His very survival had depended on the kindness of others.

Even given her present circumstance, she could feel bad for him about that.

She inhaled the scent of the air, and she yet again understood exactly what he meant when he spoke of the atmosphere in the palace versus modern architecture. It was different. You could smell the age and the walls, not unpleasant, but certainly unmistakable. It was clean, but this was not something that would get wiped away.

Right now, it was all a bit overpowering to her. Her senses had become notably enhanced over the past week or so, and at the moment smells were an assault.

She moved through the antechamber, and down a corridor, and that led to a room that was made entirely of windows. The light was so bright here, pouring in from outside like buckets of gold, bringing both warmth and a sense of space to the room.

That was when she noticed that toward the back of the room, the two panels in the middle weren't windows at all, but doors.

That was what she needed. To get outside. To clear her head.

She began to walk across the room when the same woman from last night came in. "Miss," the woman said. "Mr. Costa is looking for you."

Of course. The master desired her presence, and therefore she was fetched and expected to comply. She was not in the mood.

"Then Mr. Costa will simply have to keep looking for a while," she said, feeling stubborn, a little bit nauseous and really not in the mood.

"Miss, I don't think that is a good idea."

"If Mr. Costa would like to speak to me, he can come out to the garden."

The woman looked ashen at the very idea of someone defying Mr. Costa. "Mr. Costa does not come out to the garden."

But Charlotte was resolute. "Then Mr. Costa will have to wait."

She walked with a purposeful stride to the doors, then wrenched the first one open. She could tell that it hadn't been used in a long while. Again, not her concern.

Rafe had spirited her away to his castle out in the middle of Germany, and it was not her job to be a compliant captive. She had done so long enough. And while she was grieved to discover that Rafe was more like her father than he had once been, she knew that he wasn't going to throw her off the top of the castle for insubordination.

She stepped outside, closing the door behind her, allowing the chill autumn air to wash over her.

It was a garden, but it certainly wasn't kept up.

Everything was overgrown, in a state of disarray. There were great stone statues with vines growing up around them, making everything look as though nature was trying to reclaim it, drag it back down into the earth and render it to dust again.

She breathed out, her breath lingering on a cloud. It was so quiet here. The only sound was the occasional rustle of the leaves overhead, a few birds flitting here and there, chirping to their mates.

She had often found solace in nature. Actually, this moment reminded her of when she had first escaped into the woods after her father's men had taken her captive. They had not imagined that she would run to the woods. Because they had thought her too cosseted. What they had not understood was that it was the only thing that kept her sane all that time she'd been captive in her own home.

Walks on the estate, where she didn't feel so much like she was under the watchful gaze of her father.

She kept on walking down the little path that was well overgrown, until she found a stone bench. Then she sat down, closing her eyes and letting the breeze ruffle her hair, which was up in its usual bun.

She hadn't had a chance to do anything else with it yet. To cut it off.

She had fully intended to after her night with Rafe. And then she just…hadn't. There had been other things. The will, and making sure her apartment was in order. Hair had been a low priority. Then she had started feeling unwell. And after that, it had become clear that she needed to do some research on that unwellness.

And then there had been the pregnancy tests. And the doctor. And Rafe. It seemed to always come back to Rafe.

She let her eyes flutter closed, and she felt exhaustion sweep over her. Even though she had just woken up, she was feeling unaccountably run down. Pregnancy was hard.

And now she felt like her head was swimming. Just thinking about pregnancy. About the fact that it meant there would be a baby… No, two babies.

She laid her head down against the bench, the cool stone a vague comfort as anxiety overtook her. She just needed to rest. Just for a moment. And then maybe everything would be slightly clearer.

"Where is she?" he asked, addressing Della, his housekeeper.

"She went outside hours ago," Della said. "No one has seen her since."

Rage spiked through him. She had defied him earlier, and he had allowed it in the interest of being less of a tyrant to her. He wanted to seduce her after all. To forge a bond between them. For there he would find true control.

Overtly raging at her over every defiance would not accomplish that.

But this…he could not allow this.

"And you did not think to come and tell me before this?"

"Forgive me, Mr. Costa," she said, her voice sounding not in the least bit contrite. "I was not clear as to whether or not our guest was in fact a prisoner. It did not occur to me that she could not make her way around the grounds if she did not wish to remain inside."

"She is a flight risk," he said, his voice hard. "And she is carrying my children. Therefore, her safety and her whereabouts are of the utmost importance to me."

Della let out a small, shocked sound. That, at least, he found satisfying. At least something rattled her.

"She went out to the garden?"

"Yes, sir."

He could easily send a member of his staff out there. But it was not what he wished. Because she was defying him, openly. She would have to learn that he did not bring her here to play games.

He attempted to remind himself of his earlier conclusion. That he needed to tread lightly with her. That he needed to try to seduce her—emotionally and physically. But it was lost somewhere in his rage.

He had brought her to this place that he knew better than anywhere else, and she had taken herself off to the portion of it that he did not frequent.

He made his way to the solarium, and across to where he knew the doors were. The third and fourth panel down from the end of the room. He pressed his hand against it, made certain that it was in fact the exit, and then walked through it into the outside. He listened. But he heard nothing. Not any sound of movement at all. Just the wind in the trees.

She could not have run away. There was no way. It would be an impossible walk to civilization, and he was under the impression she was suffering from morning sickness.

Of course, *she* didn't know how far the nearest town was. That was part of the problem. She wasn't familiar with this place. And when she had run from her father…

He curled his hands into fists, uncomfortable with that thought. That he could possibly compare her running away from her father, running away from her forced marriage, to this.

He wasn't going to force her into anything.

No, you're simply going to manipulate her into it.

He scowled, and then continued to walk across the dilapidated garden. He swept the ground with his cane, making sure that he wasn't surprised by any uneven terrain. His cane struck something hard that protruded from the ground. A rock or brick in an unkempt path perhaps.

He could call her name. And perhaps, she would answer. But that would only work if she wasn't actually hiding from him. And he suspected that she was. More than *suspected*, he was *certain* that she was. Anger and a sense of helplessness washed over him. He hated this. Hated feeling like he couldn't tackle something on his own, but he was starting to think that he was going to have to walk back to the house and ask for assistance.

Fortunately, he had a strong sense of direction, where he had come from. That was imperative in his situation.

He stopped for a moment, taking stock of the direction the breeze was blowing. He tilted his head upward, a gold circle appearing on his vision. The sun. He could sense changes in light.

It was helpful. Of course, as Charlotte was not charting any kind of natural course, it was of no help to him. Charlotte was simply being difficult.

He continued walking down the path, and then his cane hit something hard. He swept it up, got the impression of a long slab of something—most likely stone— with another slab laid over the top. A bench. That was the most likely item.

"Be careful!" Someone grabbed hold of the end of his cane. And he recognized Charlotte's grumpy voice instantly.

"Charlotte?"

He heard shifting, and then the rustle of leaves. "I fell asleep. How did you…how did you find me?"

He was so relieved to find her here his knees nearly buckled. So relieved she wasn't out wandering the forest. Pregnant. Alone.

"I tracked you using only your scent," he said, his tone dry. "You know, when one loses their sight their other senses are heightened."

"I don't believe that."

He lifted a shoulder. "It's true."

"No, I believe your other senses are heightened, but I don't believe you tracked me like a bloodhound." He heard a small, shuffling sound and a little snort and he thought she was probably scrubbing her face. He wanted to laugh because the image it created was a cute one; he couldn't deny it. "I don't smell," she protested further.

He begged to differ with her there. She did smell. It was exactly how he had recognized her the first time he had seen her. That sweet floral scent that he had only ever associated with her.

"If you say so."

"I just needed some time outside the house."

"Charlotte, you cannot leave the castle."

"I'm sorry, Rafe, but I will leave the castle if I choose to. I can't be kept captive in there."

"Yes, you can. Because you have no idea where you are out here."

There was a pause. "No, I think you have no idea where you are out here," she said, far too astute for his liking.

"I found my way just fine."

"But you don't *know* it. You don't know this whole terrain. And you don't like that."

"Charlotte…"

"I am not a *thing* that you can manipulate at will, Rafe Costa. I never have been. I don't understand how you can do this to me knowing what my father did."

The wind kicked up again, the scent of damp leaves and low-hanging clouds on the air. "I'm not your father."

"You're treading dangerously close to being cut from the same cloth."

"Except were I your father, I would be fashioning some way to punish you grandly for your insubordination. He enjoyed that. Punishing people."

She laughed, a kind of crystalline sound that sounded easily broken. And if it did break, he had a feeling it could cut them both.

"You don't think I know that?" Her voice trembled. "Of course, he didn't ever physically harm me. I was a bargaining tool, and he didn't want to damage my beauty. But he kept so much from me. The outside world. He did his best to make sure that were I ever to try to go out in it, I would be hobbled. Unable to function without his say-so. I'm well aware of the kind of mental torture my father was capable of putting people under."

"Physical torture, as well," Rafe said, his tone grave. He wasn't in the mood to play nice with her. Moreover, he wasn't in the mood to be sensitive about her feelings. Despite what she might feel, he was not her father, and she would do well to remember it.

"He had people hired specifically to torture anyone who went against him. To break bones."

There was a long beat of silence. "Did you ever do that?"

"No," he said simply. "But I saw it."

He heard leaves rustling. Charlotte fidgeting. Choosing her next words with care, he imagined. "This is what I don't understand, Rafe. Why didn't you stop any of this? Why were you with him at all?"

Much like the story of his blindness, there was no reason to keep this from her either. "I was forced into it. As I said, money is power. Your father saved me from being put in prison back in Rome when I was caught stealing. Not only did he do that—he offered me an education. He paid for my mother to have housing. We had been homeless for a long time by that point."

"If it were any other man, then I would say that was quite generous of him. But not with my father."

"He was only buying a sycophant," Rafe said, "and he knew that once he held my mother's fate in his hands, he had a great deal of power over me."

"What happened to your mother after you…"

"That's the thing. Once he thought I was dead, he had forgotten that he was paying to put my mother up. When he was no longer using her for leverage, there was no reason for him to throw her out onto the street just for fun. If there was no one around to be hurt by her demise, he didn't have a taste for it. Or he didn't have a thought about it. And, once I gained my own position of power, I installed her in a home where she very happily lives now."

"Do you see her?"

He laughed, hard and bitter. "No. I have no desire to. She only asks for more money, and while I do not begrudge her a certain amount…"

"You never spoke of her. When we were together. You never told me about your mother."

"There are a great many things I never told you about."

"Yes," Charlotte said. "And I wonder why. You risked yourself to be with me… But then, it makes me wonder if you really did? If you assumed that we were doomed, I suppose it was much easier to play at love. Much simpler."

"I am not playing games with you now," he said, her words striking him somewhere unsettling. "I will not be denied my children, Charlotte. I will not allow you to dictate the terms here." He made an attempt to soften his tone. "You could be happy here. With me."

"If that were true, don't you suppose I would have been happy in the tower that my father made too?"

CHAPTER EIGHT

RAFE SUCCESSFULLY AVOIDED her for the next week. Or maybe he wasn't avoiding her; that was always a possibility.

But she doubted it.

He was far too much in control for anything to be accidental. If Rafe had wanted to see her, then she would have seen him. For the man left absolutely nothing to chance, and there was nothing that he did not manipulate in his domain.

She sighed heavily, pacing back and forth in the solarium, which she had come to think of as her room. She did still go out to the gardens, in spite of the discussion that he'd had with her last week. He might have taken her hostage, but he was not going to dictate what she did with her time in her gilded little cage.

There was nowhere for her to run, after all, and she was not going to forgo fresh air.

Today, though, it was raining, and she was taking advantage of what weak, pale sunlight was coming through the windows.

She grabbed hold of one of the settees and pushed it across the highly polished marble floor, positioning it in front of the window. Then she got the side table and did the same with that. It was much nicer with everything right by the window. For a while, she just wanted to sit and gaze out at the view; she wasn't in the mood to go and brave Rafe.

After a while she decided that it would be better if she had a cup of tea. She could ask one of Rafe's staff members to get it for her. They were very attentive, and she often got the feeling that Della—his head of staff—disapproved of his keeping her here.

It made her feel…if not safe, then at least as though she had an ally. It was nice to have an ally.

Not that Della could do anything about it either. She needed the job, presumably. And going against Rafe would mean the loss of a job. He did not run a democracy. This was a dictatorship—no doubt about it.

But Charlotte was feeling surprisingly good today, and she didn't want anyone to wait on her. She wanted to get tea by her own power. She just needed to do something.

That was the problem with being cooped up in this place. It reminded her too much of the past. And it gave her far too much time to think.

There was a lot of brooding, of course. A lot of unhappiness about what Rafe had become. But then, inevitably, it led to memories of their time together. Bittersweet and painful feelings. How he had made her feel cared for, loved, for the first time in her memory.

And that was why it was so difficult to hate him now. Why it was hard not to hope whenever she heard footsteps that it was Rafe coming into the room to see her.

Because he was the one who had taught her what it meant to be cared for. And perhaps it had all faded, broken apart in the ensuing years. The lies from Josefina, the damage done in his injury and the time apart were all too much for that fledgling love to survive.

It was as if they'd gone through a cold winter. A deep freeze. And that tender blossom had been killed.

But nonetheless, she remembered it. As if it were the only flower she had ever seen.

He was her only reference for it. And that made it...

She couldn't hate him. Even if she should.

She wandered into the kitchen, found a pot of boiling water on the stove and set about making herself a cup of tea.

When she arrived back at the solarium, she walked in to see Rafe, making his way across the room, and she saw the accident without enough time to prevent it. He charged straight through the center of the room near the windows, and then went over the end table that she had placed just by the settee, his knee going straight through the top of the thin wood as he, and the furniture, crashed down to the marble floor.

Charlotte's heart leaped up into her throat, and she released her hold on her cup of tea, the porcelain shattering on the ground, her penance, in some ways for what had just happened. For the broken table. That she needed to break something too. So that he wasn't alone.

It didn't make sense; she knew it. But then, she didn't have sense in her head right now. She had feeling. And nothing more.

Regret. Anguish. That she had cost him his pride just now. And that he might be hurt.

He was swearing in Italian, the words sharp and vile, even if she couldn't understand them all. The intent was clear. And she was frozen.

Then he extricated himself from the table, his dress pants torn, the skin beneath bloodied. He had obviously hit his forehead on something; a dark red circle was forming there.

"I am so sorry," she said, her voice trembling.

"Did you move this?" His voice was terrifyingly cold. Arctic.

She nodded, then realized he couldn't see. And she almost broke. Just like the teacup. "I wasn't thinking. I moved it so that I could sit closer to the window, and then I went into the kitchen to get a cup of tea. I didn't think about you walking in. We haven't crossed paths in a week. I thought the odds of you coming into the room where I was would be unlikely."

That wasn't true. She hadn't thought at all. Hadn't thought that of course it would be dangerous to move something out of one of his well-worn paths.

Of course Rafe knew the castle. If he didn't, he would not be able to navigate it as he did. Most of the time she had seen him wandering the halls, it had been without his cane even. So she had to assume that to a degree, he had muscle memory associated with the place. And of course that meant things couldn't simply be moved from their spots.

"That isn't true," she said. "I was thoughtless. I'm sorry."

He crossed the room in her direction, following the sound of her voice. And she froze. He looked like a madman, enraged, almost out of his mind with it. His dark eyes were wild, fixed on nothing. His lip curled into a sneer.

"Rafe…"

He reached out, wrapping his arm around her waist

and hauling her up against him. Then he gripped hold of her chin with his thumb and forefinger, holding her steady for a moment. He held her like that for one heartbeat. Two.

Then his fingertips began to drift down the side of her neck, and he curved them around her throat, pressing his thumb against the place where her pulse was beating rapidly.

"Are you afraid of me?" he rasped.

"I'm afraid *for* you," she said, her voice trembling.

"There is no need to be afraid for me, *cara*. But if you truly think that I am like your father, then perhaps, fear of me is the reason that your heart should be racing so fast."

"You're not my father."

"You must never move things in my home. This is not your domain. This is mine. We are not sharing this. It is not a happy household. You do not have free rein of it. You cannot go where you wish. You cannot touch just anything. It is not up to you to decide what goes where. This is *mine*. Mine alone."

She lifted a trembling hand, touched the side of his cheek, then reached up to his forehead, trying to soothe the angry red welt there. "I'm sorry," she whispered.

CHAPTER NINE

RAFE'S BLOOD WAS pumping, his pride burning more than anything else. He despised this. Despised how easily it was for him to be made to look like a fool. A bumbling idiot in his own home. How dependent he was on others doing exactly as he bade them. How remarkably like a child he felt at times. It was as appalling as it was enraging.

And she was *sorry.*

His blood was running hot. Rage over his injury. Desire from her nearness. That intoxicating scent that was only Charlotte.

"If you want to show me how sorry you are, perhaps it would be best for you to start on your knees." The words were hard-edged and cruel, and he expected very much for her to slap him across the face.

Except she did not slap him. She continued to touch him as though he were a fragile thing and she was attempting to make sure he had not been cracked or dented.

For God's sake, he had been thrown from a tower and he had not allowed it to break him. This indignity—witnessed by one small woman—would not leave him reduced.

He wrapped his fingers around her wrist, holding her like an iron manacle. Stopping her from stroking him as if he were a puppy.

"I will not be placated," he said. "Do you want to make up for your transgression, or not?"

She was trembling now, and he didn't know if it was from fear or from something else. He wasn't sure if he cared.

"You know I'm attracted to you," she said, her voice thick. "But is this how you want it? You want to demand it? In anger?"

"Yes. This is how I want it. You can always leave if this disturbs you. Otherwise, I suggest you apologize to me using that lush mouth of yours, and no words."

He expected her to run then. Expected her to flee his wrath.

Instead, she began to lower herself before him. He curved his hand around to her hair, and almost as if on a reflex he pulled the pin from her long, silky locks.

"Don't," she said. "I will keep that for myself."

He lowered his hand then, not trusting himself to comply with her wishes if he did not. And why the hell *should* he? He was the one who was injured. He was the one who had been made a mockery of in his own home.

He was not the one who should feel guilty. She should feel guilty. She should feel full of contrition. She ought to be lowering herself in front of him. It was no less than he deserved.

And yet, no matter how forcefully he spoke those words in his mind, he did not believe them.

She did not touch his belt. Did not touch his zipper. Instead, he felt the thin fabric of his pants, being swept aside where they were torn at the knee.

"You're bleeding," she said softly.

She leaned in, blowing cool breath onto the wound, the sensation both soothing and arousing.

"I know," he responded, the words hard.

"You're bleeding, and it's my fault." Her words were choked. "And I understand why you think you need to make me bleed too."

"I don't want your blood," he spat, the words savage. "I want your mouth. On me."

"And I have no problem giving you that. But I suppose that robs you of something. I suppose that takes away the punishment."

But she didn't move. Instead, she continued to blow on his knee, as though he were a child and she was soothing him as if he were having a tantrum after an injury.

But then, then she moved. Letting her hand slide up his thigh and inward, cupping his arousal, moving her palm along his hardened length.

"You're angry at me, but you still want me," she said. "How's that for control?"

"I did not ask for a commentary," he bit out.

"No, certainly not," she murmured.

"Your mouth should be busy."

He felt her shift, move up higher as she undid his belt, then undid the closure of his slacks. He heard her breath hiss through her teeth as she took his erection into her hand.

He would give an inestimable amount of his fortune in that moment to be able to look down and see the way that she appeared then. Her blond hair wound into a tight coil of spun gold, her cheeks undoubtedly flushed from anger if not from arousal. And once she started to work on his arousal, her lips becoming slick and red. Swollen.

Just the idea made him jump in her hand.

She tested him with the tip of her tongue, the movement slow and slick and tantalizing, a lush glide into madness. And then the heat of her mouth engulfed him as she took him deep. As she gave an apology with her lips, her tongue and the controlled edge of her teeth. She gripped him firmly as she worked him just the way he had taught her all those years ago. She had not forgotten.

And he knew there had been no other men. She had come to his bed a virgin, just as he had left her.

Waiting for him. *Waiting for him.*

It didn't matter if it wasn't true. It was the war cry that raged through his blood as Charlotte pleasured him. As his whole world broke apart and fireworks flashed in his mind, his entire being lighting up even while his vision remained dark.

He spent himself. Pleasure a feral creature inside him tearing at his gut, dragging him down into an abyss that he could find no way out of. An abyss he wanted to stay in.

And then, there was nothing but sound of their fractured breathing in the empty room, and he could think of nothing but the picture it must present. Charlotte on her knees before him, a broken cup—he presumed—on the floor nearby. Splintered furniture. And him standing there with torn dress pants and a bloodied knee.

He was supposed to be seducing her. Seducing her body. Seducing her heart. And what had he done? He had growled at her like a bear and then forced her to give him pleasure at the first sign things were not going according to his plan. He had avoided her for the past week, and then at first contact he had done this.

He had no control with her. He had made a plan, but he could not seem to stick to it, and that was untenable. Incomprehensible.

And so he bent down and swept her up from the ground, holding her close to his chest.

"Rafe..."

"Is there anything else you've moved?"

"No..."

He swept through the solarium, back toward the quarters of the house where nothing had been touched. And at last he felt powerful again. At last he felt like the master.

Carrying Charlotte. Like she was weak and he was strong. She was clinging to him, her arms around his neck, her body frozen. Probably in fear.

Probably deserved.

He had to fix this. One way or another. He had to find a way to make it so she would stay with him.

She was carrying his children, after all, and it was imperative.

He would not become his father.

Never.

He moved quickly down the corridor, then up a curved staircase, counting each stair in his head as he went, nearly unconscious exercise, and then finished perfectly, expectedly, before carrying her down another long corridor toward his chamber.

He pushed the door open, took them across the threshold and then deposited her at the foot of his bed.

"Do you see why things must never move?"

"I see," she said, her voice sounding thin.

Something in him hurt, a sharp pain in his chest that outdid the one in his knee and forehead. "I didn't hurt you, did I?"

He found that he actually cared what the answer was. Found that it actually would bother him if he had harmed her in some way.

"I'm fine," she said, still sounding somewhat dazed.

"This distance between us cannot be," he said, his voice rough.

This was only part of his plan. He had to repair now what he had broken, and clearly he could not be trusted to do it by interacting with her. Clearly, if they spoke, he was going to destroy it. He did not know how to say the right things. But he could pleasure her. That much he knew he could do.

He did not need to see to know the map of the castle. And just the same, he did not need to see in order to know the map of Charlotte's body. It was burned into his mind. The last woman he had ever seen naked. He would remember her always, and even if he had seen a thousand women after her he would imagine that would be the case.

"And what underwear do you have on today?" he asked.

"They're quite plain," she said.

"A pity. But then, you won't mind taking them off for me."

"Did I say that I would take them off for you?" He supposed he deserved that.

"Will you?" A request, which was painful, but necessary at this point.

There was a slight hesitation. "Why?"

"So that we can…so that we…I'm the one who's

blind," he said. "I should think that you would be able to see quite clearly exactly what my body wants." Unfamiliar shame lashed at him.

"You want to have sex with me, but I want to know why. Is it to satisfy yourself, or do you want something else? Because I have been a weapon for men for a very long time, Rafe, and I would like this to be about something else. Something more than manipulation. Something more than just satisfying you."

He would be a liar if he told her it wasn't about manipulation. But then, he had never fancied himself a man of great integrity. What did it matter? What did it matter if it was what she wanted to hear? If it would make her happy with him? Selfless reasons, after all.

"What I did downstairs," he said, "that was selfish. That was for my own pleasure, and more than that, for my ego. Because falling like that is never easy for a man like me. But now, now that I am seeing clearer…"

"Orgasm does that for you, does it?"

"Perhaps," he responded drily. "Nonetheless, I want to pleasure you now. To give you a gift, as you just gave to me."

"Your knee looks terrible. You'll hurt yourself."

"I don't care."

He lifted her up against him, wrapped her legs around his waist and then lowered them both to the bed. The brocade of the comforter rubbed into his wound, and he gritted his teeth, hating to acknowledge that she was right.

"I told you," she said softly, touching his face, and then tracing a path down his chin, down his neck, her fingertips landing at the base of his throat. "Your heart is beating fast," she said.

"Because I want you," he said.

He reversed their positions, bringing her to a seated pose over the top of him, so that she was astride him. "If you're so concerned for my knee, you can always do it this way."

He heard rustling, and he knew she had taken off her shirt. Then her bra. He put his hands on her hips, felt the waistband of her jeans and where it bordered soft skin.

"Quite casual attire for a palace," he remarked.

"Yes, well. Some dresses were purchased for me, but today it's awfully cold."

"I should like you to wear a dress for me."

"Would you?" He heard a smile in her voice.

"Yes. Because I should like very much to remove one from your body again. To push a skirt up over your hips and take you that way."

"I didn't realize this had become a standing arrangement."

"I didn't realize that you talked so much."

She huffed out a laugh. "I feel I should be offended by that."

"But you aren't. Because you're too turned on. You want me too much to be angry with me."

"You're very arrogant," she said, but she wiggled her hips in a way that let him know he was correct.

"Yes," he responded. "Very arrogant. But at this point in my life would you like my ego to be any more wounded than it already has been?"

She pressed a quick kiss to the corner of his mouth. "No."

She pressed a firm hand to the center of his chest, then braced herself as she lifted up away from him.

She wiggled, and he figured that she was trying to get out of her jeans. So he thought he would make himself useful.

He gripped her hips with both hands, then took hold of the waistband of her jeans, lifting her slightly as he pulled them down her thighs. She squeaked, then began kicking them the rest of the way off.

Then she took her position back over the top of him. She began to work his shirt, pulling it from his body, then shoving his pants down the rest of the way. Leaving them both naked.

He slid his hands up from her hips, letting them glide over the indent to her waist, and up farther to her breasts. He skimmed his thumbs over her tightened nipples, then tested their weight in his hands.

Visions of pale skin, curved lines and silk bled through the black in his mind. Bright pops on dark velvet, laced through with the sounds of her bliss. And somehow he could envision it all.

She gasped, a sound of sweet benediction that he let wash over him like a baptism. He felt new. In this moment. Didn't feel quite so stained by the past. By the anger that had consumed him in the solarium. By the anger that had consumed him for years.

He moved his hands back down to her hips, tilted her forward slightly and settled her over the head of his aching arousal. She gasped, rocked herself forward experimentally, then back again, taking part of him in, then settling herself down, inch by excruciating inch.

She pressed her forehead against his, her breath warm against his lips as she shuddered, rolling her hips, pleasure like a lightning strike that started at the base of his spine and shot upward. She was electric. And he could only absorb that energy.

Then he lost control. Lost the ability to simply lay there, at the mercy of her electrical storm. He gripped her hips, bucking upward, bringing her down hard onto him. She gasped, then sobbed, grabbing hold of his shoulders, her fingernails digging into his flesh.

Pleasure and pain wrapped themselves around his mind, a bold red slash he could visualize, cutting down through his soul.

"Tell me," he ground out. "Tell me you want this. Tell me it's good."

"It is," she moaned.

He would give anything to see the desire written across her face. To see how it looked when her lips parted as she sounded her pleasure.

But he shut that down. Because it was no use wanting that. No use thinking about it. Instead, he focused on the feel of her skin beneath his hands. The way those soft hips gave beneath his touch. The sounds she made when she breathed. The way her breath increased when he did something she liked particularly. The soft hitch in the back of her throat.

And he could smell her. Sex, desire, mixed together with flowers and Charlotte. He was lost in that. In the way all of his senses lit up when he was with her like this. He could feel. Deeply. Exquisitely. That slick glide of her body around his erection. The way the pads of her fingertips felt on his skin, and the little half-moon fingernails digging in. He imagined she was leaving marks behind. He would never see them with his eyes. But he could feel the shape of them. The depth. Could see it in his mind as a color. Could hear, somehow. The sound of her indrawn breath. A gasp of need.

He reached between them, slid his fingertips along her inner thigh until she shook. Until he found the sensitive notch of flesh at the apex of her thighs and rubbed in a circular motion until he felt her begin to pulse around him. Until he felt her release hold on her control and give in to the powerful orgasm that shook her entire body.

But he wasn't done. Not even close.

He'd come once already. He would not leave this unequal.

He reversed their positions, uncaring now about the way the brocade bedding bit into his wound. It only added to all this. It felt like a knife. Tasted like metal. More feelings. More.

He craved it all.

Rafe pulled back, then rocked forward slowly, tormenting them both with long, slow strokes.

He lowered his head, nuzzled her neck, just beneath her chin, and down to her breasts. Then he took one sweet nipple into his mouth, sucked hard, before turning his attention to the other one.

She was everything beautiful. Ripe and luscious, and all that he wanted. All that he needed.

Light danced across the darkness of his vision, streaks of heat pouring down over his veins. She made him see light. More than that, she made him feel it. All the way down into his soul. Touching the darkness that went deeper than blindness.

And after that, he had no control left. He needed her to come again. Needed to do something to make amends for what had happened earlier. But he couldn't hold back. Not anymore.

"Come for me," he said, the words fractured. "Please," he said, begging now, and he didn't even care.

He felt her arch beneath him, her entire body going stiff as she cried out, her second release like a raging storm, catching him up in the tide, consuming them both. His own orgasm was torn from him, as painful as it was pleasurable. And when it was over, he felt like he had lost something vital of himself, and replaced it with something just as essential. He had no idea what that feeling could possibly be. That intense feeling of loss, of surrender, coupled with a satisfaction like he had never known.

She curled up against him, a warm, soft weight of her body playing havoc with him. With his sense of time and space. He knew that it was early in the day. And yet he very much wanted to stay in bed. Very much wanted to allow the post-sex lethargy to carry him under. To hold her against him.

To embrace the darkness that surrounded him, always, and allow it to create a kind of intimacy between them. A closeness. To allow her to steal the careful control he exerted over his world. If only for a few hours.

His routine had become very important to him over the past few years. To train his internal clock so that he didn't make mistakes about when he went to bed, and when he woke up. He was dependent upon alarms and timers, but he also had worked very hard to instill the feeling of time into himself.

He didn't care right now. He cared about nothing but the way she felt, draped over him, pressed against him.

And so, he let himself drift off to sleep.

* * *

When Charlotte woke it was late in the afternoon. She was surprised that she had slept for so long. And even more surprised that Rafe was asleep by her side.

Carefully, she slipped out from beneath the covers, quietly moving to collect her clothes. She felt raw. Raw and fragile, and she needed to go away to clear her head. She knew that, given the circumstances of what had occurred between them earlier, her hiding from him might not be received very well.

If he sent someone after her, she would go speak to him. She just needed a little bit of time. She needed… something.

"To not fall in love with him?" She whispered those words to herself after she closed the door to his bedroom behind her and began to walk as silently as possible down the corridor.

Yes, she would really appreciate not falling in love with him. Not again. Because Rafe—as he was now—did not seem to be the kind of man who understood love.

The way he had behaved with her in the solarium…

She should be angry. But then, in order to be angry she'd have to convince herself she had been forced. And she had made her choice. He had given her the chance to turn away, but she had wanted to meet his challenge head-on. Had been determined that she would get her own back by stealing his opportunity to punish her. By proving to him just how much she wanted him.

And then…then they had gone to his bedroom. And what had happened there had been nothing short of soul shattering.

Rafe wanted control. And honestly, she could understand. She wanted some too. Which put them dangerously at odds, since he seemed to think that in order to control any aspect of this he had to control her entirely.

She went back into the solarium and saw the mess had been cleaned up. Saw that the couch had been moved back to the position it was in before she had foolishly adjusted it.

And she stood there, realization of what she had done—not earlier, but just now when she had left his room—washing over her.

She looked around, hoping that she could find a member of staff. She walked outside the solarium, toward the kitchen, where she saw Della.

"Della," she said. "Do you have a first-aid kit?"

"Yes," the older woman said.

"I need one. For Mr. Costa. He was injured earlier. Because I was an idiot and I moved the furniture."

"I'll get you one. Would you like me to see to him?"

Charlotte shook her head. "No. I think that I should."

"For the record," the housekeeper said, "I think it is good for Mr. Costa to not have everything go his way."

"I think he's had quite enough not go his way," Charlotte said, her heart clenching.

Della shrugged. "In some ways. But not in all ways. Wait here."

CHAPTER TEN

WHEN RAFE WOKE, he was disoriented, and there were cool, delicate hands against his skin.

"What..."

"I'm bandaging your leg." Charlotte, of course. His body had recognized her before she'd even spoken to him. "Don't be difficult."

"Why did you assume that I would be difficult?"

"Because difficult is your only setting as far as I can see, Rafe Costa." He felt something sticky and cold against his skin. It had to be medicine. She was tending him. He wanted to be angry. Angry that she was treating him like this again.

But she was touching him. And he could not find it in him to be enraged when she was touching him.

"You have to be at least as hard as life, don't you think?"

"No," she answered. "I don't think."

"And why do you disagree with me?"

"Because. That just makes me think of banging two rocks together."

He laughed, then winced as she added yet more medicine to his knee. "That is how you get a spark, is it not?"

"Sure. But what's the point of it? I mean, in the end, all you're doing is sitting there banging two hard things together. There's no nuance in that. There certainly isn't any joy. There's more to life than just getting through. At least… Rafe, I hope so much that there would be. Because I have spent a very long time just getting through. I was never able to just become hard. I insulated myself. Like somebody wrapping a heavy coat around themselves and walking through a storm. But I want more than that for myself now."

"And you think I'm offering you nothing more than survival? I would think that my castle was better than a storm."

She sighed heavily, then smoothed a bandage over his skin. "I didn't lack luxurious surroundings when I was growing up. We've already discussed this."

"Yes. You compared this experience to growing up with your father. And yet I find that it is not so. I have never threatened your safety."

He was surprised when a cool hand touched the side of his face. "But it's not freedom, is it?"

"And what would you do with freedom, *cara mia*?"

"I'm not going to take your children away from you. At a certain point, you will have to trust that."

"Trust is not a simple thing for me."

"Why not?"

She moved back to his knee, removing her hand from his face.

"We grew up in poverty, Mother and I. After we were thrown out of my father's house."

He felt her stiffen. "What?"

"My father threw us out of his house. When his wife returned."

It was silent, her hands moving over his knee, brisk, cool and certain. He wanted to know who else she had bandaged. Another man? He would kill him. Children? Imagining her with children made it feel like his chest was breaking open.

"I didn't know about any of this," she said softly.

"No," he said, keeping his tone casual. "Because I didn't tell you."

"Well. You should have. What did we talk about five years ago, Rafe? How is it we know so little?"

"We were blinded by lust." He laughed. "And now I am just blind."

"I still feel a fair amount of lust," she said, humor lacing her tone.

He reached up, searching for her face. He took hold of her, sliding his thumb over her cheekbone. "Good."

"But you were telling me about your father."

He let his hand fall back down to his side. "The topic of lust is more interesting."

"And lust is the reason we don't know each other."

"My father was a rich man. A married man. He had a house in Rome. And until I was four we lived there. He was not often in, and I had the run of the house. Master of the manor, as it were. But then, he came and told us his family would be moving in. And that meant we had to go."

"He just sent you away with no…provision made for you or anything?"

Rafe shifted beneath her touch, uncomfortable with the topic. He did not like to think about this. Did not like to reflect on it at all. "He was…not deeply in- volved in my life, you understand. Even when I lived in his home. I was raised primarily by nannies, and I was all the better off for it. But…I loved the house. It was beautiful. And it had so many lovely things in it. I loved to look at them. I was particularly transfixed by a large fish made from carnival glass. It was a whole rainbow of color and movement." He smiled slightly, remembering the trinket. Blue with flashes of purple and green. "I didn't ask to take any toys with me when we left. I asked for that damned fish."

"Oh, Rafe…"

"My father picked it up from the side table where it sat and held it out to me, and as I reached for it, he let it fall. It smashed into a million pieces on the marble floor. Blue, purple, green and destroyed beyond repair."

As he had been in that moment. A small boy, broken, utterly and completely by the rich man who'd fathered him.

"Rafe…how could he…how…?"

"Are you honestly questioning how a father could harm his own child like that? Your father tried to sell you into marriage."

"I know. It says something about me, I guess, that this still shocks me."

"That you are much better than most of the world," he said, his voice rough. "And that our children are lucky to have you."

He did his best not to visualize his father's home. He still remembered it in such detail, and memories were often more invasive now that he didn't have the sight of the world around him to distract him from images of the past.

Still, he could see the marble floors, the rugs he had sat cross-legged on when he was a boy. The large bed he'd sprawled in, like a king. And then after that…

Sleeping on the streets. The beautiful fish smashed to pieces. All his toys gone. His stomach always aching from hunger.

He shoved those thoughts away.

His own children would want for nothing. Of that he could make sure. He had the power now. All of it. And he would not use his power to harm the ones in his care.

But wasn't Charlotte in his care? And wasn't he holding her against her will now?

"You will not leave me," he said, the words much more a rough command than the question he'd intended.

"Rafe, I don't know what I want from life. All of this…the twins… Twins, Rafe. I just…I can't think past them. And here in the castle, at least it's quiet. And I've had a lot of time to myself. It feels like time is standing still here, and in some ways that's good. But one thing I can promise you is this: I will never take your children from you."

"And you?" he asked.

She shouldn't matter. It should be all about the children, and yet, here in his bed he found keeping her was just as important somehow.

"I…I'll stay. For the babies." She added the last part quickly.

But all that mattered was that she had promised to stay.

"My friend, Prince Felipe, is having a party next week."

"What?"

"Was I unclear?" he asked.

"Well, no. But it was an abrupt subject change."

"Not at all," he said, sitting up. "You said you would stay with me. And if you promise to stay with me, then

I do not have to keep you here. That means we can go away to Felipe's country and attend his wife's art gallery."

"Oh, well that's very generous of you," she said. He did not miss the sarcasm in her tone.

"I'm not pretending I'm generous. I'm informing you of the change of plans."

"This is your friend who also owns a castle? The reason you had to buy yours?"

"Yes," he said. "Also my other palace-owning friend, Adam, will be there."

"I'm very excited to meet your friends," she said. "I'm excited you have friends."

He growled, grabbing hold of her and pinning her down to the mattress. "I am charming."

"Obviously I'm not immune to you, or I wouldn't be here."

He kissed her, and he could taste the laughter on her lips. "That is good. It is very good." Finally, he was succeeding at his goal. Finally, he had secured her promise she would stay.

He ignored the disquiet in him. Ignored the echoes of other promises he'd heard as a child. That he would be warm tonight. That he would be safe.

That he would always have a home.

He ignored those broken promises and clung to Charlotte.

The problem was that the past looked bright and clear, and the present was full of darkness. But at least she was here. And he could hold her in his arms.

CHAPTER ELEVEN

"Rafe," Charlotte said one evening over dinner. "Do you often bring women to events?"

He lifted his head, arching a brow. "Never," he responded.

Charlotte frowned. "Well, do you think that bringing me is going to cause a little bit of a stir?"

"Oh," he said, sounding unconcerned. "Undoubtedly."

"Is my pregnancy a secret?" she pressed.

He raised his shoulders. "Why would it be?"

She held back an exasperated sound. Talking to him was like pulling teeth sometimes. He had all the plans for everything in that brilliant head of his and he seemed to not think sometimes about sharing them with the people they affected.

"I have no idea," she said drily.

"It is not a secret."

She cleared her throat. "How will I be introduced?"

He sighed heavily and reached out, picking up his glass of wine. "As Charlotte Adair, I would suppose."

Charlotte took another bite of her chicken. "All right. Rafe, how come you've never brought women to events before?"

"Because. I haven't been with a woman other than you since my accident."

He said the words so casually, so offhandedly. As he had done every other tiny bit of information given in his short sentences over the course of the meal. But this one…this one held a wealth of information and also raised a thousand questions.

It had never occurred to her that Rafe hadn't been with another woman. He said that she was the last woman he had seen naked, and once he had given context for his accident, that made sense. But that had not meant that she was the last woman he had actually *been* naked with.

"You haven't been with anyone?"

"Neither have you."

"Well. No." But she had been desperately in love with Rafe. And he had broken her heart. Considering she had spent so many years under the impression that he had abandoned her, it had certainly not occurred to her at all that he hadn't moved on. Plus, in the tabloids women did talk about him. Oh, none of them went so far as to claim they had had an affair with him, but they certainly spoke of him in the kinds of reverent tones that one would expect if a man had made them see God. And, she knew from firsthand experience that Rafe possessed that kind of power.

"I just would have thought—"

"I like control," he bit out. "I would have to know someone quite well in my present circumstances in order to have a physical affair with them."

"You didn't know me. When I came up to you at the ball all those weeks ago, it wasn't as if you actually *knew* me."

"Well, failing knowing the person well I thought perhaps getting you out of my system, finally having some recompense for what happened between the two of us, would fix something inside of me."

"And are you fixed?" she asked.

"Not at all," he responded, his tone dark.

She looked back down at her dinner. "Are you going to be expected to dance with me?" She wanted out of this vein of the conversation. It was oddly painful, and a bit too personal. Because he wasn't telling her what she wanted to hear. What she wanted to hear was that he had abstained from other women because he could not stop thinking about her. Because nobody compared to her.

It was much more likely that he didn't want to be vulnerable with someone after all the physical vulnerability he had endured surrounding his accident.

Still. She liked the fantasy version. One where she mattered.

"We might be," he said. "But I have never done what was expected of me."

"Would you like to?"

"What?"

"You like control, as seems to be the theme of many of our discussions, and our interactions. If you go, and you don't dance, I suppose people understand why. But if you did…"

"You are suggesting that I go all out and surprise people?" he asked.

"You are finally bringing a woman to an event. A woman who happens to be pregnant with your twins. I would think that you might as well go for a triple threat in terms of shocking the world."

Admittedly, she wanted to dance with him.

She wanted to be out in public with him. To not be hiding in her tower room. To not be hiding at all. It had been so long. So many years. Her entire life's worth.

If her future was going to be tied to Rafe's, and it was clear at this point that it was, then she wanted... She wanted it to be bright, beautiful and in the spotlight. She wanted her lover to hold her close on the dance floor, to lay claim to her in public. Without fear of retribution. Yes, her dearest wish was to finally have *everything*.

And for everyone in the whole world to see it.

She had been kept locked away, and then she had been in a prison of her own making. She was tired of that. Tired of living her life dictated by others. By fear.

"Unless you think it would be too difficult," she said, knowing that she was goading him. "Everything can be accomplished through practice. It takes me a bit more practice sometimes than it does others, but I am not afraid of hard work."

"Then I suppose we had better start practicing."

They finished their dinner, and Charlotte suggested they go to the solarium.

"I'm going to move the furniture up against the walls," she said. "I will make sure to let Della know to have it moved back by tomorrow."

"That is fine," he remarked.

"I don't have any music," she said, reaching out and taking hold of his hand.

The corners of his mouth tipped upward, and she wanted to kiss him. "But you know how to dance?"

"All right, in truth, I've never danced with anyone.

But I thought maybe you might know how. You know, since you did go to that fancy private school."

"Your father sent me to private school," he said, his voice deepening, getting rougher, his forehead wrinkling as his brows drew together. "He did not send you to school?"

"I had tutors. I did not go uneducated. He felt that any of the men he might want to marry me off to would not accept a woman with no education at all. But of course, he did not want me too highly educated. Because men don't like that either."

"Your father did damage and in a million inestimable ways, didn't he?"

"I think that we can both agree the most damage was done to you."

"I am not so sure. He used me. Blackmailed me. But he gave me much more freedom than he ever gave you. I think, in some ways, he considered me a son. Though, when a man would hold the threat of death over his own biological child, it is clear that it is not a high compliment to be considered such."

"I suppose he did," she said softly. "No wonder the two of us feel so broken."

"I feel less broken just at the moment," he murmured.

She took a deep breath, trying to shift the weight in her chest. Instead, she felt something like a jagged piece of her soul cut through to her heart. "You do know how to dance?"

"I do." He smiled, the expression somewhat rueful. "Though I have not done so in about thirteen years. And when I did it was under sufferance."

"Well, perhaps it's like riding a bike."

He laughed. "I haven't done that in a long time either."

"We can try," she said. "At least we can try."

He began to lead, his movements firm and strong, and if they weren't moving to any kind of beat, if their steps made no sense, it didn't matter to her. There was no music. There was almost no sound at all.

For him, she knew there was no sight either. And so, she closed her eyes too. Closed her eyes, and trusted him. Allowed him to lead them. Just sweep them both off in this dark, silent dance where she felt as though her feet weren't even touching the ground anymore. She clung to him, her entire body feeling like it was on fire. Her heart feeling like it would burst through the front of her chest.

And when they stopped spinning, when they stopped moving altogether. When it was just the two of them standing there breathing hard, their hearts thundering heavily. She had to acknowledge that shattering sensation in her chest whenever she breathed. To name it for what it was.

Love.

She loved Rafe Costa. And in all likelihood had never stopped loving him. No matter that he had broken her heart. No matter that he had left her—or so she'd believed. No matter that there were five years standing between them, five years of lost time, and so much pain was an uphill climb.

She loved him, and she always had. The evidence was in the simple fact that she had not been able to cut her hair. And also in the fact that she had not been able to take it down for him since they had found each other again.

Because it felt like a symbol of all they had been. The way she had revealed it to him, only to him. How it had felt like a gift, rather than something she was forced to keep because her father considered it an asset.

"I think that will do," she said softly.

"Perhaps it will be much harder when there are other people on the dance floor," he pointed out.

She hadn't thought of that. Of course, in an empty room, they had both been able to close their eyes.

"You lead," she said, "and I will follow. Everyone else can get out of the way."

He smiled, and Charlotte felt as though she had won something. Won back something she had thought lost forever.

In those dark, lonely years she'd spent in hiding she had not imagined she would ever find Rafe again. She had not imagined being with him. She had certainly not imagined that she would be having his children. But they had found each other. They had, and this was the outcome. It was a miracle in many ways, so perhaps they would get one more miracle. Perhaps they could be happy together. He might learn to trust. He might learn to love.

It was an unlikely thing, and she knew it. But, she supposed, it was no more unlikely than their beautiful dance in the dark. And that had happened. So perhaps, the rest would happen too.

"Rafe," she said softly, "I'm ready for bed."

CHAPTER TWELVE

RAFE HAD NEVER been one for large parties. He had always felt somewhat out of place. At the boarding school he had attended with his friends, he was one of the only students who was not from an aristocratic background. Yes, there were some from new money, but most had come from the aristocracy. Princes, like Adam and Felipe. Plus a host of lesser nobles, lords and other obscure titles.

But as far as he knew he was the only one who had come up straight from the gutter. And he had always been aware of the fact that it wasn't through any merit that he was there.

No, he had done nothing good to find himself in this place. Nothing at all. In fact, he had committed a crime, and been taken in as the indentured servant of a crime lord. So, his background had never been anything he had shared freely.

Rafe had always been aware of the inequality, and he was still aware of it. Even now that the money he had was his own, he was aware of it.

There would always be something that distinguished him from everyone else. It had been his humble beginnings at school, and now, it was his blindness. Whatever the reason, these sorts of things had never been his cup of tea, and now he had to go to them even more often than before, because of his status. And because Felipe never took no for an answer.

At least he had Charlotte by his side.

If nothing else, because he had the night after the party to look forward to.

He held on to her hand as they ascended the steps of the museum and walked in. Charlotte leaned over, murmuring softly, "This is a great, open room. It is quite full of people. You can probably hear that."

"Yes," he said, tightening his hold on both her and his cane. "I can."

He could also do a fairly good job of gauging the size of the room based on the acoustics. It was not perfect, but it was educated, at least.

"There are a few tables set up in here, and waiters holding trays of drinks and food. There are a couple of sculptures. Mostly of people. I assume this is the classical art of the country. Your friend was talking about that being part of the exhibition, wasn't he?"

"Yes," Rafe said. "His new wife, Briar, is quite fascinated by art. And when they married, she was put in charge of resurrecting the arts in this country. She brought a great many pieces long thought destroyed out of basements in manor houses and old universities. And she has now done her first exhibition of original art, as well."

"Wow," Charlotte said, feeling a twinge of something.

Could it be jealousy? Envy? That made her feel small and slightly petty, but it was the most likely feeling. It was just that a young woman having such an effect on her adopted country—having such drive—was enviable as far as Charlotte was concerned. Her life had been reduced to survival for so long, and she had so rarely had the chance to make her own decisions.

"She must be quite an amazing woman," Charlotte said.

"She is. She also happens to be the long-lost princess of a country."

"Really?" Charlotte asked.

She supposed she was a long-lost daughter of a crime lord, but that was not anywhere near as glamorous.

She looked across the room and saw a striking couple, a tall, elegantly dressed man in a black suit with his black hair slicked back. By his side, a petite brown-skinned woman with full, curly hair and a shimmering golden ball gown that set off her complexion.

"There is a very good-looking man. Tall. Black haired and an easy smile standing at one o'clock. And next to him is an extremely beautiful woman wrapped in gold."

"I would imagine that is Felipe and Briar. Felipe draws the eye of women quite effortlessly."

"Well," Charlotte said, "my eye is drawn."

"I have, of course, never actually seen his wife, but he is never anywhere without her, so I suspect that is the woman standing next to him."

"They have just been joined by another couple," she said. "But this man is not as handsome. He is…well, he has terrible scars. The woman is pregnant."

"That is Prince Adam Katsaros. And I would assume he is with his wife, Belle. Adam had a terrible accident some years ago. You might say it runs in our group of friends. Only Felipe has escaped unscathed.

But then, I suspect Felipe is only unscathed in a physical sense. Though, I think his wife has gone a long way in healing those wounds."

That Rafe could acknowledge that made Charlotte feel hopeful. That he could see that his friends had been healed by the power of the love they had found with their wives. Perhaps, then he would acknowledge that it could be the same for him. Maybe. Just maybe.

"Do you suppose we should go and talk to them?"

He laughed. "I have no doubt. And, if we didn't, Felipe would certainly cause a scene."

"Well," she said, "we don't want to cause a scene. Until we are ready to."

He laughed, and that made her feel like she was doing the right things. Like she had accomplished something. It made her feel as though she might be closer to her goal than she had thought before.

She took his arm, and the two of them walked to where his friends were standing.

His scarred friend Adam kept his emotions carefully guarded, while Felipe looked at them with open interest. The women were smiling, and introductions were made all around.

Charlotte felt…well, it made her yearn. For things she didn't have. For a chance to be a normal couple. A real couple like the two in front of them.

"So is this the missing piece to the puzzle?" Felipe asked.

"Puzzle?" Charlotte asked.

"The puzzle that is Rafe," Felipe said. "He has always been incredibly quiet about certain aspects of his past. The time that we had no contact with him between school and adulthood. I have always assumed that there was a woman involved. And I see now that I was correct."

"You don't know that she's from my past," Rafe said. "I didn't say."

"I suppose I don't know. But my intuition is pretty good. And, you have never brought a woman with you to any event like this. As far as I know, you have essentially lived like a monk for the past five years. You are welcome to correct me if I'm wrong."

Rafe looked annoyed for a moment, then schooled his expression into one that was carefully controlled. "Very well. Charlotte is a woman I've known for a great many years."

"Did you kidnap her? Because you were exceedingly judgmental when Adam and I kidnapped our wives."

"Did they kidnap you?" Charlotte addressed Belle and Briar, who exchanged long-suffering looks, then nodded.

"Well, Adam took me prisoner, technically," Belle said.

"Felipe definitely kidnapped me. From a hospital."

Charlotte blinked. "Well." She cleared her throat. "I'm not his wife."

"But are you kidnapped?" Felipe asked. "In my opinion that is the most important bit of information."

"Not anymore," Charlotte answered.

"Not anymore," Adam said drily. "So you did kidnap her."

"Unbelievable," said Felipe, shaking his head. "You would think that two princes and a billionaire would be able to find wives without having to resort to force."

"I'm not his wife," Charlotte repeated.

"So you said," Felipe responded.

"Though, you should be the first to hear," Rafe said, "that Charlotte and I are having twins."

Adam's eyebrows shot up, and Felipe grinned. "Congratulations."

"Congratulations is the right sentiment, yes?" Adam asked.

"Yes," he responded, sounding annoyed now.

It was a funny thing to see Rafe with friends. She had never imagined him having any. Because at her father's he was in a very isolated place, as was she. And in the time since she had continued to be isolated, so even though tabloid stories had painted a different picture, she had imagined him that way in some regards. Yes, she had imagined him with lovers, but not with relationships.

"Well, we do expect to be invited to the wedding," Felipe said. "Since, as you continue to point out, she is not your wife. Which means she will be eventually."

"He hasn't asked me," Charlotte said.

That earned him heated glares from the women.

"It was nice to meet you, Charlotte." Princess Briar extended her hand. "I have to go and make the rounds now. As is expected of me. But we will see each other again, I think."

The princess gave a slight curtsy, then wandered back into the throng.

Felipe chuckled. "I had better make the rounds too. I must ensure that my wife is adequately fêted. As is fitting of her status." He walked off then, following Princess Briar's path.

Leaving Charlotte and Rafe with the darker, quieter presence of his friends Adam and Belle.

"I think I need something to eat," Belle said, looking apologetic. "And drink. It's hot in here."

Charlotte felt like she was looking into her future just then.

"Of course," Adam said, his expression one of concern. He was so clearly besotted with his bride, it warmed Charlotte. And only made her slightly jealous.

He left then, and that left Charlotte alone with Rafe.

"Your friends seem nice," she said. "Surprisingly so. All things considered."

"Which things considered?"

"Your personality?"

He laughed. "You don't seem to mind it."

"I don't." She looped her arm through his, and they walked through the gallery and into the first room that was set up for dancing. The music was playing, swelling around them, and her heart began to beat faster. "Dance with me?"

"We have practiced for it, have we not?" He paused next to the wall, and leaned his cane up against it before tightening his hold on her.

"Yes, we have."

And then he was the one leading her out onto the dance floor, blazing a path through the crowd, a man who clearly expected for everyone else to part the way for him, so that he would have no concerns about where he should stand. "I suppose we are about to make that scene we were just discussing."

"Possibly." She put her hand on his face. "That's why they'll stare."

"Or they will probably stare if I step on people."

"Well, likely not. You're a powerful billionaire, after

all. They would probably just decide that they should step on people too. You know, in case it's a trend."

Then they were moving, and in perfect time with the music. Charlotte kept her eyes open this time, making sure that they didn't actually step on anyone. People were watching them. Probably because Rafe Costa never brought women out in public. And possibly because he was dancing. But she didn't care why. She only cared that she was finally out with the man that she loved. Being held in his arms for all the world to see. That there was nothing to hide, nothing to be ashamed of. That this was a moment denied her for so many years, finally happening now.

Maybe she didn't have a grand plan. Maybe she didn't have drive like Prince Felipe's wife. But she had this. And it was new, and special, different. She had that great, ill-fated love. The one that had broken her heart. The one that had broken the man she had cared for. They had kept it hidden, and had touched only ever in secret.

But not now. Not this time. It made it all feel bright. New and possible.

He spun her, then brought her back into his body, his hold firm, his steps unerring. He spun her until she was dizzy, breathless, until they might as well be the only people in the room, as they had been back in his castle.

Then, with every eye on them, they walked through the ballroom hand in hand, into the art gallery.

He stood behind her, his hands placed possessively on her stomach. He bent down, whispered in her ear. "Tell me about the paintings."

"This one here, directly in front of us, is an evening scene. There are rolling hills set behind a large, expansive field. Nestled into the hills are houses. There are lights on in the windows. It's probably dinnertime. Dark outside but not late enough to sleep. Families all gathered around the table. I bet it's winter. And early. Cold the way that those evenings get, where the chill bites into your skin. And the warmth in the house makes your cheeks tingle when you go inside. All of these people that live in the houses, I bet they have families they're sitting with. Talking to. Telling them about their days."

"You see all that?" he asked, his voice gruff.

"I don't know. Not really, I guess. It made me feel it, though."

"Even if I had my sight I don't think I would see that," he said. "I would just see lights on in houses. Not families. Not happy homes. That you still have the ability to imagine such things, that you do it so easily, is nothing short of a miracle."

"I don't feel very special," she said. "Or very miraculous. I'm only Charlotte. I haven't…put together an amazing gallery like the princess here. I haven't done anything at all. I was set free, and the first thing I did was come to find you."

She looked up at him, and saw that his face had gone pale.

"Rafe," she said, "what is it?"

"Nothing," he responded. "Though I do believe you're the first person other than your father—who wanted me dead—to ever seek me out. And so, I would not call it nothing."

They continued walking down the hall, and she continued to describe the scenes in the paintings for him. She did so until her throat ached, until her feet were tired. And until she was about ready to fall asleep standing up.

"We had a long day of travel," Rafe said, "and I know that Felipe has set aside a room for us. Perhaps, it is time we went back to the palace?"

"My second palace in only a couple of weeks. It all feels quite extravagant."

"I should like you to have extravagance. Though, every time I promise you extravagance you remind me that your father gave it to you, as well, and that it was little more than a comfortable prison. And so, I'm at a loss as to how to present you with such things."

"Being with you is not a prison," she said, feeling guilty, because he was right. He had offered her things, and she continually played them down. Because they weren't what she wanted, not really. She wanted him. He was very willing to give things, but he held parts of himself back.

So controlled was his existence. So controlled was he. She wanted more, but she had a feeling that were she to ask for more he would claim he had already given everything.

She allowed him to guide her back to the front of the museum, and she waited as he spoke to a man out front about getting them a car. They rode in silence back to the palace.

Once they arrived, they were escorted to a side entrance that led them the most direct route to a room—or rather a series of rooms—that was tucked back behind all of the others. It felt like a private little retreat. Something intimate enclosed inside the mammoth space.

Once the doors closed behind them, Rafe turned his focus to her, his dark eyes glittering. And she saw it there. The spark of something completely uncontrolled. Wild. Animal even. She felt goose bumps rise up on her skin, and her entire body shivered beneath his unseeing gaze.

"I have but one request, darling Charlotte," he said, his voice hard. "Let down your hair."

And this time, Charlotte wanted nothing more than to comply. She wanted to give him this. Give it to him with all of herself, with no coercion at all. Because all this time she had saved that hair for Rafe. And she had held it back over the past weeks because she had been holding back her heart. But if she wanted all of him, then she could hold nothing of herself in reserve.

She could no longer protect herself.

She was—in so many ways—jaded. Her own father had not loved her. Had treated her like a thing. A prize pawn in a game. She had been emotionally abused. Had lost the only man she had ever loved—imagined herself abandoned by him. And then she had spent five years living in a strange kind of isolation.

But she also felt…so green, so inexperienced. As if life held a great many wonders that she had not yet seen. That she was desperate to see.

She didn't know how she could hold both of those feelings inside of her. Both the bone-deep sense of world weariness and a fascination with the same world.

But she did. It was all a part of her, whether it made sense or not.

She reached up and worked one of her hairpins free, allowing the pin to drop to the floor as one silken curl unwound itself and fell, thick and heavy down her back.

A muscle in his jaw ticked, his expression going hard as stone.

Then she removed another pin, and another, letting them all drop to the floor, the small sound swelling in the otherwise silent room.

Her hair fell in long, heavy coils, the blond waves falling down well past her waist. Hair that had felt like a burden, that had felt like part of her imprisonment, something that belonged to her father and never to her, until Rafe.

Until he had changed it. Changed her. Changed her entire perception on the world.

"Only for you, my prince," she said, once the task was finished.

She didn't wait for him to come to her. Instead, she moved across the space and wrapped her arms around his neck, pressed a kiss to his lips. He lifted his hands, threading them through her hair, winding around his fist, holding tight and tugging as he tilted her head back and deepened his exploration of her mouth, his tongue sliding against hers, his teeth scraping the edge of her lower lip.

She moaned, reveling in this, in this prelude to something that she knew was going to destroy her. Change her irrevocably. And even knowing that, she couldn't regret it. Didn't want to stop it.

She wanted all of this, all of him. Every single thing that he would offer, she would take.

And perhaps, that was her gift. Perhaps that was her. The thing that made her special. This ability to love, this ability to hope in spite of all that she had been through. It had seemed like nothing. Like something commonplace. And yet, having met his friends, having seen Rafe himself, she knew that it was not. Love and hope could be burned out of a person by the dark, cruel things in the world.

And that she had been subjected to some of the worst of it, and yet had continued to hold it in her heart. While she was in exile. Even knowing that it was doomed, she had fallen in love with Rafe. Had continued to love him deep inside of herself in spite of what she had thought to be a betrayal.

She knew that she could be a mother to her children. Knew that she would love them unconditionally, with unfettered grace in spite of the transgressions that had been committed against her by her own father.

In spite of the fact that she had never known a mother, she knew that she could be one.

She had not considered those gifts. She had not considered it having a sense of direction for her life. And yet it was. It was a miraculous thing, a wonderful thing, and it'd been inside of her all along. Opening herself up now, allowing him all of her, allowing him this moment, this moment of reckless love that she wanted to pour out on him regardless of what he might give in return, made her feel more whole, more complete than she could remember ever feeling.

It was a risk. And she knew it. But it was necessary. Without this. This freely given gift. This wild and reckless love, she would always be in a cage. A cage of her own making. She refused to give her father that. Refused to give that to her stepmother. She refused to let them beat her.

She refused to be hidden.

She had stood in the light earlier with Rafe on the dance floor, so she would stand in it now. With him.

"I want you to tell me about this beautiful dress

while I take it off your exquisite body," he murmured against her lips.

"Of course," she complied. "It's a dark, rich purple, with long sleeves that fall off the shoulder. There is a zipper in the back."

He reached around behind her, taking hold of the zipper and lowering it slowly.

"The skirt flows away from my body. Doesn't give very much away. It's quite discreet."

"I like that. That I am the keeper of your secrets."

She looked up at him, pressed her thumb to the line on one side of his mouth and smoothed it. "You are. And I hope that I am yours."

He said nothing to that. Instead, he released his hold on her hair and pushed the rich velvet dress from her body and consigned it to the floor.

"What about your underwear?" he asked.

"That…is less discreet. I chose them thinking about describing them to you. They're black. And thin."

As if to test her claims he lifted his hand, brushing his thumb over her nipple, achingly sensitive through the sheer lace bra.

Then he unhooked it, and moved his hands down over her curves, to her hips, pulling her panties down and discarding them too.

Then he turned her around abruptly so that she was facing away from him and pressing his hand between her shoulder blades, stroking all the way down, over her back, over the silken curtain of her hair.

"So beautiful," he said. "So soft. It is like silk in my hands. And if I remember right, it is the color of raw spun gold. I dreamed of this. Of touching you like this. You and all your soft, incredible beauty. Your hair, which is like no other woman's ever."

"I kept it for you," she said, feeling like now was the time to tell him that. Now that she was no longer holding back. "Only for you."

"Because you knew I liked it?"

"Yes," she said. "Because something inside of me refused to give us up. In spite of what I had been told. In spite of…everything. There was a large part of my heart that could never let go of you."

And it never will.

But she didn't speak that last part out loud.

He gathered her hair up into his hand, twisted it around his fist again. Then he drew her up against his body, and she could feel the hard, insistent arousal pressed against her rear.

She gasped, wiggling against him, feeling as though she would die if she didn't have him. All of him. His hands, his skin. His full possession.

She was naked, and he was still fully clothed. It felt far too real. A too-honest appraisal of the entire situation. That she was ready to expose herself. Utterly and completely, and he was still holding back.

But she had no time to protest. He leaned in, his voice rough, fractured. "Tell me about the layout of the room."

She could hardly think, let alone offer him a description of the space. But, she did her best to gather her thoughts. To do as he asked. "The bed is directly in front of us," she said. "Over to your right is a door, I assume that leads into the bathroom."

"Is there a vanity?"

"Yes," she responded. "To the left, in the center of the far wall. There is."

Keeping his hold on her, he began to move in the direction she'd said the vanity was in. "Take us to it," he asked her roughly. She complied. Moving to stand in front of it.

"Brace your hands on the top," he commanded.

She complied, pressing her palms flat against the shining mahogany surface, her heart thundering as she did. She heard him working his belt, then undoing the zipper on his pants.

He coiled her hair more tightly around his fist, pulled tight, so that her head was forced backward. She looked at their reflection. Rafe, looming large and dark behind her, looking like an avenging angel. The sight of her pale, bare body in the mirror, with his hands gripping her hips tight enough to leave marks behind on her skin made her entire body shiver with erotic anticipation.

This was something that probably would have frightened her five years ago. Something that would have reminded her of being tethered. Being held back. But, with all of her recent revelations, it didn't bother her at all. It excited her. Because she knew her own power here. With him. She knew exactly what she wanted. And she knew that even though he was the one with all the physical strength, that he was the one holding her tight, pinning her in this submissive position, that she possessed her own kind of strength.

That she had the power to bring this man to his knees.

Only she didn't want that.

He had been brought to his knees already. Had been wounded. Betrayed. Left for dead by both of the men who had played the part of father figure in his life.

She would not ask that of him.

She would never require it.

He positioned himself at the entrance of her body, rocking his hips forward, pressing her more firmly against the edge of the vanity.

"I want you to watch us," he said. "There is a mirror, yes?"

"Yes," she said, her voice trembling.

"Watch us," he commanded. "Tell me what you see."

He thrust completely inside of her, and she gasped, looking up as he had asked her to do. "I…"

He thrust harder, increasing the pace, and though she wanted to obey him, she didn't know where to begin. Didn't know what to say. The woman looking back at her was clearly in the throes of ecstasy. Her cheeks a heightened color, her eyes glistening with need.

Her breasts moved each time he thrust into her body, her nipples tight. And then there was him. Big, muscular and perfect. His dark eyes were full of black fire, his jaw tight, his teeth clenched, his lips curled into a near snarl.

She lowered her head, resting her cheek on the cool surface, trying to cool her heated skin. She waited for him to reprimand her, but it didn't come.

She moaned as he claimed her, over and over. The wood bit into her skin, and her scalp prickled. He pulled her hair hard, forcing her to look back up at her reflection in the mirror. She probably would have looked like an angel falling from grace to anyone who saw her now.

But she thought it looked a lot more like finding salvation. Finding freedom. There was nothing here to be ashamed of. Nothing here to hide.

When she made helpless sounds of pleasure, she wasn't ashamed. When the furniture hit the wall as he thrust home, she only wanted more. Wanted the whole room to fall apart around them. A testament to the changing landscape inside of her.

To them changing their surroundings, rather than being changed by them.

They had been locked up for too long.

"Take me," she whispered. "Please. Harder. I need you."

He growled, complying, his movements becoming uncontrolled. Almost violent. And she reveled in it. In the shades that came with making love. The uncivilized. The base and raw. The soft and beautiful. Gentle and rough. Pleasurable and painful.

He stopped, suddenly, withdrawing from her body and turning her, then picking her up. "Direct me to the bed," he growled.

"Straight behind you," she said, breathless, her legs like jelly.

Without Rafe holding her she would have melted completely to the floor.

He crossed the room slowly, and she told him when he'd reached the edge of the bed. He laid them both down, brought her down on top of him, her hair shielding them both, falling down over his chest.

He reached up, stroking her hair, threading it through his fingers. "My whole world is darkness," he rasped. "But when you're with me. When I'm in you, I see light again. And it doesn't matter that it's not out here. It doesn't matter that it's only in my mind. It's the only light I have."

A tear slid down her cheek, and she was grateful

that he couldn't see it. Because he wouldn't like her crying for him. Not even a little. Not at all. He would get angry and tell her that he wasn't fragile. And he wasn't. She knew.

Charlotte rocked up and down on his body, driving them both wild. Taking them closer to the edge of madness. Tears flowed freely from her eyes as pleasure twisted inside her stomach, unleashing a tidal wave inside of her.

His hold on her hips was nearly painful, but she didn't mind. She welcomed it. Welcomed the lack of control. Welcomed the way that he growled as he thrust deep inside. Welcomed the swear words in both English and Italian that fell from his lips as easily and readily as endearments and encouragements.

Her world was shrunk down once again. And the only people in it were Rafe and herself. That should frighten her. Because she had lived in a shrunken world before. But it wasn't full like this one. And it wasn't her choice. This was a world of her own making.

A world of their making.

And it wasn't about control. It wasn't about stifling, limiting or oppressing. It was about love. At least for her, it was about love.

Her release shuttered over her like a pane of glass, the glitter dust shimmering all around her, through her, cutting deep into her skin, and her soul, with the brilliant kind of terrible beauty that went on and on as she pulsed around his hardness.

His own release came on a feral growl as he slammed her body down on his while thrusting up, spending himself deep within her.

She collapsed over him, going limp against his

chest, her hair a tangled cloud of silk around them. He stroked it, sliding his fingers through the golden strands. She closed her eyes, reveling in the feeling. The way that he touched her made her feel precious. It didn't make her feel owned. Didn't make her feel as if she were a thing.

In his arms, with an uncertain future and a pain in her chest, she felt more herself than she ever had.

Back when she had been eighteen, when she and Rafe had been little more than children, at least emotionally, she had been lost and saw what it meant to be in love from her point of view alone. The excitement, the danger. It had been real, but it had been one-dimensional.

He had also been the only man in the vicinity. That was not the case now. She had spent five years traveling all around, and in that time she'd found no one that appealed to her in the same way that Rafe did. She had gone to London to seek him out. She had made her choice. He might have kidnapped her and taken her to a castle; pregnancy might have, from certain points of view, forced them together.

Except, there was no force involved. Not really.

She had chosen Rafe a long time ago. And the way things had played out over the past few months had only confirmed that.

Another tear fell from her eyes, landing on his chest, and this time she knew he would be aware of it. But that was okay. It might make him angry, but then she would simply deal with his anger. Because she wasn't here for happiness alone. She wasn't here simply to please him. That wasn't love.

Love was all of it. All of him, and all of her. Yes,

certain parts of him were jagged and rough, and bits of her were cynical, while some remained woefully inexperienced. But together, she was confident that they could find a way to fit.

That they could find a way to be everything. For each other. And for themselves.

"Rafe," she whispered, pressing a kiss to his chest. "I love you."

Rafe felt as if the world was crashing down around him. Breaking off into tiny pieces that he could not collect as quickly as they were undoing themselves. He felt as if the very walls around them were caving in.

He moved away from Charlotte, jackknifing into a sitting position, his heart pounding so hard he thought it might explode.

"You do not love me," he said, the denial ripped from him.

"Oh, really? I don't? Why do you suppose I'm here with you, Rafe? Do you think it's just because I like castles? Or have I not made my position on those things clear?"

"You have. But what you feel isn't love."

"Oh, really?" She sounded angry now, and he supposed he couldn't blame her. But there was a desperate beast roaming through his chest, and he could not control it or stop it. He hated that. Hated that this made him feel not only out of control but utterly and completely at the mercy of something that he could not see or touch with his hands.

Vision would not have helped in this moment. Even with his sight he could not have dealt with this any easier.

Love. Love was pain. It was only ever that. It was only ever false hope.

A beautiful glass figurine held up in front of you and then smashed onto the floor just as it was being placed in your hands.

A body that functioned just fine until it was pushed over the edge of the balcony and smashed on the ground below. As if it was glass, just like that long-ago statue.

He was far too familiar with this brand of pain. Far too familiar with the ultimate end.

How many times did a man have to be shown the fate of love before he began to believe it?

The end of love—and there was always an end—was pain. Always. And forever.

"I do not love you," he said, his voice hard. "So you can call it whatever you wish, and you can demand whatever you want, but you will not get those words from me, Charlotte Adair."

"That doesn't make any sense," she said. Of course, his Charlotte would not let this go easily. She never did. She was inquisitive, and she poked at him. She always had.

She had no sense. Any other woman who had spent her life under the autocratic rule of a madman would be much more afraid of him; that was certain. She would be much less likely to speak her mind, much less likely to risk herself, and yet Charlotte seemed to have never taken on board the fact that her spirit should be dented, if not crushed after her experiences.

The foolish woman.

She had no sense to protect herself.

And it made no sense to him. None at all.

"It doesn't need to make sense to you in order for it

to be," he said. "What is love, Charlotte? When has it ever served either of us?"

"Will you not love your children, Rafe? And if not, then what is the point of laying claim to them? What was the point of laying claim to me? Just to keep us as possessions? In that case, how are you different from my father? You profess that you're not like him. You swear it to me. And yet, if all you want to do is have me so that you can control me, have your children so that you can control them, how does that not become the same twisted thing that my father had. At the end of all the years, how do you keep it from turning into something sadistic?" She moved away from him, and he felt the bed shift, assumed that she had gotten out of it. He heard bare feet on the stone floor, and it confirmed his suspicions. "I have come to the conclusion that love is the thing that keeps us all human. It is the thing that makes us free. Brave. Good. Otherwise we turn inward. If we cannot love, we become small, selfish things who look out only for our self-interest."

"Self-interest is important," he said. "Without it, God knows I would be dead."

"But it can't be the only thing. Self-interest is the kind of thing that spurs men to build empires that do nothing but wound and oppress. Self-interest is what creates men like my father. Love is what destroys them."

"Then perhaps I am more like your father than we think, because all love has ever done is destroy me."

"Rafe…"

"I loved my father. I loved our life. I loved our home. And yet, in the end it netted me nothing except pain.

I loved you. And what did it get me?" He laughed, a short, humorless sound. "You say that love gives, but in my experience it only takes. I nearly died for our love, and what did it get me? Where were you in the end? You believed in my defection so easily."

"And you believed in mine. But you have such a convenient out here, Rafe, that I can have this argument with you. I was hiding. Afraid for my life. You were physically wounded and absolutely unable to come for me. And I understand that. But the minute…the minute I was no longer afraid for my life I came for you. It was the first thing that I did."

He gritted his teeth, shame lashing at him. To accuse Charlotte of abandoning him was unfair all things considered. But he did not feel fair. He felt…broken and raging, and utterly helpless to do anything to stop it.

"What does love matter, Charlotte? In the end, what does it matter?"

There was a pause, and then she made a small, choked sound. "It's everything. Don't you understand that? It's absolutely everything."

"I understand that it was the key component in the most terrible losses I have suffered. Me believing myself to be loved. Trusting in that. Trusting anyone but myself. I believe in money. I believe in things I can create. Things I can control. Nothing else."

"Can you believe in me, Rafe?"

And he knew. That in many ways he was standing on the edge of that balcony again. Teetering on the edge. That this was one of those moments that would either build something or destroy it. And he had a choice to make.

But he had been bruised. He had been abandoned. And he had fallen.

He could not submit himself to that again.

"I can't," he said, his voice rough.

He heard the soft rustle of fabric, and he knew that she was getting dressed. Knew that she was getting ready to leave him. And it enraged him.

"So," he said, his voice hard, "you love me, and yet you're going to leave me. Abandon me, because I cannot give you exactly what you've asked for. How is that love, Charlotte? It seems a weak and selfish thing."

He heard shoes on the floor, and he knew that she was ready to leave. That no amount of striking out at her now was going to stop her.

"I don't know," she said. "Maybe it is. All I know is that I have lived in the tower before, Rafe. Alone. Isolated. I have shrunk myself down, hidden my heart. And I just don't want to do it anymore. I do love you. But I don't think staying with you and pretending that I don't is going to do either of us any favors. And I think right now loving you has to mean walking away. Because in order to love you the way that I want to, the way that I need to, I need to take care of myself. My own heart. I need to do that for our children too. I will never block you from seeing them—you have to understand that. I am not taking them from you. But I am taking myself away. Because I can't…"

She took a deep breath, and he imagined what she must look like standing there. Frail but strong. And it broke him.

"I can't hide anymore," she continued. "I can't go back. Having now opened myself up I can't close myself off again. And I won't. This world is so cruel. It's hard and it isn't fair. But I…I'm brave enough to love you knowing that. I feel very much like I deserve the same. Like I shouldn't have to accept something less."

And then, she was gone. He heard her footsteps carrying her farther and farther away. And he sat there for a moment, unable to decide what to do.

Then he stood, righting his clothes, hastily making it so that everything important was covered before flinging the door open and tearing off down the hall.

He didn't have his cane. He didn't know which direction she had gone. He strained his ears listening for the sound of her footsteps, but he could hear nothing. Nothing.

And the darkness closed in around him. Charlotte had been his light, and now she was gone. He had no idea what in hell he was supposed to do now. How he was going to survive. How he was going to move on.

The simple fact of the matter was he didn't want to. He wanted to have her with him. Wanted to have her love him without having to give anything up in return. Because that's all love could ever be to him. Loss.

But this loss was one far beyond any of the others he had experienced. When he had fallen from the tower, he had been left broken and bleeding, in very much the literal sense. But he felt it just as keenly now. Like he was going to bleed out onto the stone floor of the castle, his heart a ravaged, damaged thing that was hemorrhaging with every beat.

He heard movement, and he began to run. But he did not realize there was a staircase until he was falling.

He struck his temple on the edge of something hard, and a blast of pain shot through his skull, down his spine. And for a moment, he knew nothing. Felt nothing.

And when he came back to himself and opened his eyes, a shaft of light broke the darkness.

CHAPTER THIRTEEN

CHARLOTTE WASN'T HIDING from him. And thankfully, he hadn't come after her. Or, she tried to tell herself that she was thankful about that. Really. It kind of hurt.

Because of course initially he had kidnapped her and dragged her to a castle in Germany. Now she was just sitting at her flat in London, right where Rafe could easily find her if he wanted to, and he hadn't.

Her love really was repellent, apparently.

At least her morning sickness was starting to abate a tiny bit. So, there was that. Of course, she still didn't want to get out of bed.

She had been heartbroken by Rafe before. But this was different. Because this had been her choice.

She could have stayed with him forever. She could have stayed with him, and she could have tried to make herself be all right with the fact that he didn't love her back. She could have kept her love hidden. Could have kept it quiet, never spoken of it. She could have made it the nonissue that it was.

But she hadn't done that.

She had demanded love. Had demanded it, insisted upon it, and had refused to hide the love she felt for him.

It hurt so badly that convincing herself it was a good thing was difficult, but in her heart, she knew it was right.

She took a deep breath and opened up her laptop. She had been looking into some things. Enrolling in classes.

It would be difficult with the twins; she knew it would be. But she wasn't destitute, and she needed to figure some things out.

She couldn't sit around and do nothing.

Well, she supposed she could, but she would go insane. She needed to have some focus, a goal. She needed to at least figure out what she was interested in. Because she had spent so much of her life unable to do that.

Perhaps she could do some online schooling while the twins were little. It would give her a chance to find out about what she might want, and that would be helpful. And her education had been so tightly controlled by her father, it would be good for her to expand her horizons.

She wanted to stay in London, of course, because no matter that Rafe had broken her heart, she needed to be in proximity for the sake of the children.

She felt a stab in her chest. She was going to be a mother, but she was not going to have a husband. And actually, the husband part didn't really matter. She didn't want some generic groom that could be any old cake topper. She wanted Rafe. As her husband, as her boyfriend, as her captor. Pretty much any way she could get him.

But she had walked away from him.

She had demanded love, in spite of the fact that part

of her wasn't even certain yet she deserved it. She had certainly never been given it freely in her life.

Rafe, in fact, had been the only person to give it to her easily. But that had been five years ago, and when her stepmother had killed the dream of the two of them being together, when she had taken his sight from him, she had apparently stolen that last bit of his ability to love, as well.

She hated her for that. Hated her and hated her father. And hated Rafe's father for good measure. For throwing him out. For breaking a beautiful thing Rafe loved out of spite. But all of that hate didn't fix it.

But then, her love didn't either, so she felt that reserving a small corner of her heart for anger at those particular people was fair enough.

She took a deep breath, and looked out the window. She still had seven and a half months before the babies would be born. And she really did need to find something to occupy herself.

She wasn't locked in this apartment. She wasn't locked up anywhere.

Resolutely, she walked toward her front door and put on a long winter coat. Then she grabbed her plaid scarf and tossed it over her shoulders, wrapping it around her neck.

She made her way down to the city streets, doing her best to enjoy the cheer and sparkle of the Christmas decorations that were already beginning to go up in late November.

She didn't feel very cheerful, but the city looked cheerful. And she had the freedom to move about in it as she chose. So, she supposed there was something cheering in that.

She kept on walking past a row of tall, rusty brick buildings with bold white trim and a beautiful little park. The narrow streets were quiet until they opened up to a larger intersection, and she realized exactly where she'd been wandering all this time.

To her very favorite department store for window-shopping. The large store was bedecked with Christmas lights, and they were like a welcome sign as far as Charlotte was concerned.

Suddenly, she was seized with a bit of inspiration. It was the holidays, and undoubtedly there would be stores that needed more help. She had always enjoyed working in shops. She liked talking to people. It was better than sitting around feeling morose—that was for sure. And all right, maybe it wasn't a long-term plan. Or maybe it was. It was easy to get into this idea that if she didn't perform an entire country's art program, or get higher education that she wasn't doing anything. But she enjoyed working in retail. After so many years by herself it gave her a chance to be with people. It made her happy. When her life had been bleak, it had brought her joy.

Well, her life was damned bleak now.

At least she could look at other people who were smiling for the next few weeks. She could enjoy the hustle and bustle of Christmas. Get out of her own head.

And so, resolute, she marched right beneath the green awnings and into the shop, and decided she was going to ask for a job.

"It's difficult to explain, Mr. Costa, but then your particular injury always was." Rafe's doctor was looking at

CAT scan results in front of him. "It seems to me that you injured your brain again in your most recent fall. And that the trauma and swelling of the brain tissue, coupled with this new healing has given your brain the chance to right some of the previous damage."

He stared blankly at the man in front of him. The man with gray hair and deep lines on his face. Dr. Keller was the same physician he'd been going to since he'd first come to London, but he'd never actually *seen* the man before.

He could now. He could see everything.

"So basically," Rafe said, slowly, "it did what you hoped my brain would do on its own in the aftermath of the original accident?"

"Yes."

"Will it reverse itself? As it keeps healing? Will it just go back to how it was?" He'd expected each morning since to open his eyes and be met with darkness. Instead, there had been morning light filtering through his window. And he'd been able to see it.

But Charlotte was still gone.

The doctor lifted a shoulder. "I can't answer that. I don't see why it would, but then, I would not have told you another knock on the head would have fixed your sight, or I would have suggested we hit you with a hammer a long time ago."

The doctor was joking, but Rafe did not feel like laughing.

It had been a week since his fall at the castle had resulted in his first glimpse of light in over five years. A week since Charlotte had left him. And in that time, his vision had been growing steadily clearer. At first, it was just an increase in light and shape. But as the swelling from the impact had receded, his vision had begun to return in force.

His vision still wasn't perfect, or so he was told. It looked good enough to him. But then, his frame of reference wasn't so great, considering he had seen nothing more than vague, muddy gray on black for half a decade.

He should be…he didn't know. He should be happy. He could see light again. But the light in his soul had gone out. Charlotte was gone, and his vision was back. And if there was anything on earth more ironic than that, he could not think of it. As if he had had to lose her in order to gain this.

It hurt. Everything. His head, from the injury. His chest, from the loss of her.

And he knew that he was supposed to sit here and smile and be happy because he was some sort of medical marvel and miracle, just in time for the holiday season. And undoubtedly, once the tabloids seized hold of all of this, he would be expected to give commentary.

He had no commentary. Not for anyone or anything.

He scowled, and did his best to thank the doctor before heading out of the office and back onto the streets. He had chosen to walk today, simply because he could. Without a guide or aid of a cane.

He *hated* the Christmas decorations. The lights strung overhead. It was all a mockery of turmoil that was happening in his soul. The general cheer of the place.

That there was anyone smiling in the world at all when he felt like he did.

It was his own fault that Charlotte had left him, and he knew it. He just…he could not face any more loss.

And he had been certain that love was the poison that seemed to generate loss in his life.

But then, Charlotte was gone. She was gone, and it hurt now. Whether or not he had ever said those words to her. Whether or not he had ever truly taken it on board when she had said them. Saying he didn't believe in it. None of it mattered at all. Not when he felt like he was being crushed beneath the weight of his despair.

He walked through the lobby of his building with barely a glance at the opulent settings. A strange thing. But he could hardly be bothered to take in the details of the place that he had not acquired until after he lost his vision.

The one thing he had enjoyed in the ensuing week was the view from his office. He had chosen well. Even if he had chosen out of a kind of petty need to keep something from other rich men. He was enjoying it now. As much as he could enjoy anything.

He got into the gilded lift—which, he thought, was a bit gaudy actually and he was going to have it changed—and pushed the button that would take him up to his office floor.

When he got out, his PA was sitting at the desk looking agitated. "You have visitors," she remarked.

She looked worried, and he was not used to having the sense that his PA was ever worried. But then, he wondered if she was just very good at keeping her voice calm, and if she actually frequently looked worried and he just hadn't known it.

"Why did you allow visitors in? You know I'm not in a good mood."

"Well," she said. "As terrifying as you are, I wasn't really sure how I was going to refuse two princes."

He muttered a vile curse beneath his breath. Of course, Adam and Felipe were here.

"There is, of course, no way you could refuse either of them. They're royal asses. But I will deal with them. Don't worry."

He passed through the antechamber, and into his office, where Adam—who was indeed hideously scarred—and Felipe were waiting.

"You look terrible," Rafe said by way of greeting.

He had never actually seen his friend since his accident had left him scarred.

"It's true, then," Adam said, his expression fierce. "You can see?"

"Is that the going rumor already? I've only just started to accept it as fact. I didn't realize it was common knowledge."

"It is not common knowledge," Adam said, sounding imperious. "*I* am not common. But Belle was in touch with your housekeeper at the German castle, and, it may have come up."

"I should fire Della for her indiscretion."

"You won't," Felipe said simply, a bit too cheerfully.

"I just might," he returned.

"You can *see*," Adam said, "but you are in a worse temper than when last I saw you. Which leads me to believe that the other rumor is also true. You have lost your hostage."

"She was not a *hostage*," Rafe said. "But to confirm your suspicions, yes. Charlotte has moved back to her own home."

Charlotte, whom he had made a concerted effort *not* to see since his vision had returned. Were he to actually lay eyes on her, he would lose himself completely. Promise her anything. There were limits to his strength.

"Well, she was with you, and then she was seen running out of my palace very late at night a week ago, and no one has seen her since."

"I'm sure *someone* has seen her since," Rafe said drily.

"This is why Belle was digging around," Adam said. "Because Briar heard that she had fled the castle. They were concerned."

"And none of you thought to ask me?"

"You're a grumpy bastard," Felipe said. "We didn't want to have to talk to you about it until we could force you to."

"Some friends I have."

"The very best," Adam said, his tone hard. "Which is why I'm here to ask you if you're stupid."

"Do I look stupid to you?"

Adam appraised him, his dark eyes hard. "Yes, you do look rather stupid. Because you're standing here without that woman. And she clearly cared for you. Is having your children, and... What did you do?"

"She *left me*," Rafe said, his voice a growl. "I did not send her away. She left of her own free will."

"For no reason?" Felipe asked.

"No reason that truly mattered," Rafe answered.

"Except, clearly it mattered enough for her to leave."

"The two of you, you get married, and you think you know things. But you had to kidnap your wives. So, perhaps you don't know any more than I do, and you just got lucky."

"What happened?" Adam asked, his voice growing sincere.

He disliked all of this even more with Adam being sincere.

"She told me that she loved me. She demanded that I love her in return." His friends only stared at him. "I don't love her."

"Well, that's a bunch of bull—" Felipe said.

"You're an expert on love now?" Rafe cut in.

"More so than you," Felipe said. "Clearly."

"Love has never done a damn thing for me in my life. Specifically, loving Charlotte cost me my sight. It is a cosmic joke, or perhaps a message from the universe that my sight was restored after she left me."

"Or perhaps not. Perhaps it is simply a coincidence, and you are looking for any reason you can find to keep yourself from being happy." Felipe was simply standing there, regarding him far too closely with his enigmatic gaze.

"I do not want to keep myself from being happy," Rafe insisted. "That would be madness. Obviously, I would like some form of happiness in my life. If I didn't care about that, why would I have gone to all this trouble to earn all of this damned money. To buy all of these damn things."

He picked a figurine up off his desk, one that reminded him of that best-beloved item his father had broken before throwing him out.

He hurled it against the wall.

"There, you see? And because I have money it means nothing to me. I can replace it. That is happiness."

"You are utterly full of rubbish," Felipe said. "You don't want to be happy. Because God forbid you feel anything good. Then it might be taken away from you."

"I like things I can control," Rafe said. "Do not tell me for one moment you aren't exactly the same."

"I was," Felipe said. "I was exactly the same as you, until I realized that a life you can control is empty."

"You think I don't understand?" Adam asked. "I have loved someone and lost them. I loved my first wife," he continued. "And she died. And falling in love with Belle was the most wretched, unwelcome thing that had ever happened since. I did not want to open up my heart. Not after everything I had lost. But I have. And it's worth it. It's worth it, because I have found the kind of happiness that I didn't know I could feel ever again. A kind of happiness I didn't know was possible."

"I'm not going to submit myself to certain loss," Rafe said, digging in. "Love costs too much. I've been there. I have done it. I have no desire to ever experience it again."

"And what about your children?" Adam asked. "Will you hold yourself back from them? What kind of father will you be? Will you be just like your own father?"

Rafe reached out, and he saw exactly where he could grab his friend by his jacket. Because he could see now. So really, Adam should be more careful. "Your face has already experienced damage, and I would hate to add to it," Rafe said. "But I will."

"I'm only saying," Adam said. "It seems to me that your father, your biological father, was emotionally stunted enough to kick out his mistress and his son. When you insulate yourself, you turn into a monster. Believe me—I know. I have been the monster in the castle, Rafe. Hiding away from the world. Shutting everyone out, doing terrible things. And love—Belle— that's how I found my way out. You are being offered salvation. A way out of the darkness. Maybe that's your metaphor."

Rafe took a step back, releasing his hold on Adam's jacket. "I will be there for my children. But this…is too much to ask."

"Because someday you might lose her?" Felipe asked.

"I lost her once," Rafe said, "and it quite literally nearly killed me."

"So you end things with her now? Before she could end them. Before something bad happened to her." Adam looked around the room; then he crossed to the desk and picked up a pointed letter opener. "I feel that perhaps you should go ahead and gouge your eyes out."

Felipe arched a brow. "I can't decide if I'm disgusted or truly impressed by this turn of events."

"I'm just saying. If you're going to try to prevent yourself from loss by causing the loss yourself, then you want to gouge out your own eyes. You have no guarantee you won't lose your sight again. Or perhaps, if that's too extreme, just tape them shut. While you have the ability to see, perhaps you should simply live the life of a blind man so that just in case something happens and this miracle is taken from you, you won't be disappointed."

The two men stared at each other, and Rafe said nothing.

Adam set the letter opener back down. "Or perhaps, my friend, for as long as you have sight, you should allow yourself to see."

"Damn," Felipe said.

"I'm ready to go," Adam said.

And with that, his scarred friend stormed out of the office.

Felipe lingered for a moment, regarding Rafe carefully.

"He has a point," Felipe said. "It pains me to admit it, but he does. He also had a point when I sent Briar away. About darkness and light, and the choices we all must make. The three of us have spent a fair amount of time standing in darkness, Rafe. Adam told me I had a choice to make. To continue to live in the shadows, or to walk into the light. You have that same choice now. You can have her. So you'd better damn well take her. If not, you aren't the man I believed you to be all this time. You are not the man I thought I knew." He reached out and touched the letter opener on Rafe's desk. "I know that you always felt unequal to us at school. Because we were royalty and you were from the gutter. But you were always a man whose stature exceeded that of nearly everyone around us. A man who had everything required of him to be a king. If you don't exhibit that now, then I am not sure if I ever really knew you."

And then it was Felipe's turn to walk out, leaving Rafe there with nothing more than a hollow ache in his chest.

Slowly he walked to the window and looked out at the view. At the sprawling vista of London below. Those iconic landmarks and the pink-and-orange sunset, slowly illuminating the waters of the Thames. Color. Light. He could see. And if it was taken from him again, it would surely be a deep, dark grief. To be reminded of the beauty that the world held only to lose it was unthinkable. But so was robbing himself of even a day without his sight now that it was back.

To gouge his eyes out now would be a foolish thing; there was no denying it.

To send Charlotte away when he had her love…

How was it any different? He was choosing to stand in the darkness when he could have the light. Was choosing to be isolated when he could have love.

But if he went after her, if he saw her, he would be lost to himself. There would be no controlling it. There would be no controlling his emotions, no regaining dominion over his heart. If he allowed himself to love her, then he was at the mercy of things that he could not control at all.

And so he had a choice. He could stand here with that semblance of pride, of being intact, and he could be alone. Or he could throw himself at her mercy and take the risk of being broken again.

The very idea was anathema to him. The idea of such a risk, the idea of such a loss.

But he thought of his life as it had been before when he'd had love. The warm house he had lived in, the time spent in Charlotte's arms. It was not the love that was lost. Love was the warmth. It was the color. It was the light.

Rafe had been given light again. But it was his choice as to whether or not he would remain in the darkness.

He was done with darkness.

He turned away from the window and strode out of his office.

CHAPTER FOURTEEN

CHARLOTTE WAS EXHAUSTED after a full shift. The shop was busy with people for the holidays, but she was enjoying working behind the food counters very much. She had never seen such a thing. All those lovely pastries stacked behind glass cases, like an edible rainbow that she wanted to eat in its entirety.

In fact, she had brought home a little box of cakes to enjoy for her dinner. Because she was sad, and she was pregnant, and if she could not have Rafe, then she would have cake. Because quite frankly a woman should have love and good sex or pastries.

Ideally a woman would have all three, she conceded as she flopped down onto the couch and opened up her box of cakes.

But she was not a woman in possession of all three. And so there would be cake.

She sighed, and lifted one of the treats to her lips, then froze when the buzzer for her door sounded. She stood up, sighing, and then getting spots of powdered sugar all over her black dress. She frowned, brushing at it uselessly, and then the buzzer sounded again.

She jumped and got even more powdered sugar on her. Giving up any semblance that she might remain somewhat unmussed, she popped the rest of the cake into her mouth, creating a small cloud of white that settled down onto the nice fabric.

She made her way over to the door and pressed the intercom. "Yes?"

"Charlotte," a very familiar, rich voice said. "It's me."

"What are you doing here?" she asked.

She had expected that he would come at some point. It wasn't as if she had thought she would never see him again. They were going to share custody of their babies; he would no doubt come to some of the doctor appointments. At least the ones with ultrasounds. So really, his presence was an inevitability that she was going to have to deal with. But she really didn't want to deal with it while she was covered in powdered sugar and exhausted from a work shift.

It did not appear that she had a choice.

"Why don't you come up?" She hit the button allowing him entry, then scurried into the bathroom to quickly brush her teeth.

It would not do for her to have bad breath when she saw him for the first time since he had cruelly stomped on her heart.

She scurried back out into the living area, then looked down and saw the white splashed across her black dress. She started to wipe the powdered sugar, then remembered he wouldn't be able to see her state, so she stopped messing with it.

There was a light knock at the door. "Come in," she called.

The door opened, and for the space of a breath, they just stood there with an expanse of floor between them, staring at each other.

"Rafe," she said finally, wishing that she hadn't breathed his name out like she was a teenager meeting a rock star.

"Charlotte," he said. There was something different about his expression, something haunted, ravaged. He was staring at her, she realized. Really staring at her. As if…as if he could see her.

"Rafe?"

"Charlotte," he said her name again. "Charlotte." And then he was moving across the floor toward her, that expression going sharp and intense. He hauled her into his arms and he was kissing her before she could protest. Before she could do anything, say anything.

"Rafe," she said, repeating his name stupidly, because she didn't know what else to say.

"Charlotte. You…you're beautiful."

He looked haunted. And he looked nearly destroyed. Most important…he was looking.

"You can *see*?"

"I can. I…when you left me…I fell and I hit my head. The doctor thinks I reinjured myself in such a way that it has reversed some of the damage of my previous injury."

"That… Rafe…"

He took a deep breath, pushed his hand through his dark hair. "It happened a week ago. And it's why I have been avoiding you. Because I knew that if I saw you… Charlotte, now that I have seen you." He gripped her chin, holding her face steady. "Those blue eyes, just as I remember them. Hair…even more beautiful. The pink in your cheeks, the same as that color in your lips. Charlotte…I love you."

"What?"

"I love you. And I never stopped. Not in all these years. I could give any number of reasons for why I did not pursue a physical relationship with another woman. Not wanting to be with someone when I couldn't see. But most people make love in the dark, Charlotte, and frankly being with a woman as a blind man wouldn't have been such a terribly vulnerable thing. But I had excuses. And it was all because I couldn't imagine touching anyone that wasn't you. I couldn't imagine giving myself to somebody who wasn't you. I had found the one that my soul loved, and anything else would have been a farce. Would have been dishonoring what we had."

Her heart was hammering so hard she couldn't breathe. Her entire body was trembling, tears spilling from her eyes. It was a miracle that Rafe was here. A miracle that he was standing there with her. And that he could see. That he could see her. That was an even bigger miracle still.

"I never wanted anyone but you," she said. "I could never even consider it."

"I was so afraid to admit that I loved you. And I was…humbled by your bravery. Part of me felt like I didn't deserve it. Because you're right. In the face of all that you've been through your ability to love is nothing short of a miracle. But…we have miracles, Charlotte. I have a miracle. I can see you. God willing I'll be able to see our children. If this lasts. I have no guarantee that it will. It is somewhat unexplainable, and therefore there is no guarantee. Much like love. In life, we are given fragile, wonderful things. And…we may not get to keep them. But I would rather take a risk. I would rather have the happiest of days, however many there may be, than insulate myself and stay in darkness and isolation. I want to stand in the light. I want to stand in it with you."

"I want that too," she said. "I want to be with you. And I don't know what else I want to do. With all of this newfound freedom that I have. But I know I want to love you. It is the one thing I have always known. Since I was eighteen years old and I was risking my life to do it. You were my first dream. And you're still my dream. Always."

"I had forgotten about dreams. As a little boy I was shown that nothing in life was certain. And as a young man, I lost the only person that I cared for. You. I've lived in darkness ever since, and that has nothing to do with my vision. But you have taught me how to dream again, Charlotte. You have taught me how to love again. And this is not the first time you've taught me that. You taught me when I was twenty-five. You're teaching me again at thirty. I daresay you'll teach me again at forty. Sixty. Ninety. But it is my great joy to learn from you. For all the rest of my life."

"And it is my joy to teach you."

He pulled her into his arms, and he kissed her. And when he lifted his head, he looked deep into her eyes and he said, "Let down your hair."

EPILOGUE

CHARLOTTE WAS EXHAUSTED. The birth had not been an easy one. Hours of labor that had resulted in a C-section anyway, which Rafe had found to be a deep injustice and a test of his ability to remain calm.

Loving something put you at terrible risk. And watching his wife struggle as she had to bring their children into the world had certainly tested his sanity.

But now Charlotte was resting, and the babies were here.

A boy and a girl. The most perfect things Rafe had ever seen.

And he could see them.

He looked down at their pink, wrinkled faces, both babies cradled against his chest, one in each arm, and he felt his heart swell with pride and love. When he looked down at Charlotte, who was starting to drift to sleep, her pale golden lashes over her cheeks, her long golden hair loose around her shoulders, he thought his heart might burst altogether.

This was love. This was his family.

This was the truest and most real power in the world. It was not money. It was not status.

Rafe Costa had learned that the long and hard way. But thank God he had finally learned it.

"I have a present for you," Charlotte said, her tone sleepy.

"For me?" he asked. "That doesn't seem fair—you did all the work."

"Well, it's for you. And for the babies, as well. They're in my bag over there. If you open it up, you'll see them."

Frowning, he turned toward the far wall and went to retrieve her tote bag. In it were two small parcels, wrapped in plain paper.

"Unwrap them," she said.

He complied, slowly opening the paper, a flash of blue appearing as he tore the wrapping. It was a fish made of carnival glass. And in the other package was one identical to the first. Nearly identical to the one that had been destroyed by his father.

His chest constricted. It was almost impossible to breathe. "Charlotte…"

"We can't change the past, Rafe," she said softly. "But we can make our own future. No one can take this from us."

"I think these will be perfect in the nursery," he said, looking at the shimmering fish for a moment before placing them gently on the shelf nearest to him, already adorned with flowers sent by their friends.

"That's what I thought too." She looked down at the babies. "And hopefully they'll like them."

"If not, they can go in my office."

"Sounds good."

"Have you thought of what you want to name them?" he asked.

"The fish or the babies?" she asked.

"The babies," he responded, holding back a laugh.

Charlotte smiled, her full pink lips curving upward. "I did," she said sleepily.

"All right, what are your ideas?"

"Well, I was thinking that we ought to name them Adam and Philippa. You know, after your very good friends who suggested you either return to me or poke your own eyes out."

"Well, that is a suggestion," Rafe said, laughing.

But it was more than just a suggestion. His bride was quite adamant. So Adam and Philippa they were.

Which always created humor around the various gatherings over the years, as Adam and Belle and Felipe and Briar remained the best of friends with Rafe and Charlotte.

And whenever they were mentioned, it could truly be said that all of them lived happily ever after.

* * * * *

If you enjoyed
THE ITALIAN'S PREGNANT PRISONER,
why not explore the first two parts of
Maisey Yates's
ONCE UPON A SEDUCTION...
trilogy?

THE PRINCE'S CAPTIVE VIRGIN
THE PRINCE'S STOLEN VIRGIN

Available now!

"I am the boss, Miss Andrews," Hugo reminded her from between his teeth. **"You are the employee. Everything about the way you are speaking to me is disrespectful, not to mention foolish. Why would you try to antagonize the person who pays your spectacularly generous salary?"**

Eleanor's frown smoothed out a bit, though it didn't precisely soften. And still Hugo wanted to taste that faint crease between her brows, where the edge of her fringe kissed her skin the way he wanted to do.

"In point of fact I won't be paid for two weeks," she said after a moment, as if she couldn't help herself.

Maybe she really couldn't. He couldn't have said why that notion washed through him like a new sort of heat.

"A notable distinction," Hugo murmured.

And then, because he loved nothing more than complicating any given situation beyond repair, the better to make it worse, he kissed her.

And then they were in real trouble, because she tasted like magic.

USA TODAY bestselling and RITA® Award–nominated author **Caitlin Crews** loves writing romance. She teaches her favourite romance novels in creative writing classes at places like UCLA Extension's prestigious Writers' Program, where she finally gets to utilise the MA and PhD in English literature she received from the University of York in England. She currently lives in the Pacific Northwest, with her very own hero and too many pets. Visit her at caitlincrews.com.

UNDONE BY THE
BILLIONAIRE
DUKE

BY
CAITLIN CREWS

MILLS &
BOON

First Published in Great Britain 2017
By Mills & Boon, an imprint of HarperCollins*Publishers*
1 London Bridge Street, London, SE1 9GF

© 2017 Caitlin Crews

ISBN: 978-0-263-92540-1

UNDONE BY THE
BILLIONAIRE
DUKE

To Maisey Yates and Nicole Helm
for encouraging my flights of fancy—
like rearing horses and billowing cloaks…oh, my!

CHAPTER ONE

ELEANOR ANDREWS WAS certain that she could handle the likes of Hugo Grovesmoor, and no matter that no one had ever quite managed to do so before in living memory. As the papers shrieked daily, the Twelfth Duke of Grovesmoor was not only known to be a terrible villain in every salacious way imaginable, he was *impossible*. Too wealthy. Too full of himself. And worse still, so appallingly and egregiously handsome that he'd essentially been born spoilt through, and had only descended further from there.

Into pure, hedonistic, and ruinous devilry. Usually with pictures.

And Eleanor was delivering herself directly into his clutches.

"Don't be so dramatic," her younger sister Vivi said with a sigh, sending her long and lively brunette curls slithering this way and that every time she exhaled. When all Eleanor had done was express the tiniest hint of concern about her brand-new role as governess to the poor seven-year-old in notorious Hugo's care.

As occasionally trying as Vivi was—and if Eleanor was honest with herself, it was more *often* than *occasionally*—Eleanor couldn't help but love her. Desperately. Vivi was all she had left after their parents had been killed years ago in the tragic car accident that had nearly claimed young Vivi's life, as well. Eleanor never forgot how close she'd come to losing Vivi, too.

"I don't think I was being dramatic at all," Eleanor replied. She chose not to point out that the opera heroine histrionics were usually Vivi's department. Surely that went without saying.

Vivi was addressing Eleanor through the mirror in the bedroom of the tiny, crowded, so-called "one-bedroom" flat they shared in one of London's less fashionable neighborhoods. The "one bedroom" in question being the space on the far side of a bookcase in the long room with a cramped kitchenette slung beneath the eaves on the other end. Vivi was applying a third, slick layer of mascara to her lashes, the better to emphasize the eyes one of her many boyfriends had once called *as warm and bright as new gold.* Eleanor had heard him—as had half the street in the village where they'd grown up as their distant cousin's charity cases after their parents had been killed and Vivi had finally gotten out of the hospital—given that the poor sod had been shouting it toward Vivi's window long after the pubs had closed, as pissed as he was poetic.

Vivi lowered the mascara wand and rolled said *new gold eyes.* "You won't actually *see* Hugo. You're going to be the governess of his ward who, let's face it, he can't possibly like that much. Given all that messy history. Why would he give either one of you the time of day?"

A dismissive wave of her hand encompassed all the salacious details everyone knew about Hugo Grovesmoor, thanks to the fascination the tabloids had always had with him.

Eleanor knew the three main points as well as anyone. The dramatic on-and-off relationship with beloved society darling Isobel Vanderhaven, whom everyone had been certain Hugo would ruin with his shocking brand of committed wickedness that even Isobel's innate goodness couldn't cure. The way Isobel had left him for good when pregnant with his best friend's Torquil's child, because, everyone agreed, love had finally triumphed over wickedness and Isobel deserved better. And Isobel's celebrated marriage to and subsequent tragic boating accident with said former best friend, which had resulted in famously reluctant Hugo being named the legal guardian of the child whose very existence had wrecked his chances with the lovely Isobel forever.

All this while the nation jeered, applauded, and mourned in turn, as if they knew all of these people and their pain personally.

"A man as rich as Hugo is dripping in properties and can't be expected to visit even half of them in the course of a year. Or even five years," Vivi said with the same nonchalance, and Eleanor reminded herself that her sister would know.

After all, Vivi was the one who'd spent time with Hugo Grovesmoor's sort of people. She was the one who'd attended the posh schools and while she hadn't exactly distinguished herself academically, she'd certainly had a sparkling social calendar that had carried over to her life in London. It was all in service to the glittering marriage they were both certain Vivi would manage to score any day now.

Vivi was eighteen months younger than Eleanor and the beauty of the pair of them. She had the sort of slim-hipped, smoky-eyed, lush-mouthed prettiness that left men struck dumb when they beheld her. Literally. Her wild curls gave the impression she'd just rolled out of someone's bed. Her just-wicked-enough smile hinted that she was up for any and all adventures and suggested that if a man played his cards right, that bed could be his.

And to think that after the accident, the doctors had doubted she'd ever walk again!

Vivi had proven herself to be more or less catnip for a certain sort of man. Usually one endowed with a great many estates and a bank account to match, even if, so far, she hadn't quite managed to break out of the "potential mistress" box.

Eleanor, on the other hand, went to very few parties while working at least one job and sometimes more, when things got rough. Because while Vivi was the pretty one, Eleanor had always been the sensible one. And while she'd had her moments of wishing she, too, could have been as effortlessly charming and undeniably pretty as her sister, Eleanor was twenty-seven now and had come to a place of peace with her role in life. They'd lost their parents and Eleanor couldn't bring them back. She couldn't change the many years of hospitals and surgeries that Vivi had survived. But she could take on a bit of a parental role with Vivi. She could hold down decent jobs and pay their bills.

Well. Vivi's bills. There was no point gussying up Eleanor in the sort of slinky, breathtakingly expensive clothes Vivi had to have to blend in with her highbrow friends—and *that sort of thing* required money. Money Eleanor had always made, one way or another.

This latest job—as governess to the most hated man in England—would be the most lucrative yet. It was why Eleanor had resigned from her current position as a front desk receptionist at a bustling architecture firm. Vivi had been the one to hear of the governess position through her high-flying set of friends, since men like the Duke did not exactly pin up adverts in the local pub. More important, she'd heard what the Duke intended to pay his governess. It was so much more than all the other jobs Eleanor had taken—combined—that she hardly dared do the math, lest it make her dizzy.

"The rumor is the Duke has dismissed all the governesses he's been sent. Being a distraction is apparently the top reason for getting sacked and, well..."

Vivi had shrugged with a regret that had not struck Eleanor as being entirely sincere. Her small, perfect, perky breasts had moved enticingly behind the filmy little silk dress she'd worn to some or other desperately fashionable soirée that evening, as if in an approving chorus.

"But you *might just be perfect!"*

The sleek agency that had handled the interview had agreed, and here Eleanor was, packing up her case for the trip into the wilds of the Yorkshire moors to what had to be the most overwrought of all the ducal properties in England. Groves House, as the sprawling dark mansion was quaintly called as if it wasn't large enough to merit its own postal code, had been looming over its vast swathe of the brooding moors for centuries.

"A governess is a lowly member of his household staff, Eleanor," Vivi was saying now, with another eye roll. "Not a guest. It's highly unlikely you'll encounter Hugo Grovesmoor at all."

That was more than fine with Eleanor. She was immune to star power and the sense of self-importance that went along with it. She told herself so all the way up on the train the next morning as it hurtled at high speeds toward deepest Yorkshire.

She hadn't gone to the north of England since she was a child and their parents had still been alive. Eleanor had vague memories of traipsing about the walls that surrounded the ancient city of York in a chilly summer fog, with no idea, then, how quickly everything would change.

But there was no point heading down that sort of sentimental road now, she told herself sternly as she waited in the brisk October cold at the York rail station for one of the slower, more infrequent local trains out into the far reaches of the countryside. Life went on. That was just what it did, wholly heedless and uncaring.

No matter what anyone might have lost along the way.

When Eleanor arrived at the tiny little train station in remote Grovesmoor Village, she expected to be met as planned. But the train platform in the middle of nowhere was empty. There was nothing but Eleanor, the blustering October wind, and the remains of the morning's fog. Not exactly an encouraging beginning.

Eleanor cast a bit of a grim eye at the case she'd packed with what she'd thought she'd need for the first six weeks she'd agreed to spend at Groves House without any break. It was only the one case. Vivi needed to travel with bags upon bags, but then again, she had a *wardrobe*. Eleanor had no such problems. And no excuses. It took a second or two to pull up a map on her mobile and find it was a twenty-to-thirty-minute walk to the only stately manor in the area. Groves House.

"Best set off, then," she muttered to herself.

She heaved her heavy shoulder bag higher up on her shoulder, grabbed the handle of her roller bag and tugged on it, and strode off with every confidence in the world. Or every appearance of confidence, anyway, she amended when she walked for five minutes down the road only to realize she should have headed in the opposite direction, away from the quaint little town arranged on either side of a slow river.

Once headed in the right direction, Eleanor tried to

channel Maria Von Trapp as she trudged along the lonely country road that wound further and further into the fog and the gloom. She marched on, aware of her breathing in the otherwise still afternoon and very little else. She'd lived so long in the hectic rush of London now that she'd almost forgotten the particular quiet of country lane, particularly one that seemed to be swallowed up by moors in all directions and peaks here and there that she expected would have names. If only she'd researched them.

She found the turnoff for Groves House between two stone pillars and started up the drive. It wound about just as much as the road had, and was only differentiated from the lane she'd left behind by its absence of hedges and proper stone walls. And its slight incline straddled by lines of stout and watchful trees. She'd lost track of how many turns she'd taken and how far she'd gone from the road when she looked out in front of her and saw the house at last.

Nothing could have prepared her.

The house loomed there on the far ridge. It was rambling, yes, a jumble of stone and self-importance, but none of the pictures she'd seen had done it justice. There was something about it that made a raw sort of lump catch there in her throat. There was something about the way its interior lights scraped at the gloomy afternoon that seemed to speak to her, though she couldn't think why.

She found she couldn't look away.

It was not a welcoming house. It was not a *house* at all, for that matter. It was much too large and starkly forbidding. And yet somehow, as it gleamed there against the fall night as if daring the dark to do its worst, the only word that echoed inside Eleanor's head was *perfect*.

Something rang in her then, low and long, like a bell. She didn't know why she couldn't seem to catch her breath when she started walking again, her case seeming heavier in her grip as she headed further up the hill.

And that was when she heard the thunder of hoof beats, bearing down on her.

Like fate.

His Grace the Duke of Grovesmoor, known to what few friends he had left and the overly familiar press as Hugo, found fewer and fewer things cleared his head these days. Drink made his skull hurt. Extreme sports had lost their thrill now that his death would mean the end of the Grovesmoor line of succession after untold centuries, tossing the whole dukedom into the hands of grasping, far-removed cousins who'd been salivating over the ducal properties and attendant income for perhaps the entire sweep of its history.

Even indiscriminate sex, once his favorite go-to for obliteration on a grand scale, had lost its charm now that his every so-called "indiscretion" went rabbiting off to the papers before the sheets had gone cold to tell further tales in the nation's favorite narrative. Evil, soulless Hugo, despoiler of saints and heroes, etc. He was either glutting himself in excess to hide from his dark regrets or he was so extraordinarily shallow that a shag or two was all he was capable of. The stories were all the same and always so damned boring.

It galled him to admit it, but the tabloids might actually have won.

The particular horse he rode today—the pride of his stables, he'd been informed, as if he gave a toss—liked him as little as he liked it, which meant he found himself rampaging across the moors very much as if he'd sprung forth from a bloody eighteenth century novel.

All he needed was a billowing cloak.

But no matter how far he rode, there was no escaping himself. Or his head and all his attendant regrets.

The vicious creature he rode clearly knew it. They'd been playing a little domination game for weeks now, raging across the whole of Hugo's Yorkshire estate.

So when Hugo saw the figure slinking along in the shadows up the drive to Groves House, all he could think was that it was something *different* in the middle of an otherwise indistinguishably gray afternoon.

God knew Hugo was desperate for anything different.

A different past. A different reputation—because who could have foreseen what his shrugging off all those early tabloid stories would lead to?

He wanted a different *him*, really, but that had never been on offer.

Hugo was the Twelfth Duke of Grovesmoor whether he liked it or did not, and the title was the important thing about him. The only important thing, his father had been at pains to impress upon him all his life. Unless he bankrupted his estates and rid himself of the title altogether, or died while engaged in some or other irresponsible pursuit, Hugo would simply be another notation in the endless long line of dukes bearing the same title and a healthy dollop of the same blood. His father had always claimed that knowledge had brought him solace. Peace.

Hugo was unfamiliar with either.

"If you're a poacher, you're doing a remarkably sad job of it," he said when he drew close to the stranger on his property. "You really should at least *try* to sneak about, surely. Instead of marching up the front drive without the slightest attempt at subterfuge."

He reined in the stroppy horse and enjoyed the dramatic way he then reared a bit right in front of the person creeping up his drive.

It was then that he realized his intruder was a woman.

And not just any woman.

Hugo was renowned for his women. Bloody Isobel, of course, like a stain across his life—but all the other ones, too. Before Isobel and after. But they all had the same things in common: they were considered beautiful by all and sundry and wanted, usually quite badly, to be photographed next to him. That meant fake breasts, whitened teeth, extensions to thicken their silky hair, varnished nails and careful lipstick and fake lashes and all the rest of it. So years had passed since he'd seen a real woman at all, unless she worked for him. His crotchety old housekeeper, for example, who he kept on because Mrs. Redding was always as deeply disappointed when he appeared in the tabloids as his father had been. It felt so comfortable, Hugo often thought. Like a lovely, well-worn hair shirt tucked up next to his skin.

The woman who stared up at him now, looking nowhere near as shocked or outright terrified as Hugo imagined he would be if he'd found himself on the underside of a rearing horse, was not in the least bit beautiful.

Or if she was, she'd gone to significant lengths to disguise it. Her hair was scraped back into a tight brown bun that made his own head ache just looking at it, without a single flyaway to suggest she was actually human. Even her fringe was ruthlessly cut across her forehead to military precision. She wore a bulky, puffy sort of jacket that covered her from chin to calf and made her look roughly the size of one of the grand, gnarled old oaks dotting the property. She clutched a large black bag over her shoulder and tugged a rolling case along behind her, and she had death grips on both. Her cheeks looked flushed with the cold and there was no denying she had a delicate nose a great many of his own ancestors would have envied, given the curse of what was known as The Grovesmoor Beak that seemed to afflict the females in the line unfairly.

But most of what struck him was the expression on her face.

Because it looked a great deal like a scowl.

Which was, of course, impossible, because he was Hugo Grovesmoor and the women who usually crept onto his various properties without invitation found the very idea of him—or to be more precise, of his net worth—so marvelously attractive that they never stopped smiling. Ever.

This woman looked as if she'd crack in half if she attempted the smallest grin.

"I'm not poaching, I'm a governess." Her voice was cool, and something else that Hugo couldn't identify. "My ride from the train station didn't materialize or I assure you, I wouldn't be marching anywhere, much less up this very long drive. Uphill."

It dawned on him then. That "something else" in her voice he hadn't been able to place. It was *annoyance*.

Hugo found it delightful. No one was *annoyed* with him. They might hate him and call him Satan and other such tedious things, but they were never *annoyed*.

"I should have introduced myself, I think," he said merrily, as the bastard horse danced murderously beneath him. The woman did not appear to know her own danger, so close to sharp hooves and the thoroughbred's temper tantrums. Or, more likely, she didn't care, as she was too busy trying to win a staring contest with Hugo. "Since you're lurking about the property."

"It is not lurking to walk up the front drive," she replied crisply. "By definition."

"I am Hugo Grovesmoor," he told her. "No need to

curtsey. After all, I'm, widely held to be a great and terrible villain."

"I had no intention of curtseying."

"I prefer to think of myself as an antihero, of course. Surely that merits a bow. Or perhaps a small nod?"

"My name is Eleanor Andrews and I'm the latest in what I've been told is a long line of governesses," the woman told him from the depths of that quilted monstrosity she wore. "I intend to be the last, and if I'm not very much mistaken, the way to ensure that happens is to keep my distance."

Hugo was used to women making similar announcements. *You're terrible,* they'd coo, lashes batting furiously. *I'm keeping my distance from you.* This usually led directly to the sort of indiscriminate evenings from which he was now abstaining.

He had the lowering realization that this woman—wrapped up in a hideous puffy coat with her chin jutting forth and a scowl across her face—might actually mean it.

"Your Grace," he murmured.

"I beg your pardon?"

"You should address me as Your Grace, particularly when you imagine you are taking me to task. It adds that extra little touch of pointed disrespect which I find I cannot live without."

If Eleanor Andrews was appropriately mortified by the fact she'd addressed a peer of the realm—who happened to also be her new boss—so inappropriately, she gave no sign. If anything she seemed to pull herself up straighter in her vast, quilted shroud, and made no attempt to wipe off that scowl.

"A thousand apologies, Your Grace," she said crisply, as if she wasn't in the least bit intimidated by him. It made something in Hugo…shift. "I was expecting a ride from the train station. Not a walk in the chilly country-side."

"Exercise improves the mind as well as the body, I'm told," he replied, merrily enough. "I myself was blessed with a high metabolism and a keen intelligence, so I've never had to put such things to the test. But we can't all be so lucky."

There was enough light that he could tell that there was a remarkable sort of honey in the brown of this woman's eyes as they glittered furiously at him. He couldn't imagine why that shocked him, but it did. That there should be anything soft about such a bristling, black-clad, evidently humorless female.

That he should notice it.

"Are you suggesting that I am not as lucky as you?" she asked, with exactly the sort of repressed fury Hugo would expect to hear from a woman he'd just obliquely called fat.

"That depends on whether or not you imagine that the storied life of a pampered duke is a matter of luck and circumstance. Rather than fate."

"Which do you think it is?"

Hugo nearly smiled at that. He couldn't have said why. It was something to do with the way her eyes gleamed and her surprisingly intriguing mouth was set, flashing more of that annoyance straight at him.

"I appreciate you thinking of my well-being," she said with what he was forced to concede was admirable calm, all that flashing annoyance notwithstanding. "Your Grace."

Hugo grinned down at her, hoping she found having to look so far up at him as irritating as he would have.

"I wasn't aware that the last governess left, though I

can't say I'm surprised. She was a fragile little thing. All anime eyes and protracted spells of weeping in the east wing, or so I'm told. I'm allergic to female tears, you understand. I've developed a sixth sense. When a woman cries in my vicinity, I am instantly and automatically transported to the other side of the planet."

Eleanor only gazed back at him. "I'm not much of a crier."

Hugo waited.

"Your Grace," he prodded her again when it was clear she had no intention of saying it. "I wouldn't insist upon such formality but it does seem to chafe, doesn't it? How republican of you. And really, Eleanor, you can't expect to mold a young mind to your will and provide fodder for the therapy bills I'll be expected to pay out from her trust if you can't remember the courtesy of a simple form of address. It's as if you've never met a duke before."

She blinked. "I haven't."

"I'm not a particularly good representative. I'm far too scandalous, as mentioned. Perhaps you've heard." He laughed when she did a terrible job of keeping her face blank. "I see you have. No doubt you're an avid fan of the tabloids and their daily regurgitations of my many sins. I can only hope to be even half as colorful in person."

"And it's Miss Andrews."

It was Hugo's turn to blink. "Sorry?"

"I would prefer it if you call me Miss Andrews." She nodded then, a faint inclination of her head, which he supposed was as close to any kind of recognition as he'd get. *"Your Grace."*

Something moved in him then, far worse than a mere shift. It felt raw. Dangerous.

Impossible.

"Let me clear something up from the start, Miss Andrews," he said, while his terrible horse tried to trick him into easing his hold on the reins. "I'm exactly as bad as they say. Worse. I ruin lives with a mere crook of my finger. Yours. The child's. Random pedestrians minding their own business in the village square. I have so many victims it's a bit of luck, really, that the country still stands. I'm my own blitzkrieg. If you have a problem with that, Mrs. Redding will be happy to replace you. You need only say the word."

If that affected this maddening woman in any way, she hid it behind her mountainous coat and that equally dour gray scarf.

"I told you, I have no intention of being replaced." He couldn't say he liked the exaggerated note of patience in her voice then. "Certainly not of my own volition. Whether you wish to replace me or not is, of course, entirely up to you."

"I might." He arched a brow. "I do detest poachers."

She eyed him as if he was her charge, not his ward. *His ward.* He hated even thinking those words. He hated even more the fact that Isobel had done exactly what she'd spitefully promised she'd do, time and again: kept her hooks in him even from beyond the grave.

"You should do as you please, Your Grace, and something tells me you will—"

"It is my gift. My expression of my best self."

"—but I might suggest you see how I handle the child before you send me packing."

The child. His ward.

Hugo hated that he was required to think about anyone's welfare at all when he cared so little for his own. He had extensive staff in place, paid handsomely to think about the health and happiness of all his many tenants and other staff members and various employees, leaving him free to lounge about being as useless as he liked.

Which—he'd read in the papers and heard from a chorus of people who would know, like his own dearly departed father—was all he was good for.

The girl, however, was a different sort of responsibility than real estate in Central London or a selection of islands in the Pacific or a coffee plantation in Africa or whatever else was in his holdings.

To say Hugo bitterly resented this was putting it mildly.

"What an excellent idea," he murmured. "I'll see she's waiting for you in the great hall when you finally make it to the house. It shouldn't be long. Five minutes' walk if you keep a good pace."

"You must be joking."

"Fair enough. Ten minutes' walk if your legs are shorter than mine, I suppose. I'm afraid I can't tell, as you appear to be wearing enough goosedown to leave the entire goose population of the United Kingdom shivering and bare. Assuming that's what's making you so…" He nodded at her voluminous black tent. "Puffy."

"Your hospitality is truly inspiring, Your Grace," she said after a moment, and the fact she managed to keep her face and voice smooth…poked at him.

He didn't like it.

Just as he really, *really* didn't like the fact that he couldn't remember the last time anyone or anything had managed to get beneath his skin.

"That is, as ever, my only goal," he replied.

And then, because he could—because he'd dedicated himself to being every bit as awful as he was expected to be, if not worse—Hugo spun the horse around, galloped off, and left the problematic Miss Eleanor Andrews there to find her own damned way to his house.

And his ward.

And this life of his that he'd never wanted, but had inherited anyway. Some would claim he'd earned it. That he deserved it and more.

That it really was fate, not luck, after all.

Hugo knew it didn't matter. He was trapped in it all the same.

CHAPTER TWO

FIFTEEN MINUTES LATER, Eleanor trudged up to the front of the house at last.

The front door itself rose forbiddingly up over a circular area directly in front of it that was paved with smooth stones and accented by the remnants of a garden turning brown as winter approached.

It seemed like an omen. Though Eleanor did not permit herself to believe in such things, of course.

The closer she'd got to the house, the more she'd wondered exactly why she'd agreed to any of this in the first place. Was it truly necessary that she isolate herself in this creepy old manor house? Was all that lovely money really worth marooning herself in Yorkshire with a man she'd never imagined she'd meet face to face—and didn't want to meet again, thank you?

And why couldn't Vivi do something for herself for a change?

But such thoughts made her feel disloyal. A little bit sick to her stomach. It felt like an act of betrayal when Vivi had come so close to losing her own life in that terrible accident. And had fought so hard to stay here. And walk again. Eleanor had been the only one left unscathed.

Sometimes she felt the guilt of that as if it was her own scar, slashed bright and hot across her whole body.

"Stop feeling sorry for yourself," she told herself briskly, pulling herself together as best she could. "You already took the position."

She rang the great and imposing bell that hung beside the door before she could think better of it, tugging on the slick old pull once. Then again.

It sounded long and low and deep, like some throwback to medieval times. She half expected knights in shining armor to come cantering up, wittering on about old King Arthur and ladies in lakes.

She was coming over all fanciful. That was what that man had done to her with his smirk and his amusement and his *mouth* when he was nothing but the same unsavory character she'd read about in the papers all these years. Only worse.

The fact that he was infinitely better-looking than any picture she'd ever seen of him didn't help. Worse, he was not nearly as fatuous as she'd imagined and he'd been entirely too sardonic besides. Her knees hadn't felt right since.

But as the door swung inward, she found herself staring not at a disgraceful duke in all his questionable glory, but down into the bright blue eyes and suspicious face of a little girl.

A little girl with silky red-gold hair plaited on either side of her head and a brace of adorable freckles across her nose. A little girl who made Eleanor's breath catch, because it was impossible to look at her and not see her very famous, very dead mother. Isobel Vanderhaven of the sunny smile and titian hair, who'd looked like everybody's best friend and the girl next door—if, that was, you happened to live next to one of her parents' rolling vineyards in South Africa.

"I don't need a governess," the child announced at once. In a tone that could only be called challenging.

"Of course you don't," Eleanor agreed, and the girl blinked. "Who *needs* a governess? But you are lucky enough to have one anyway."

The little girl considered her for a moment, as the October wind blustered and moaned, rushing in from the moors smelling of rain and winter.

"I'm Geraldine." Her lower lip protruded just slightly, and made her look her age, suddenly. "But you probably know that. They always know that."

"Of course I know your name," Eleanor said briskly. "I couldn't very well take a job if I didn't know the name of my charge, could I?"

It was clear to Eleanor that this child would keep her standing on the doorstep until the end of time if she didn't do something about it herself. So she pushed open the door with her free hand, and brushed straight past Geraldine, who watched her with a mixture of surprise and interest.

"They usually just stand in the drive, texting and whingeing," she piped up.

"Who is 'they'?" Eleanor reached past Geraldine once she'd stepped inside and shut the door, firmly, which took some doing because it outweighed her by approximately seven tons. And when she turned around to face the hall that had been waiting there behind her, she was glad the little girl didn't appear to be paying strict attention to her.

Because she was standing in a bloody castle.

Or close enough, anyway. Groves House had looked so grim and brooding from the outside, but here in the spacious foyer, it gleamed. Eleanor couldn't tell how it was doing that, precisely. Was there gold in the walls themselves? Was it the way the chandeliers hit all the paintings and the elegant furnishings and the rest of the things that seemed to clutter up rich people's foyers, that she'd only ever seen before on episodes of *Downton Abbey*?

"Everyone knows my name," Geraldine was saying with all the self-possession of the very young. "Sometimes they yell it at me in the village. You're the fifteenth governess so far, did you know that?"

"I did not."

"Mrs. Redding says I'm disobedient."

"What do you think?" Eleanor asked. "Are you?"

Geraldine looked a bit thrown by the question. "Maybe."

"Then you can stop, if you like." Eleanor eyed the mutinous little face before her and didn't see any disobedience. She saw a lonely little girl who'd lost her parents and had been sent off to live with a stranger. Eleanor could certainly relate. She ducked her chin so her face was closer to Geraldine's and whispered the thing that no one had ever bothered to say to her when she'd been heartsick and orphaned, waiting to find out if Vivi would make it through her latest surgery. "It won't matter either way, you know. Whether you're good or bad. I can already tell we'll be great friends and that means we always will. Friends don't change their minds about each other when things get tough, after all."

All Geraldine did was blink. Once, then again. But that was enough. Eleanor started unzipping her big coat.

"She's not any more disobedient than any other small human creature," came a male voice Eleanor wished she didn't recognize, wafting down the length of the hall as if it, too, was made of gold. And was set to shine. "She's seven. Let's not put the child in a cage so quickly, shall we?"

It took her a moment to find Hugo in all the dizzy bril-

liance of the bright foyer. But then there he was, saunter-
ing out of one of the connected rooms toward the front
door as if he hadn't a care in the world.

Because of course, he didn't.

He looked nothing like a duke should, Eleanor thought
darkly. No Hooray Henry red trousers or Barbour slung
just so for the most hated man in all of England. Not
for Hugo. He came towards her in an old, battered pair
of jeans. He had his hands thrust into the pockets like
some kind of slumming American celebrity. He wore a
T-shirt, cleverly ripped here and there, like those Eleanor
had seen in the posh shops that Vivi preferred. It was the
sort of T-shirt that would've looked like a soiled tissue
on a lesser man. But Hugo hadn't been lying about his
metabolism. Or anyway, that was how Eleanor tried to
view the magnificent specimen of male beauty walking
toward her then: in terms of his metabolism.

Because everything on Hugo Grovesmoor's body was
cut to perfection as if he was another piece of statuary
in his own hall. His chest was ridiculous, broad at the
top and narrow near his hips and stunningly ridged in
between. He looked as if he should be racing about in
a loincloth, banging on about Sparta. Instead, his dark
eyes were the precise shade of a lazy glass of whiskey,
his dark hair looked very much as if he'd been galloping
around in a bedchamber instead of on horseback, and
that little curl in the corner of his mouth was nothing
short of disastrous.

Because Eleanor could feel it everywhere. Lighting
her up in places she'd long since forgotten about.

She didn't know what that dark, edgy thing was that
wound around inside of her then. What she did know was
that it was Hugo's fault.

"The child is already in a cage," Eleanor retorted before she could think better of it. She flicked a glance around the vast hall, which was even bigger and more magnificent at a second glance, and just as dizzying, from the plump chandeliers to the acrobatic sconces on the walls. "A large one, I grant you."

Hugo kept moving toward her, eventually coming to a stop a few feet away. And then they were all three standing there in various degrees of awkwardness, right in front of the big front door.

It was worse when he was close, Eleanor was forced to admit. It made her feel raw and unsteady inside. It had been bad enough when he was up on the back of that giant horse, hooves flailing every which way and that mocking voice of his like a weapon, but Hugo even closer was confusing. Eleanor eyed him balefully, as if that might do something about that bright nonsense sloshing around inside of her and making her feel…things.

Way too many *things*.

In entirely too many places.

She told herself that it was only that she still had her big, heavy coat on. The coat was the reason she was flushed. Too warm. Almost itchy, somehow. It had nothing at all to do with him.

Next to her, Hugo did nothing to change the impression she'd had of him from across the hall. Or up on that horse, for that matter. And once the shock of his astonishing male beauty wore off—or, if she was more precise, dimmed a slight bit when she managed to breathe—she found that what really exuded from him like his own, very rich and unmistakable scent was all that arrogance.

That smile of his only deepened then. It was as if he could read her mind.

But he directed his attention to Geraldine. "Well?"

The little girl only shrugged, a sullen look on her cute little face.

"No point letting this one settle in like the others, if you're only going to complain about it later." Hugo's voice was...different, Eleanor thought. Not exactly softer, but more careful.

She was so busy trying to figure out what the difference was that she almost missed what he'd said.

"I beg your pardon. Are we discussing my employment?"

Hugo slid that gaze of his back to her. Too lazy. Too hot. She could feel it in too many places. More than before, and hotter.

"*We* are." He raised a dark brow. "It appears you're doing nothing but eavesdropping."

Eleanor's teeth hurt, and she unclenched them. "It would be eavesdropping if I was hid behind one of the flower arrangements, blending into all this feverish decor." She forced herself to smile, and the fact that it was difficult made her uneasy. More than uneasy, but she did it anyway. "*I* am not eavesdropping. But *you* are being remarkably inappropriate."

"It's a bit of bad form to hurl accusations like that at an innocent child, don't you think?" Hugo asked lazily, and Eleanor had the strangest thought that he was teasing her.

But why would the Duke of Grovesmoor tease anyone, much less someone as insignificant as Eleanor, a governess he apparently no longer wished to hire? She thrust that aside and concentrated on the only part of this bizarre interaction that she could control. Or try to control, anyway.

"I think all three of us are perfectly aware who I'm speaking to." Eleanor gazed down at Geraldine then, and this time her smile was genuine. "It won't hurt my feelings if you'd like me to leave, Geraldine. And I don't mind it if you say so to my face. But the Duke is very deliberately putting you in a position where you can act out his bad impulses, and that isn't fair."

"Life isn't fair," Hugo murmured, a bit too dark and smooth for Eleanor's peace of mind.

Eleanor ignored that, wishing it was as easy to ignore him. "It's also perfectly okay not to know," she told the little girl. "We met all of five minutes ago. If you'd like to take a little bit longer to make up your mind, that's fine."

"You say that with such authority," Hugo said. "Almost as if we stand in your house instead of mine."

Then he looked around as if he'd never laid eyes on the hall before in his life, when Eleanor knew full well that he'd been born here. Apparently, the Duke liked a bit of theater. She filed that away.

"But no," he continued, as if anyone had argued with him. "It's the same hall I remember from the whole of my benighted childhood, when governesses far stricter than you failed entirely to make me into a decent man. Portraits of my dreary ancestors lining the walls. Pedigrees as far as the eye can see. Grovesmoors in every direction and back again. Which would suggest that the authority lies with me and not you, would it not?"

"Funny," Eleanor said coolly, keeping her gaze fixed to his as if she wasn't the least bit intimidated. Because she certainly shouldn't have been, and why should it matter to her that his gaze felt as intoxicating as it looked? "The agency is under the impression that in this situation, Geraldine has the authority."

"Do you think so?" Hugo asked with a dangerous sort of laziness in his voice, then.

She didn't know what he might have said then. Something like temper stormed about in that gaze of his, making her breath feel heavy and tight in her chest.

But she knew, somehow, that it wasn't temper. Not quite.

"I like her," Geraldine chimed in then. "I want her to stay."

The Duke didn't shift his eyes from Eleanor's.

"Your wish is my command, my favorite ward," he said in that same careful tone, and maybe Eleanor was the only one who could hear all those undercurrents. Or feel them, anyway. Swishing around inside of her as if she'd had entirely too much to drink.

As if he was a new brand of spirit served in far more than the usual measures.

Everything felt hot. Entirely too sharp, as if there were some unseen hand clenched around them, gripping them tight. This close, Eleanor was sure that she could feel the heat of the Duke's body, making that T-shirt of his seem sensible. Making her feel that much warmer and uncomfortable in her own skin.

It's only the coat, she told herself desperately, but he was still so close. And much too tall. He towered over her the same way he had on that damned horse, and she assured herself there was no particular reason she should have the image of its flailing hooves, rearing up over her, when it was only a man standing in front of her in an entryway. Just a man. No dangerous animal in sight.

She was sure he almost said something, but he didn't. Instead, he shifted. He pulled one hand out of his jeans pocket, and lifted it. That was all. If she'd seen a stranger do it on the street, she wouldn't have thought of it as any kind of gesture. It seemed accidental.

But it wasn't, she realized the next moment, because suddenly the hall was filled with people.

Geraldine was swept away in the care of two clucking nannies. Someone took Eleanor's bags, another person took her coat, and then suddenly there was a very neatly dressed, efficient-looking older woman bearing down on her with a tight smile on her mouth and her steel gray hair tucked back in a bun that looked a great deal like Eleanor's own.

"Mrs. Redding, I presume," Eleanor said as the woman drew close.

"Miss Andrews." The woman greeted her in the same briskly matter-of-fact tone Eleanor recognized from the telephone calls they'd had. "If you'll come with me."

As Eleanor followed her deeper into the depths of the great house, she realized that the Duke was nowhere to be seen. Then he'd disappeared in all the commotion.

She told herself she was relieved.

"I do apologize that there was no one waiting to collect you from the station," the housekeeper said as she strode through the maze of halls, not pausing for an instant to give Eleanor a glimpse of the splendor closing in on all sides. Eleanor found she was grateful. She was afraid that if she stopped or stared for too long at any one thing, in any of the many beautiful rooms they hurried past, she'd be mesmerized for days. "It was an oversight."

Eleanor doubted that, for some reason. Or she doubted that this woman made any oversights, perhaps. But this was her first day, and she had the distinct impression she'd already irritated her employer, so there was no reason to dig that ditch any deeper.

"I had a lovely walk," she said instead. "It was a nice chance to take in the area. And quite atmospheric."

"The moors are nothing if not filled with atmosphere," the housekeeper said, an undercurrent in her voice that made Eleanor's ears prick up. "You'll want to be careful of the winds, however. They crop up out of nowhere and howl terribly wherever they go. They have a way of getting under your skin, you'll find. Whether you're aware of it or not."

Eleanor didn't think Mrs. Redding was talking about the Yorkshire wind. Or not only about the Yorkshire wind.

"I'll be certain to dress appropriately for the elements, then," Eleanor said after a moment, her tone even.

The woman led her down an endless hallway, then stopped at the far end.

"These are your rooms," Mrs. Redding said, waving Eleanor into the waiting suite. "I hope it will be sufficient. I'm afraid it's a bit less spacious than some of the previous governesses were hoping for."

Eleanor wanted to tell the woman she had been expecting a closet, or perhaps a cot down in a basement. Wherever the servants were kept in a place like this.

But she couldn't get the words out of her mouth, because she was too busy being overwhelmed. Again.

Mrs. Redding had said *rooms* not *room*, and she hadn't misspoken.

The flat she shared with Vivi could easily have fit into one part of the large room she walked into first, and it took her long, stunned moments to realize that it was, in fact, her own sitting room. And Mrs. Redding was still going, straight into the next room, which it took Eleanor another long beat to realize was a great closet. For the grand wardrobe she didn't possess.

The bedroom itself was on the far side of a huge bathroom that looked like a spa to Eleanor's untutored eyes, and as she walked into it, trailing behind Mrs. Redding, Eleanor was certain that this was the biggest dwelling space she'd ever been in.

One side of the room was dominated by a massive four-poster bed with carved wood posts and more carved wood as a canopy over top, like some kind of queen's bower. There was another fireplace, and more places to sit around it, as if the whole sitting room wasn't enough.

Eleanor's breathing had gone a bit shallow. But she pulled it together, and smiled serenely at Mrs. Redding.

"It will do," she murmured, trying her best to sound dry and sophisticated and professional. Instead of like an overexcited child in a candy store.

After the older woman left her, with instructions about where and when Eleanor was to present herself later for a tour and a breakdown of her duties, Eleanor found herself standing in the middle of this bedroom she couldn't imagine ever calling her own. If possible, she felt more out of place than she had downstairs, where somehow the Duke's arrogance had made her forget herself and Geraldine's fierce, obvious loneliness had caught at her.

But here in these sumptuous rooms, she had nothing to fight. No one to defend. Only elegant emptiness all around.

Nothing but herself.

Whoever the hell that was.

CHAPTER THREE

HUGO HAD NO idea what had gotten into him.

He didn't know what it was about starchy, overly puffy-coated Eleanor Andrews that scraped beneath his skin. But there was no denying the fact that he, Hugo Grovesmoor, who had never chased a woman in his entire life, had been *lying in wait* for this one.

It was extraordinary.

Hugo told himself he needed to see what on earth was hidden beneath that enormous coat of hers, that was all. That not knowing might keep him up at night. Was she a marshmallow creature like the monster in that old movie? Or had she hid her true, svelte form away in a billowy suit of armor?

And he knew when she didn't back down in the foyer or unzip that great horror of a coat more than an inch or two that he needed to retreat back to his part of the house, carry on living the life of ease and leisure and loathing the whole of the world begrudged him these days, and forget all about his ward and the governess she'd decided to favor on sight. He knew it.

So he had no explanation for why he found himself lurking about in the wing he'd given over to Geraldine because he knew Mrs. Redding was giving Eleanor a tour and showing her where and how she'd be expected to do her work. The governess's quarters were in this same wing, one floor above, right up the nearby stairs— a fact that there was absolutely no reason at all for Hugo to keep reciting to himself.

"I didn't expect to see you, Your Grace," Mrs. Redding said when she swept out of the nursery that was now a playroom and found Hugo inspecting the rather horrifying paintings hanging on the walls in the hall that he remembered from his own childhood.

"I can't imagine why not, Mrs. Redding." Hugo kept studying the garish painting in front of him as he spoke. "I do own the house and am known to be in residence. Surely I could be expected to turn up sooner or later."

"In the child's wing? Unlikely." The older woman could still manage to infuse every syllable with genteel condemnation. A true skill, he'd always thought. "And yet here you are."

Hugo turned then, smiling faintly at Mrs. Redding as he looked behind her to where Eleanor stood.

And he understood in an instant that he'd made a terrible mistake.

Because Eleanor was not as puffy and large as her coat had suggested. Nor was she as whipcord-skinny as a gazelle's thigh, as many of her predecessors had been, eyes gleaming with avarice and ambition.

Quite the opposite, god help him.

The damned woman had the body of a goddess. A naughty fertility goddess. Eleanor had lush hips and generous breasts, sweetly separated by a tiny waist that made him hunger to test the span of it with his own hands. She was dressed in a perfectly conservative and appropriately opaque blouse over sensible trousers with a cardigan tossed on besides, and she still looked like an old pinup model. Her body was so markedly opulent that it made her harshly scraped back hair all the more intriguing—in that Hugo wanted to get his hands in it. Or feel it all over his naked body while she was engaged in other things, none of them involving any sort of harsh scraping at all.

Hugo knew he needed to stop. Now.

He needed to turn around this minute and get himself away from her, especially when she frowned at him from behind Mrs. Redding, and from beneath that fringe of hers. The legions of other women who had come this house and tried it on with him had pouted at him. They'd simpered and giggled. They'd made eyes at him over his ward's head and had dressed in preposterously inappropriate clothing while supposedly out taking walks on the grounds in the middle of rainstorms in the hope of attracting his notice.

Eleanor Andrews, on the other hand, barreled about in the ugliest coat he'd ever beheld in his life as if she didn't care whether or not she was found attractive, made no secret of the fact she held Hugo in rather low regard, and aimed disapproving frowns at him while she stood on his property as if she didn't expect to receive her salary from his accounts.

It was almost as if she didn't want anything from him.

That notion was so revolutionary it shook him a little. He found himself very nearly frowning himself, but caught it just in time. Hugo Grovesmoor did not *frown*. That might indicate he had thoughts, and that would never do. He was considered nothing more than a vessel of pointless and predatory evil, sent to earth to ruin every good thing in it at will.

He'd learned his place a long time ago.

And yet, "I'll finish giving Miss Andrews her tour of the premises," he heard himself say.

And then wondered if the rest of his admittedly impure thoughts were being broadcast on his face when both women stood there staring back at him. Then again, that was the benefit of owning half of England, wasn't it? He could bloody well do as he liked.

"Was I unclear?" he asked softly.

Mrs. Redding huffed slightly at that, but excused herself in the next moment because bristle as she might, the woman knew her place. And that left Hugo exactly where he shouldn't be, under any circumstances. Alone with Eleanor.

His ward's latest governess who happened to have the kind of body that made him feel like an adolescent boy all over again, all cock and delicious promise.

"How remarkably kind of you to take time out of your busy schedule to welcome a lowly member of your staff, Your Grace," Eleanor said as Mrs. Redding's steps faded away, down the stairs and off into the busier parts of the house. Leaving them alone with nothing but the wind outside and the far-off sounds of Geraldine at her dinner on the other end of this hall, chattering away with her usual brace of nannies. "When I assume you must have any number of urgent ducal matters that require your attention."

"Dozens at every moment," Hugo agreed cheerfully, when what he actually had was the good sense to hire excellent people to handle such things. "And yet here I am, ready to wait on you hand and foot like a good host."

She smiled. It was a frozen sort of smile that shouldn't have hit him like that. Like a lick of heat in the place he was entirely too hard already.

"But I am not a guest, Your Grace," Eleanor said stiffly, as if he'd insulted her by suggesting otherwise.

"I'm certain I heard explicit criticism regarding my hospitality, did I not? Outside, when there was some question as to whether or not you were poaching from the estate?"

"There was never any real question about whether or not I was poaching, surely."

"And yet I felt as if I had many questions, none of which were answered. And many more of which were complicated by your performance in my foyer."

She made no apparent attempt to keep herself from frowning at him all the more furiously. "My 'performance'?"

Hugo waited, brows raised expectantly, and her frown deepened.

"Your Grace," she managed to get out, sounding even stiffer than before.

Hugo tried as hard as he could to keep his mind free of any thoughts about Geraldine. Lest they stray from the girl he'd been called upon to care for, and end up on her mother instead.

And the less he thought about Isobel, the better.

The less anyone thought about Isobel, the better, in his opinion. Not that anyone had asked Hugo's opinion on Isobel in quite some time.

But as was to be expected, thoughts of Isobel and the damage she'd done—and still did despite the fact she was dead and buried—only made him angrier.

Not that he was angry, of course.

Hugo Grovesmoor was never *angry*. Angry was for people who had emotions, and it had been established long ago that he lacked that particular human frailty. In every paper possible. Over and over again.

"I don't know what else to call it but a performance." He felt his gaze go narrow. "Perhaps you can explain to me why you gave a little girl such false hope. Is that your angle?"

"Geraldine is a lovely young girl," Eleanor said in her prim way that made Hugo feel more of the sorts of things he was famous for never, ever feeling. In a great mad rush that made his fingers itch to touch her. "She does seem lonely and a bit lost, if I'm honest." Eleanor's startling gaze, frank and sturdy on his, made an interesting sort of heat pool inside of him. Hugo didn't like it. But not liking it, it turned out, didn't make it go away. "I look forward to being able to help her in some way. Assuming, of course, I'm allowed to do that."

"Do you imagine I would prevent you from doing the job for which I hired you in the first place? You have the most curious notions, Miss Andrews. Quite a fanciful imagination, it appears. Are you entirely certain that you are the best choice for a little girl you consider lost and lonely?"

The unfathomable woman shrugged as if it was no matter. "Whether I'm a good choice or bad choice, it appears I'm the only governess here."

"A circumstance that could change in an instant. On a whim. My whim."

Another shrug. "There's nothing I can do to control your whims, Your Grace. Is there? Best to muddle along and hope for the best, I think."

"The best being today's display? Telling a vulnerable child you'll always be her friend before you've taken off your coat or unpacked? Without knowing if she even likes you?" He shook his head. "Most women in your position play their games with me, Miss Andrews. They tend to leave the girl alone."

She stood there in her frumpy little outfit that should have made her look dumpy and instead made him think that he'd never seen a woman more magnetic. Especially since she didn't seem to be the least bit aware of it.

"All the more reason that someone ought to pay attention to the poor thing," she said briskly. "She's thirsty for a little companionship, clearly."

Eleanor was still eyeing him as if he was something distinctly unsavory as she spoke. And there was absolutely nothing new about that look. Hugo had seen that particular expression on more faces than he could begin to count. Friends, family members—or what few of each remained, anyway—and strangers on the street alike. He wasn't usually a receptacle for friendly glances, a fact of his existence he'd become inured to long since.

But for some reason, seeing that same old look on this woman's face dug into him. As if that *you are judged and found wanting* gaze she kept trained on him was attached to a sharp implement and she was raking it over his skin, if not jabbing it straight into his gut.

"Why do you want this job?" He didn't know why he bothered asking when he already knew. There were two reasons women applied for this position and Eleanor clearly wasn't thinking she'd angle her way into bed, which was a crying shame any way he looked at it. That left the money.

"Why wouldn't I want this job?" she asked, very coolly, in reply. "Fourteen other women had this job before me. It's obviously very popular."

"That's not an answer. And I can actually tell the difference between an answer and a nonanswer, which I accept may come as something of a surprise to you." He smiled at her, and made sure to show all his teeth. "I'm not just a pretty face, Miss Andrews."

If possible, her frown darkened even further. "I'm not following this conversation at all. Have you decided, now that I've actually moved into this house and have already met your ward, that it might be a good time to conduct a personal interview?"

"And if I am?"

"I think it's a little late. Don't you?"

"And I think, unless I'm very much mistaken or have succumbed to death without my knowledge—which should make this conversation significantly more upsetting than you seem to find it at present—that I am your employer. Or am I lost in some kind of dread fever dream, imagining myself the Duke of Grovesmoor?"

Hugo didn't know exactly when he realized he'd moved a little too close to her. Or perhaps she'd moved to close to him, he couldn't tell. All he knew was that they were no longer standing across from each other on different sides of the wide hallway. Instead they'd somehow closed the distance, and had met in the middle now.

Entirely too close to each other for Hugo's peace of mind, or whatever passed for that state. Because when he was closer to her, he was even more fascinated by her. He'd entertained the notion that it was the novelty of that hideous coat she'd worn earlier that had intrigued him, but no. He was still intrigued now.

More so.

The goddess curves didn't exactly help the situation, especially when she put her hands on her hips, which only made her lush figure that much more impossible to ignore.

"I don't know if you're imagining it or not," Eleanor said in a tone that only just managed to qualify as polite, "but if you're not the Duke of Grovesmoor, you've certainly managed to take on an identity with a remarkable amount of baggage."

Even that little swipe at his history intrigued him, because it was so direct. She was unlike any woman he'd ever encountered, even without that eyesore of a coat. It was something about the way she stood, wholly unimpressed and unintimidated by him, hands on her hips and her brown gaze utterly clear of any attempt at feminine wiles. It was the belligerent tilt of her jaw and the way she was clearly endeavoring to look down her nose at him from beneath her razor-sharp fringe. He imagined she did the same with her charges when they got uppity, and it didn't seem to matter to her that she was much shorter than he was.

And Hugo realized in that moment that he was perfectly content with being hated. He was used to being the focus of any number of dark feelings, vicious rumors, and random character assassinations. But he wasn't used to outright defiance. And certainly not to his face. For a man who had always considered himself entirely too modern for his circumstances, Hugo found that there was more than a little Ancient Duke in him than he'd ever imagined before. Because he wanted to pull rank. Badly.

Except it was more than that. He didn't want to crush *her*. The truth was, this woman made him *hungry*.

Hugo wanted a taste of her so badly that he could feel the need of it marching inside of him, as if his body was staging a full-scale mutiny. He didn't think he'd ever felt anything like it in his life. Hell. He knew he hadn't.

He was ravenous.

"I would suggest, Miss Andrews," he said, very carefully and very deliberately, and he kept his damned hands to himself despite the fact it took a Herculean application of self-will, "that you endeavor to recall which one of us is the Duke and which one the governess."

If Hugo expected her to be cowed by that, he was in for a surprise.

"I am not likely to forget that anytime soon," Eleanor replied without appearing to take even a moment to pause or rethink a thing. Not her belligerence or the way she stood there and took him on, exactly as she had outside. And certainly not her position—here in this house, much less here, in his grasp. "I was promised very little interaction with the owner of the house, Your Grace. That you were not available, ever, was made abundantly clear in all of the interviews."

"Most of the enterprising women who apply for the position want to see me, Miss Andrews. You must realize that it's the primary reason they condescend to grace these halls with their presence. And the primary reason they are sacked shortly thereafter."

She tilted her head slightly to one side. "And what did they do to get sacked?"

"I will leave that to your imagination."

"Did you chase all of them down on the grounds of the estate, charging about on a great big horse?"

He almost laughed at that. And it might have been that which floored him the most.

"And I ask again, why do you want this job? Because you don't seem to understand the usual boundaries that govern a woman in your position. Or have the faintest sense of self-preservation."

"I beg your pardon, Your Grace," she said in that same brisk tone, as if she thought she was managing him. As if both he and Geraldine were under her care, and he was the more difficult one by far. "All I'd like to do is start working. There's a little girl having her tea at the other end of this hall and it would be nice to get to know her a bit before our lessons start. If there isn't anything else…?"

"I am the boss, Miss Andrews," he reminded her. From between his teeth. "You are the employee. Everything about the way you are speaking to me is disrespectful, not to mention foolish. Why would you try to antagonize the person who pays your spectacularly generous salary?"

Her frown smoothed out a bit, though she didn't precisely soften. And still, Hugo wanted to taste that faint crease between her brows, where the edge of her fringe kissed her skin the way he wanted to do.

"In point of fact, I won't be paid for two weeks," she said after a moment, as if she couldn't help herself. Maybe she really couldn't.

He couldn't have said why that notion washed through him like a new sort of heat.

"A notable distinction," Hugo murmured.

And then, because he loved nothing more than complicating any given situation beyond repair, the better to make it worse, he kissed her.

They were standing so close that it seemed almost impossible to avoid for another second. Maybe that was his excuse. He slid his palm over her cheek, marveling at the sensation of such sweet, silken skin beneath his hand despite how severely she'd been regarding him all this time, and then it was the easiest thing in the world to hold her fast and claim her mouth with his.

And then they were in real trouble, because she tasted like magic.

CHAPTER FOUR

ELEANOR HAD NO idea what was happening.

He was kissing her.

Hugo was *kissing* her. The hated Duke of Grovesmoor himself had his *mouth* on hers.

And nothing about that was all right. It was dangerous and it was terrible and it was shocking—

But even worse, she liked it.

She more than liked it.

There were no words—and least none she knew—that could begin to describe how much she liked it.

It was like fire. It was an explosion, and only the fact that he was holding her against him kept her from shattering into a million pieces, she was sure of it.

What Eleanor knew about kissing could be summed up in two very short words: not much. But the single adolescent fumbling she'd subjected herself to at a mortifying school disco years and years ago bore no resemblance to this.

Hugo's mouth on hers was untroubled, somehow. Unhurried. He sampled her lips as if he planned to keep on doing so for hours. Days, perhaps. He seemed entirely and wholly unrushed, teasing her and tasting her, then licking his way inside to do it all over again.

With a devastating thoroughness that made her tremble. Everywhere.

And she didn't know what was worse, that mouth of his licking fire into her in ways she could hardly begin to process, or the heat of his hand as he held her face to his. Her cheek felt as if it had been branded, as if he was still pressing a red-hot iron to her skin, but for some reason she had no desire whatsoever to step away.

And still he kissed her.

As if a kiss was not a finite thing, a buss on the cheek or halfhearted peck, easily given and more easily forgotten. A real kiss—because Eleanor had no doubt that what Hugo was doing to her was the real thing, something she'd had no idea even existed all this time—was more of a slow burn.

It was longing made physical, then slowly kindled into an ache.

And oh, how Eleanor ached.

She didn't know how she'd ended up standing so close to him in the first place. She'd told herself repeatedly to keep her distance from the man, because no good could possibly come of their proximity when she was so *aware* of him, and then there she was. Stood in the center of the hallway with her hands on her hips as if she'd half a mind to scold the man, or as if she'd forgotten herself completely and was dressing down *the Duke*. Eleanor had no idea what had come over her. It was like an out-of-body experience. As if she was being haunted by some stroppy, mouthy ghost that was taking her over and making her act as if she very much wanted to be fired on her very first day…

She hadn't the slightest idea what she thought she was doing.

And now this.

Whatever *this* was, that was setting her on fire and tearing her apart at once.

But then it hit her, as his impossibly addictive mouth moved on hers, making her feel as if a lightning flash had been trapped between them. This was Hugo Grovesmoor. *This was what he did.* She hadn't expected him to be as articulate as he was, it was true. She'd expected his dark good looks to seem seedy and tatty in person—and she'd imagined she'd barely see him. But it occurred to her that she should have expected this kind of thing from him.

Hugo was a man who was willing to use his body to get what he wanted. Anything he wanted. Particularly if it was harmful to others. How could Eleanor have let herself forget? The fact that his kiss felt like a revelation was something that should have filled her with shame.

It would, she was certain, just as soon as she had time to collect herself.

Somewhere that lightning wasn't burning her alive.

Eleanor pushed at his chest, and that was problematic too, because he appeared to be made of more of that iron. Worse, he was much too hot beneath that soft T-shirt, and she had no desire whatsoever to let go.

No matter how she knew she should.

Lazily, taking his time, Hugo raised his head. His whiskey-colored eyes gleamed as he gazed down at her and Eleanor could feel that, too. She could feel so many things she thought she might collapse. Part of her wanted nothing more than to let all that emotion take her straight down to the floor, but she was made of sterner stuff. She'd had to be. She had Vivi to think about.

"Is this why all fourteen previous governesses left?" Eleanor demanded, and she was horrified to hear her voice shake. "Is this a test?" She swallowed, hard. "Geraldine is only just down the hall."

Something flashed in those dark eyes of his, but he dropped his hand. And Eleanor told herself that what rushed in her then was relief. Triumph. Not something a great deal more like loss.

She could feel the way he kissed her everywhere, in ways that made no sense. There was a twisting, melting ball of sensation deep in her belly. There was a rawness in her chest. Her breasts felt weighted, heavy. And there was a dampness behind her eyes that she knew perfectly well was too complicated to be simple tears.

"I enjoy nothing more than living down to each and every one of a person's low expectations of me, of course," Hugo said in that mocking, cut-glass way of his. "Do you not find me entertaining, Miss Andrews? Could there be anything more delightful than to discover I am exactly as you imagined I'd be? Depraved and indifferent and thoroughly spoiled, inside and out?"

Eleanor had been thinking along those lines herself, but somehow, hearing him say it all out loud like that— with such bitterness, and something she could have sworn bordered despair—made something inside of her turn over.

But she shoved it aside, because none of this should have happened. Not with her. She wasn't the sort of woman men grabbed and kissed in spontaneous bursts of passion. That was Vivi's life. Her sister was forever fending off male attention wherever she went. That was how Eleanor knew that there was no reason for a man like Hugo to put his hands on her unless that was just something he did as a matter of course, the way the tabloids had always claimed—or if he was making fun of her, somehow.

She'd never heard of mockery by kiss, but what did she know? She'd spent her life working rather than socializing, and she'd never bloomed into a needy curiosity of the opposite sex the way everyone had claimed she would.

Something that made her profoundly grateful, as what she didn't need or even wonder about, she couldn't miss.

"I think it's best if we pretend this never happened," she said, as evenly as she could, pleased to find she'd managed to strip the tremor from her voice.

Hugo regarded her from the near foot of height he had on her, and the fact he was dressed so casually, she realized, did nothing to take away from that matter-of-fact power he seemed to exude even so. How had she not noticed that before?

Because he hides it, a voice from deep inside of her replied with far too much authority. *In the same way you lie to yourself about the things you need.*

Eleanor didn't like that at all. She ignored it.

"That will make it difficult, you understand, to sell your salacious story to the tabloids," Hugo was saying in a cold sort of tone, as if he was discussing something that wouldn't affect him one way or the other.

"I couldn't do that if I wanted to, which I don't." Eleanor thought her voice softened at the end there, so she tried to even it out again. She put her spine into it. "I signed an extremely comprehensive nondisclosure agreement, Your Grace. Surely you must be aware of it."

"What I am aware of is that the penalty for breaking that nondisclosure agreement is a certain amount of pounds sterling. Should the tabloids offer, say, twice that amount, it might well be worth it to break the agreement. To a certain type of person, of course."

"I…" Eleanor very rarely found herself a loss for words. She didn't understand the sensation warring inside of her. That strange longing, or the fact she had to curl her hands into fists at her side to keep them to herself. She, who was not the sort of person who liked to touch others or even to be touched herself. She, who had never had to fight *not* to touch someone in her life. She was baffled. "I would never do that."

"Because you are such a good person, naturally. My mistake."

His sardonic tone could have stripped the paint from the walls and Eleanor nearly checked to see if it had. But didn't, because she could feel her reaction in the flush that heated her cheeks, and she thought that was more than enough of a response.

"Because who would do that?" she asked, almost helplessly.

The expression on the Duke's face was all razor-sharp amusement, but all Eleanor could feel in the space between them was more of that same bitterness that cut a little too close to despair. Dark and thick and everywhere.

Hopeless, she thought, and didn't know why that made her ache again, the way she had when he'd kissed her. Only sharper.

"Everyone has their price, I assure you," Hugo said quietly.

As if he was making a prediction. A terrible one.

"Do you?" Eleanor dared to ask.

The expression on his face then made her heart kick at her, then sink into that same sharp ache. But his laugh was worse, dark enough to fill the hall, if not the grand house arrayed all around them, too.

"Especially me, Miss Andrews," he told her, almost gently. Though his dark eyes blazed, and were anything but gentle. Anything but soft. "Me most of all."

Eleanor woke in a room fit for a princess and told herself that the unsettling scene in the hallway that had kept her awake and that kiss that had invaded her dreams hadn't happened.

Because surely she could not possibly have been so stupid as to go full *Jane Eyre* on the very first day of her new job, within hours of meeting the Duke and his ward. Before she'd even unpacked her case or figured out what her new job actually entailed. Eleanor had never been that kind of silly. She'd never had the time or, if she was honest, the inclination to fling herself headlong into the sort of mad passions and silly entanglements the bright young things all around her seemed to flock to so mindlessly, like moths to a wholly avoidable flame.

Until last night, Eleanor would have confidently asserted that she simply didn't have those sorts of feelings or bodily reactions. That she wasn't wired that way.

She decided she would treat that kiss as if it hadn't happened, because it shouldn't have. And because she had no idea how to handle all the things she *felt*. As if she was a moth battering itself against a light after all.

But she soon found that it didn't matter how she handled what should never have happened, because the Duke was nowhere to be found over the next few weeks.

Eleanor told herself that was a good thing.

Geraldine was a bright, often funny kid, and even on her less than stellar days, it was far more interesting to work with her than it was to answer ringing phones and take the odd bit of abuse from walk-ins and disgruntled clients and snarky deliverymen. Far better Geraldine than her last immediate supervisor, Eleanor thought more than once.

"I feel terrible that I pushed you into taking this strange job," Vivi told her a few days into her time at Groves House.

"It's actually a good fit, believe it or not. I like it."

Vivi plowed right on, her voice merry and sharp. "I

bullied you into it and now you're trapped in the bowels of Yorkshire in some moldering old stack of stones."

Eleanor was sunk deep into her luxurious bathtub, bubbles high and the hot water silky against her skin. She had a book on her little bath tray, a glass of wine and some fine cheese she'd never tasted before, and a fire crackling in the other room. She and Geraldine had spent the day investigating the sciences and giggling uproariously for no particular reason, until Eleanor had delivered her to the nannies who supervised the little girl's tea and bedtime.

"The poor tyke can't go to a proper school, can she?" the slightly friendlier of the two notably unfriendly nannies had said out in the hall after Geraldine had run into her rooms, as if Eleanor had argued otherwise. "Those worthless journos won't leave her alone for a minute. If I knew who sold them stories about the Duke I'd give them a piece of my mind, believe me."

As if Hugo was a good man who merited that kind of defense.

The other woman had huffed off after Geraldine. Leaving Eleanor finished with lessons—and thus finished with her work for the day—at four-thirty. Which was late, as they were usually finished hours sooner unless they'd taken a little trip further afield.

Eleanor had never had such easy, comfortable hours.

But for some reason, she didn't tell Vivi any of that, and not only because that sharp merriment in her voice suggested her sister had been tossing back spirits.

"I'm fine, really," Eleanor said instead, like a proper martyr.

And felt terrible about herself as Vivi mouthed a few more drunken apologies, then rang off.

But not terrible enough to correct her sister's impression that she was muddling through dire circumstances in their next conversation. Or the next. Or, for that matter, let Vivi know that she had in fact met the disgraced Duke himself. More than "met" him.

She told herself that because that kiss had been such an egregious misstep, and because the Duke had disappeared thereafter, it hadn't happened. So there was no need to tell Vivi about it, as her sister would only leap to the wrong conclusions.

But something deep inside her whispered a different, darker reason.

Eleanor ignored that, too.

The truth was that Eleanor had wanted to become a teacher years ago, but hadn't thought she could make enough money at it to serve Vivi's purposes and hers—and certainly not without heading back to school to get the proper certification. There had obviously been no time for that. *I can only be dazzling for a few years, after all,* Vivi would say. Working with Geraldine was a lot like fulfilling an old dream. It was like a little glance down the road not taken, which, Eleanor found, she liked as much—if not more—than the one she'd been on all this time.

And with her focus on Geraldine and the new lessons she plotted out every night on her laptop, she hardly noticed the absence of the Duke.

Until she fell asleep, that was, when that kiss haunted her dreams.

And Eleanor woke each morning flustered and red-faced, and entirely too warm. Because in her dreams, vivid and wild, they didn't stop at a single kiss.

CHAPTER FIVE

"HIS GRACE WILL not be returning from Spain today as planned," Mrs. Redding announced one morning, when Eleanor had dropped by the housekeeper's office off the kitchens to go over Geraldine's schedule of excursions so the cook and staff could be kept informed.

Eleanor blinked. "Oh?"

Later, Eleanor thought immediately, she'd be furious with herself for sounding something other than blandly disinterested. But all she could do now was gaze back at the disapproving older woman and pretend she hadn't sounded a little too intrigued.

Maybe more than a little. She hated herself for that, too.

"We expected him in residence today," Mrs. Redding said matter-of-factly, very much as if she hadn't heard anything in Eleanor's voice. Eleanor told herself that *of course* she hadn't. It was all in her head, because Eleanor was the one wandering around with the guilty conscience—and the memory of that kiss. Not Mrs. Redding. She hoped. "But his plans have changed, and he will be making a brief trip to Dublin before returning."

"I didn't realize he wasn't in residence now," Eleanor lied, her voice as bland as she could make it. She punctuated it by taking a calm sip of her tea.

Mrs. Redding eyed her as if she knew the tea was a prop. "When the Duke is in residence, he likes to have Geraldine presented to him at least every other week at dinner. By the child's current governess, so he can assess both Geraldine's and the governess's progress."

"Well, I suppose that explains why the Duke has appeared so hands-off since I arrived." Eleanor managed a laugh. "I thought perhaps he didn't have much interest in his ward."

The temperature in the room seemed to plummet at that. Eleanor watched Mrs. Redding's gaze frost over right there before her.

"It would be wiser to put a little less stock in what people say about His Grace from afar," the housekeeper said, as if each syllable cut the roof of her mouth on the way out. "That tabloid creation bears no resemblance to the man I've known since he was a child. A man who took in an orphaned child out of the goodness of his heart and is still painted a villain for it."

Eleanor took her time placing her cup of tea back in its saucer, surprised at the vehemence in the older woman's voice.

"Having a ward thrust upon one and being expected to raise them must be something of an adjustment," she said after a moment.

Mrs. Redding shifted behind her desk, and gazed at Eleanor for a moment over the top of her eyeglasses.

"We are a mite protective of the Duke here," she said with the same quiet intensity, and Eleanor couldn't tell if that was a warning or an explanation. "It's a rare stranger indeed who has his best interests at heart. He has been so long in that spotlight that the spotlight is all anyone sees, but we see the boy who grew up here." Her gaze edged back into chilly territory. "The whole of England might be dedicated to telling nasty stories about His Grace, but they are never told here. Ever."

Eleanor couldn't help feeling as if she'd been slapped again. And harder, this time. As if the fact no one had met her at the train station when she'd arrived had been a test, not an oversight. She wanted to ask Mrs. Redding directly but didn't quite dare.

It was the same with all the staff in Groves House, she found as the days passed and the weather grew more blustery and grim. Each day was bleaker than the one before. The trees grew ever more stark and the rain fell colder. Icier. And the other members of the household were as uninterested in Eleanor's presence weeks into her residence as they'd been at the start. She ended up eating her meals alone in her own rooms because when she entered the common staff areas, all conversation stopped, which did not exactly aid the digestion.

"What do you mean they're all offish?" Vivi asked in one of their phone calls. She sounded distant and preoccupied, the way she often did when Eleanor called her instead of the other way around. As if she had her mobile clamped to her shoulder while she bustled about doing other things. Much more important things, her distracted tone suggested.

Eleanor told herself, brusquely, that it wasn't entirely fair to attach meaning to Vivi's *tone*. They each played their parts, after all. If she had a problem with that, she'd had years to say so. She could have objected years ago when their reluctant, distantly related cousin had eyed the pair of them as adolescents and set the course of their lives.

"Might as well marry a rich man as a poor man," she'd tutted at them one afternoon. *"You two have noth-*

ing in this world but Vivi's pretty face. I'd use it to better yourselves, if I were you."

"I mean exactly that." Eleanor said now, scowling at the memory. As if Vivi hadn't already been a miracle, walking the way she had when the doctors thought she never would. And it wasn't entirely true that all they had was Vivi's face, was it? Because what was Vivi's face without Eleanor's financial wizardry and prowess with a sewing needle? "They're a closed group. No newcomers."

Eleanor had taken to walking in the evenings and tonight she'd taken the back stairs that led from the kitchen into a wing she never been in before. She'd climbed up to the second floor and found herself in a long hallway that doubled as an art gallery. Obvious, recognizable masterpieces worth billions were flung on walls next to what looked like very dour and period-appropriate versions of Hugo. But she concentrated on her phone call, not the wigs and funny hats and companion animals in the portraits before her.

Vivi sighed, which definitely put Eleanor's back up, and no matter that she tried to pretend otherwise. "Are you there to make friends, Eleanor?"

"Of course not." She could hear the tension in her voice, and forced herself to take a breath. "I know why I'm here, Vivi. All I'm saying is that it wouldn't be the worst thing to have a friendly face about the place. That's all."

Vivi, clearly no longer feeling guilty or bullying or drunk, sighed again.

"Don't go moping about the place. No one likes an Eeyore."

Eleanor found she was scowling at the painting in front of her, biting her tongue. As in, literally pressing it against her teeth to keep from saying something back in the same dismissive tone.

"I should think you ought to feel grateful that you're not required to work so hard for the friendship of people you won't know in a year's time," Vivi said dismissively.

It hadn't really occurred to Eleanor to think about the people here—or her position here or whole solitary little life here, really—as temporary. But of course it was. Even if all went well, a girl only needed a governess for so long.

"I think I have a few years before I can happily drift off into the sunset," she pointed out, and she was proud of herself for sounding as if she was smiling, not scowling. "Geraldine is seven, not seventeen."

Vivi laughed. "You're not disappearing into the north forever, Eleanor. You're supposed to make us enough to cover our bills and then come back."

"I didn't realize that was the plan. Especially when the longer I stay, the more I'll make."

"Eleanor, please," Vivi said, her tone light. But there was something beneath it that wedged its way into Eleanor's stomach and sat there. Heavily. "I can't possibly do all this without you. You're on holiday, nothing more."

Eleanor finished off the call, and found herself staring blankly out one of the windows in this strange art gallery hall, her stomach still not quite right. Because it was tempting to pretend that Vivi couldn't do without her emotionally, that she missed Eleanor herself, but deep down, Eleanor suspected that wasn't true. Just yesterday Vivi had been in a panic about how to pay all the bills and get the rent in, and she'd moaned something about what a tip the flat was since there was no one to tidy it up.

Because, of course, the person who usually handled all those things was Eleanor.

It was a good thing Vivi thought Eleanor was suffering in a pile of debris in the middle of a moor. Because if her sister had any idea how luxurious Eleanor's lifestyle was at present, Eleanor had no doubt Vivi would contrive a way to get herself up to Groves House so she could enjoy it herself.

And Eleanor was obviously far more deeply selfish than she'd ever imagined, because for once in her life, she didn't want to share something with the sister she'd always loved to the point of distraction.

She stuck her mobile in the pocket of the black trousers she wore and moved over to the windows. The gallery was set up over the back of the house and looked out over the tangle of the back gardens that led straight into the brooding moors. There was a full moon tonight, tossing a spooky sort of silvery light here and there, silently moving in and out of the clouds, and making the whole of Yorkshire seem to gleam.

If gloomily.

Maybe it was because she was tucked away in this desolate old house. Maybe it was because the halls were always empty, the locals were unfriendly, and the nights were already starting to seem as if they lasted three times as long as the day. Maybe it was because she felt a bit too much like a gothic waiting to happen, locked away in here.

But when had she decided that she was so all right with being alone? Her goal had always been Vivi's great marriage. She'd never thought about what *she* would do once that happened.

She shivered as she thought about the Duke's mouth on hers, firm and commanding. And if the highlights of her circumscribed life were the potent, powerful dreams that shook through her every night, all featuring Hugo in searing detail, well. That was more than some people ever had. Maybe it was enough.

Eleanor took a deep breath and vowed it would be. It would have to be.

"Dare I hope that your unexpected appearance outside my private rooms is an invitation, Miss Andrews?"

Eleanor told herself she was hallucinating. Auditory hallucinations, which were really just another part of a regular old haunting, according to all the scary films she'd seen in her time.

She took her time turning to check. And it was worse than any run-of-the-mill haunting.

Hugo stood there at the other end of the long gallery. And this time, he looked exactly like a duke. Exactly like every fantasy Eleanor had ever had of a man that powerful, for that matter. He was dressed all in black and looked vaguely historical. It took her a shattering beat of her heart or two to realize it was because he wore a top hat that should have looked absurd over a long black cloak that did. Or anyway, should have. *Would have*, even, had another man worn it.

But Eleanor was very much afraid, as her throat went dry and her stomach twisted into something that wasn't quite anxiety, that there was nothing Hugo could do that was truly absurd. Now when he looked the way he did.

And certainly not when he was looking at her.

"You appear to be dressed as if you've been off visiting Regency England," she said dryly. And only she had to know that the dryness in her mouth was more physical response to him than any attempt on her part to sound indifferent.

"Naturally," Hugo said, as if an agreement. "I've been out terrifying the tenants and topping barmaids in my stagecoach." He raised a brow. "Or possibly I was attending a Halloween party, complete with fancy dress. You must be aware that it's the end of October."

She was aware of almost nothing but him. That was the terrifying truth that seared its way through her then, making her entire body feel…different. As if there was a fire in her bones, and it was changing her. Or had already done so, dream by dream, without her realizing it.

Hugo moved toward her in that graceful way of his, as if he was half liquid. When he drew too close, Eleanor desperately wanted to think of something appropriately boring and dampening to say—but instead found that she still couldn't seem to think of anything at all but the sensation of his mouth on hers.

His gaze darkened, as if her thoughts were written all over her face, but if they were he didn't say a word. He only kept moving, brushing past her and indicating that she should follow him with nothing more than a supremely arrogant tilt of his chin. And yet Eleanor found herself obeying.

As if this was as close to happy as she was likely to get.

Hugo stopped at the door at the far end of the gallery and looked back over his shoulder.

"Come," he said, and Eleanor didn't know if she was tempted or terrified. Or some far more potent combination of both.

All she knew was that she picked up her pace, on command.

And Hugo's dangerous mouth curved. "Perhaps it's time I conducted that interview, after all."

Hugo felt like the big, bad wolf.

It was not exactly unpleasant. God knew he'd had nothing to do these past years save sharpen his fangs.

And the distance he'd put between him and this governess who shouldn't have tempted him hadn't dulled a thing. Not the impossible lushness of her curves or that tiny waist that mesmerized him. Not her apparent inability to cower before him like almost every other person he encountered in this house.

Above all, it had failed to dull his reaction to her.

He was hard and needy in an instant, and inviting her into his private library was only going to make it worse. He knew he shouldn't do it. He knew better than to tempt himself—because when had he ever resisted temptation?

But when his hand was on the door, she stopped, and she looked at him as if she was fighting her way out of a magic spell.

"I can't… Is that your bedroom?"

Hugo was merely a man. And not a good one. It took everything he had not to throw her over his shoulder and carry her off to his actual bedroom.

"That tone of voice would be so much more effective if you were clutching a strand of pearls, I think," he said instead, like a bloody saint. Maybe that was why he sounded so gruff. "As it is, the offended virgin act needs a little bit of work."

Eleanor blinked, and straightened. "So I should take that as a yes, this is in fact your bedchamber."

There was no earthly reason why Hugo should be baring his teeth in a poor semblance of a smile, far too much wolf and very, very little of him—even that less than stellar man he usually was.

"If you are so eager to take to my bed, you need only ask. These games are so unbecoming, Miss Andrews. Do you not think?"

"Your Grace…"

But she didn't turn tail and run.

Hugo smirked at her, because it was that or touch her, and once he started he doubted he'd stop for at least a week. Maybe three. She'd haunted him across the planet, with her defiant gaze and her unimpressed mouth and all of her mouthwatering curves. He'd decided that if she was going to torture him, she might as well do it in person.

"Relax. This is my library. Not a den of iniquity." His lips twitched. "Depending, I suppose, on what books you choose to read."

He threw the door open and strode through. He did not look behind him to see if she followed because that, too, was tempting fate.

If she was walking away from him, he didn't know what he'd do.

The very thought appalled him. Who *hadn't* walked away from England's most reviled man? He welcomed it. He thrived on it. He certainly shouldn't care in the least what this governess did.

But once again, she followed him, and he was forced to admit he liked it. And that there was something else simmering in him when she shut the door behind her. It felt a bit too much like relief, though Hugo knew that couldn't be it. True villains felt nothing, through and through. They were made of stone and had no regrets.

Everybody said so.

He waved his hand at the comfortable leather chair before the crackling fire, and allowed himself a small, triumphant smile when she sat. Obediently. Despite that look in her dark eyes that suggested that at any moment, she might break for it.

Hugo told himself he wouldn't chase her if she did. Of course he wouldn't. But as he rid himself of the top hat and his great cloak, he wasn't entirely sure.

"I've been in the grand library downstairs," Eleanor

said after the silence drew out. "This is built on a smaller scale, but is no less impressive."

"I'm delighted you think so. I did wonder."

She was looking at his books, not him, but he was sure he saw her lips move as if she was biting back a smile.

"Fat mysteries next to battered paperbacks," she murmured, gazing around the room. "Ruminations on astral physics and—is that philosophy?—next to the entire series of Harry Potter books."

"Signed first editions, obviously."

"Careful," Eleanor said softly, still not looking at him. "Books tell a whole lot more about a person than the things they say. Or the things others say. Well-worn books tell all manner of inconvenient truths about their owners."

Something rushed through Hugo then, almost as if he was lightheaded. Or drunk.

Foreboding, he thought grimly.

As if, were she to look too closely at the truths his books told about him, she'd know what was real and what wasn't. And everything would change. *He* would change.

And Hugo was perfectly content to stay exactly as he was. Hated and all the more powerful for it. The more they made him into the bogeyman, the happier he was.

Because all those people who had bought Isobel's act deserved to imagine that the love child she'd made with that idiot Torquil was forced to pay for her parents' sins in the grip of a monster like him. They deserved to worry themselves sick about it, torturing themselves as they imagined scenes of neglect and abuse, because that was the least that could be expected from the villain Isobel had created.

"Every good story needs a villain, darling," she'd told him archly that first time.

That being the first time Hugo had woken to find a version of himself he didn't recognize in the papers. The first time he'd had the sickening realization that the fake version was more believable. That even when he tried to clear his name or at least tell a different side to the story, no one wanted to hear it. Terrible Hugo was far more compelling than the real one ever could have been.

He remembered the time he'd tracked her down across the planet in Santa Barbara, California, to demand that she stop the insanity, years into her game. That she stop telling those lies. That she leave him out of the sick games she liked to play with people's lives—and not because it bothered him. He'd long passed the point where anything she did could bother him. But his father had still been alive then, and it had wrecked the old man.

"Hurting your lovely old father isn't my goal, of course," Isobel had murmured, out by one of those impossibly still and blue California pools, all hipbones and malice in a tiny bikini. She'd smiled at him over her oversized sunglasses. *"It's a happy bonus, that's all."*

"There is nothing you can do to me, Isobel," he'd told her fiercely then. *"You cannot take my heritage from me. You cannot siphon off a single penny of my fortune. Whether I am liked or I am hated, I will still become the Duke in due course. Grovesmoor will carry on. Don't you understand? I'm bulletproof."*

But she'd only laughed at him.

"And I'm a better storyteller," she'd said.

Hugo had borne the brunt of that damned story of hers for years. He still did. But now he had his own weapon in the form of a child everyone assumed he hated and the world's endless censure.

And he had no intention of giving it up.

Certainly not to a governess with the body of a screen

idol and too much uncertain temper in her dark eyes. A woman who looked for truth in his books and didn't know when to back down from a fight she couldn't win.

No matter how much he wanted her.

CHAPTER SIX

ELEANOR COULD ONLY stare at the Duke's book collection for so long before it became awkward. Or rather, a little too obvious that she was going out of her way to avoid looking at him directly.

She told herself she was simply appreciating the amount of literature he kept on his shelves and at hand at all times, that was all. The truth was she'd never lived in a place where she could keep more than her absolute most favorite books on what little shelf space she could spare. She wouldn't have minded spending a few hours getting lost in this place.

But, of course, her employer had not called her into his library to offer her the chance to browse.

Pull yourself together, Eleanor, she chided herself.

She sat on the edge of a buttery soft leather chair, afraid to let herself sink back into it. Afraid she'd never pull herself out again. But when she was finally sure that her expression was nothing but serene and dared to look at him again, everything had gotten much worse.

Much, much worse.

Because while Hugo had removed that top hat and cloak that made him look like something out of the sort of fantasies Eleanor had never had before coming to Groves House, Hugo in nothing but exquisitely fitted dark trousers and a white shirt that opened at the neck was infinitely more dangerous.

And tempting in all kinds of ways she'd never experienced before in her life.

She could feel each and every temptation as if it was a separate strand of heat, swirling around inside of her and making her feel like a stranger to herself.

Hugo moved from the great desk where he'd carelessly tossed his coat and hat, and stalked across the room toward her. Of course he wasn't *stalking*, Eleanor told herself sharply. The man was simply walking from one end of the library to the other. The way people did when they wished to cross a space.

There was no reason at all that she should find herself holding her breath the way she was. Or clenching tight every single muscle in her body as she perched on the edge of that heavy chair, until she thought she might snap in half.

Hugo dropped himself down into the leather chair across from hers. He did not exactly sit nicely. Instead, of course, he sprawled. He was bigger every time she looked at him, it seemed, and his solidly built body covered more than simply the chair. His legs were long and he thrust them out before him, eating up the thick rug that was all that sat between their chairs.

He wasn't simply *sitting there*, Eleanor thought, with a mounting sense of unease. He seemed to claim the entire room with that offhanded masculine grace of his. As if he was the hazard, not the fire, which crackled away beside them and yet seemed to dim everything that wasn't Hugo.

It would be a lot easier, Eleanor reflected with no little hysteria, if the man was as seedy and dissolute as he'd always seemed in the tabloids. Instead of finely chiseled everywhere and exuding entirely too much sheer, powerful certainty the way other men reeked of cologne.

"How fares my ward?" Hugo asked.

So politely, so mildly, that Eleanor thought she must have been imagining the strange currents that seemed to fill the room—and her—with such an odd, electric sensation. It was clearly her, she told herself sternly. She was the one who was having some kind of allergic reaction to being in this man's presence. Or perhaps it was all those centuries of Grovesmoor influence and authority that he wore so easily when he was meant to be nothing but a layabout. Eleanor supposed it could even be the broad span of his shoulders, entirely too sculpted and athletic for a man so famously devoted to his own leisure.

But when she met his gaze, she understood that she wasn't suffering from some allergy to the aristocracy. Or if she was, he was too. Because his dark eyes burned with a bright, intent fire Eleanor didn't recognize, but could feel. Everywhere.

"Geraldine is very well," she said before she forgot to respond. Which wouldn't do at all.

Thinking about the little girl was the way to survive this, clearly. Eleanor made her spine as much of a straight line she could bear without actually hurting herself, and folded her hands neatly in her lap. She found that if she gazed at Hugo's chin instead of directly into his overwhelming, challenging gaze, she could pretend to be looking at him without actually risking too much direct eye contact.

And that little disconnection made it possible for her to catch her breath. To keep her heart from beating entirely too fast. Or anyway, pretend that she had herself under control, which would have to be enough.

"She's quite intelligent. And funny, it turns out. Not

all little girls are funny, of course." Eleanor felt herself flush slightly, because she sounded a great deal as if she was babbling. And she never babbled. "Not that I have vast experience with seven-year-old girls, but I was one."

Hugo looked boneless and hungry, and the combination made Eleanor's pulse dance.

"Some time ago, if I'm not mistaken," he said.

"A lady does not discuss her age, Your Grace."

"You're a governess, are you not? Not a lady in the classic sense, if you will excuse the pedantry. But more to the point, you're entirely too young to become mis-sish and coy about your age. Surely that is the province of women significantly longer in the tooth than you."

Eleanor found she was meeting his gaze, and had no idea when she'd given up the chin offensive. It was a mis-take. She felt as if she'd sat out in the sun too long and was now a miserable prickle everywhere she had skin.

"I'm twenty-seven, if that's what you're asking. And I hope that you're not asking that. Because that would be unpardonably rude."

Hugo's lips twitched. "The horror."

"And I'm surprised that a duke of England should bother himself to pull rank. Surely in the absence of a Windsor lurking about, that's a bit redundant."

"You cannot be surprised, Miss Andrews." The cor-ner of Hugo's mouth tipped up, but if that was a smile, it was entirely too dark. "I have yet to encounter a single story ever told about me that did not make it clear I am the worst kind of person. A stain upon the nation."

"Are you suggesting that I believe everything I've read about you? My understanding—" culled entirely from books and television and supermarket checkout queues, which she did not plan to share with him "—was that most celebrities claim that the things that are written about them in places like the tabloids are lies."

Something in his expression shifted. Eleanor couldn't put her finger on it. It was as if he turned quietly to stone, everywhere, even as his gaze changed. Melted, she would have said, if she were the fanciful sort. Into a far more powerful spirit, more intense than his usual whiskey.

"And if I were to tell you that, indeed, nearly everything that has ever been written about me in the press is a lie, you would believe that?"

Hugo wasn't exactly smirking, but there was no mistaking the challenge he'd thrown at her or the way he lounged there in the chair opposite her while he did it. His oddly intent gaze was taut on hers while one long finger tapped the side of his jaw, rough now instead of clean-shaven.

He looked decadent. Sinful.

Eleanor had absolutely no trouble believing every wicked thing she'd ever heard about him. Ever.

And it did absolutely nothing to diminish his appeal.

"Your reputation precedes you, of course, Your Grace," she said briskly, fighting to keep her wits about her when she couldn't seem to pull in a full breath. "But it is not your reputation that concerns me. It is your ward's education."

"A clever dodge, Miss Andrews, but I'd prefer it if you answered the question."

Eleanor reminded herself that this was not a situation that required her honesty. This man was not interested in her frank opinion of him. How could he be? Hugo was the Duke of Grovesmoor. And her employer. If he wanted to pretend that the stories about him were lies, it was only in Eleanor's best interest to agree.

Because, as her sister reminded her almost every

night, this was about the money. It was most certainly not about that odd weight in her chest that urged her to do the exact opposite of what she knew to be necessary. And smart.

She ignored that weight. She shoved it aside and pretended she couldn't feel it. She made herself smile. Politely.

"Everyone knows the tabloids are filled with lies," she murmured, hoping that placated him. "All smoke, no fire."

Hugo shook his head as if he were disappointed in her. "I believe you are lying, Miss Andrews, and I am shocked onto my soul." That curve in the corner of his mouth deepened. "And yes, I do have one. Clouded and murky though it may be."

It was entirely too easy to drift off, staring at this man in all his dark, threatening beauty, as if he was an approaching storm and the worst that could happen to her was that she'd get a bit wet. But she had to stop thinking of him that way. She had to do something about the strange signals her body sent off that made her entirely too nervous. That tightness in her breasts. The knotted thing in her belly. And that odd, melting sensation lower still.

She had to remember what she was doing here. It was about the money and it was about Geraldine, and all these strange electrical moments were distractions, nothing more.

Because of course they couldn't be anything more.

"I've given Geraldine a series of tests and have found she's well above her year in most areas. Whatever the previous fourteen governesses might have lacked, they were clearly decent tutors. She's very bright and quite advanced."

"I'm delighted to hear it." He did not sound delighted.

"I believe she will make you proud," Eleanor said, and realized almost instantly that it was the wrong thing to say. Of course it was the wrong thing to say. The child was not his. Geraldine was his ward, not his daughter. It was entirely possible that the only proud day of his life would be the day she reached her majority and was no longer his responsibility.

And none of that was her business, as Mrs. Redding had suggested.

"I'm sorry," she said quickly, before he could respond. Then, as if the apology needed explanation, she pushed on. "I always wanted to be a teacher when I was younger, but then I took a little bit of a detour."

"Into a number of office positions in London," he said, without consulting any notes. Meaning he just knew that. Eleanor told herself that wasn't strange at all, and there was absolutely no reason that prickling feeling should intensify until she felt goose bumps on her arms.

"Yes," she confirmed. "This governess position is new to me. Perhaps in my enthusiasm, I've overstepped."

For a long moment, Hugo said nothing. But it wasn't as if his silences were empty. On the contrary, everything felt thick. The air. That raw thing that kept expanding inside her chest, until once again, she didn't think she could pull in a full breath. But the longer she stared at his mesmerizing face, and those unholy eyes of his, the less she cared.

"You do not treat me like a monster, Miss Andrews." Hugo's voice was a smooth lick against the quiet that surrounded them. "I find it disconcerting that you do not, when everyone else does. Why don't you?"

Eleanor felt her lips part at that, and quickly snapped her mouth shut. "I don't know what you mean."

"I think you do. Women normally approach me in one of two ways. They either fling themselves at me, desperate for my touch and my attention. Or they cower, certain that a stray graze of my finger will ruin their reputations forever, and more importantly, leave them mere, shivering wrecks of their former selves thanks to my supposed evil powers—but not in any fun way. Yet you do neither."

There was a note in his voice that she didn't understand, but it seemed to wind its way through her like honey. Or something far more intoxicating.

"I apologize, Your Grace," she managed to say. "I was unaware that a certain reaction was called for the part of the job. To you, I mean. Perhaps it's silly of me, but I thought my relationship with Geraldine was the point."

"No one takes this job for the child. One way or another, they always take it for me. The fact that you do not wish to admit this only makes you more curious. And I should not have to tell you that making yourself the focus of my attention…has consequences."

Eleanor was clenching her hands together entirely too tightly, something she only noticed when they went numb. She forced herself to unlace her fingers and sensation came back in a rush. She ignored it when they began to sting.

"I would prefer not to be crass, Your Grace, but you give me no choice."

"I am all ears, of course. I enjoy crassness very much. You must realize this."

"I'm sure you're a very nice man. Deep down," she added at his snort. "But of course you must realize that the position's salary is what's attractive. While you have a certain charm, I suppose, that really isn't why I came. I told you before. I was assured—repeatedly—that I would never see you."

"I have a very large and extraordinarily healthy ego, Miss Andrews, and yet it withers before you. Most women would scramble up the Cliffs of Dover if they imagined they might catch a glimpse of me."

"I suspect your ego is quite robust and will survive handily. And I am not most women."

"You most certainly are not."

Eleanor caught herself before she flung something back at him. There was no call to come over all caustic and acerbic, which seemed to be her happy place where the Duke was concerned. It wouldn't help her in any way to actively antagonize him. Hugo might have been eyeing her in very much the same way a large, indolent house cat might an extremely foolish mouse. But that didn't mean she should scamper out there of her own volition and show him her belly.

Think of the money, she told herself sternly. *Think of Vivi.*

She surged up and onto her feet at that. "It's late, Your Grace."

"It is not yet midnight." He didn't bother to glance at the watch on his wrist, which Eleanor could tell must have cost a fortune or two, since it looked like it belonged on the side of an old town hall in Prague. "It is scarcely ten."

"Which is late for those of us who rise with small children in the morning."

"There it is," he said softly and, if she was not mistaken, with some satisfaction. "There is that fear of me I recognize."

"It's not fear, it's anxiety," she corrected him. "It makes me anxious to have these confusing conversations. Surely you can understand that. I work for you."

"Of course I can't understand any such thing. I've never worked for anyone in all my days."

Eleanor waved a hand at the stuffed shelves on all sides. "Thank goodness you have all these books, then, to allow you a different perspective than your own."

"I think you're lying again, Miss Andrews," Hugo said, and his voice had gone silky. Dark. Something much worse than simply decadent.

And it shuddered through Eleanor. It made her ache. Everywhere.

Her pulse fluttered about weakly and she thought perhaps she shouldn't have had those prawns for her tea. Then she wondered what had become of her that she was standing here, actively wishing she was ill. Instead of the alternative.

"You've lost me once again," she told him. Faintly.

"What you're feeling right now is not fear," Hugo told her, and there was that certainty again. Pouring out of him as if he'd never suffered a moment's doubt about anything in his charmed life. "Or anxiety about speaking to your employer. You can feel how quickly your heart beats, can you not? And that hot and restless yearning in the pit of your stomach?"

She flushed hot and, she feared, red. "No."

"The funny thing about a man like me is that I cannot abide lies to my face. There are too many in print." He smiled. "Try again."

"I'm a bit overtired, actually. I'd like to be excused so I can take to my bed, please."

"Bed is the cure, Miss Andrews, but I'm not talking about sleeping. And I think you know it."

Eleanor found she was gaping at him. Again. And this time, she didn't have it in her to do anything about it.

"Are you... You can't..."

And Hugo laughed, stealing the heat from the fire and the air from the room.

Then, worse, he unfolded himself from his chair and rose to his feet. And suddenly, the library seemed like a closed fist—a vicious and unbreakable grip all around her. Forget breathing—Eleanor wasn't sure she could stand. But she also couldn't seem to move away the way everything in her screamed she should. It was as if she was frozen in place, though there wasn't a single part of her that was cold.

Not one.

"You look very much like a woman who can think of nothing at all but the way I might kiss you," Hugo said softly.

"That can't happen," Eleanor breathed.

"It already has. It will again. I'm afraid it is inevitable."

He reached over and fit his hands to her cheeks. And as if that was not bad enough, he used one thumb to trace slowly, lazily over her mouth, as if he was learning the contours of her lips.

If he'd doused her in gasoline and lit a match, she could not have burned hotter. Or brighter. And god help her, it was all so *wrong*.

"See?" His voice was so low, so sure, it seemed to interfere with her ribs. "Not fear at all."

He shifted, lifting her chin and her face toward his, and Eleanor panicked. Or anyway, that was what she thought that was, that blinding rush of sensation that was too electric and too impossible to be borne.

"I'm asexual," she blurted out.

She expected that announcement to stop him. To stop everything. To make all of this stop pulsing and whirling and make a little sense again.

But Hugo made a noise, deep in his throat, that sounded like a cross between a laugh and a sort of growl.

He didn't let her go. If anything, his hands held her faster. And she felt them in even more places.

"Are you?" He didn't sound particularly fussed.

"Well, yes." This close, it was almost impossible to remember what she meant to say—it was those eyes of his. And worse, his mouth. His lush, wicked mouth, that hovered far too close to hers and made everything in her a molten sort of heat. "I always have been, I suppose."

"Have you?"

"Yes," she said, with a bit more asperity. She would have kicked herself if she could. And if she could remember how to operate her legs. "I don't feel things, you see. I'm sorry if that makes things awkward."

"It would," Hugo agreed. He moved closer to her, making his impossibly well-formed chest part of the whole... problem. "But I think you feel quite a lot."

"I most certainly do not," Eleanor retorted, despite the fact that she did indeed feel entirely too much. Everywhere. And constantly. And she couldn't tell if she was sick or panicked or something in between. But she was certain there was some other explanation than the heat she could see in his whiskey-colored eyes.

"I suspect that what you've been, little one," Hugo murmured, his voice a low rumble that she could feel inside of her like a kind of earthquake, "is bored."

And then he set his mouth to hers, and proved it.

CHAPTER SEVEN

THIS KISS WAS different from the last.

Eleanor would not have imagined in a million years that she would ever be in a position where she was noting the difference between kisses, having never expected to spend much time kissing anyone, but here she was. This one was different than the lazy way he'd taken her mouth in the hall outside the nursery.

Much different. Much…hotter.

There was urgency this time. Bright fire and driving need.

Or maybe, she thought with no little wonder, that was her.

Hugo dropped his hands from her face and slid them down her back. He pulled her up against him, and it was as if everything inside her head simply went white. Blank. She disappeared into the sound of her heart, clattering wildly against her ribs, and the impossible, wild beauty of his mouth on hers.

Over and over again.

In some distant part of her mind, Eleanor knew this was a mistake. *She knew it.* But she couldn't seem to stop herself. She didn't *want* to stop herself. He angled his head and took the kiss deeper. Hotter. Wetter and wilder.

And she was content to let him guide her. Teach her. Take her over and burn her alive.

He kissed her again and again, bending her backward as he did. One of his hands found the small of her back and held her fast against him as he continued to use that mouth of his like some kind of slick weapon. Eleanor found her arms around his neck, but had no memory of putting them there. Maybe there was something inside of her that knew she needed to hold on. Or be lost forever in this storm she should have had the good sense to avoid.

But she didn't want to avoid it. She wanted to dance in it. She wanted to shout down the thunder and let the rain wash her clean.

She didn't even know what that meant, but she wanted it, and every time he dragged his lips across hers, she thrilled to it.

And then there was what he did with his hands. She couldn't work out which was worse, that he seemed to know her so much better than she knew herself, or that she was afraid she might explode with every sizzling new touch.

He slid his free hand down her side as if he was testing her shape, spilling heat wherever he went, then sliding around to grip her bottom and pull her even closer.

"Perfect," he muttered against her mouth, and a sheer, shivery sort of reaction burst inside of her at that.

Pleasure, she thought. *Pure pleasure.*

She had never allowed herself that sort of thing before. She hadn't known it existed, if she was honest. But Hugo's hands on her body opened up a new window into near-unimaginable delights and Eleanor couldn't seem to keep herself from tossing herself headfirst into them. Whatever they were. Whatever the price.

"More," Hugo said in a low, dangerously gruff voice, moving his mouth down the line of her neck.

And when the world seemed to shift, the floor moving beneath them and the fire spinning in a giddy loop, it took Eleanor a moment to realize that it was because Hugo was doing it. She didn't think her feet hit the ground as he picked her up and swung her around until her back was to the bookshelf.

Then he pressed himself against her as if he couldn't bear another inch of separation between them.

Eleanor supposed she should have objected to that—to all of it—but she was entirely too busy being overwhelmed by him. All of him. Her mind could hardly keep up with what was happening to her body. What he was *doing* to her body.

And what her body was doing to her, every time she shivered. Every time she surrendered. Every time she let out sounds she didn't recognize.

Hugo's mouth was a torment. A reward. Both at once.

He stroked his hands down the length of her arms and threaded his fingers with hers. Then, never breaking contact with her lips, he lifted her arms up above her and pinned her wrists to the bookshelves at her back.

"Stay still," he ordered her.

And it didn't occur to Eleanor to do anything but obey him. She was quivering too much. She was too undone. She was lost in this, whatever it was, and she wasn't sure she could make her way out of it.

Scarier still, she wasn't sure she wanted out in the first place.

Hugo muttered something that she couldn't quite make sense of, and then he shifted back slightly so he could look down at her, moving his hands so that one rested on each side of her face. In some far-off corner of her mind it occurred to Eleanor to worry that he might find her lacking. That looking at her the way he was might break this spell, whatever it was. Because this was a man who could sleep with any of the great beauties of their age at will. And had.

But when he finally dragged his gaze back to hers, all thoughts and insecurities vanished. Because Eleanor might not have done this before. She might have no idea how this had happened or what she was meant to do next. But she'd never seen anything so hot or so needy in all her life as that look on Hugo's face.

It was so intense it felt like a kind of devastation, rolling over her and flattening her and changing her, but she was still standing.

Somehow, she was still standing, and she couldn't seem to step away from him. She couldn't even bring herself to try.

Hugo moved then. He traced his way down her neck, then moved his hands to cup her breasts, making her breath desert her in an audible rush that embarrassed her, it was obvious. But there was something reverent in the way his hands curved around her, testing her through the layers she wore and dragging those expert thumbs of his over her nipples—and the crazy part was that she could still feel the heat of his palms. Flooding into her. Making her feel even more needy and wild.

He made another one of those distinctly male noises deep in his throat, low and somehow untamed, that made everything inside Eleanor bristle into a kind of liquid awareness. Shocking and bright, even as it pooled low in her belly.

"Later," he said, and it sounded like a promise.

Eleanor had no idea what he was talking about. And she didn't care, because he kept going. He bent closer to her as he traced his way down the length of her body, finding the indentation of her waist and then the swell of her hips and taking his time learning both.

And then he found his way to the fastening of her trousers, and it was as if everything inside of her toppled over and crumbled into dust. Just like that.

"I told you not to move your hands." Hugo's voice was dark, demanding.

And it wasn't until he spoke that Eleanor realized she'd brought her hands down toward his shoulders. To push him away? To draw him closer? She had no idea. But she did as he asked, because she couldn't think of what else to do, and she raised her arms back up over her head again.

And Hugo simply pulled the fastening of her trousers open, then dipped his hand inside, as if it was inevitable.

It felt as if it was.

There was no sound in the library. There was the snap and rustle of the fire, and then a harsh sort of noise that it took Eleanor long moments to realize was her own breathing. Panting, more like, that she could barely hear over the noise in her head that she thought was her heart. Beating madly.

But if Hugo heard any of it, he liked it. That was what that hard smile on his beautiful face told her. She could feel it wash over her like its own sort of glare, making her feel exposed. As if he could see things she wasn't even aware she was showing.

"I'm pleased that you're allowing this experiment, little one," he said, a certain satisfaction in his voice that should have alarmed her. She knew it should have, but she couldn't quite bring herself to react to it. "Given how well you know your own desires."

"I don't know what you…"

"Hush."

Once again, Eleanor obeyed him. Because he was sliding his fingers down, down, all the way into her panties, and that made everything in her…constrict. Shudder.

And then he curved his fingers around to cup her where no one else had ever touched her.

Eleanor realized as her legs went to jelly that she lacked the ability to stand.

But Hugo was holding her up with that big body of his and one hard hand at her hip. Even when he let out the sort of laugh that should have been outlawed as a public safety hazard, he kept her upright.

"I must tell you, Miss Andrews, you are remarkably wet for one who claims she is asexual."

"Wet?" she asked. On a choppy little breath.

"Very, very wet," Hugo amended, his voice little more than a dark growl.

And then he began to stroke her.

Sensation buffeted her from all sides. He was all around her. He loomed above her, and his shoulders blocked out the rest of the house, and more, the world she could hardly recall outside it. She could smell him, an intriguing male scent that put her in mind of the fire behind them and soft, buttery leather, only much warmer. She could taste him in her mouth, like the kind of spirits she only dared sip at Christmastime, and then only in minuscule quantities.

And she could feel him. Good god, could she feel him.

He moved the hand at her hip back to her jaw, smoothing his palm around to hold her where he wanted her. And there was a smile on his face when he lowered his head to take her mouth once more.

Eleanor could taste that, too. And god help her, he was like a bottle of the good stuff, with every demanding slide of his tongue against hers.

And all the while, he stroked her. He slipped in and around her folds, slippery and hot when she'd never felt anything like it before. When surely it should mean something was wrong, but nothing *felt* wrong.

Eleanor couldn't think. She couldn't control herself. She was lost between his mouth and his hand, and she simply followed the rhythm he set as he built that storm in her.

Higher and higher. Darker and wilder.

And she didn't know when it dawned on her that it was going to break. That the tightness in her belly and the need and the hunger could only go one way, and it was going to happen whether she wanted it or not. That the wall that seemed to bear down on her was entirely unavoidable, and coming much too fast—

"Don't fight it, little one," Hugo murmured. He lifted his mouth from hers the slightest little bit, so Eleanor could taste his words on her lips.

"I'm not fighting anything," Eleanor gasped out. Crossly.

But then it was happening.

It was like a golden sort of crash, fast and slow at once. A shower of fire and sparks, magic and longing, as debilitating as it was delicious. It roared through her, from the top of her head straight down to the tips of her toes that she dug into the floor beneath her feet as if that could keep her holding on.

She bumped against his marvelous, wicked hand and she threw her head back, and still his mouth was there against her neck, urging her on. Taking her wherever he wanted to take her, and all she could do was let him.

He was even laughing slightly, she noticed with something like panic, as she fell and fell and fell.

And hoped like hell that Hugo would catch her on the other side.

* * *

Making his starchy little governess come apart beneath his hands was the hottest thing Hugo could remember doing.

Ever.

The little sounds she made. The dazed wonder in her wide eyes. Even that frown at the end, and her sharp little voice before she broke to pieces.

He didn't understand how it was possible when he should have no further to sink, but Eleanor Andrews was ruining him.

But Hugo shoved that aside. For any number of reasons, not least of which was the fact that he had already been ruined. A long, long time ago. There was no lower place for Hugo Grovesmoor to go. He should know. He'd tried to find it over and over again.

And no innocent woman deserved a man that self-destructive. Especially not a woman like this one, who had confused her own inexperience for disinterest. That was how little she knew of men.

He would eat her alive.

And it said something about him, didn't it, that he rather liked that idea.

She was limp and dazed and breathing heavily, so he shifted her off the bookcase and swept her up into his arms, entirely too aware of the way she melted against him. He carried her over to the wide sofa and settled her on it, more than a little concerned about how uncharacteristically gentle he was with this woman. Automatically. When he was not exactly known for his sweet bedside manner. He did not lounge around, shyly reading verses of poetry from slim volumes and softly asking permission to touch a lover's ankle.

Please.

Hugo had always assumed that what poetry was in him was rough and raw and best expressed with his hands. And his body.

And the dark things he could do with both. And did, again and again.

He'd never had any complaints. In person, that was. The tabloids were a different story, but even those fabricated fantasies never claimed he was a bad lover. Simply that he was a very, very bad man.

But still. Untried innocence was not his thing. No matter how sweet the taste, still there on his tongue. Driving him that much closer to madness.

He made himself stand, something furious in his chest and all that leftover heat and hardness making his trousers feel too tight, and waited for her to come back to him.

It took her a long time. And it occurred to him that a woman who fancied herself asexual and was so obviously a stranger to her own body was perhaps significantly less experienced than he'd been thinking. Almost as if she was something more than "inexperienced." Almost as if...

But that was impossible, of course. This wasn't the dark ages.

"Are you a virgin?" he asked, perhaps a bit too abruptly.

On the deep leather couch, Eleanor stirred. She looked around as if she didn't know where she was, and didn't recognize the library either way. Or him. She sat a little bit straighter as she took him in. Her hands went first to her head and she smoothed back the one or two strands that had dared to come loose from that ruthless bun she always wore. Only then, when she'd secured her dark hair in its cage, did she shift against the seat, look down, and note that her trousers were still wide open.

And Hugo found he was captivated by the red flush

that took her over, staining her cheeks and making her brown eyes gleam from beneath her fringe with that hint of honey that he thought might be his undoing.

Eleanor swallowed, hard, and he saw a frown etch itself between her eyes again. But she didn't say anything. She only fastened her trousers and sat a bit straighter. Only then did she look up at him, and something about the steady way she did it made him feel like the monster he knew he was. More so than usual, that was.

She looked breakable.

It should have made him hate himself all the more, that he should so effortlessly stain whatever he touched. But that was not his primary reaction to the mounting evidence that no one had touched Eleanor but him.

Indeed, what he was feeling—in every part of him, like a thread of wild heat—was significantly more primitive.

"Whether I am or am not a virgin, I can't imagine how that's any of your business at all," she said coolly. Her brows rose slightly. Arrogantly, he would have said, had anyone ever managed to outdo him in that arena. "Your Grace."

And Hugo stopped feeling badly about the whole thing.

"That is not a very nice tone to take with a man who just made you come," he pointed out, all silk and threat. "So hard you nearly broke off the shelf of an ancient bookcase."

"The bookcase appears to be holding up just fine."

"Given that you had your back arched and your eyes closed while you rode my hand, I rather doubt you have the slightest idea how close you came to bringing down the whole of my collection on your head."

"I wish it had," she said, and while her gaze grew

darker, her tone only chilled further. "Everything that's happened here is almost too inappropriate to bear. I will tender my resignation in the morning, of course."

Hugo lifted one shoulder, then dropped it. "If you wish. But it will be a wasted effort. I won't accept it."

She scowled at him. "Of course you will."

He didn't know why she amused him. She shouldn't have. He'd fired many of her predecessors for far less than this. The one who'd tracked him down in the gardens to let him know she was without her undergarments. The one who'd pouted prettily at him over Geraldine's head when the child had needed a doctor. The alarming one who'd left lavender-scented unmentionables all over the house, for servants and Hugo alike to find in the most curious of places. He hadn't thought twice about sacking any of them.

He should have welcomed Eleanor's resignation. Hell, he should have demanded it himself the moment he'd seen her outside the nursery, divested of that awful coat and obviously a problem. With killer curves.

Hugo had no idea what the hell was wrong with him.

"I fear I must remind you—and not for the first time— that I am the Duke of Grovesmoor."

"I know who you are. Everybody knows who you are."

"Then you should know how pointless it is to argue with me." He watched as she rose to her feet, and didn't bother to hide his satisfaction when she had to reach out a hand to steady herself. "Instead of discussing resignations that will never come to pass, why don't you tell me why you insist on scraping your hair back into that painful-looking bun?"

"Because it's professional," she snapped. "And also none of your business."

Hugo kept his gaze trained on hers. Very slowly, very

deliberately, he lifted his hand and put the fingers he'd sunk deep inside of her softness into his own mouth. Then licked them clean.

Her mouth fell open. Her pretty face went pale, then red.

"I can still taste you, Eleanor," he said, a bit more roughly than planned, because she affected him too damned much. "It's a bit too late for boundaries, don't you think?"

Eleanor flinched. And he wasn't at all surprised when she turned around, then fled the library and his presence, coming as close to running from the room as a person could without actually breaking into a sprint.

Hugo didn't blame her at all.

He blamed himself. And the fact he really could taste her, sweet and sharp and intoxicating, was his own cross to bear as the night wore on. As he sat in his library and brooded into his fire and contemplated just how destroyed he was. How much of a monster was he, really, if he'd become the disreputable, distasteful Old Duke locked away in his ancient house, terrifying virgins? Why not simply start belching out flames and singeing the livestock, while he was at it?

But when the next day came and went with no resignation letter on his desk and Eleanor still in residence, his commitment to his self-flagellation…shifted.

Because it was one thing to lure an unwilling virgin into his dragon's lair.

It was something else again when she knew who he was, and what he might do…and stayed anyway.

CHAPTER EIGHT

"You have a visitor."

Eleanor looked up from the textbook she and Geraldine were poring over in the grand library to see Mrs. Redding standing over them, looking more crisp and disapproving than usual. Which was quite a feat.

"A visitor?" she echoed, trying to work out from the other woman's expression what that could possibly mean. Eleanor didn't know anyone in the area. Aside from a few rambles about the village with Geraldine, she hadn't spent much time off Hugo's estate in the five and a half weeks she'd been here.

"It is not encouraged for staff to invite friends and family to the estate," the housekeeper said coldly, as if she'd caught Eleanor throwing a party like an errant teen. "We are not guests of His Grace. We are members of his staff. I'm certain this was covered extensively in the interview with the placement agency."

"I haven't invited anyone," Eleanor protested, but it was no use. Having rendered her judgment, Mrs. Redding had already turned and was making her brisk way to the door, every line of her body showing her offense at Eleanor's transgression.

Eleanor gave Geraldine a reading assignment to keep

her occupied, then followed Mrs. Redding's crisp footsteps toward the front of the house.

There was only one person who knew where she was, but there was no way Vivi would be here, surely. Vivi preferred to stay in the bright lights of London, or in the posh homes of friends abroad. She certainly didn't venture into the north of England. Under any circumstances.

That's a bit harsh, isn't it? she chastised herself as she walked.

Something was the matter with her. It had been growing inside of her since that terrible night in the Duke's private library a week ago. As if he'd infected her with his touch. With the things he'd made her feel. She found herself tense and strange. Snappish with Vivi on the phone and even less able to sleep than she had been before.

It was her horror with her own behavior, she told herself stoutly as she made her way toward the great foyer. She'd allowed herself to be compromised and worse, she kept letting it happen.

The Duke hadn't touched her again, which meant it was all she thought about.

But what he was doing was worse. Dropping by Geraldine's lessons as the mood took him, for example, when Eleanor had assumed he was off somewhere else being Hugo on his usual international stage.

"This does not sound like the Latin I was forced to learn," Hugo had said from behind her, out in the back gardens one unexpectedly fine morning, making Eleanor jump as she walked and then instantly try to conceal her reaction from Geraldine.

"It's French," Eleanor had said sternly.

"I am aware of that, thank you," Hugo had replied as he'd moved to walk beside her. In French, which had made Geraldine giggle.

And Eleanor had wanted nothing more than to ask him to leave them to their walk and French conversation, but, of course, she couldn't. It was his property. And his ward, for that matter. But she'd been psyching herself up to demand he respect Geraldine's lesson time when he started talking to the little girl directly.

In perfect French, unlike Eleanor's, which had been cobbled together from her time in school and the job she'd had for a year when she was barely twenty at a French company based in England.

And he kept it up for the better part of the next twenty minutes, as if Eleanor wasn't there.

It had made her heart beat a little too fast in her chest. And it had made Geraldine glow, which was worse—because Eleanor had no defense against her scrappy charge.

And when he took his leave he bowed to Geraldine and only pinned Eleanor briefly with an unreadable look in his dark whiskey eyes. That had haunted her long after.

"Come have dinner with me," he'd said another afternoon, appearing in the library when Eleanor had thought she and Geraldine were on their own.

Eleanor had instantly checked to see where the little girl was, but she was still at one of the tables in the center of the huge library, poring over a dictionary as she picked ten vocabulary words to use in the new story she was writing in the journal Eleanor had her keep.

"I appreciate the offer, Your Grace," she'd said as frostily as possible. *"But I'm afraid that's impossible."*

"For all you know I intended to whisk you off to Rome for the evening."

Eleanor scowled at the book in front of her, though she'd stopped seeing the words on the page in front of her the moment he'd materialized at her side. *"That would be almost incomprehensibly inappropriate."*

"I would hate to be incomprehensible," Hugo had murmured in that sardonic tone of his that made her think of his body pressed against hers and his clever hands between her legs. *"My private dining room will have to do."*

"That is equally inappropriate," she'd said sharply.

"But more comprehensible."

"Your Grace—"

"It's a bit late for that, Eleanor," he'd said quietly. *"Don't you think?"*

"I do not think," she'd retorted, struggling to keep her voice in a whisper. She'd glanced at Geraldine, then back at Hugo again. *"This is a game to you. But it's a job to me. And more people than just me depend on it."*

Hugo's impossible mouth had shifted into one of those half smiles that haunted Eleanor when she slept. And when she wasn't sleeping, too.

"If I hadn't tasted your innocence myself I'd assume that meant you had a child of your own hidden away somewhere."

"I don't have a child, I have a sister," Eleanor had said in an undertone.

"A younger sister?"

"Vivi is twenty-five."

"And she is unwell?"

Eleanor had frowned at him. *"No, she isn't unwell. But I'm the one who pays the bills."*

One of Hugo's brows rose. *"You pay for your twenty-five-year-old sister?"*

And it had occurred to Eleanor that she'd never had to explain her situation to anyone before. Most people didn't ask such impertinent questions and if they had, she wouldn't have felt compelled to answer them.

"It's complicated," she'd said after a moment. *"Vivi is very talented, but it's not always easy to find the right*

*place for her to shine. Once she does, everything will
seem a good deal more...balanced."*

There had been something entirely too perceptive in
Hugo's gaze, then.

*"Are you trying to convince me?" he'd asked. "Or
yourself?"*

When Geraldine had called out that she was finished,
breaking the tight little knot that had seemed to hold
them both where they stood, Eleanor had been unrea-
sonably grateful.

Hugo made her feel like she no longer fit in her own
body.

Not that she felt much like herself now, she was forced
to admit as she hurried along the main floor toward the
foyer.

Who exactly are you? a little voice asked from deep inside her, and to her shame it sounded a little too much like
Hugo's. *Who exactly are you so desperate to hold on to?*

She shook her head to get that voice to shut up, for a
change. And then she turned the final corner that delivered her into the great foyer and stopped.

Because Vivi was standing there.

For a moment, Eleanor couldn't make any sense of it.

There was no reason on earth for Vivi to be in Yorkshire, much less in the grand foyer of Groves House. Back
in London, when Eleanor had asked if her sister planned
to come up and visit her when she finally got a break
after her first six weeks, Vivi had been noncommittal.

*I can't possibly know what I'll be doing so far in the
future,* she'd said. Dismissively, Eleanor thought now.
But at the time she hadn't thought much of it. That was
Vivi's style, after all. So effervescent and carefree that
she never knew what she was going to be doing from

one moment to the next, much less six weeks out. *But I doubt very much that I'll have any business in Yorkshire.*

But she'd said *Yorkshire* the way some people might say *nuclear waste facility.*

Eleanor told herself she had to be mistaken, but the woman who stood at the other end of the foyer was indisputably Vivi. She was microscopically thin, the better to show off the excruciatingly expensive designer jeans she wore thrust down low on her jutting hipbones. The denim licked down her minuscule thighs before disappearing into a pair of recognizably chic boots. She wore the sort of coat and scarf that would not look out of place in Sloane Square, and she wore her hair in the usual temperamental way. It was wild and wavy, pouring down her back and over her shoulders in an artful sort of tangle that was meant to look as if it never saw a brush or a styling tool, when the fact was, it took hours for Vivi to make it look just so. As she moved closer, Eleanor could see that her sister's lips were pursed slightly as she took in the wealth on display across every inch of the deliberately jaw-dropping entryway. More, she had a particular gleam in her eyes that Eleanor recognized all too well.

Avaricious, that voice inside her whispered.

Eleanor told herself to stop. She was being severe and unfair. She should have been delighted to see her little sister. She was. Of course she was.

"Vivi? What are you doing here? Is everything all right?"

Vivi took her time meeting Eleanor's gaze. Her own lingered on the walls, on all that gold and gilt, stretching out in all directions. Statues and flowers and paintings that went all the way up to heaven and back. And that was just the foyer.

"Aren't you the dark horse," Vivi murmured.

"You don't look as if anything terrible has happened," Eleanor continued, telling herself that there was no need to read into her sister's dark tone.

Vivi eyed her, her hands stuck into the back pockets of her jeans and her hips thrust out in what could only be called an aggressive posture. Eleanor ignored that, too.

"You told me this place was a tired old mausoleum. A crumbling pile of rocks, plunked down in the middle of a moor with heather growing all over it like a weed." Vivi sniffed and jutted her chin at all the lavish displays before her. "Apparently not."

"You were the one who called it a pile of rocks," Eleanor pointed out, still keeping her voice calm and even and something like soothing. "I just didn't argue."

"I had no idea you were so secretive, Eleanor. Is that a new personality trait?"

"Surely you didn't really think that the Duke of Grovesmoor lived in a crumbling pile of stones." Eleanor made herself smile. "Given that he owns the better part of England."

"It's quite intriguing that you've decided you need to keep secrets from me now that you work in such a posh old house, isn't it?"

There was no denying the fact that there was more than little attitude in her sister's voice. But Eleanor ordered herself to remain calm, and not only because she never called her miracle of a sister out on anything, much less *tone*. But because she couldn't trust the things that were happening inside of her.

The truth was that she hadn't felt much like herself since Hugo had kissed her that first time. Maybe Vivi was right and Eleanor had gone squirrely and secretive. She'd never done anything like that before.

And when, exactly, were you permitted to have any

kind of a life before? that voice inside demanded. *Or have you forgotten that your whole existence is catering to Vivi's life, not yours? She just doesn't like imagining that anything might have shifted.*

It was possible that Eleanor didn't really like it all that much, either.

"If I failed to tell you something it wasn't for any nefarious reason," she said, still keeping her voice even. "I thought you knew everything there was to know about this position. You're the one who recommended I interview for it in the first place."

Vivi shook her hair back from her face, though none had fallen forward. "I assumed he'd thrown the kid in some second-rate cottage somewhere rustic. Not *this.*"

Eleanor did not rise to the defense of *the kid.* She did not dig into Vivi's assumptions about rustic cottages. And she did not ask herself why it was apparently perfectly all right for her to live somewhere not quite as nice as Groves House. Because Vivi didn't mean it. Vivi came across as thoughtless, but only because every thought that moved through her head came out of her mouth, not because she harbored any ill will. It was part of the larger-than-life charm that Eleanor had been grateful for every single moment since Vivi hadn't died in the car accident that had claimed their parents.

She reached out a hand to place it on her sister's arm and build a bridge, but Vivi pulled away.

"Vivi, whatever is the matter?" she asked.

And she wasn't surprised when her sister's expressive eyes filled with emotion. Not quite tears, but their glassy precursor. This felt like normal, suddenly. Like common ground again. Vivi had problems and Eleanor fixed them. That was the way the world turned.

"Everything." Vivi's voice was ever so slightly husky,

as if from the force of her feelings. "The rent wasn't paid. The credit card is full. The flat is a *complete* tip. I can't find anything and what I can find is filthy and I don't know what to do about any of it."

"You didn't pay the rent? And you went over the maximum on the credit card?" Eleanor shook her head, feeling dazed. "But I left you the money—"

"And that's not the worst of it. Peter's asked Sabrina to marry him." Vivi stared at Eleanor as if she should have an explosive response to that bit of news. Eleanor only blinked and Vivi made a frustrated, impatient sort of noise. "*Lord* Peter, Eleanor. Hello. Only the man who's been crucial to my happiness for as long as I can remember."

"As long as you can remember," Eleanor repeated dryly.

Vivi waved a hand. "This past month, anyway. We've been *quite* close."

"And by this past month," Eleanor said, trying her best not to panic at what Vivi must have done to their finances in so short a time, "do you mean the month that I've been here, in this house that you might have noticed is miles and miles away from anything, teaching lessons to a seven-year-old child?"

"The point is that everyone thought that I was in with a chance," Vivi complained. "But he chose *Sabrina*, of all people. The cow. She's no better than she has to be and who cares if her father has all that money? But everything's gone pear-shaped." Vivi held Eleanor's gaze for a moment, then shifted to look around the foyer again, almost as if she was calculating something as she did. "It was time to make myself scarce, that's all. I thought I'd hole up with you for a little while."

"Vivi," Eleanor said softly. "What did you do?"

Her sister shrugged, though it was more of a defensive gesture than anything else. "Some people need to learn how to have a bit of a laugh, that's all."

Eleanor suddenly became very aware of where they were standing. The foyer appeared empty, but Eleanor had been in Groves House too long now. She knew that the Duke's staff were everywhere. That every word was being watched, recorded, judged. That whatever Vivi might have done, the whole house didn't need to know about it.

Though it was entirely possible that all of England would, if she'd got up to her usual tricks. And found her way into the tabloids again. Of course, Vivi would likely view that sort of exposure as a great success.

"Come on," Eleanor said, reaching out once more and this time, actually taking hold of her sister's arm. "This is not the place to talk about this. We'll go somewhere a bit more private."

Vivi certainly didn't evidence any sense of urgency as she sauntered along, letting Eleanor keep hold of her as they walked. Eleanor didn't know why it made her teeth clench, hard. This was nothing new. This was who Vivi was. She never thought things through. The rent, the credit card, whatever idiotic thing she'd done to Lord Whoever and his new fiancée. She expected the whole world to revolve all around her, and because of that, it usually did.

Or Eleanor's did, anyway. It always had.

But Groves House wasn't the place for Vivi, something deep and dark in Eleanor's gut insisted. She couldn't let her sister take—

Eleanor was ashamed of herself. There was nothing here that was hers. There was nothing anyone could take from her, especially not the sister she loved. The sister she would give anything to if she had the chance. The sister who had somehow survived that accident, and kept Eleanor for being all on her own.

That was what she was telling herself, fiercely and on repeat, when she turned the corner that led toward the nursery wing where her rooms were and nearly ran straight into Hugo.

And she knew who she was then, in an instant. She knew too much about the feelings she'd been telling herself were uncertain for so long now. Particularly after what happened in his library a week ago. Oh, the lies she'd told herself to explain it all away...

But there was nothing but truth here, pouring into the hallway like the diffident light of the afternoon outside.

Eleanor did not want Vivi to meet Hugo.

There was something inside of her, hunched and ugly, all claws and spite. And it was dragging all of its sharp edges around and around in the pit of Eleanor's stomach, because it wanted to avoid this. It would have done anything to avoid exactly this.

She did not want Hugo to behold her vibrant, charming sister who wrapped men like him around her fingers.

Or tries, anyway, that ugly little voice hissed.

But it was too late.

Because Vivi recognized Hugo instantly. Of course she did. Eleanor knew her sister, but even if she hadn't she'd have understood the change in her sister's body language. Suddenly everything was languid, easy. Suddenly Vivi's eyes seemed smoky, and the little giggle she let out was the same.

Eleanor had never wanted to slap her hand over her sister's mouth before. Or at least, she'd never wanted it this badly.

"I had no idea, Miss Andrews," Hugo drawled, coming to a stop a few feet away, his dark gaze unreadable, "that governesses could multiply in the space of an afternoon. Like geese. How extraordinary."

Eleanor watched that gleaming gaze of his flick over her sister, and was more than a little surprised when it returned to her. But perhaps he was outraged. Perhaps he was looking for an explanation as to why he'd been kissing the likes of Eleanor when all the while he could have had Vivi.

And that ugly thing inside of her grew thicker. Burrowed deeper. But there was no stopping a speeding train, and Vivi had always been far more dangerous than any high-speed rail.

"Your Grace," Eleanor said stiffly, especially when Vivi seemed to melt into her side, holding on tight to Eleanor as if she was her very own plush toy. "May I present my sister, Vivi."

"You may," Hugo said in that same sardonic drawl that made heat bolt through Eleanor, but didn't seem to have the same effect on Vivi. "If you feel you must."

Eleanor frowned at that, but her attention was drawn by her sister, who couldn't seem to stop that damned giggle.

Be kind, Eleanor told herself sternly. Hugo was an overwhelming man. Anyone would be expected to overreact to the sight of him.

"I am honored, Your Grace," Vivi simpered. Then she batted her eyelashes at Hugo. "And here I thought every duke in the land was over the age of fifty."

"It only feels that way," Hugo replied with that liquid ease of his that made the bottom of Eleanor's stomach disappear. "It is the obsequiousness that ages a man, not the title."

Eleanor flushed on her sister's behalf, but it was a

wasted effort as Vivi hardly seem to notice that the Duke had just taken her down a peg or two. Or perhaps she did notice. Perhaps that was her sister's true secret weapon, all this time. Maybe Vivi got her mileage out of pretending not to notice the very clear signals sent all around her.

But in either case, Eleanor frowned at Hugo, because she wasn't pretending anything.

"If you'll excuse us," she said, perhaps too severely, "I must show my sister to my rooms and then return to my duties."

"I'm sure Geraldine can manage," Hugo said offhandedly.

"Have you been supervising her reading, Your Grace? I had no idea you had taken such an active interest."

"I have been supervising my accounts," Hugo said in a faintly chiding tone that made Eleanor flush slightly. Again. "Which is how I know that I employ a veritable fleet of overpriced nannies. The child is more than fine. Always."

Vivi laughed again then, though there was nothing to laugh about in Eleanor's opinion. Then she let herself flop a bit toward Eleanor, as if she was giving her a hug from the side.

"You must forgive my sister, Your Grace," she said merrily. "She's ever so serious. She always has been. It won't surprise you to learn her favorite color is gray."

Eleanor told herself there was no reason for it, but that didn't stop the feeling of betrayal that swept over her. And the injustice of it, to have Vivi cut her down like that and call her *gray*, of all things, when it wasn't even true.

But there was nothing to be gained by arguing the point. There was no arguing with Vivi.

"My favorite color is not gray," Eleanor heard herself say, to her own astonishment. And once she'd started it seemed silly not to carry on. "On the contrary, I prefer a bright and cheerful red. It just so happens, however, that one cannot march about life forever dressed like a cardinal."

Next to her, Vivi slid Eleanor a cool look. She pretended not to see it.

But she was certain Hugo did. Just as she was certain that Vivi was about three seconds away from hurling herself across the space that separated them to make a complete fool of herself. All over him.

And the truth was, Eleanor could hardly blame her. She'd made a fool of herself over him herself, hadn't she? Such a fool of herself, in fact, that she hadn't even realized she was doing it until now.

When it was much too late.

Hugo was devastating. Full stop. Today he was affecting his international rock star look again. His dark hair looked messy, the intriguing kind of messy that made Eleanor want to test it with her fingers. His dark eyes were lit with that suppressed humor of his, dark and sardonic. He wore another one of his battered T-shirts that left nothing of his perfect chest to the imagination and another pair of jeans that hugged him in all the wrong places, as if he aspired to give the two-fingered salute to the fusty dukedom with every breath and outfit. And as if there were no autumn drafts snaking along the halls and no wind rattling the windows, come to that.

Or as if he was immune to all of it, because he was that darkly beautiful.

But Eleanor was quite certain that all Vivi saw when she looked at him were pound notes.

"If you wish to wear red, I would not object," Hugo said, a current of dark laughter in his voice. "There is no required uniform, Miss Andrews. I hope Mrs. Redding didn't mislead you on that score."

"Oh, you silly old thing," Vivi cut in then, with a little trill in her voice, and though her eyes were on Hugo she was clearly speaking to Eleanor. Or pretending to, anyway. "You know that red doesn't suit you."

Hugo's attention swung back to her sister, and Eleanor was glad, because she felt stricken straight through. Ashamed, if she was honest with herself at last.

Had she really imagined that she was anything to a man like this but a diversion while he was bored? Even for a moment?

She knew the way of the world. There was a reason Vivi was the one who flitted about with people of Hugo's ilk, and it wasn't only because she was thinner and prettier. It was because she bloomed in such circumstances. She came alive. She stole all the light from the room.

Men like Hugo were destined for women like Vivi. Women like Eleanor were destined to be exactly what she was here in Groves House: staff. And that was all right, she told herself fiercely as she watched her sister show her dimples to Hugo. Some people were meant for the shadows and Eleanor had long since accepted that she was one of them. She didn't know what had happened to her over the past nearly six weeks, stuck away in this rambling old house with only a seven-year-old to talk to. She'd started believing in the sort of fairy tales she read to Geraldine. Or she'd been tempted to, anyway.

She'd even let Hugo touch her.

When she knew—when everyone knew—that he was a man who toyed with others. And so what if he'd claimed the tabloids had lied about him? That was what he would say.

She didn't understand how she'd allowed herself to

feel so many impossible things inside and then lie to herself about it. Because if she'd been as unaffected by Hugo as she'd claimed she was—as she'd been so sure she was—nothing Vivi was saying or doing could possibly have bothered her.

And that was the trouble. It bothered her a lot.

"You must bring your sister to dinner, Miss Andrews," Hugo said, snapping Eleanor back to the issue at hand, and she tried to stop noticing that his eyes looked like overpriced whiskey. Especially when she couldn't read the expression in them, as he looked from Eleanor to Vivi and then back again. "In my private room. Tonight."

"I would love to, Your Grace," Vivi trilled—but Hugo was already walking away.

Eleanor pulled her arm away from Vivi's then, and hated herself for it.

"There's no need to respond," she said matter-of-factly. "He is the Duke and this is his house. That was not a request or an invitation, it was an order."

Eleanor set off again then, aware that her sister was following behind her. And that Vivi was laughing softly under her breath, which the tight, thickening thing inside of her knew could only bode ill. But she refused to look over her shoulder to see. She refused to give in to the dark things sloshing around in her gut.

She refused to be the person she'd apparently become.

Eleanor finally reached her rooms, and threw her door open, beckoning for Vivi to come inside.

And then had to ask herself why she was surprised that her sister entered the room very much the way she had, back when she'd arrived. Staring all around at the sheer luxury. Eleanor found herself standing there in the sitting room, rooted to the floor as Vivi gave herself a tour, feeling awkward and angry and deeply disappointed in herself.

"My, my, my. This just gets better and better."

Vivi's faintly accusing voice floating in from one of the other rooms struck Eleanor in the heart. Because the truth was, she felt guilty. Horribly guilty.

And she knew why.

Her sister would have been here like a shot if she'd had any idea the sort of opulence that was on display at every turn in Groves House. That alone would have encouraged her. But Hugo's presence? Her sister would have done anything to meet the Duke of Grovesmoor. And Eleanor still couldn't explain to herself, not reasonably anyway, why she hadn't let Vivi know from the start that Hugo was in residence.

"You fancy him."

Eleanor's head shot up at that. She found Vivi leaning in the door that led from the sitting room to the bathroom, a considering look on her pretty face.

"Don't be absurd," she said. "He's my employer."

Vivi shook her head, and there was a sharp light in her eyes that Eleanor couldn't say she cared for at all. "Why else would you have lied to me?"

"I've never lied to you, Vivi. And you still haven't told me why you're here. Not the real reason."

"I missed you."

Something pointed seem to lodge in Eleanor's side, because she wanted that to be true. And she also knew it wasn't.

"I don't think so," she said quietly. "You've had scandals and overdrawn bank accounts before without getting on a train. What makes this different?"

"I don't want to talk about London. It's so boring. What's not boring is you holed up in this gorgeous house with Hugo Grovesmoor. Something you failed to mention to me, night after night after night. If that's not a lie, Eleanor, I don't believe I know what one is."

"You were certain I would never encounter him," Eleanor replied, and she was aware of the fact that she was trying much too hard to keep her voice even. Though she allowed the slightest hint of impatience, as if this was one of Vivi's flights of fancy that she was called upon to temper. Because it should have been. "And I saw no reason to tell you of his comings and goings, because I hardly know when or if I'll lay eyes on him."

"You met him before today."

"Yes, I met him. If you consider being presented to him like any other member of staff 'meeting' him." She made quote marks in the air with her index fingers, and shook her head at her sister. "I think when you meet men it's a little more momentous than when I do."

She expected Vivi to argue. But instead, her sister only smiled. Which did not make Eleanor easy in any way, because she knew Vivi. There was always a scheme. There was always the next plan. The smile was never acquiescence.

Or worse, that little voice chimed in, *she agrees.*

When had she become so awful about her own sister?

And anyway, Vivi was changing the subject. "Why have I been shuffling about London, forced to spend my nights in a grotty bedsit, when you've been living it up like the landed gentry?"

"These are the governess's quarters," Eleanor said. She made herself smile. "This is what passes for a grotty flat to a duke."

"You are in terrible, terrible trouble, big sister," Vivi said, but if there was a storm, it had passed.

Once again, Eleanor saw before her the sister she

knew. With a mischievous look in her golden eyes and an infectious grin. She blinked, doubting herself. It was as if she'd made her sister into some kind of enemy the moment she'd dared walk into the house—which said nothing nice about Eleanor. It said a whole lot, however, about jealousy and envy and a whole host of other, vile things that Eleanor didn't want to admit were sloshing around inside of her.

Congratulations, she thought. *You're a terrible person.*

"I know you have to work," Vivi continued merrily. "I'll take you to task later. In the meantime, I think I'll help myself to that glorious bath."

Eleanor stood there for a long while after her sister disappeared. After she heard the water turn on in the bathroom, splashing into the huge tub. She stood there and she tried to collect herself. She tried to remember the person she'd been before she'd come to this far-off place, and more, before she'd let Hugo touch her. Change her.

Make her into that jealous, dark-minded creature who was selfish beyond measure.

She told herself that it was over. That whatever the spell was that had held her in its grip these last weeks, Vivi's appearance had broken it. It was time to wake up and remember what she was doing here.

She made the money. Vivi was the one who reeled in men like Hugo. And for good reason. She was the sort of girl who caused scandals that ended up in tabloid newspapers. She was *someone.*

Eleanor had never been anybody.

She forced herself to leave, then. She closed the door to her own rooms quietly behind her and headed into the hall. She had to find Geraldine and get back to her job, which was the only reason she was here. The fact of the matter was that Vivi should never have come here, but she had. And worse, she'd run straight into the Duke within moments of her arrival, when he could have thrown them both out.

But he hadn't done that. And Eleanor knew why.

And if something lodged in her heart, making it feel cracked straight through, she told herself it was nothing.

Nothing at all. Nothing new.

Nothing that mattered.

CHAPTER NINE

HUGO COULDN'T SLEEP.

As he was not a man unduly plagued with the demands of conscience, this was not an issue he generally struggled with. But it wasn't some newfound and unruly set of principles that kept him up tonight, roaming his own halls like his very own ghost story.

It was Eleanor.

Eleanor, who he'd come to depend upon over these last weeks. For her starchiness. Her prim disapproval. Every spicy, challenging word that fell from her notably disrespectful mouth—the very same mouth that Hugo had tasted and which haunted him more than he cared to admit to himself, even now.

He had the terrible suspicion she would haunt him forever, not that he allowed himself to think such things. Not when he refused to think about next week, much less the rest of his life. Or anything approaching *forever*.

But the Eleanor he rather thought he'd come to know had disappeared tonight.

She'd been noticeably absent when he'd run into her and her sister in the hall outside the summer salons, en route to the nursery wing. Gone was the fiercely capable Eleanor who'd been giving him hell and in her place was a far more quiet and distant version, as if she'd been trying to disappear where she stood.

Hugo hated it.

He'd never met Vivi Andrews before. But he knew her at a glance, because he knew her type intimately. It took him all of two seconds on his laptop to find entirely too much about the actual Vivi Andrews, and the sorts of shenanigans she got herself into with high-profile members of the aristocracy. The more he read about her, in fact, the less he understood about Eleanor. How was she so forthright and dependable when Vivi was anything but?

The truth was, the younger Andrews sister—who Eleanor was supporting, if he'd understood that right, which made no sense while Vivi pranced about decked out in the sorts of labels the heiresses of his acquaintance wore because their fortunes were so vast that a six-thousand-pound T-shirt was a "little treat"—was the sort of creature Hugo usually slummed around with. Vivi had showed him her true colors in their first meeting, all batting eyelashes and come-hither smiles as if they'd been in a club instead of a hallway in his ancestral home. And she'd kept it up throughout dinner while Eleanor sat beside her, subdued. Vivi had distinguished herself by being endlessly pouty, unkind at the slightest provocation, and obviously convinced that she was a great, rare beauty when the truth was, thousands of equally ambitious girls looked just like her. Her sister was the rare beauty, but he had no doubt Vivi wouldn't see it that way.

She looked nothing like Isobel, and yet the resemblance was impossible to miss. Hugo felt Vivi's attention the way he'd always felt anything that reeked a bit too much of Isobel's sort—like an oily sort of shame inside him, as if the fact a person like her was so obviously interested in him made him somehow like them.

Because, after all, it had. Given enough time, he'd become exactly who Isobel had made him, hadn't he?

He hadn't cared much for that thought, either.

"It astonishes me that you are sisters," he'd said during their excruciating dinner.

Eleanor appeared to have taken it upon herself to embody the very soul of the starchiest possible governess, with Victorian overtones. Her hair was more severe than he had ever seen it before, wrenched back from her poor face as if she was trying to pull it out, so that only her fringe offered any kind of relief. And he doubted it was a coincidence that she'd chosen to wear black. All black, save for a hint of gray in the shirt she wore beneath her cardigan, as if she was in mourning.

Or as if she was reacting to her sister's earlier claim that it was her favorite color. A poke at Vivi, he wondered? Or a twisted sort of penance?

"Don't be silly, Your Grace," Vivi had simpered at him. She'd been in a slinky sort of red dress Hugo thought would have been more appropriate for a club in Central London than a country duke's dining room. But the point was likely to draw his attention to all the skin the tiny dress left bare. "Everyone swears we are practically twins."

He was apparently not supposed to realize that she was being cruel.

But before he could express his feelings on that—which, it turned out, were extensive and a bit overprotective—Eleanor had sighed. Mightily.

"No one has ever said that. Not one person, Vivi. Anywhere." She'd aimed one of her chillier smiles at Hugo.

"My sister and I are quite aware of our differences, Your Grace. We choose to revel in them."

Vivi laughed then, long and loud. The way Hugo had then realized, belatedly, she would continue to do all night. Because she clearly imagined she was being lively and full of fun, or whatever it was women like her told themselves to justify their behavior. He should be better versed in it, he knew. He'd heard it all before.

Sometimes from his own mouth.

He'd settled himself in for an endurance event. But it had turned out that he was more than capable of blocking out the likes of Vivi Andrews. She'd brayed on about the guest suite she'd been given while she remained in Groves House and something about her feelings regarding the Amalfi Coast, and Hugo had watched Eleanor disappear. Right there in front of him. She'd simply... gone away.

It had made Hugo edgy. And something far darker and more dangerous than that.

And now he was wandering his own damned halls, scowling at the portraits of men who looked like him, wondering why the plight of a governess and her family were getting to him like this.

Well. He wasn't wondering. He knew.

Watching Vivi create an entire character she called Eleanor—stiff and humorless and faintly doltish and unattractive—while Eleanor sat right there and was not only none of those things, but offered no defense against the brush that was being used to paint her, was maddening. But it was also familiar.

It was what Isobel had done to him.

He was in the grand ballroom, glaring out at the rain that lashed at what was left of the garden this far into fall, when he heard a faint noise from behind him. Hugo turned, and for a moment he couldn't tell if he'd conjured up the sight before him or if she was real.

But god, how he wanted her to be real.

Eleanor moved across the floor, light on her bare feet. She wore some sort of soft wrapper that showed him the better part of her legs and made Hugo wonder what was beneath it. But the thing that made his chest hurt was that finally, her hair was down. It wasn't ruthlessly scraped back and forced to lie flat and obedient against her skull. It was glossy and dark and swirled around her shoulders, making her look softer. Sweeter. Even that razor-sharp fringe seemed blurred.

Mine, he thought instantly.

And he wanted her so badly that he assumed this was a dream.

Until she stopped walking, jerked a little bit, and stared directly at him as if she hadn't seen him until that very moment.

"Are you hiding in the shadows deliberately?" she asked him, and even her voice was different this long after midnight. Softer. Less like a challenge and more like a caress.

"My ballroom, my shadows," Hugo said, and he hardly recognized his own voice, come to that. He sounded tight. Greedy. As if the need that pounded in him was taking over the whole of him, and the truth was, he wasn't sure he had it in him to care. "By definition, I think, I cannot be hiding. You should expect to see me anywhere you go in these halls."

Eleanor didn't respond to that. Her lovely face seemed to tense, as if it was on the verge of crumpling, and he couldn't bear that. He couldn't stand the idea of it. He'd told her that tears were anathema to him. He'd told her he put distance between himself and the faintest hint of them.

And yet he found himself moving toward her, his gaze trained on her as if he expected her to be the one who turned and ran.

"Why are you looking at me like that?" she asked, her voice a small little rasp against the thick, soft air in the old ballroom. The chandeliers were dim high above and it made the room feel close. Somehow intimate.

"You should not allow your sister to treat you like that," he told her, his voice much darker than it should have been. Much more severe. But he couldn't seem to do anything about that when it was taking everything he had to keep his hands to himself.

But Eleanor only shrugged. "You don't know Vivi. She doesn't mean anything by the things she says. Some people don't think before they open their mouths."

"You are mistaken," Hugo said, stopping when he was only a foot or so away from her, and still managing not to touch her. He expected her to move away from him. To bolt. Or square off her shoulders and face him with that defiance of hers that he'd come to look forward to in ways he couldn't explain to himself. Not to his own satisfaction. And not tonight, when neither one of them should have been here in this room where no one ventured by day. "Poison drips from every word she hurls at you. And you believe it. Sooner or later, you believe all of it."

Eleanor shook her head, though her gaze was troubled. "Vivi's young. She'll grow out of it."

"She's what? A year or so younger than you?"

"You don't understand the sorts of people she knows. Viciousness is a sport. When she's not trying to imitate them, she's really quite sweet."

But Eleanor's voice sounded so tired then.

"I know exactly how this story goes," Hugo told her quietly. "I've heard all these excuses before. I used to believe them all myself."

"You don't have a sister. And you don't understand. I almost lost her when we lost our parents. Who cares about a few thoughtless words?"

But Hugo cared. And the undercurrent in Eleanor's voice suggested she might, too, whether she wanted to admit it or not.

"I had a best friend," Hugo said softly. "And despite the fact we knew each other in the cradle, I eventually lost Torquil to the same poison that made me a villain in the eyes of the world. That's the trouble with the sort of hatefulness your sister seems so comfortable with. It doesn't go away. It doesn't fade. It corrodes."

"Isobel," Eleanor whispered.

Hugo didn't like her name in Eleanor's mouth. As if that alone could poison the woman who stood before him against him. Just the mention of her.

"Isobel and I dated, if that is what it can be called, for two weeks." He couldn't keep the bitterness from his tone. The truth was, he didn't really try. Because what was there now besides that bitterness? What was left? Only the stories Isobel had told about him, his inability to refute any of them, and the long game of revenge he was playing against all those who'd chosen to believe it. "Two weeks, that is all. There was no on-and-off nonsense, stretching on for years. There was barely any affair to speak of. There were two entirely physical weeks when I was too young to know better, and then I cut it off."

Eleanor's gaze searched his. "I don't understand."

"Of course you don't understand. I assure you, I do not understand it myself. Isobel didn't like the fact that while she wanted our relationship to be something more than it was, I did not." He felt his mouth flatten. "And she didn't see why she should have to accept any reality that she didn't like. So she made her own."

"You can't mean…" Eleanor took a deep breath that made her hair move about on her shoulders. And Hugo couldn't keep himself from reaching out then. If he was honest, he didn't try too hard.

He reached over and ran his fingers through the fall of her hair, dark and enticing. It felt warm against his fingers, as if she was giving off heat like some kind of sun, and as soft as he'd imagined. And when he was finished running his fingers through it—at least for now—he didn't let go. He held on to a hank of her hair, as if he needed it. As if it was some kind of talisman.

Or she was.

"At first it was just sad." He didn't like talking about any of this. It only occurred to him then that he never had before. Because who could he have told? Everyone had already come to their own conclusions. "She would contrive to be somewhere I was and the next thing I knew there was a photograph in a tabloid, and breathless speculation about whether or not we were back on. At first I didn't even realize that she was the one calling the paparazzi herself. But as time went on, of course, the coverage took a distinctly darker turn."

He didn't know what he expected from Eleanor. An instant refusal, perhaps. After all, Isobel had been a sunny ambassador of goodwill. Everyone said so. She had been all that was light and good and the only strange thing she ever done in her life, according to the coverage of her that she'd manipulated constantly, was try to date a monster like Hugo. It wouldn't have surprised him if Eleanor had argued with him. If she'd tried to deny the story that he was telling.

But she didn't say a word. Her solemn gaze was fixed to his, and she seemed ready enough to hear him out.

No one else had ever given him that courtesy. Hugo felt something sharp, wedged there in the vicinity of his heart, but he had no name for it.

"As time went on Isobel became more and more unhinged. She got together with Torquil, of course, but that wasn't enough for her. Because the truth was, she knew that wouldn't hurt me. If he wanted to be with her that meant nothing to me either way, and that was what she couldn't stand. It was right about the time she convinced my friend, who'd known me all his life, that I'd treated her abusively in private that it occurred to me her only real goal was to hurt me. However possible."

"If you didn't care for her at all," Eleanor said softly, "and you weren't even involved with her in the ways she claimed, how could she ever have hurt you?" She seemed to think better of that as she said it. "Your friend's betrayal must have hurt, of course."

Hugo shrugged. "Sometimes a woman comes between friends. To be honest, I wasn't worried. I thought that he'd come out of it with continued exposure to her."

"I can't pretend to know how it feels to have lies about myself splashed all over the paper," Eleanor began.

"It was my father."

It sat there so starkly. That ugly little truth that Hugo had never dared utter out loud before to anyone but Isobel, and only that once. And not only because there was no one else to hear it. But because naming it gave it power and he had never wanted to do that. He had never wanted to give Isobel the satisfaction—not even in death.

"I was all the old man had," Hugo managed to say, aware there was a kind of earthquake in him, tearing through him and reducing him to rubble. And yet he stood. "And I was a terrible disappointment to him."

"I'm sure you're mistaken," Eleanor breathed, that honey in her dark eyes gleaming with sympathy. "Maybe you only thought he felt that way."

"I know he felt that way, little one." Hugo's voice was soft. "He told me so."

And he stopped trying to fight that feeling inside of him then. That sharp thing in his chest only seemed to bleed out more at that stricken look on Eleanor's lovely face. As if she couldn't imagine such a thing, that an old man could think so little of his only son.

But Hugo knew he had.

"My father was prepared to put up with a certain amount of foolishness, because he was old-school and he'd had what he called his 'day in the sun.' He very much believed that boys were indeed boys." Hugo felt his mouth curve, though it was no smile. "But his expectation was that such conduct unbecoming in a Duke of Grovesmoor would end. If not during my university years, then shortly thereafter. Except I met Isobel two years after I left Cambridge, when I was still committed to every wild oat a man could sow. And that was when she started her campaign."

"Surely your father didn't believe the tabloids."

"Of course not. My father would never sully his eyes with such trash. The trouble wasn't the tabloids themselves. It was that everyone who did read the tabloids accepted everything they read in them as fact. And it wasn't only the scandal rags. There were cleverly disguised hit pieces in more reputable magazines that made me seem seedy and vaguely disgusting. And soon enough, that was how I was discussed. Not just in salacious news programs, but right here, in my father's own home. To his face."

"Who would do something like that?" Eleanor asked, and if he hadn't been looking right at her, with her eyes wide and filled with distress, he might have imagined she was faking. "And why would your father believe the kind of person who would slander his own son directly to him?"

It was an excellent question, and one Hugo wished he could ask the old man.

"Sometimes a rumor is far worse than a fact," he said instead. "Facts can be proven or disproven, most of the time. But rumor can live on forever. It commands a life of its own and dignified silence doesn't refute it. And sooner or later, whether you mean to or not, you find that you're living in it. Against your will."

"There was nothing you could do?" She shook her head as if to clear it. "No way you could tell the truth?"

"That's the thing about rumors like that, little one," Hugo murmured. "They're *more* believable than the truth. My father was a man of the world. He'd flirted with his own share of potential scandals in his day. It made no sense to him that a pretty girl like Isobel, who could have anyone, would waste her time pretending to have a relationship with the one man who didn't want her. And I think you'll find that it didn't make sense to anyone else, either."

"But surely you could prove it."

"How?" Hugo wasn't surprised when Eleanor didn't have an answer. "Where there's smoke, people always look for a fire. And the more that fire burns, the more everyone believes that you must have had a hand in setting it, or you'd put it out. But Isobel had no intention of ever letting it die down."

He thought of that endless blue afternoon in all that Santa Barbara sunshine. The way Isobel had smiled at him.

You'll always be mine, Hugo. Always. No matter where you go or what you do, no one will ever see you without thinking of me.

"I'm surprised you didn't date her just to keep her quiet," Eleanor said then, scowling furiously—but not, for once, at him. "Just to make her stop."

Hugo let out a low noise. "I thought about it, of course. But I didn't want to be anywhere near her. And then, of course, came Geraldine."

"None of this is her fault," Eleanor said at once. Fiercely.

"Of course not," Hugo said shortly. "I don't bear the child any ill will."

"But—"

"But I don't mind if the world thinks I do," he finished for her. He shook his head. "Before there was Geraldine, there was Isobel and her pregnancy. And believe me, she used it like a hammer." He dropped that piece of Eleanor's hair then, because his hands were curling into fists and he thought he'd better keep them to himself. "She told my father the child was mine."

"She left you. She married your friend. How could it be yours?"

"She didn't leave me." Hugo realized he'd growled that out like a savage, and fought for calm. "We were never together. But she told my father that we had been. And then she told him that I refused to do my duty. That I told her to get rid of it. That I was, in short, every bit the callous and unfeeling character she'd painted me in the tabloids. And in those rumors."

"You must have insisted on a blood test to prove that you're not the father."

"I did," Hugo bit out. "But he died before I could show him that proof. He had heart failure and never recovered, and doctors can use any terms they wish to explain what happened. But I think the shock killed him."

He'd forgotten that they were standing in the middle of the ballroom. Because all he could see was Eleanor, and that terrible look on her face. As if there was nothing in the world but the two of them and the way they stood so close together, as if what he was telling her here was far more important than a mere story. As if it was something infinitely more critical than the past he was still paying for.

It was, he understood. He was telling her the truth about the most hated man in England, and she believed him.

She believed him.

Eleanor moved then, tipping herself up on her toes and fitting her palms to his chest. One of them right there where his heart still hurt.

As if she knew.

"I'm so sorry, Hugo," she whispered, her voice intense and low. "I'm ashamed to say I believed the stories, too."

Hugo felt a kind of bitterness twist through him then, though there was a warmth in it this time, as if it was something a little more complicated. He reached up and covered the hand over his heart with his.

"Do you know," he said quietly, "that you are the only person I have ever met who's apologized? When you are the one who's done the least damage."

She bit her lip, and electricity pounded through him, reminding him of all the ways this woman got to him. All the ways she was clearly the death of him.

"I've spoken to you as if I knew you. As if the stories I read were the truth, when of course they couldn't be.

The truth is never so black and white, is it? No heroes, no villains, just people."

"Perhaps. But there are also Isobels in this world. They prey on others because they can. It gives them pleasure. And Eleanor, your sister is one of them."

She tried to pull her hand away, but Hugo held her fast.

"You don't understand," she said, her voice fierce again.

"But I do." Hugo moved closer then, until there was only the scantest bit of air between the two of them. "Tonight you're barefoot, your hair is down, every inch of you is feminine and soft."

"I didn't expect to run into anyone in what I wear to bed."

He took his free hand and placed it over her lips. He smiled down into the crease between her eyes. He felt things he'd never thought were real, before tonight.

"Eleanor. Who told you feminine and soft is bad?"

"Not bad," Eleanor said against his finger, sending delicious little licks of heat spiraling through him. "But not me." Her frown intensified. "It's cruel of you to pretend that you can't see it, now that you've met Vivi. I'm not the pretty one. I never was."

"Your sister is pretty, yes," Hugo said, dismissively. "In a very particular way that would, I imagine, appeal to a very particular man. But you?" He shifted his hands, smoothing them over her cheeks and then down to curl into the nape of her neck. "Little one. How can you not realize that you are beautiful? Stunning? There is no comparison."

Her marvelous eyes filled with emotion. Her perfect mouth trembled.

"You don't have to lie to me, Your Grace," she whispered.

And Hugo didn't know what to do with a woman

who'd believed that he was a better man than anyone had believed him to be in years—making everything inside him shift and change—but not that she was the most beautiful creature he thought he'd ever beheld.

So he did the only thing he could. He kissed her.

CHAPTER TEN

IT WAS LIKE DANCING.

Eleanor wasn't sure she should let herself fall into something that felt a little too much like a fairy tale here in the middle of a ballroom, but his mouth was on hers again and she couldn't seem to think of anything else. Or she didn't want to think about anything else.

She didn't want to think about how little she'd cared for her sister tonight, which made her feel small. Petty. Selfish beyond measure.

But not enough to stop.

She didn't want to think about the fact that she'd left her room after tossing and turning for hours, and despite what she might have let Hugo think, she knew that she hadn't been dressed like a governess should have been. Or even as a guest should have been when she'd eased her door open and crept down the hall. She been filled with a kind of despairing recklessness, a restless need that had urged her to *do something* with all the pent-up hurt and betrayal she'd felt after dinner. She'd convinced herself that it was an excellent idea to wander the halls of Groves House half-dressed. Hair down. Bare feet.

Had she wanted this all along?

But she didn't really care if she had, because it felt like dancing.

Hugo kissed her and he kissed her. His hands moved from the nape of her neck, smoothing their way down the line of her back, and fastened thrillingly at her hips, drawing her against him.

He kissed her as if there was nothing else but that. Nothing in all the world but the slide of his mouth on hers.

"I can't get enough of you," Hugo muttered against her lips, as if it hurt him to say that. "I can't get enough."

And when he bent, then lifted her into his arms, Eleanor knew she should have protested. Nothing had made this any less wrong than it had been yesterday. Or a week ago. Or ever. She was still his employee.

But he was Hugo Grovesmoor. And Vivi was right here, in this house, but he hadn't chosen her.

He'd chosen Eleanor. He'd called her beautiful and he'd kissed her, *after* meeting Vivi. After Vivi had launched a full-scale offensive, in fact, and gotten nowhere.

For the first time in her life, someone had chosen Eleanor.

She didn't have it in her to pull away.

Hugo carried her through the house. Eleanor had no concept of what time it was, only that the last time she'd heard the clocks chime, it had been after midnight. But as far she was concerned, the night could last forever. She hoped it would.

She rested her head against Hugo's wide shoulder, and let the house drift past her as he carried her. Through the halls and up the stairs that led to his private wing. And this time, he did not take her to his library, or to that dining room of his where she'd spent all evening feeling as if she didn't exist, but further on. Down to the end of that same hall, and into the rooms that waited there.

She had a dreamy sort of impression of magnificence.

Bold, masculine furnishings, dark woods and impressively large paintings and rugs so lavish it seemed a shame to walk on them. A massive stone fireplace that made her think of medieval castles, and that was only the living room.

But Hugo kept going. And with every step he took toward what had to be his bedroom, Eleanor's heart kicked at her. Harder and harder.

And then they were there, standing by the side of a massive bed that would have dwarfed a room any smaller than this one, and Hugo was shifting her. Placing her down on the edge of his mattress as if she was infinitely precious to him.

And Eleanor felt shivery. Fragile all the way through.

Because she couldn't think of another time in her life that anyone had treated her like that, as if she mattered. Oh, she assumed her parents had. But the truth was that she couldn't remember any longer. What she remembered was taking care of others.

She tilted her face up, so she could study Hugo's gorgeously male expression—hungry and intense—as he gazed back at her. He made her feel like she was dancing even when she was still. He made her feel small in all the best ways.

The truth was that he made her feel like the kind of girl she'd never been. Light, airy. Charming beyond measure.

He made her feel the way she'd always imagined it felt to be Vivi.

Eleanor still couldn't believe that she was the one sitting here, on the edge of the Duke's bed. That he hadn't picked Vivi when he'd had the chance.

But she had no intention of throwing this away. This was her chance at last. To experience everything she never had before. To be that girl some part of her had always dreamed she could have been, maybe, if things had been different.

"I would tell you I don't bite, little one," Hugo said in that smokily amused way of his. It reverberated up and down her spine, then pooled somewhere low in her belly, where it began to pulse. "But that would be a lie."

"I'm not afraid of you," she managed to say.

Hugo looked amused. Something like delighted.

"No, you are not. And it is one among many reasons you are under my skin." He studied her. "But still, you're still looking at me as if you expect me to eat you alive."

"Oh," Eleanor said softly. "I thought that was exactly what you intended to do."

Hugo let out a breath. Or perhaps it was a laugh. Either way, it shimmered in Eleanor like light.

"You'll be the death of me," Hugo muttered.

And then he was moving. He hooked an arm around Eleanor's waist and hauled her along with him as he crawled toward the center of the bed. And then, marvelously, he stretched out on top of her and settled the whole of his lean, hard body between her legs.

"Breathe," he told her, and she knew she wasn't mistaking that unholy amusement in his dark gaze. His eyes looked even more like whiskey tonight, or perhaps it was just that this close, she couldn't pretend that she was anything but drunk.

On him.

"I'm breathing," she whispered.

"See that you continue," Hugo ordered her in his lazy, aristocratic way. "I haven't killed a virgin yet."

And Eleanor loved the fact that he knew. That she didn't have to make any long, drawn-out confession. When she'd thought about this moment—in those few and far between moments when she still imagined that this was any kind of possibility, that she might give herself to a man—she'd always assumed that she would have to offer extensive explanations. She would have to tell a reasonable story about why a woman her age had never quite managed to get here before, horizontal on a bed. She would have to talk about how distant she'd always felt from others her age, in part because she'd felt so responsible for Vivi, and how that had always seemed to leave her on her own. And she'd never been able to conjure up a way to tell someone that story without coming across as some kind of freak. Better to lock all that away. Better to convince herself that not only didn't she care, but she didn't feel the same things others did.

But Hugo didn't seem to care about any of that. Not why she was a virgin at twenty-seven. Not how. The only thing he seemed to care about was that he was the one braced over her, gazing down at her as if she was a treat. As if he wanted nothing more than to bury himself in her.

As if it was only a matter of time before he did.

It took Eleanor long moments to realize what that sensation was that snaked his way through her. A blistering sort of relief.

Because she felt safe. Somehow, someway, Hugo Grovesmoor made her feel safe, here in his bed where that should have been the very last thing she felt.

She hadn't known that was possible.

"Stop thinking so hard, little one," he said then.

"That's easy for you to say," she retorted. And his mouth was at her neck, so she felt it when he smiled.

"This is very simple," he told her, and there was a serious note beneath all that lazy heat. "If I want you to do something, I'll tell you what and how to do it. Otherwise, all you need to do is enjoy yourself."

Eleanor frowned at him, and he must have sensed it, because as he looked up that smile of his widened.

"That sounds very selfish."

"Eleanor, please." Hugo shook his head. "You cannot possibly be more selfish than I am. I promise you."

And then he put his mouth against her skin again, and Eleanor stopped thinking about anything.

Hugo took his time.

He tasted her everywhere. First he ran his hand over every part of her he could touch. He traced her collarbones. He tested her figure, spending a lot of time on her waist and the generous curves above and below. He made her writhe side to side beneath him, and when he had enough of that, he stripped her of her wrapper and her silky little nightie, and he did it all over again.

But this time, he used his mouth too.

He took her nipples in his mouth and sucked on them until she sobbed. He played with her. He made her arch up against him and cry out, over and over, and only when she felt limp and outside herself did he shift down the length of her body.

And then put his mouth between her legs.

Shattering the world into a white hot panic.

He licked into her. What he'd done with his fingers in the library had been astonishing enough, but this was worse. Better.

This was unlike anything Eleanor could possibly have imagined.

And when that wall came at her this time, she wasn't afraid of it. She let him throw her over the edge once, then again, and she shook and shimmered all the way down.

When she opened her eyes again, Hugo was naked too. And he was crawling his way over her again, his eyes locked to hers.

"You're holding up beautifully," he said, that curve in his lips. "I haven't even had to tell you to lie back and think of England."

"I always thought that would be unsanitary," she blurted out. That curve in his mouth bloomed into a real smile.

"You may well be the death of me, Eleanor. Here. Tonight."

"It always sounded so…" She trailed off, aftershocks still shuddering through her.

"It is *so*," Hugo told her. "That's what makes it so much fun."

And then Eleanor's attention was stolen away by the way Hugo settled himself against her once more.

And this time, she could feel everything.

That beautiful chest of his, chiseled and perfect and hot to the touch. But more than that, there was that heavy, foreign part of him that she could feel nudging up against the place where she was soft and melting. It made her shudder.

She reached down between them and wrapped her hand around him. His breath hissed out of him, hard. And there was that strange glitter in his eyes.

Eleanor pulled her hand away. Guiltily. "I'm sorry," she said hesitantly. "I didn't mean to hurt you."

"You didn't hurt me." Hugo's voice was strangled. "I promise you, there's no possible way you could hurt me. But hold off on that for now."

Eleanor realized in the next instant what she'd done. She did read, after all. And she had certainly watched enough television in her time. But nothing had prepared her for how different it was in real life. Hugo was big and sculpted and stunning, and still he shuddered when she touched him. How could she have known? A thousand

Hollywood movies were nothing next to the feel of his body above hers, and the way that silken length of his had burned itself into her palm.

Hugo shifted. She felt the tip of him nudge its way between the folds he'd licked, and then begin to move. Up and around. Nudging against the place that made her shiver the most, wilder and wilder each time.

"Will it hurt?" she asked.

Hugo's dark gaze glittered. "Hideously."

"Is that meant to be reassuring?" she asked him, and it was hard to catch her breath. But not because she was afraid of the potential pain.

"You strike me as a woman who appreciates the truth, Eleanor. Are you not?"

"Surely it can't be that bad or people wouldn't do it all the time."

"If you already know," Hugo drawled, "then why did you ask?"

Eleanor scowled at him. She opened up her mouth to snap something at him, and that was when he slid himself inside of her.

All the way inside of her.

Eleanor choked back whatever she might have been about to say. Pain lanced through her—

But it wasn't pain. In the next instant, she realized that it was sensation, certainly, and almost too much of it. Still, it wasn't *pain*.

It was somehow sharp and full at once. She felt exposed, even though Hugo covered the whole of her body with his. She felt shaky and taken, and still, somehow, fragile and precious at once.

"Did it hurt?" Hugo asked, his voice little more than a growl.

Eleanor tested it. She shifted her hips a little bit this way, then that. Then again.

And each time she moved, the sensation changed. The fullness remained, but the sharpness eased. Until she started to suspect that the fullness was warmth. She tried it again, and again, and sure enough the more she moved, the warmer it got.

And it spiraled out from that place inside her, and set the rest of her on fire.

"Hideously," she whispered up at him.

Hugo grinned. And then he began to move.

And Eleanor understood that she'd only known sparks. This was the fire.

Hugo was thorough. He set a slow, easy pace, and Eleanor met it as she wrapped herself around him. And then she mirrored him. She did what he did.

He put his mouth on her skin and she returned the favor. When he thrust deep into her, she lifted her hips to meet each stroke. And the more she did it, the less smooth and studied he became.

Until he seemed as out of breath and outside himself as she was.

Something cracked wide open inside of her. She felt it happen as he slammed into her, sending that impossible joy dancing all through her veins.

"What the hell you doing to me?" Hugo whispered fiercely, his face in the crook of her neck.

And that crack only widened further, and filled with light.

He'd chosen her. And here, beneath him, with him deep inside of her and everything fire and need and all that beautiful hunger, she couldn't help but believe that maybe he needed her, too.

Not because she was a woman to scratch some itch.

He was Hugo Grovesmoor. He could have any woman he liked for that kind of thing, she knew that. But because she was her, specifically.

Because together, they were *them*.

And that was more precious than anything, even all the priceless things cluttering up this rambling old house.

With every deep stroke, every life-altering thrust, she believed it more.

And when she found herself falling this time, cracked wide open and full of him, it felt like love.

Especially when Hugo followed her over, shouting out her name.

CHAPTER ELEVEN

It was very early the next morning when Eleanor finally slipped from Hugo's bed, placing her unsteady feet on the floor beside the massive bed where she'd slept in snatches and learned a whole lot of things about pleasure.

Dark, delirious, wondrous things that still moved in her, making her flush hot and red all over again, just remembering.

She ached everywhere, she realized as she stood. Places she'd had no idea *could* ache were half on fire, making her feel as if she'd woken up in someone else's body. There were tugs here and vague abrasions there, and she could remember something wild and carnal and inexpressibly beautiful to explain each one.

Eleanor thought she ought to be ashamed. Maybe she would be, later. When the reality of last night had time to settle. But right here, right now, she didn't regret a thing.

She found the nightclothes she'd worn last night and pulled them back on, trying hard not to remember exactly how Hugo had pulled each of them off her. Trying hard not to slip off into that same red haze again, all flushed and needy.

She peeked over her shoulder at the bed again, some part of her still unable to believe that any of this had happened. One red-hot image after the next chased itself through her head, in case her body couldn't tell her what had happened, inside and out. But if she'd had any lingering doubt, the sight of Hugo sprawled out there across the better part of his bed got rid of it.

She had tasted every inch of him. She'd taken that enormous length of his deep into her mouth, and had learned how to taste him and tease him the way he'd done to her. He'd taught her how to kneel up over him, and had taken her that way. He'd taught her all the wicked things he could do with his hands, and she'd tried to do the same to him. Over and over again.

She had no idea there were so many different ways— an infinite number of ways, apparently—to do the same thing. Crack apart like that and fall together, sleep entangled, then wake to do it again.

And the greedy part of her wanted to experience all of them. Every last possible way to explode like that. Here and now, though she was a little bit stiff and still achey. Eleanor didn't care, as long she got to experience it all with Hugo.

Hugo, who lay on his back with his arms splayed wide, as commanding in his bed as he was out of it. Hugo, who looked more approachable when she slept. No smirking. No mocking tone of voice. No reminders that he considered himself the biggest monster in England, because everyone else did.

Everyone except Eleanor, that was.

She tucked her hair behind her ears and forced herself to turn around. To walk toward the bedroom door, and then, harder still, to walk out and leave Hugo there behind her when that was the last thing she wanted to do.

Because whatever else happened, she had a job to do. A little girl who had enough of people in her life abandoning her in one way or another, and didn't need more of that from Eleanor.

And if there was a part of her that didn't want to be there when Hugo woke, well. She told herself that was nothing but her inbred practicality. The man might not have had the relationship everyone thought he'd had with Isobel Vanderhaven, but that didn't mean he been a saint.

Eleanor refused to be that silly virgin she'd certainly read enough about and seen too many times on-screen. The one who fell head over heels at the first hint of a man's interest and made a complete fool of herself.

There wasn't much she could do about the first part of that, but she'd be damned if she'd make a fool of herself. Not if she could avoid it.

Once outside of Hugo's rooms, she ducked her head down and moved as quickly as she could through the house without actually breaking into a run. It was still early, so she thought it was likely that no one would be up and around yet. Even so, she took the back stairs whenever possible, the better to be sure no one saw her wandering around, so far from her own rooms, in her revealing sleepwear.

"Better safe than sorry," she muttered to herself.

And then she let out a huge sigh of relief when she made it to her door. All she could think about, then, was that enormous tub in her bathroom and slipping her whole, sweetly aching body into the deep embrace of it. She pushed her way through the door, already piling her hair on the top of her head in anticipation.

"Where have you been?"

Eleanor flinched at the sound of that voice. It startled her so badly that it took her longer than it should have to realize that it was Vivi, of course. Because who else could it be?

She dropped her arms, the hair she hadn't quite managed to put into a knot tumbling down around her shoulders, and she told herself she had no reason whatsoever to feel guilty. About anything.

And yet that was exactly what she felt as she found her sister standing there in the doorway to the bedroom, her arms crossed and a flat sort of look on her face.

For a moment, they stared at each other across the stillness of the early morning.

"Sometimes when I can't sleep," Eleanor said with as much quiet dignity as she could manage, "I walk in the halls. It gets the blood moving, at the very least."

Vivi let out a small sort of laugh that suggested she didn't find anything funny at all.

"You can't possibly expect me to believe that, can you? I'm your sister, not your seven-year-old student."

"What are you doing here, Vivi?" Eleanor asked softly. "The guest suites are clear across the house."

Vivi's mouth was a taut line, and that flat look was still making her new gold eyes look a bit more tarnished than usual. "I went looking for you. I was after a little bit of sister time. And guess what? You haven't been here for hours."

"You wanted sister time in the middle of the night?" Eleanor asked, and she didn't try too hard to keep the skepticism out of her voice. "Did you imagine that I would be awake? Or did you think you would wake me up, even though I have to get up and work in the morning?"

Neither one, she was well aware, said great things about how her sister saw her. Hugo's words swirled around in her head, and it seemed she couldn't banish them the way she wished she could. And something sour was sloshing around in her belly, making it worse.

Because Eleanor didn't know that it would really be all that out of line if Vivi *had* assumed that Eleanor would be perfectly all right with being woken up at all hours. Wasn't that what her role had always been? And there was only one person who had demanded Eleanor stay in that role. Eleanor herself.

She had always been so desperate to be needed, because love was tricky and people died and took their love with them. Need was better. Need made her indispensable.

But it had never made her feel as alive as Hugo had. As if she'd been sleepwalking for years.

"Do you think I can't tell what you've been up to?" Vivi asked. Her voice was strange. As flat as her gaze, and yet there was that sharp undercurrent. "How could you do this?"

"I don't know what you think I've done." Eleanor squared her shoulders and forced herself to ignore the part of her that had always been afraid to square off with Vivi. Because if she lost Vivi on top of everything else she'd lost, what would she have? She clarified. "To you."

Vivi shook her head. "All the things I've done, all the trouble I've gone to for *us*, Eleanor. And you can't even tell me the truth."

"I think that's unfair."

"If you had something going on with the Duke, you should have told me, so I wouldn't have bothered making a fool of myself at that dinner last night." Vivi shook her head. "Am I just a party trick you like to trot out to amuse yourself and your aristocratic friend?"

The sweeping injustice of that was almost enough to knock Eleanor back a step or two.

"I don't have any 'aristocratic friends,' Vivi," Eleanor managed to say, her voice on the verge of trembling. It felt a lot like anger, something she'd always swallowed down before. Something she'd always pretended she didn't feel, no matter what. "I think we both know that's you, not me. I work at Groves House. You're on holiday. It's been years since we decided it would make sense for you to make like a socialite and land a rich husband, and all you've done since is go to parties and spend the money I make. Which one of us is the party trick?"

She heard her own words hanging there in the quiet of the room, and could feel them shaking around inside of her, like a new kind of shivering. And she didn't know if she needed to lie down. Or possibly get sick. Or apologize, instantly.

But she didn't do any of those things. She should have said something years ago. She'd bitten her tongue and she'd bitten her tongue—and it was funny, wasn't it, that it took Hugo teaching her all the other, more fun things she could do with it to loosen it at last.

Eleanor waited to feel shamed by that, but it didn't come.

"This is why they call him a monster," Vivi said softly. "You know that, right? He ruins everything he touches. Even us."

Abruptly, Eleanor was finished with this conversation. She'd had enough. She straightened herself up and reminded herself that she was a grown woman. Not a teen who'd been caught sneaking about after curfew. She didn't have to stand here and offer explanations.

And she certainly didn't need to listen to her sister's malicious and uninformed thoughts about Hugo.

"I don't need an interrogation, Vivi," she said then. Not unkindly. Just matter-of-factly. "I really do have to work in a couple of hours."

"You can't possibly think—" Vivi began, a scornful sort of note in her voice that Eleanor didn't like at all.

"I don't ask you to account for yourself, do I?" she retorted, cutting Vivi off as she moved across the floor toward the doorway her sister stood in. "I choose to believe that everything you do, you do with both our best interests at heart. I don't understand why you can't extend me the same courtesy."

She brushed past Vivi then, half expecting her sister to grab her arm and escalate things the way she'd been known to do in the past, but Vivi only watched her—closely—as she made her way into the bathroom. Eleanor turned on the taps, ran her fingers through the water as she fiddled with the temperature, and pretended everything was normal. That she was still a virgin. That she was still the same person she'd been yesterday.

That she hadn't spent her night so full of Hugo in every possible way that she could barely breathe now.

The truth was, she didn't want to breathe.

And love her sister as she might, she didn't want to share what had happened with her. Eleanor wanted to keep it to herself. She wanted to hold it tight.

She wanted to hoard it, a bright, gleaming evening set against the rest of her practical life.

"He will chew you up and spit you out," Vivi said darkly from the door. "That's what he does, like it's his job. Because he doesn't have a real job."

Eleanor shook the water off her hand as she straightened. There were so many things she could say to that. For example, she could point out that Vivi had dressed for dinner last night as if she was perfectly willing to risk a few tooth marks. But she didn't. She only walked to the bathroom door and she smiled at her sister.

"Are you concerned for me?" she asked quietly. "Or is this something else?"

Vivi flushed at that. Her eyes narrowed. "Of course I'm concerned for you. What else would it be?"

"I can't imagine."

"I'm not jealous of you, Eleanor, if that's what you mean."

"Perish the thought," Eleanor said dryly.

"The truth is, I know what men like Hugo Grovesmoor are like. You don't. I've spent years around his type while you've…"

"Yes." Eleanor nodded. "While I've scuttled about in the shadows like the help."

Vivi let out a breath, and if Eleanor wasn't mistaken, the look in her new gold eyes then was pity.

Something in her froze solid.

"If you don't like your life, you should change it," Vivi said quietly. "I'll help. But Hugo Grovesmoor isn't a change, Eleanor. He's an atom bomb. And I understand that you're hopped up on hormones right now and feeling lavish, but I don't think you're prepared for the damage a man like him will do."

"I love you, Vivi," Eleanor managed to say past the sudden, sinking feeling inside of her, because who was she kidding? She knew nothing about men, much less men like Hugo. Why was she so certain she was right and Vivi was wrong? "You know I do. But I have to get ready for my day."

"I love you, too," Vivi retorted. "And don't worry. I'm going to prove it. I'll take care of you. I always said I would."

Eleanor didn't know what that meant and more, she was certain she didn't want to know, especially once Vivi left.

She ran her bath and she sat in it for a long time, until the water grew cold and the clock in her living room told her it was time to move. Then she climbed out, toweled off, and got dressed for her usual day with Geraldine as if she was still the same old Eleanor in the same old body she'd had before.

Because she was, damn it. No atom bombs. No damage.

She was exactly who she'd always been, despite her ill-considered words to Vivi. She castigated herself for each and every one of them as she took Geraldine through her lessons, the last she'd have for a few days now that Eleanor's initial six weeks were up and Eleanor was due a brief holiday. They talked about what Geraldine would do over her break. They talked about the books Geraldine was reading and Geraldine's many adventures with Pono, the rooster plush toy she liked best.

They did not see the Duke. Eleanor told herself she was grateful. Because she didn't want to be that silly virgin—the one even her own sister seemed certain she already was—and that meant she'd needed the day to regain her equanimity.

"You're fine now," she told herself stoutly as she climbed the stairs from the nursery that led to her rooms. "Perfectly fine, as ever."

But when she let herself into her rooms, Vivi was waiting. Again.

"You should have just had a cot brought in," Eleanor said mildly.

"I think you'd better pack, love," Vivi replied. "We'll need to leave tonight."

"No need for that, surely," Eleanor said. She sank down on the nearest upright, Elizabethan chair. "We can leave in the morning. More chance of a train, I'd think."

"You don't understand," Vivi said, and while her voice was patient, her gaze was not. Her eyes fairly danced, too bright and a bit too sharp, as if she'd been at the spirits again. "You're not going to want to be here in the morning."

Eleanor discovered that she was tired. Very, very tired. That was what happened when a person got all of about twelve minutes of sleep all night long. She couldn't say she regretted it. But it had obviously dulled her brain, because she wasn't following Vivi at all.

"Vivi," she began, "I really don't..."

"I told you I would take care of you and I meant it," her sister said stoutly. "There are certain tabloids that are so desperate for a story about Hugo that they'd pay anything for a fake one. Which means they'd pay twice that for a real one."

Eleanor was glad she was sitting down, because she thought that if she hadn't been, she might have fallen.

"No," she managed to say from a far distance, while her ears buzzed at her and her lunch threatened the back of her throat. "I signed a nondisclosure agreement. I can't sell anything."

"You can't," Vivi said with a hard sort of shrug. "But I can. There's been nothing new on Hugo in ages. Everyone's tired of speculating what horrors he's visiting on that poor kid. A sex romp with the governess is exactly what they'd expect, isn't it?"

"I forbid it," Eleanor snapped, and she hardly recognized her own voice. Or the fact she'd surged to her feet and had balled her hands up into fists.

Vivi only eyed her from across the room, that pitying look on her face again.

"I thought you'd say something like that."

"You thought correctly."

"Which is why I didn't consult you." Vivi shook her head. "It's done, Eleanor. We have five hundred thousand pounds in our account and you don't have to say a word. Or do another thing. Our troubles are over. But the story is running tomorrow." Vivi tilted her head, taking in the house all around them. This life Eleanor had known better than to get too attached to—hadn't she? And Hugo, whose name seemed to detonate inside of her, shaking through her. Shaking her. "And if I were you, I wouldn't be here when he reads it."

CHAPTER TWELVE

ELEANOR HAD BETRAYED HIM.

What bothered Hugo most was that somehow, this entirely predictable turn of events surprised him.

"Off to catch the last train," Mrs. Redding had said yesterday afternoon when Hugo had actually lowered himself to ask where Eleanor was, with her usual disapproving sniff. "A bit keen to celebrate her time off, if you ask me."

"No one did," Hugo had replied, with a smile. A cheeky one. Which had done absolutely nothing but make the old woman roll her eyes. Their love language, he'd told himself.

But that had been before the tabloids published their usual filth and innuendo in the morning. That had been when he was still looking forward to seeing her. Craving it, if he was honest. He'd woken yesterday morning to find her missing from his bed and it was as if he was missing a limb. As if they'd spent every night of a good five years sleeping wrapped around each other in the same bed, and her sudden absence hurt.

Hurt.

He didn't understand it. Or perhaps he didn't want to understand it. Yesterday, all he'd wanted was to lose himself in her innocence. Her sweetness. And all that intoxicating heat.

Somehow he'd forgotten to be cynical where Eleanor was concerned.

An unforgivable oversight.

Because sometime yesterday, when he'd still been lying in his bed surrounded by her scent and marveling at the notion that innocence could be so addictive—transformative, even, which should have appalled someone as calcified in his own bitterness as Hugo had been for years—Eleanor had not been doing the same. Instead, she had been sharing what had happened between them with her sister. Reporting back, perhaps, that their plan had worked? And sometimes after that, Vivi had sold an extraordinarily salacious and sordid tale to the most shrill and suggestive of the tabloids about *Horrible Hugo*, the *Most Hated Duke in England*, and his *Sexcapades with his Governesses*.

Really, Hugo could have written it himself.

What astonished him was that he hadn't. He'd let his guard down for the first time since Isobel had gotten her hooks in him—hell, he'd even told Eleanor the truth. As if she was someone he could trust. As if, when she'd sounded so appalled at the very notion that anyone could sell him out to the tabloids, she'd meant it.

Hugo couldn't trust anyone. Ever. How many times did he need to learn it?

The truth was, he'd handed Eleanor and her sister all the ammunition they'd need. Fourteen previous governesses, all unceremoniously sacked. When the suspiciously unknown sister of a periodic tabloid bit of arm candy, the overly ambitious Vivi—whose desperation repeatedly led her to all sorts of entanglements that found their way into tawdry little tell-alls—had turned up, Hugo should have seen this coming.

Why hadn't he seen this coming?

Hugo treats his governesses like his own private harem!

That was what the paper screeched, in that awful tone they used when they were putting words into people's mouths. Then again, he imagined a woman who could giggle aggressively the way Vivi Andrews had could turn a pointed phrase or two when she had a mind to.

He doesn't give a toss about poor Isobel's baby, preferring depraved sex romps in his country estate to changing nappies.

It was nothing he hadn't read before a thousand times. It wasn't even particularly well done, in his opinion, given he was now a kind of connoisseur of tabloid hit pieces. A giant spread with vague accusations about unsavory sexual practices, a glamour shot of Vivi as if she was the governess in question next to a picture of what might have been Eleanor in a hooded something or other, and an excuse to fling pictures of lost, sainted Isobel and Torquil all over the place. Along with everyone's favorite picture of toddler Geraldine—all gap teeth and copper curls, looking lost and in need of nappy-changing—as if she'd been preserved forever at an age when Hugo's neglect could have resulted in her toddling about in her own filth.

He was tempted to ring up Vivi Andrews himself and demand a cut of what must have been a very tidy profit. But he couldn't do that, could he, because that would mean very coldly and calculatedly discussing when and how Vivi and her sister had decided to set him up so beautifully.

And then asking the question he wanted to know the

answer to but was afraid to ask: How had they known that Eleanor's brand of stroppy innocence would send him crashing to his knees? He'd had women throwing themselves at him his entire life. Some were desperate for the title. Others only wanted a little turn in the tabloids. He'd have said that there was no possible approach he hadn't grown tired of years ago.

But somehow they'd picked the one that worked.

He had a lot of questions for Eleanor. He was even tempted to question whether her virginity had been real—but no. He knew better. He'd been there. The betrayal was real, but so was that night. So was what had passed between them.

Hugo might not know much, but he knew that.

Not that it helped. He still found himself stalking around his damned house in the gloomy twilight, like a sepulchral poet or something equally tragic.

Hugo couldn't remember the last time he'd surrendered so completely to self-pity. He made his lonely, nauseatingly melancholic way into his library, broodingly eyeing the shelves he'd once told Eleanor she'd nearly knocked down. Tonight he was tempted to knock them down himself. With a bottle of whiskey and his own hard head.

Because he never learned.

He was the monster of all of England's most fervent fantasies, paying out his penance in his rambling out house, alone. Forever.

Nothing could change that. Not his own disinterest in the narrative. Not the fact his ward was, despite all wailing to the contrary, a healthy and relatively happy child. Not a scowling, insufficiently respectful governess who'd treated him as an irritant to be borne, much like the sulky moors all around.

He might have imagined that things had changed that night and that wildly optimistic morning after, but that was only more proof that he was an idiot of epic proportions.

"Nothing new in that," he muttered to himself, not even bothering to scowl at the fire. "It's the bloody story of my life."

As was the certainty that somehow, he would pay for this, too.

The door to the library opened then. Hugo watched, bemused, as it scraped its way inward across the thick rug on the floor. Almost as if the person entering the room wasn't strong enough to move it.

He blinked when he saw the figure standing in the door then. It was Geraldine, who never sought him out of her own accord, and never here. She usually suffered warily through her dinners with him, eyeing him suspiciously from her place down the table. Tonight she looked less like the celebrated daughter of a world-renowned beauty and more…like a kid. Her copper-colored plaits stood out at odd angles from her head, she was dressed in a jumper and jeans like any random child might have been, and her little face was drawn into a frown.

She looked sturdy. And surly, Hugo couldn't help but notice.

"Yes, my ward?" he drawled. He lounged back in his chair before the fire and raised his brows at her, doing his best, as ever, to sound like a proper guardian instead of the world's favorite scandal.

The little girl screwed up her nose while the corners of her pudgy mouth turned down, but she kept her scowl aimed right at him.

Evidence of Eleanor's teaching, clearly, he thought, and hated the lancing sensation of something that couldn't be pain—because he refused to accept pain—straight through him.

"Nanny Marie says Miss Andrews is never coming back."

Hugo waited for her to continue, but Geraldine only stared at him. Rather challengingly, actually.

"I am at a loss as to where *Nanny Marie*," and he utterly failed to keep the sardonic inflection from his tone at that name, "would get the impression that she has access to staffing decisions."

"I like her."

"Nanny Marie? I couldn't identify her in a lineup, I'm afraid. Much less determine whether or not I cared for her one way or another."

"Miss Andrews."

Geraldine sounded testy, but definitive. And that was the trouble. Hugo liked Miss Andrews, too. Definitively.

Even now.

He'd told Eleanor things he'd never told anyone. He'd expected her to understand him when no one else had, ever. And then sure enough, she had. Meanwhile, she'd held on to her innocence far, far longer than most women her age, and she'd gifted it to him. *Him.* As if it had never occurred to her that Hugo the Horrible wasn't a suitable recipient for such a gift.

As if she'd felt completely safe with him, which should have been impossible.

And as if that wasn't enough, Hugo wasn't entirely sure that she was the one who had been rendered fragile by what had happened that night. There were parts of him that no longer fit the way they had before. Parts of him that scraped at all the walls he'd built inside, as if *he* didn't fit anymore.

He had been perfectly content here. Happy enough to

live out the consequences of Isobel's decisions far away from prying eyes and telescopic lenses. Perfectly willing to let the country shake in horror at the notion of what he might be doing to their lost saint's precious little girl. No small part of him had thrilled to the idea that he was literally some people's nightmare. Every single night.

He'd taken pleasure in that. They deserved it.

Hugo couldn't understand where all that had gone. How it had disappeared in the course of one very long, very thorough exploration of a prim governess's astonishingly curvy body.

What was it in him that couldn't shrug her off the way he had all the others? Why was it so impossible to draw a line under the latest tabloid scandal and move on? When his past mistakes had aired out his laundry in front of whole nations, Hugo had been unbothered.

He had the sinking, lowering notion that all this time, he'd never known real ruin at all.

"You didn't fire her, did you?" Geraldine demanded, reminding him he was not alone with his brooding.

Hugo eyed her. The little girl had moved further into the room. Now she stood near the fireplace, her hands on her little hips, glaring at her guardian without a seeming care in the world. As if she thought, should there be an altercation, she could take him.

He had tried so hard these past three years, since the accident that had taken Isobel and Torquil. He'd kept his distance from this child. He had tended to Geraldine's needs, but not in a way that could ever hurt her. Or compromise her. He'd been certain—as certain as his critics, if not more so—that left to his own devices, he could only do harm.

That was what he did, he knew. Harm.

He certainly hadn't allowed himself to like Geraldine. Or anyone.

But all he could see was Eleanor, then. Her face, so lovely and so fierce, as she'd stood up for Geraldine. *It's not her fault,* she'd told him.

And Hugo knew that. He'd gone out of his way to make sure he never brought his feelings about Isobel into any interaction he had with Geraldine. But it hadn't occurred to him until today—until Eleanor—that he hadn't let his feelings enter into anything in a very long time.

Because the fact of the matter was, he rather liked this little girl. He liked how unafraid she was. He liked the fact that she was seven years old and yet had no apparent second thoughts about walking straight into her guardian's library and confronting him. And the more he stared at her, the less she seemed to care. Her little chin tilted up. She even sniffed, as if impatient.

She was a fighter. How could he not adore her for it? Especially when he'd stopped fighting so long ago.

"If I did fire her, that would be my decision as your guardian and would not require a consultation, Geraldine," Hugo said reprovingly. But when her face looked stormy, he relented. "But I didn't let her go."

He crooked his finger and then pointed to the leather chair across from him. Geraldine made a huffing sound that did not bode well for her teen years, but she obeyed him. With perhaps a little too much stomping, and more attitude than he would have thought possible from a sweet little child, she moved from the fireplace to climb up into the big leather chair. The big piece of furniture seemed to swallow her whole, but that didn't bother Geraldine. She slid back, stuck her feet out straight in front of her, and crossed her arms over her chest.

Mutinously.

"Where is she if you didn't get rid of her?" Geraldine asked as if she'd caught Hugo out in a dirty lie.

"I feel certain Miss Andrews told you that she was taking a few days' break. She does get one, you know. We can't lock her away in a cage and force her to stay here all the time."

Though the idea held some appeal.

The little girl's chin jutted out. "Why not?"

"Excellent question."

"We should go get her back, then," Geraldine said, with a wide gesture of one hand, as if Hugo really was an idiot and she was leading him to the right answer because he was taking too long to get there himself.

And the damnedest thing was, Hugo admired that, too.

Geraldine was not yet ten and yet she was showing more fight than he had in the past fifteen years.

Why had he allowed Isobel to paint him the way she had? Of course there was no fighting a slanted story or a nasty rumor, but he hadn't tried and he hadn't done anything else, either. He hadn't pointedly lived a life completely opposed to the one Isobel claimed he did. He'd never even defended himself. He'd told himself it was because he was too proud to dignify her claims with a response, but was that truly it? Or was it the same sort of martyrdom he'd always abhorred when Isobel faked it?

Had he been waiting all this time for someone to look at him and see him and believe that he wasn't the things that had been said about him?

Maybe there was some virtue in that. Or there could have been—had his father not died believing the very worst of him.

The fact of the matter was, Hugo had never seen the point of fighting battles he'd decided in advance that he couldn't win. He'd never righted a single wrong. He'd simply sat here and taken it. And to what end?

Whether the public loved him or hated him, he was the only parental influence in this child's life. And despite that handicap, Geraldine appeared to be thriving. She was flushed with indignation, and if he wasn't mistaken, love.

Love.

It thudded into him. Then again. Like another fight he was destined to lose. But this time, he didn't intend to go down alone.

Was it virtue to act as if he was a punching bag for all these years or was it an especially noxious version of self-pity?

Hugo didn't know. But he did know this. He was a creature of temper and mood, unable to control himself at any time, the tabloids said.

So he saw no reason to start now.

"Yes," he said slowly, smiling at Geraldine. Until she smiled back, as if they were together in this. Because they were. "We really should get her back. What an excellent idea."

CHAPTER THIRTEEN

RETURNING TO LONDON was like being slapped in the face with the pitiless palm of a little too much reality. But there was nothing to do but grin and bear it.

Eleanor gritted her teeth, figuratively and literally, and set about cleaning up Vivi's mess.

Not the big mess, of course. Not the mess that haunted her, making her feel sick and small and ashamed. Or shaky every time she saw the *Daily Mail* in a newsstand. Not the mess that rolled around inside of her, making her feel as oily and greasy and horrid as what Vivi had done, every time she drew breath—

No, there was no fixing that. Vivi had sold Eleanor's story as her own and asserted, repeatedly and proudly, that she would do it again. She claimed it was for both of their own good, though that prickly, ugly thing inside of Eleanor thought different and left marks every time it did. But it made no difference. It was done.

And Eleanor was just one more scar Hugo would add to his collection. One more lie to add to the rest.

Eleanor concentrated on the things she could fix.

She placated their landlord, pleading their case as sweetly as she could. She did not take Vivi's advice to simply tell the suspicious old woman where she could stuff it, because all that money that Vivi had been promised had yet to come through. She cleaned. Everything. From what passed for baseboards in their tiny tip of a flat to the windows and back. She cleaned every cup and saucer, plate and utensil. She even cleaned out the terrifying old tea mugs, coated in tannins as evidence of their long years of use.

She cleaned as if she was on a mission.

As if it was penance.

And none of that seemed to do a single thing to make her feel better.

Eleanor suspected that there would be no feeling better. That there would be no recovering from this. It didn't matter how she'd come to betray Hugo, surely. It only mattered that she had. Not only had she betrayed him, she hadn't even had the decency to look him in the face and let him know she'd done it.

She hadn't even said goodbye.

Instead, she'd snuck off into the gathering fall evening with her case and her sister, like some kind of thief in reverse.

That was the part she didn't think she could live with. That was the part that scraped to her belly like some ravenous beast with sharp claws. Over and over again.

"You're being a bit dramatic, no?" Vivi asked one evening.

The way she had back in that other life, when Eleanor had never met Hugo Grovesmoor and hadn't had the faintest idea how he would upend her life. The way she did with a little too much frequency, to Eleanor's mind, given her penchant for making an opera out of all and sundry.

Eleanor eyed her sister over the pile of mending that she'd been ruthlessly going through for days now that the flat fairly sparkled. Vivi's trousers. Vivi's poncey skirts. Vivi's lovely and expensive clothes that Vivi herself didn't bother to treat with anything resembling reverence. Or even the bare minimum of care, it appeared.

"While tending to your sewing?" Eleanor asked mildly, which was getting harder to do all the time. "I didn't realize it was possible to be theatrical while mending."

Vivi lifted herself up from the bit of floor in front of the telly, where she'd been flinging herself this way and that to a DVD of some shiny-toothed and alarmingly narrow American celebrity trainer.

"Everyone's obsessed with this workout," she'd informed Eleanor as she'd contorted about.

Eleanor had responded by finishing off the last packet of chocolate biscuits. *At* her.

Now Vivi plunked herself down on the small sofa next to Eleanor, making the cushion dip alarmingly and a pile of her waiting mending tip over. Eleanor thought she'd switch the telly over to a show and drown her mood out, as she been doing since they'd returned, but instead she twisted her body around so she could look her sister straight in the face.

"I know you think you hate me," Vivi said, her voice serious and an unexpected wallop. "I understand that. I even accept it. You don't have any experience with these things."

Eleanor's teeth ached. She made herself unclench her jaw.

"If you mean making up tawdry stories and selling them to the highest bidder, then no. I certainly don't."

"I mean Hugo." Vivi's voice was soft. Worse, kind. "I mean men."

Eleanor bent her head to the blouse she was attempting to repair. She kept her attention furiously focused on her needle. But she was sure that it was no use, that Vivi could see the flush that crept up the back of her neck and threatened her cheeks as well. She didn't understand how a topic that she'd been so pleased to discuss with Hugo— or not discuss, as the case might be, because he'd known and he'd handled it—she had no desire at all to discuss with her sister.

"I think I'd prefer to skip the 'poor, sad Eleanor' discussion tonight, thanks." Eleanor had to order herself to unclench her jaw. Again. And do something with her shoulders before she lifted them over the top of her head. "I think it's possible that the only thing worse than the story you sold might be your pity."

"I don't pity you, Eleanor," Vivi said, and her voice was different. Almost unrecognizable. It made Eleanor uneasy. "I envy you. I don't think I've ever been soft or dewy-eyed about anything. Not even way back when you cried over me in the hospital and I didn't."

Eleanor paused. She very carefully put down her sewing. And then she turned and held her sister's gaze.

"Vivi. Please tell me you're not about to give me 'the talk.'"

Vivi's eyes gleamed then, and they really did look like shiny gold coins, something that Eleanor wished she could find more annoying than she did.

"You spent all night with Hugo Grovesmoor. I think any attempt at a sex talk at this point would be a waste of breath, don't you?"

Eleanor tried to hide the pain that flashed over her. Or that near-reflexive urge to draw in a sharp breath, as if that would ease it.

"I don't want to talk about Hugo."

It was more that she didn't want to talk about Hugo

with Vivi, if she was honest. But either way, thinking about him was painful enough.

"I know you're not going to believe me." Vivi reached over and put her hand on Eleanor's leg, and all Eleanor could seem to do was stare at it. "I know that I'm too selfish and take you for granted and anything else you want to accuse me of. It's all true. I know it's true. But that doesn't mean I don't love you, Eleanor. And I get to protect you, too."

Eleanor frowned at that hand on her leg. Hard. "Is that what you were doing, Vivi? Protecting me? Are you sure?"

Eleanor didn't know how she dared ask that—especially because she wasn't sure she wanted to know the answer. Beside her, Vivi blew out a breath. And when Eleanor looked up, something else glittered in her gaze.

"That's fair enough. I can't deny that I reacted a bit poorly when I arrived at Groves House. I guess it all took me by surprise."

"You were jealous." Eleanor held her sister's gaze, and dared her to refute it.

But Vivi only shrugged, making the curls she'd piled on the top of her head bob a bit. "I don't know what I was. I've worked hard, for years."

Eleanor wanted to argue that, but something made her hold her tongue. Vivi's gaze darkened.

"I've put up with people you wouldn't tolerate for the length of a simple conversation, thank you. I thought we were on the same page. I thought we had specific roles to play. And then it looked as if maybe everything I was doing was beside the point and I didn't know how to handle that." She shook her head. "I'm sorry I'm not as perfect as you are."

"That's not fair."

"You could have told me how much you liked him."
Vivi's voice cracked slightly, startling them both. "You
could have told me that, Eleanor."

"I didn't think you would have listened if I had."

Vivi shook her head, as if that had hurt her and she
was reeling. "Of course I would have listened. *You're my
sister.* It's you and me against the world, remember?"

"I remember," Eleanor whispered. "Of course I remember."

They sat there for a moment, and something shifted
inside of Eleanor as they did. That ugly, clawed weight
seemed to dissipate a little.

"But this is what I wanted to talk to you about even
if it makes you turn red. You don't know about men like
Hugo, Eleanor. I do."

"I was under the impression that there were no men
like Hugo."

She knew that was true for her. She thought it might
also be true for the world, given the way they talked
about him as if he'd rounded them all up, abused them
horribly and personally, and then booted them out of a
speeding vehicle.

"Men are more alike than not." And there was a weariness in Vivi's voice that pricked at Eleanor. She'd been
so concentrated on herself. So focused on all the ways
she felt overlooked. Taken advantage of. Why had it never
occurred to her to wonder if her sister felt the same way?
"Keen to take what they can get. No matter what. But it
doesn't necessarily mean more than that."

And Eleanor wanted to argue. She wanted to tell Vivi
that she was wrong. That she didn't know Hugo. But
the fact was… Neither did Eleanor. She'd lived in his
house, true. He'd flirted with her, she'd given him her

virginity—but despite what that meant to her, it was likely all in a day's work for the likes of Hugo.

She believed that he wasn't the monster the tabloids had made him out to be. But that didn't make him a monk. It didn't make her any less of a fool. She felt her eyes fill up, and ducked her head to hide it. And blink the tears back before they could fall.

"I feel like such a fool," she whispered.

"I can't think of a woman who wouldn't fall for Hugo Grovesmoor," Vivi said, distinctly. "Not one. He's gorgeous and evil and everyone knows he's wild in bed. You never stood a chance."

She could talk about more of this than she'd thought, it turned out. But she couldn't talk about Hugo's reputation in bed. There was only so much she could be expected to handle, surely. Without cracking apart into little pieces, all over the floor, that she knew her careless sister would never sweep up.

"And what now?" Eleanor asked instead, lifting up her hands and then letting them drop back to her lap. "What am I supposed to do now?" She moved one hand in a lazy, circular motion that encompassed the whole of her chest. "With all of *this*."

Vivi laughed, then. It was that merry laugh of hers that still warmed up the room. It astonished Eleanor how welcoming she found the sound.

"That I can help with." Vivi got to her feet and reached out her hand, beckoning for Eleanor to join her. "Come on, then. The night is young and filled with trouble for us to throw ourselves into."

"Oh, no," Eleanor said then, with a frown. "I don't get into trouble. I—"

"You don't have a job that you have to go to bed early for. You have nowhere to be in the morning."

"Well—"

"And unless I'm mistaken, you're a bit of a scarlet woman, fresh from a shocking affair with the most hated man in England."

"But it's a Wednesday," Eleanor said. Scandalized.

"Ah, grasshopper," Vivi replied mischievously. "I have so much to teach you."

And that was how Eleanor found herself out at one of those desperately chic clubs that Vivi spent so much of her time in. This one was so new it was considered a coup to get in, Vivi informed Eleanor as she got them waved past the line that snaked off down the block and around the corner. On a blustery Wednesday.

Inside, it was a cavernous place, filled with too many dizzying lights and far too many people dressed sleek and sharp. Not exactly the sort of crowd Eleanor felt at home in. But Vivi had asked Eleanor to trust that she knew what she was doing, and Eleanor had agreed to do it.

That was how she'd ended up in the ridiculous outfit her sister picked out for her, sourced more from Vivi's closet than her own.

"I told you it would fit," Vivi had said with great satisfaction when she'd finished her handiwork back at the flat. "It's quite Cinderella, isn't it?"

"If Cinderella was a bit of a tart."

Eleanor ran her hands over the slinky, stretchy dress that gave her curves absolutely nowhere to hide. For the seventeenth time, and it still accomplished nothing. She was still all breasts and hips. There was only one person alive who had ever made her feel beautiful—

But there was no use thinking about Hugo. The sooner she accepted that, the better. He wouldn't have wanted to deal with an overly sentimental virgin for long anyway. That was what Eleanor kept telling herself. No one liked clingy, especially in an employee. Vivi's tabloid story had only hastened the inevitable.

Strange how that failed to make her feel any better.

"There's nothing wrong with a tart," Vivi had admonished her, then flashed one of her grins. "It's all in the quality of the pastry, I promise you."

Eleanor didn't know what that meant. Or, rather, she opted not to pick up on her sister's innuendo. What she did know, within seconds of entering the club, was that she was most certainly too old for this scene. Perhaps not chronologically. But she had nothing in common with the blissed-out, gleaming creatures who danced madly and drank deeply and didn't seem remotely aware of the fact that there was a world outside where people were already tucked up in their beds, ready for the next morning.

And yet, as soon as she recognized that she wasn't built to enjoy flinging back spirits and then leaping around the dance floor like Geraldine on too much sugar, she really rather enjoyed herself. It was too loud to worry about Hugo. It was too dark to worry about herself and what on earth she planned to do with her life. It was too noisy and too chaotic to do more than smile and then duck away from the strange men who tried to speak to her now and again.

Maybe tottering around town on a random Wednesday was exactly the medicine she needed, come to think of it. Eleanor decided it was, and let the night wash over her.

It was coming on three in the morning when Vivi was finally ready to leave her pack of posh friends and their innumerable dramas. Eleanor was quite pleased with herself for contriving to keep her eyes open the whole of the night, even if she'd lapsed into a strange state where she couldn't tell if she was actually asleep or not. It hadn't seemed to make much of a difference.

Vivi was chattering, as much to herself as anyone else as far as Eleanor could tell, about summoning a taxi driver with her mobile and about which of her circle she'd rowed with over the course of the evening. And Eleanor let it all wash over her, too. Because yes, she thought she really was half-asleep. But also, none of this felt like life. None of it felt real.

London didn't fit her anymore. The thought slid into her head and stayed there, taking up space. Growing with every breath. She had no idea what she was going do about that, because the only place she'd felt as if she'd fit, she'd lost. Yorkshire was as closed to her as if there was a wall around it and several armies keeping her out.

Stop, she ordered herself. *Stop thinking about Hugo.*

"I cannot imagine what you think you're doing, Miss Andrews."

Eleanor froze. Surely that voice was only in her head, the way it had been all week—but no. It was still going.

"Role models for proper young ladies, the wards of dukes, no less, cannot be carousing in the streets of London at this hour. Whatever would the tabloids say?"

That voice was straight from her dreams. It couldn't be real. Eleanor didn't react—but Vivi did. She froze solid next to her.

And Eleanor let herself believe what was right before her eyes, a car or two down from where she and Vivi had exited the club.

Hugo.

CHAPTER FOURTEEN

OF COURSE IT was Hugo.

He lounged at the curb next to a gleaming sports car that was as sleek and muscular—and expensive—as he was. It was hard to tell the difference between them. Both seemed to light up the dark all around them with the same kind of danger.

She'd dreamed this a thousand times since she'd left Groves House, but now it was happening and Eleanor didn't know what to say. What could she possibly say?

"Hugo…" she whispered.

The Duke straightened, pushing away from his leaning position against the side of the powerful vehicle. He looked elegant and dangerous with the streets of London arrayed there behind him, as if his presence rendered the ancient, ever-settled city as wild and untamed as the moors up north. His dark gaze was almost too hot to bear.

And he focused on Eleanor as if she was the only other person for miles.

For a moment she thought she was.

Then Vivi cleared her throat, and Eleanor felt reality slap her again. Hard.

"I'm sure you must be very angry," Vivi began, looking and sounding as uncertain as Eleanor felt. At a later point, she might reflect on the fact that she'd never actually heard her sister sound remorseful before. But at the moment, she was too busy greedily drinking in the sight of Hugo. Right there in front of her and who cared how.

"I don't get angry," Hugo said in that low way of his that made everything inside Eleanor seemed to run liquid and hot, then shudder before starting all over again. "What is another scandalous story in the tabloids to me? One fiction after the next, without end. One life destroyed by my touch only to appear in a bathing costume in Ibiza the following summer on the arm of a film star. Who can keep track?"

It was the cynicism in his voice that almost killed her, Eleanor thought. The weariness. It felt like a knife straight into her gut.

Because she remembered. She remembered what it had been like in his bedchamber that night. She remembered the look on his beautiful face then. Open. Filled with longing and wonder and almost too much light to bear.

"You should keep track," Eleanor heard herself say, just as she heard the huskiness in her voice that she was sure told him far too much. Gave too much away. Made her far too vulnerable. She didn't care. "Someone should keep track. Someday you will make a note of all the lies and I wouldn't be surprised if apologies followed."

Beside her, she felt Vivi tense, but she couldn't spare a glance for her sister. Not now.

"Don't be so naïve," Hugo murmured, all weary cynicism and a bit of censure besides, as if he was in some snide ballroom making cutting remarks behind a quizzing glass, like the Dukes in Eleanor's favorite novels. And yet his voice seemed to fill the street, then reverberate around inside of her, too. "There are never any apologies. *Especially* when the lies are proven to be falsehoods.

No one cares about that. They care about the story, and the more salacious and slanderous it is, the better."

Eleanor stepped in front of Vivi then, because the tension in the air felt like a weapon. "It's not her fault. She was taking care of me."

Hugo smirked, and it made Eleanor flinch.

"Because I am the big bad wolf, after all," he agreed in that same dark way. "Despoiler of maidens when they are so unfortunate as to cross my path. Hunkered down in my Yorkshire cave, picking my teeth with the bones of my enemies."

"It is because you say things like that with such obvious relish," Eleanor pointed out crisply, "that it's difficult to imagine you are anything else."

"I'm not sorry," Vivi said over Eleanor's shoulder. Unwisely, in Eleanor's opinion. "Everyone knows what you're like. If you've come down here to bully us, or make things difficult because of the story, you should know that I'm more than capable of taking care of Eleanor as well as myself."

"Are you now?" Hugo's smirk could have taken chunks out of the old, listed building behind them. Eleanor was surprised it still stood. Or that she did. "Let me guess. You will smile prettily. Eleanor will frown. And before you will fall the whole of London and assorted villains just like me. With a click of your fingers."

Hugo didn't wait for an answer to that. He did that thing with his hand again. He merely lifted it, and just like that a cab came screeching to a halt in front of him. He moved from front of his own sports car to the cab, and opened the passenger door with great flourish.

"Your carriage awaits," he said.

Eleanor blinked. It seemed absurd to her that Hugo would appear before her at three o'clock in the morning only to summon them a taxi, but maybe Vivi was more right than she'd wanted to accept. Maybe men were in fact this mystifying at all times. She set her teeth in that way that was becoming a little too common, straightened her shoulders to match, and she marched toward the cab.

"Not you," Hugo said, a current of something like laughter in his voice. Or maybe Eleanor was so desperate to pretend he didn't hate her that she was imagining it. Either way, he reached out a hand and hooked her arm. "You're coming with me."

Vivi stopped on Eleanor's other side. "Oh, no, she's not. Don't go after the weak link. If you want a fight, fight me."

And Eleanor stood there on a London street in the middle of a Wednesday night that had long since become a Thursday morning, her sister fierce at her back and this maddening, intoxicating, gorgeous man before her.

It seemed as if her whole life had come down to this moment. Did she fall back into what was comfortable and let Vivi do her thing the way she always did—the way she'd done when she'd left Yorkshire without a word to Hugo, in fact? Or did she step forward into all the blistering unknown she could see shining there in Hugo's eyes—whether he hated her as he should…or didn't?

How would she live with herself if she didn't try?

There was a part of her that wanted to wait and see. She wanted to see who Hugo would choose. This wasn't a ballroom, in the middle of the night, empty of everyone save the two of them. This was a London street, and both she and Vivi were dressed for the night they'd just had. That meant skin. Skin and lean, lanky attractiveness on Vivi's part. Skin and abundant curves on Eleanor's.

There was a part of her that wanted to act as if she and her sister were a buffet. Line them both up and watch him as he made his decision, so she could see if she was the one he'd chose because she was convenient, or because he really was the only man she'd ever met who wanted her, not her sister.

And she was tired of everyone around her making decisions for her. Even if they were well-meaning. Even if the decisions were in her best interest.

Maybe it was time for Eleanor to make a choice herself.

"It's okay," she said. She kept her eyes trained on Hugo, but she squeezed her sister's hand. "You can go Vivi. Really."

"But—"

"Go," she said again, with soft certainty. "I'll see you at home."

There must have been something in her tone, then, that brooked no disobedience. Or any back talk. Vivi squeezed her hand back, hard, and then got into the waiting car. She slammed the door behind her, and the cab headed off, chugging down the street and then around the corner.

And Eleanor was left standing on a quiet street in a busy city, with the man she never thought she'd see again. Not face to face. Not anywhere but in her head and on a screen or a glossy tabloid page.

"Eleanor. Little one." Hugo shook his head, and it made heat spiral through her, charging through her where she stood as if he'd lit a match. Making the heels she wore seem that much more precarious. "Whatever are you wearing?"

"In comparison to most of the girls I saw tonight, I might as well be wearing a grandmother's cardi and a suit of armor."

"A suit of armor would be a good start."

"I'm wearing a perfectly lovely dress, thank you," Eleanor said primly, and kept herself from tugging on the hem of it by sheer force of will. "If I was working, I'd be wearing something appropriate for work."

"Your hair."

His voice sounded almost tortured, and Eleanor stopped breathing. He reached out and raked his fingers through the dark mass that Vivi had made wavy and thick.

"I hate your hair up, Eleanor. Have I told you that?"

"It's a good job it isn't up to you, then. Isn't it?"

"Are you certain it isn't up to me?"

Hugo moved closer, but all Eleanor could feel was what hung there between them. That tabloid story. Eleanor's innocence. Geraldine. Or the fact she was in love with him, just like a silly, clingy virgin in a story who didn't know enough to guard her own heart. Too many things to bear.

But Hugo moved closer as if he was as entranced she was. As if he couldn't stay away. And Eleanor stopped thinking about anything but him and the half smile on his face as he looked down at her.

"Maybe you haven't heard. I'm a great and glorious peer of the realm. My every wish is law. Or close enough."

He shifted closer. He moved so he could cup her face in his hands, his hundred-percent-proof eyes intent on hers. And everything inside her shivered. Rocked a little bit, then rolled, deep and low.

And this time, she didn't think it was the shoes.

"The tabloids…" She whispered. "Hugo, I'm so very sorry. I don't know how I can ever make it right."

"I don't care about the tabloids."

Eleanor scowled at him. "Well, you should. It's not

a small thing to have all these lies told about you. You should care and you should fight and you should—"

"But that's the thing. In this case, the tabloids are no more than the truth. I did take advantage of you. You worked for me and I shouldn't have touched you. But I did."

"I wanted you to."

"I didn't say I was sorry."

He shifted again, and there was a look on his face that Eleanor thought she'd seen before, though she couldn't quite place it. And then it came to her. It had been that night. Locked away in his bedchamber, just the two of them, with nothing outside his door between them. He'd propped himself over her, he'd sunk himself deep inside of her, and he'd looked at her. Just like this.

Her heart began to beat at her, slow and intense.

"I forgot how to fight," Hugo said. "At first I didn't care. And then I did care, but I thought I was taking the high road. And then the high road somehow became this endless act of self-immolation, acted out in the public eye as if that might make it better. It never occurred to me that the flames would take over. Or that my own father would burn."

"It wasn't your fault," she said fiercely. "This was something that was done *to* you. You shouldn't beat yourself up for the things you did to survive it."

"I'm a selfish man, little one. I want to believe you because it's convenient, not because I think it's true."

"You are not a monster." Eleanor poked her finger in his chest as punctuation, and saw that hint of a smile deepen. It was like the sun coming out. "If anyone's a monster, it's that Isobel."

"I think you're letting me off the hook," Hugo said, his voice serious again. Too serious. "And I like that about you. But the truth is, I was callous. Unfeeling. There were any number of ways I could have handled Isobel at the start to avoid all of this, but I didn't. I suspect I must have hurt her, deeply."

"That's no excuse."

"It's an explanation."

Hugo blew out a breath. Eleanor started to say something else, but he laughed then.

"You need to stop defending me, Eleanor. I'm trying to tell you what I should have realized sooner. I love you."

All the air went out of Eleanor's body. She was too hot. Too cold.

She thought it was a fever.

Or possibly joy.

"Yes," Hugo said, as if he knew every last inch of her insecure little soul. "You." There was a wondering look on his face, and she thought his hands weren't entirely steady as they smoothed over her hair to settle at the nape of her neck. "I was so busy thinking of myself as a dragon in a cave, spouting off fire nonsense whenever anyone dared approach. And then you came. And you didn't see a dragon. You didn't see a duke. You saw a man. An irritating man, if memory serves."

"Surely not, Your Grace." But her voice was barely a whisper. Barely a scratch of sound against the night.

"You treated me like a person, nothing more. Even though you read all the same tabloid stories as anyone else. You took my ward under your wing, and more than that, stood up for her. You actually put her first."

"That's the job."

"You would be shocked how few of Geraldine's governesses considered her at all. You made a lost child feel found, Eleanor." His dark eyes gleamed. "And you made a lost man feel whole. For a few short weeks, and one long night, I completely forgot that I'm meant to be the boogeyman."

Eleanor shook her head at that, her eyes feeling much too full. "I had no idea Vivi was going to do that, Hugo. You have to believe me."

"I never fought before," he told her, his voice low and intense. "I never stood up for myself. But I'll be damned if those rags will drag you through the dirt. I've already had my attorneys contact them. I am the Duke of Grovesmoor. And I am finished hiding."

"Hugo..."

"And more importantly, I love you." He laughed, and it was a sound so pure, so filled with life and light, that Eleanor forgot it was the middle of the night. "I didn't care enough to fight before, because I never loved Isobel. She was an annoyance, but she never hurt me. I only recognized how much I loved my own father after he died, disappointed in me to the end. I worked so hard to pretend I didn't care about my best friend or the fact he chose Isobel over me. And I decided I'd be damned if I'd soften toward the little girl he and Isobel left in my care. The truth of it was, I was fine."

Eleanor didn't realize that tears had started to slide down her face until Hugo wiped them away. She felt caught in a tight, hot grip. Unable to speak. Unable to do anything but float there, gleaming bright and buoyant.

And Hugo was still talking.

"But then you appeared. You marched up my drive in that ridiculous coat and you ruined everything. In the best possible way."

Eleanor ran her hands up the wall of his chest, indulging herself.

"What's the matter with my coat?" She tipped her head back and frowned at him. "It's very warm, Hugo."

That made him laugh again, and then he was picking her up and spinning her around and around, as if she was weightless. But then, he made her feel that way when her feet were on the ground.

"I don't know how to be anything but everyone's favorite monster," he told her when he stopped spinning them, though he still held her there against him in the cool, close night. "But I want to try. I want to watch you frown at me for the rest of my life. I want your dry tone and your prim little remarks and Eleanor, you need to understand me on this, I want everything."

"I loved you the moment I saw you," she told him, smiling down at him as her tears fell freely, and not a single one of them because she was sad. "On that terrible horse."

"Everything," he said again, as if he thought she might have missed it. "A ring on your finger and my babies in your belly, to start. After that, who knows? We can take over the world. I have no doubt you could topple a regime or two in a few weeks, if you put your mind to it. You did it to me."

"I don't want to do anything unless Geraldine's okay with it," Eleanor said, biting her lip as she considered his ward. "The poor thing doesn't need to feel any more abandoned."

"Geraldine will never be abandoned again." Hugo's words rang out like a vow. "She and I have come to an understanding, you see." He leaned forward and pressed his mouth to hers. "We can't rustle around in that great big house without you, Eleanor. It doesn't work. We need you. *I* need you."

"Your Grace," Eleanor whispered, wrapping her arms around this man who could never be a monster, not to her. "You know your wish has always been my command."

He kissed her on that lonely street, with only the far-away stars as witness, and tossed them straight on into forever.

And then, together, they found their way home.

Hugo married his governess in the spring, when Groves House was bursting with flowers and life, and even the screeching tabloids were as nothing next to the benevolent sunlight of a pretty Yorkshire afternoon.

Geraldine stood in as Hugo's Best Man, which was appropriate on a number of levels. Vivi was Eleanor's Maid of Honor, and it was interesting how she'd changed, Hugo thought. The new Vivi didn't have to worry about making connections or finding a husband or whatever plan it was the sisters had cooked up all those years ago.

"That's a terrible plan," Hugo had said when they'd laid it all out for him after Christmas that first year, probably because everyone was a touch too merry after their sumptuous dinner. "The worst I've ever heard."

The adults had been sitting about like overstuffed lords and ladies of old in one of Hugo's salons, waiting for their meals to digest a bit so they could stuff in a few more mince pies. Geraldine had been lying in front of the fire, her face in a book.

It was, Hugo had reflected with some surprise, the happiest Christmas he could recall. Ever.

"It's a plan that's worked to change the circumstances of impoverished women since the dawn of time," Eleanor had pointed out.

"It has significant downsides," Hugo had argued. "First and foremost, the rich man in question always knows exactly why he was found so marriageable. Believe me, he'll demand payment for that. Forever."

"There is always some form of payment," Vivi had said quietly. "That's just life."

Eleanor and Hugo had exchanged a look, but neither one of them had said anything—out loud—about that weary cynicism in Vivi's voice.

Later, when they were alone in the rooms that Hugo had moved her into shortly after he'd taken her home from London and put the Grovesmoor emerald on her finger, Eleanor had settled herself astride him and smiled down into his face.

"Is this part of my payment plan?" she'd asked mischievously.

"Of course." Hugo had run his hands along the crease where her thigh met her hip. "I'll insist on certain sexual favors, to be spelled out in the marriage contract."

"I have only one condition," Eleanor had said, very solemnly, angling herself down so her breasts filled his greedy palms and both of them could feel how slick and ready she was for him, as always.

"Name it."

"Love me," she demanded. "Forever."

On his wedding day, Hugo found that promising her exactly that came easily. So easily he laughed at the tabloids that called him all manner of names. So easily that he found even Vivi amusing, as she seemed to veer between finding the fact her sister had become Hugo's duchess romantic and armoring herself in that world-weariness she seemed infinitely more comfortable with.

"She'll come around," Eleanor said confidently on the dance floor as they'd moved together where everyone could watch them, in that ballroom where everything had changed between them previous autumn. Tonight she was dressed in a white gown and she wore his ring, but he could still see her the way she'd been then, with her hair down and her feet bare. "How can she help herself?"

Time changed everything, Hugo discovered. First Vivi, who took a solid year to relax around him. Then another year to really become comfortable in her new role, as a woman of some means with a very powerful brother-in-law.

"It's amazing how many people I thought I wanted to talk to when I was poor," Hugo overheard her telling Eleanor one lazy weekend in France at Hugo's vineyard. "And how little it turns out I like them now that they're the ones pursuing me."

"Imagine," Eleanor replied with a laugh. "You can spend time with only the people you like now."

And so, Hugo realized, could he.

He stopped paying attention to the papers, the way he should have years ago. He cultivated what friendships he had left, gratified to discover that those who'd truly known him had never believed the stories about him. And he let his beautiful wife guide him, with her quiet resolve and her cheerful determination, away from bitterness. More and more with each day that passed.

She knew the names of every staff member in his employ within a month. She continued Geraldine's schooling herself because she liked it. She quickly became popular in the village, with the no-nonsense demeanor good Yorkshire folk appreciated and that kindness of hers that Hugo thought could set the world alight. She took over some of the managerial aspects of the estate, because her keen mind and attention to detail far outstripped that of some of Hugo's aides.

She even built a bridge with the dour Mrs. Redding.

"She allowed as how she didn't trust me *before*," Eleanor told him, laughing, wrapped around him in their bed as she reported the conversation, "because the women ran all over you like water and none with a single thought about anything but themselves."

"Exactly the image I wish to have implanted in my wife's head."

"And then, of course, she waited to see if I drained the family coffers and attempted to divorce you for half of what wasn't mine."

"As well you should. There was no prenup. You have the Grovesmoor fortune entirely within your control, little one."

Eleanor pressed her mouth against his chest, sending a new heat spiraling through him. And that deeper weight that had nothing to do with sex, but everything to do with her. His miraculous Eleanor. "It's not the fortune I want to control. Just the Duke."

"He's a lost cause."

But he was laughing as he said it, and he grinned at Eleanor when she frowned at him.

"No," she said crisply, "he is not. And more, he never was."

And the more time passed, the more he believed it. Isobel had only ever told stories. Torquil might have believed them, but both of them had paid far too high a price for that.

Hugo didn't need to pay it, too. Not anymore.

And he certainly didn't intend to let Geraldine pay a single penny.

She was nine when she got her hands on the tabloids they'd deliberately kept from her for years.

"Is it true?" she asked, her fierce little face screwed up tight, as if she was keeping herself from sobbing by will alone. "Do you keep me only to get revenge on my mother?"

"How would that work, exactly?" Hugo asked mildly. He and Eleanor were reading in his library, but he noticed Eleanor kept very still. Letting the little girl speak to him directly. "I suppose I could lock you in a cupboard, if that would help. Beneath a stair, perhaps?"

"Do you hate me?" Geraldine had asked. She'd looked at him full on , and there was no mistaking the fact that she was a nine-year-old then, no matter how precocious she seemed at other times.

And this was how Hugo knew that Eleanor had changed him, from the inside out. He remembered sitting in opposite chairs from his ward and deciding that they should get Eleanor back. But that Hugo had been handicapped by his own distrust of everything. This Hugo knew what love was. He lived it every day.

So he reached out and pulled the little girl onto his lap, where she belonged.

"You are my ward by law," he told her gruffly, liking the weight of her solid little body against his. Liking the feeling that rose in him, thick and real, that told him he would protect this child against the world with his own hands if necessary. "But as far as I'm concerned, Geraldine, you have always been my daughter."

And as she snuggled into him he lifted his head, and saw Eleanor wiping tears away across from him, her face wreathed in smiles.

A year or so after that, Geraldine pushed her way into the library one summer evening, already slouching about as she walked, like the teenager she would be entirely too soon for Hugo's peace of mind.

"I'm certain I've asked you to knock," Hugo said mildly, his attention on the drink in his hand and his lovely wife, who was frowning intently over the book in her lap. Eleanor had decided to get the university degree she'd been too busy to get when she'd been younger, and was spending the summer with a reading list.

Hugo wasn't sure it was physically possible to love her more.

Geraldine held his gaze. "Knock, knock," she said, because she was as smart-mouthed as anyone else in this house.

"Charming," Hugo murmured.

"I've thought about it and I've come to a decision," Geraldine told him.

"Have you changed your mind about school?" Eleanor asked, lifting her head.

"I still want to go," Geraldine replied. "It will be fun to board and I'll come home all the time. But you two will be so lonely without me."

Hugo's mouth twitched. "Indeed."

Eleanor's dark eyes danced, but she nodded seriously. "I'm sure that's true."

"Well, I know what you need to do," Geraldine said, and then she smiled. "You need to have a baby. As soon as possible."

And Hugo would never know how both he and Eleanor kept from laughing at that, but they didn't. They thanked Geraldine and then, when she'd skipped back out again to enjoy the long, blue evening, they'd dissolved into the laughter they'd been holding at bay.

But they obeyed her.

Ten months later, the Duke was delighted to catch his first son and heir as he roared his way into the world. But not, perhaps, as delighted as his ward, who was sure she'd plotted out the whole thing.

And Eleanor had never done one thing when she could do three instead. That was how the future Duke of Grovesmoor found himself with a little brother and a baby sister in short order, all of them loud and rowdy and perfect.

"Look at that," Eleanor said as she shepherded their little brood through the village on a blustery sort of fall afternoon that reminded Hugo of the day they'd met. She was even wearing that hideous puffy coat of hers, that she'd steadfastly refused to throw away no matter how many glorious, sleek, and flattering coats he'd gifted her with over the years. Obstinate woman. "I hardly recognize the man in those headlines."

Hugo glanced over at the newsstand and saw his own face, but didn't bother to read whatever nonsense they'd spouted about him this time. He took his wife's hand in his and raised it to his mouth. His sons were running ahead of him toward the green, chasing Geraldine who was for all intents and purposes their older sister, and he was holding his baby girl against his chest.

"Ah, little one," he said with a deep and quiet contentment that was pressed down into his bones now, a part of him forever. "I don't believe in ghosts."

His family was complete. His heart was whole.

Eleanor looked at him as if he'd always been the man she was so proud of, and Hugo believed, at last, that he was.

And would be for as long as they were together— which would be for the rest of their natural lives and far beyond if he had anything to say about it.

Which he bloody well did. He was the Duke of Grovesmoor, after all.

* * * * *

If you enjoyed
UNDONE BY THE BILLIONAIRE DUKE
why not explore these other stories
by Caitlin Crews?

THE GUARDIAN'S VIRGIN WARD
BRIDE BY ROYAL DECREE
THE PRINCE'S NINE-MONTH SCANDAL
THE BILLIONAIRE'S SECRET PRINCESS

Available now!

MILLS & BOON®

MODER N™

POWER, PASSION AND IRRESISTIBLE TEMPTATION

MILLS & BOON®

EXCLUSIVE EXTRACT

When chauffeur Keira Ryan drives into a snowdrift, she and her devastatingly attractive passenger must find a hotel…but there's only one bed! Luckily Matteo Valenti knows how to make the best of a bad situation—with the most sizzling experience of her life. It's nearly Christmas again before Matteo uncovers Keira's secret. He's avoided commitment his whole life, but now it's time to claim his heir…

Read on for a sneak preview of Sharon Kendrick's book
THE ITALIAN'S CHRISTMAS SECRET
One Night With Consequences

'Santino?' Matteo repeated, wondering if he'd misheard her. He stared at her, his brow creased in a frown. 'You gave him an Italian name?'

'Yes.'

'Why?'

'Because when I looked at him…' Keira's voice faltered as she scraped her fingers back through her hair and turned those big sapphire eyes on him '…I knew I could call him nothing else but an Italian name.'

'Even though you sought to deny him his heritage and kept his birth hidden from me?'

She swallowed. 'You made it very clear that you never wanted to see me again, Matteo.'

His voice grew hard. 'I haven't come here to argue the rights and wrongs of your secrecy. I've come to see my son.'

It was a demand Keira couldn't ignore. She'd seen the brief tightening of his face when she'd mentioned his child and another wave of guilt had washed over her.

'Come with me,' she said huskily.

He followed her up the narrow staircase and Keira was

acutely aware of his presence behind her. She could detect the heat from his body and the subtle sandalwood which was all his and, stupidly, she remembered the way that scent had clung to her skin the morning after he'd made love to her. Her heart was thundering by the time they reached the box-room she shared with Santino and she held her breath as Matteo stood frozen for a moment before moving soundlessly towards the crib.

'Matteo?' she said.

Matteo didn't answer. Not then. He wasn't sure he trusted himself to speak because his thoughts were in such disarray. He stared down at the dark fringe of eyelashes which curved on the infant's olive-hued cheeks and the shock of black hair. Tiny hands were curled into two tiny fists and he found himself leaning forward to count all the fingers, nodding his head with satisfaction as he registered each one.

He swallowed.

His *son*.

He opened his mouth to speak but Santino chose that moment to start to whimper and Keira bent over the crib to scoop him up. 'Would you…would you like to hold him?'

'Not now,' he said abruptly. 'There isn't time. You need to pack your things while I call ahead and prepare for your arrival in Italy.'

'What?'

'You heard me. You can't put out a call for help and then ignore help when it comes. You telephoned me and now you must accept the consequences,' he added grimly.

Don't miss
THE ITALIAN'S CHRISTMAS SECRET
By Sharon Kendrick

Available November 2017

www.millsandboon.co.uk

MILLS & BOON®

Why shop at millsandboon.co.uk?

Each year, thousands of romance readers
find their perfect read at millsandboon.co.uk.
That's because we're passionate about
bringing you the very best romantic fiction.
Here are some of the advantages of
shopping at www.millsandboon.co.uk:

* **Get new books first**—you'll be able to buy
  your favourite books one month before they
  hit the shops

* **Get exclusive discounts**—you'll also be
  able to buy our specially created monthly
  collections, with up to 50% off the RRP

* **Find your favourite authors**—latest news,
  interviews and new releases for all your
  favourite authors and series on our website,
  plus ideas for what to try next

* **Join in**—once you've bought your favourite
  books, don't forget to register with us to rate,
  review and join in the discussions

Visit **www.millsandboon.co.uk**
for all this and more today!

Join Britain's BIGGEST Romance Book Club

50% OFF your first parcel

- **EXCLUSIVE offers** every month

- **FREE delivery direct** to your door

- **NEVER MISS a title**

- **EARN Bonus Book** points

Call Customer Services
0844 844 1358*

or visit
nillsandboon.co.uk/subscriptions